Weird

VOL. 2, NO. 11

Features

Stories

Poetry

Artwork

Weirdbook #41 is copyright © 2019 by Wildside Press LLC. All rights reserved. Published by Wildside Press LLC, 7945 MacArthur Blvd, Suite 215, Cabin John MD 20818 USA. Visit us online at wildsidepress.com.

FROM THE EDITOR'S TOWER

Hello Dear Readers,

Time has flown so quickly and it's time for *Weirdbook* #41, our first issue for 2019.

I just closed the submissions period for this year and received almost 400 submissions. I'll be able to fill the rest of 2019's regular issues.

In just a little over 3 years there have been a baker's dozen of *Weirdbooks*. Not bad for what one author described as "the little magazine that could"! And I promise that we are going to keep at it and publish four more issues this year of the best in today's weird fiction.

On a very sad note, we lost two giants of the field over the last four months.

Paul Dale Anderson left us on the 13th December 2018, and Wilum Hopfrog Pugmire crossed over on the March 26th, 2019. Both were *Weirdbook* contributors to whom I will forever be indebted. Knowing them has enriched my life. Both were great writers and even greater human beings. They will be sorely missed by their fans, friends and families. The world is a lesser place without them.

This issue of *Weirdbook* is dedicated to the memories of Paul Dale Anderson and Wilum Hopfrog Pugmire. Two of the last titans.

Requiescat in Pace.

—Doug Draa

Staff

PUBLISHER & EXECUTIVE EDITOR

John Gregory Betancourt

EDITOR

Doug Draa

CONSULTING EDITOR

W. Paul Ganley

WILDSIDE PRESS SUBSCRIPTION SERVICES

Sam Hogan

PRODUCTION TEAM

Steve Coupe
Sam Cooper
Shawn Garrett
Sam Hogan
Karl Würf

TONIGHT I WEAR MY CRIMSON FACE

by Adrian Cole

That night I couldn't make my mind up whether to employ my strangler's hands, exercise my psychic scalpel, or deliver the fabulous toxic kiss. Perhaps some new, even more terrible death-skill? Ah, but I could draw on so many. On stage in the delicious atmosphere of the *Theatre Verité*, it is so thrilling to exercise my art—and to such loving audiences. How they adore my manipulation of their dark desires. How I feed on my growing fame! Each performance takes me a step closer to that greater destiny prepared for me.

It was to be a special show, the culmination of a number—five in all—that I had been promised would see me well rewarded. A night to savour.

I decided it would have to be the anaconda's embrace. I had not used it for a while, but that night I felt invigorated by the thought of what would come later, in the small hours. My dressing room was reasonably spacious, not cramped like one assigned to the new recruits. Maurice de Villiers, our lord and patron, never allowed anyone to get ideas above their station. Luxuries such as a bigger dressing room had to be earned. I can say, with some pride, that I had certainly earned mine.

I had been here since my childhood, plucked from the dangerous, hostile streets where, as little more than an urchin, I had wormed my way into the underworld's embrace, destined for an inevitable early death, until Maurice de Villiers's long reach had drawn me into his labyrinth of intrigue. I think it was less a case of sympathy for my destitution and more opportunity for him to mould another creature to his flock. The world immediately outside the *Theatre Verité* was a dire place, many of its former palatial buildings now derelict, its streets neglected, its inhabitants living like roaches away from the brighter heart of the city. I was enchanted by my new environment. Our wonderful theatre was a monument, a beacon that drew its patrons like moths to its vivid flames.

I began the lengthy process of applying my make-up, turning my face into a serpentine mask, slicking back my hair and ears, and exercising my tongue until I could fork it—the audience always adores that. I wore my skin-tight scales easily enough, but my performance would requite me to undergo a transformation when I revealed the coils of the anaconda. I would have to call upon the assistance of one of my inner beings, one of the select company I had absorbed some time earlier. Using its power, I would be able to expand myself appropriately, contorting muscle and bone to create the perfect effect. I was renowned for such transfigurations, and consequently my act was always a sell-out.

When I had practiced some of my movements and felt sufficiently prepared, I donned my cape and went out through the claustrophobic corridors of the back-stage area towards the main proscenium. In common with all my fellow artistes, I was not permitted to watch any of the acts on stage—they were performed for the select audience alone. I am sure that Maurice de Villiers himself viewed everything, although he remained almost a complete mystery to his entire ensemble. There were some who had dared to suggest that he was no more than an idea, a relic of days long gone, when the *Theatre Verité* thrived in an area of singular grandiloquence, flanked by numerous similar establishments, patronised by all the upper echelons of society, including royalty.

Doubtless the history of the building was as people believed, but it was never a sensible idea to dismiss Maurice de Villiers as a mere legend. Invisible he may have been, but I have always held that he is a living, breathing entity. As to his real nature, well, I would not even begin to speculate. Those who have expressed negative views have regretted their point of view, painfully.

I waited in the shadows as stage managers and assistants slipped in and out of the curtains and sets, fussing quietly, waving and gesticulating at their hidden colleagues high on the gantry where a hundred ropes and pulleys manipulated scenery and where lights turned night into day, through all its gaudy shades. Some of my fellow artistes were in evidence, tucked away, waiting their turn. I could see the troupe of Exotics, young girls, naked as cherubs, who could perform a combined dance and acrobatics, whispering and giggling to each other, eager to get on to the stage and massage the lascivious emotions of the audience. They were due on before me and I favoured those who looked avidly, always avidly, at me, with a sultry smile. They were a perfect entrée to my act.

Every member of that audience was here by special invitation, and they had all been summoned for a reason. Maurice de Villiers manipulated them all, like a grand puppeteer. We knew little of this, only the principle, but we played our parts happily, given the rewards. As with everything relating to Maurice de Villiers, there were stories about the people who came and my favourite concerned some vast trail of revenge that he was trekking, like some modern Edmund Dantes, the celebrated fictional Count of Monte Cristo. I rather liked the concept. Others told of his deals with darker beings, of sinister pacts and bargains that had earned him, among other things, a much extended life. He was said variously to be a fallen angel, a vampire, an androgynous being and far more besides, though the truth was, no one really knew.

The Exotics performed well that night, writhing and wriggling through their routine to the sounds of the small but precise orchestra down in the pit and I anticipated an excellent audience response to my own act, which would follow on naturally to the flesh-fest that had preceded it. When I took to the stage, it had been prepared carefully by the stage hands, who knew the niceties of my requirements. Deep crimson curtains, thick velvet, hung on all sides, and the space created had a supernatural feel to it, like the lair of some fabulous creature of legend. That was my role, of course, as I entered, sleek and silent, semi-human, in my cape that initially shielded my night's guise from the audience.

They were packed in, having all been promised something fabulous. They had been especially invited by Maurice de Villiers and not one of them would have declined, nor indeed, would they have wanted to. The delights, the raptures of a night at the *Theatre Verité* were addictive, a heady concoction of glamour and magic that, once sipped, could never be denied. We appealed to their cravings, their lusts, and their endless need for stimulation. I could not see their faces, for the darkness of the luxurious auditorium shaded them and they appeared to me as shadows behind their feathered lamps. I could feel them, though, their desires drifted from them like a powerful musk or sexual perfume.

The music, which I had chosen specifically for tonight's extravaganza, began softly and sinuously and I moved about the stage in perfect time to its serpentine rhythms. The stage itself was bare, save for a long divan, draped in soft sheets, the palest pink. Subdued lighting added to the eerie effects, a single spot following my movements. Silence fell upon the crowd, though I could sense their breathing and imagined the rapid beating of their hearts. It was intoxicating! Such power.

After a few moments, one of the curtains shivered, parting to permit the entry of a young woman. She was dressed expensively, doubtless a member of a wealthy family, chosen from the audience by Maurice de Villiers, or to be precise, his representative, for our lord never revealed himself to his patrons any more than he did to us. This girl's face was framed by long braids of shining blonde hair, her expression one of awe. I could see that she had been given something to transport her into a kind of trance so that her performance on stage could be suitably moulded to my act. For her, it would have been the equivalent of a high, as if she had taken a stimulating narcotic. Only the most expensive and purest samples were available at the *Theatre Verité*.

I moved around her and she grew very still, like a nervous creature of the forest. I let my cloak fall and heard the unified gasp of the audience as they saw my physical shape, my anaconda. For most of them, this was a new experience and they thrilled to it, loving the danger and imminent threat of my glistening, muscular form. The inner demon I had selected responded well to my urgings and lent its power to my transmogrification. The trick for me was always not to let the inner creature have its head and overpower me. I had to maintain control.

That night it proved very difficult, for I could sense the demon's blood-lust. How it desired the girl! It contorted me, which was wonderful for the audience to behold. I felt them shuddering as now I danced, now I slithered on my belly, now I rose and revealed that long, forked tongue. It flicked the air lasciviously, teasing the audience, stroking their wicked longings. Music and movement blended and I brought the girl at last to the divan, stretching her out on the gleaming sheets. I enfolded her, cocooned her in what the audience would have seen as coils. It was all I could do to prevent the demon from crushing her and beginning what would have been a terrible digestion.

At the climactic moment, the lights subsided to the merest glow and I swung off the divan, slickly winding the sheet over the girl. The audience could not see what I did next, although it would have appeared to them to have been a final, fatal act. I had drawn blood, enough to smear the sheets to heighten the impression of a colourful death, depicted clearly as the lights rose again. There were shouts from the audience, even a scream or two. It had been a virtuoso performance. I leapt to the front of the stage, bowing and taking the applause. If Maurice de Villiers had been secretly watching, he would have been deeply satisfied, I am sure.

I stepped back and drew on my cape. Slowly I went to the shape on the divan and as I bent over its hidden form, the audience again fell silent. I lifted the body and with a final glance to the front, carried it soundlessly away through the crimson curtains. Beyond, in the darkness, I unravelled the sheet, standing the girl on her feet. Dazed, unable to see in the thick shadows, she put a hand on my shoulder to steady herself. Blood ran freely from that hand.

She may not have realized, but I had completely severed her small finger, using my teeth as the tool. She would have felt no pain, despite the barbarity of the act. It was the price she had to pay me for the privilege of being my co-star for the performance. It was also her indoctrination into the wonders of our theatre. She was marked now, as others before her had been, although, when she came to her restored senses and the wound had been expertly cauterised and dressed, she would be proud of her new status, as would her family. Those chosen to be so marked by the *Theatre*

Verité were exceptional. And to have been marked by one so lauded as myself, well, that was almost unique.

As for the finger, that was mine. I had tucked it under my tongue and it was only when I had returned to my dressing room that I removed it. I applied some specially prepared ointment to it, to stem the last seeping of blood—it is surprising how much leaks from a severed finger—and set it aside in a silk handkerchief. No one disturbed me while I removed my make-up and exercised the mental exercises necessary to subdue the demon within me. It had failed to best me and would lie dormant among my other captives until I called upon it again.

I had almost finished dressing, when there was a soft knock at the door. I opened it and found Nathaniel standing there. He was one of the concierges, a small fellow, stooped through a damaged spine, and he held out an envelope in a hand that shook unsteadily. He was, of course, in total awe of me, as well he might have been that night.

"For you, sir," he said with a low bow.

I took the letter and thanked him. I closed and bolted my door. Before opening the letter, I opened one of the drawers of my dresser and took from it a small, silver casket, a particularly lovely *objet d'art*. I opened it and studied the four items within it, set in a bed of satin. There were three fingers and a thumb, each having been removed from a different patron of the theatre on varying nights during specific performances over the past few months. All were in a perfect state of preservation, as if they had been severed this very night. To them I added the small finger I had taken tonight. I closed the lid and locked the casket with a tiny, silver key.

I turned to the envelope and slit it open with an ornate silver knife designed for the purpose. I confess I am fastidious about such things. It is a ritual with me, but I never underestimate the power of exactitude. Silver, of course, has magical qualities that surpass so many other, commoner metals. The letter was a single sheet of expensive vellum, and I already knew who had sent it to me. Maurice de Villiers invariably commented on the quality of his artistes' performances.

I read his words calmly. He was pleased. I had done well, and credit reflected on him and the impeccable tradition of the theatre.

"...*I understand that Lord and Lady Bellevoire were delighted with tonight's show. Alessandra is a little unnerved to find herself missing a finger, but once she understands how marvellously she will be compensated, she will recover her composure, undoubtedly. She will serve us well and the Bellevoire family will rise in society.*

You have earned your own prize, Armand. Go out and claim it quickly and return to the theatre at once. Please, do not feel tempted to utilise your new power outside these walls. The consequences could be more than a little serious. Remember who brought you here and who has been your constant guardian angel since he pulled you from that mire of human suffering beyond these walls. Remain on the path I have woven for you. Your destiny is closer than you realise."

It was an inevitable reminder, a deterrent against my natural hubris, which he understood so well. However, that final line made my head swim!

I put the letter into another drawer. I was, in a sense, a prisoner here, but tonight I must venture outside. It would be exciting, though unnerving. The being I was to meet always filled me with dread, though it had never threatened me directly.

I remained in my dressing room, and for the second time that night I diligently prepared my attire, although this was to be for an altogether different performance. I would be Lady Silver, a somewhat ambiguous creature, but the importance of the role was not so much in its sex, but in the silver. Nothing protects like silver and tonight I would need to be on my guard. Once I had satisfied myself that my makeup, jewellery and clothes—an extravagant but wholly practical suit—were as required, I left the theatre. I had with me, carefully wrapped and placed discreetly in a shoulder-bag, the silver casket.

It was a blustery night and there were few people about at this hour. The *Theatre Verité* loomed over me as I quit it, as though the Gothic pile was eager to pull me back into its embrace. Its age was unknown, although our illustrious lord claims that it was built in its current form in the late eighteenth century. There is enough evidence in its lower levels to suggest that something of its nature has been on that site for far, far longer.

Its environs were squalid and dilapidated, due to be cleared soon, according to those who ran the business of the city. It was unlikely that any such plans would include the theatre. Too many of its patrons held high office. Too many of the stage's lauded acts had been nurtured here, before going on to greater glory. I tried not to allow myself the luxury of imagining a leap to such heights, a rise to unalloyed fame, but what artiste has not harboured such ambitions? They were a spur to our efforts.

I made my way into the insalubrious heart of the area, entering one of its grimmest public houses, where the clientele were, like me, disposed to make a show of themselves, drawn as they were from as colourful and exhibitionistic a crowd as one could imagine. This was a theatre of a different kind, a human market. Many of the dilettantes were known to me and I nodded, politely declining offers to join them. On another night, I would have done so and taken pleasure from it and the admiration that went with it, but tonight I remained single-minded.

The publican was expecting me. Arrangements had already been made. I was shown to a stairwell at the back of the building, lit by a solitary, wan bulb. I descended into the thick, hot air, as though visiting a sauna. I felt my make-up becoming slightly sticky, the consistency of blood, but I gritted my teeth with resolve. There were tunnels leading off from the corridor down below, dug out of the bedrock, barely shored up with ancient bricks. If I had not been before, I would have shunned the place.

I knocked on the door at the end of the corridor and a voice beyond it, familiar but disturbing, called me in. The light was poor, the room little more than a cave. The one I had come to see sat at an ancient table, its body hunched, its face masked by shadow. I had only ever seen that face partially and to be truthful, had no wish to look fully upon it. I was glad of the silver woven into my clothing, jewels and face-paint, which was also silver.

The demon—I could think of this creature in no other guise - grinned at my outfit. I saw the teeth flash. "Armand, ever the cautious. Do you think I'm here to bring you pain?"

There was no seat for me. I stood, as calmly as I could, and inclined my head politely. "No, of course not." I said it without confidence. A cat may allow you to fondle it, but it's a fickle creature. Who knows when it will draw your blood?

"A special night, I believe," it said and its eyes glittered. There was no denying the hunger in them.

I rummaged in my shoulder-bag and brought out the silk-wrapped casket, uncovering it slowly, as though handling an egg. I placed the silver casket on the table.

The being sat back, fully cloaked in darkness, and as it did so I got the strange impression of a disembodied mouth, the rich, full lips, and the whitest of teeth. "Open it for me," it said.

I knew it would never touch the silver. It would be poison to such a beast. I did as asked, displaying the ghoulish wares within the little casket, the five fingers I had taken from various victims of my act, including, of course, tonight's little trophy.

The creature was studying them, motionless but as alert as an eagle. "Excellent," it said at last and I breathed a deep mental sigh of relief. "All from young women?"

"Quite so. Maidens, too, I suspect."

"Well, that's never a bad thing. Their youth is important, though. Good." It leaned forward now and put both arms on the table, and I saw that it had already drawn up the wide sleeves of its voluminous jacket, so that those arms were bare, their skin gleaming strangely in the light, hairless and apparently polished. I could not say what skin tone they exhibited, it being distorted in this underground lair, but it was doubtless unique to the creature's kind.

I glanced at those hands. The right hand was perfectly formed, strong and with thick fingers that suggested manual labour, though they were unblemished, the nails elongated and manicured. Its left arm, however, ended in a hand that had no fingers. It was a slightly grotesque ball of flesh, club-like and deeply unsettling. I did my best not to appear squeamish, but it ignored my sentiments.

"Remove the fingers from the casket," the creature said.

I slid the casket from the table and took out each finger slowly, laying it down on the table, between the creature's hands, until all five rested there, fanned out. After a brief moment of further reflection, it moved very quickly. I did not see what it did, and in a moment it had withdrawn again into the darkness.

I waited. I could hear its breathing, a peculiar sound, like an animal in its lair, twisting and turning. The room had become stifling and I resisted the urge to vomit.

After a while the creature thrust both arms across the table and I saw that the fingers of the left hand had been restored, those that I had brought fused somehow on to that appendage. They moved, wriggling with new energy. They should have been incongruous, a poor match, but they were not. Instead their bizarre physicality matched the nature of the beast, enhancing his lack of humanity.

It laughed at my expression, which would have been a mixture of horror and amazement. "You have done well, Armand, - so very well. I have waited a long time for this moment. Maurice de Villiers has trained you well. He will be proud of you."

Yes, I imagined my lord would be rewarded for his part in this business. It was the meat and drink of his existence. He, too, served a greater power.

"I have the promised gift for you in return. Go back to the *Theatre Verité*. You will be followed. There is someone I want you to meet. And don't look so frightened. Enjoy what is coming."

I wasted no time in quitting the place. Getting away, the business in there over, was enough for me. If there were to be more such unnatural bargains struck in future, well, I would deal with them in due course. For now, I just wanted to get back to my small apartment adjacent to the theatre and wait for my reward.

Many of Maurice de Villiers's protégés were housed in the building, which could only be entered and exited from the theatre. Some laughingly called it a prison, but I was far too diplomatic to be as loose with comments. Our lord had long ears.

Out in the night, hurrying through the packed darkness, I went home more by instinct than anything else, like a bat homing in on its lair. I used my usual route and it took me down a long alleyway between tall, abandoned storehouses, lit by an occasional light high up on the walls. Almost entombed, I heard the promised sound of pursuit. It was soft, barely audible, but it was a footfall. I knew I could not hope to avoid a meeting.

I turned, waiting. My silver had partially shielded me from the demon I had visited. I had no reason at all to suppose I was under threat now, but putting one's trust in the people of the night, as I had done, did not come easily or naturally. I was not yet one of them. My instincts were to flee the place, and only my sharp desire for a reward steadied my nerve.

It was a girl, probably in her late teens. She was barefoot and wore crimson, an elegant mix of modern fashion, silk scarfs and a simple dress that gave her an ethereal quality. As I stopped, so did she, her movements mirroring mine. Still I waited. I could see her face, smudged and dusty but nevertheless quite beautiful, framed in a halo of very dark hair that had been combed up into an aura.

Slowly she came forward, smiling. Inside my shirt, I clutched a silver chain instinctively. I felt my fingers growing hot, too hot, burned by the metal, as if I, like the dark beings I warded off, had become susceptible to the silver's power. I let the chain fall and stood, transfixed. I both longed for and dreaded what was to come.

The girl reached me and she looked now little more than a spectre, a phantasm, composed not of dimensional flesh and blood, but of something far less substantial. Mesmerised, I allowed her to close with me, her arms going around me, her hands coming up behind me, fingers digging into my hair. As we kissed, I felt an intoxication, even more puissant than my previous experiences of such beings. We held that kiss until slowly she began to melt into me, become one with me, until I had absorbed her completely.

I stood there, transfixed, my eyes closed, my entire body on fire. I don't know how long I remained like that—I would have been terribly vulnerable to anyone passing by. When I opened my eyes, the symbiosis was complete. Ah, but this was not a punishment, no, not at all. Foolish of me to have thought so, but each time it had happened to me, I had endured the same uncertainty, a human failing. Maurice de Villiers had steered me to higher levels of fulfilment. I had a new character within me, an extension to my troupe. For a while I was a little unsteady on my feet, as if I'd been drinking strong wine.

As I made my way back to the *Theatre Verité*, I became conscious of an unfamiliar pain, which seemed to have taken hold of no particular part of me, and yet pervaded me. Had I contracted some sudden illness, a virus? I had visited enough insanitary haunts often enough not to consider such things. Eventually, back in my rooms, I undressed, assiduously removed my Silver Lady make-up, and showered. I had an odd feeling about the silver. It was exacerbated when I went to hang my discarded clothes up in a wardrobe.

I could not bring myself to touch them. It was the silver, I realised. Formerly my protector, it had become somehow tainted, almost like a pollutant.

I stood, naked, before my full length mirror and studied myself, especially my face. I could see the girl there, softly superimposed behind my own features. We smiled at each other. Hers was a smile of such promise. I would call her act, my crimson caress. I lifted my left hand to touch my face—and hers—but in the mirror, the hand had no fingers. It ended in a kind of fist.

I had seen such an abnormality earlier that night. I looked at my actual hand. It was complete and yet the fingers were a little numb, as though all sensation was ebbing from them. And as the slow transformation took place, I understood the real nature of the changes about to shape my future.

It was a knowledge that suffused me with a new joy.

✗

BELTANE
By K.A. Opperman

The wicker man is burning
Upon the verdant green.
The Witches' Wheel is turning,
We hail our Maytime Queen.

We crown ourselves with flowers,
And prance the maypole round,
Until the twilight hours,
While cries of death resound.

Triumphant flames of summer
Leap off the looming pyre;
A rabbit-maskèd mummer
Adores the raging fire.

The wicker man is burning,
We pay our yearly due.
The Witches' Wheel is turning,
From death comes life anew.

THE HOUSE OF THE WITCHES

by Darrell Schweitzer

The House of the Witches perched precariously on a basalt spire, far out in the depths of space, an infinite distance from the mundane world, where star-clouds broke against black stone like the froth of an infinite sea. This was not a place that could be reached by any vessel or contrivance of mankind, only by magic, on a broomstick, in an enchanted cauldron, or in the ecstasy of a vision induced by forbidden ointment; though demons fluttered around the high windows like sparrows, and dragons coiled slowly and lazily beneath the eaves.

Still, the house crouched, like a drunken, living thing. It creaked and tottered in extra-cosmic winds, but it somehow never fell: an immense and perhaps always growing pile of wooden gables and balconies, of stone towers and battlements, of brick faces, and even a vast ivory portal carven of a *single piece*. Sometimes the floors swayed and rocked. The windows rarely looked out on the same vista twice, and the house flowed and grew and shifted, like the creation of a mad dream.

You had to be a witch to find the place comfortable. But witches did, either as an occasional resort or a permanent residence. On one high balcony, semi-enclosed behind gingerbread trimmings carved in the delicate likenesses of leaves and flowers and writhing, damned souls, there dwelt three witches of particular note. Jezebel, the oldest, could remember Babylon. That was not actually her name, but she had taken it when wicked names were all the rage. She'd known the original Jezebel and thought well of her: "Great lady," she would reminisce. "Very elegant, with a real queenly presence, even if she did wear too much makeup." The witch Jezebel had grown vast and soft and pasty-faced over the course of centuries, favoring as she did among the Seven Deadly Sins these days Sloth and Gluttony above all others. She could argue with the subtlety of a theologian that those two were just as bad as any of the rest, for all they required less exertion. "If you've got a problem with that," she'd say, "just shut up and think impure thoughts for a while."

She seldom moved now, but lay on her wide couch with her feet up on the balcony's railing. Far below, the fires of Hell burned infinitely hot, but at this distance they warmed her feet comfortably.

On a low table before her, in a space cleared amid the lavish feast that was perpetually spread out before her, she played endlessly at a game like knucklebones. She could have used it for divination, to delving into mighty secrets if she'd wanted, but now it was more of a habit. When not doing that, she often slept, dreaming iniquities and little misfortunes, which she sent wafting out into the universe like a plague of boils. As long as she could trifle with worlds and with fate, lie there and nibble on delicacies, and rattle her knucklebones, she was content.

Salome, who joined her in the game, had taken that name, too, after a series of others. She was considerably younger, little more than a slip of a girl when she and her parents had escaped from the unpleasantness at Salem in 1692. Now she was middle-aged in appearance and had a stern, solemn look about her. But she was Jezebel's boon companion.

The third witch, Annabel, whose name was not particularly wicked, more chosen for the rhyme, was less and a hundred, raised in Brooklyn among gangsters and speakeasies, pale and slinky and still addicted to nearly transparent flapper fashions and sometimes inane phraseology; but to the others she had her uses.

It was Annabel who sat apart from the other two, warming her hands with a cup of hot brimstone-flavored cocoa (something only witches have a taste for) when she noticed the surface of the beverage rippling.

"Ooh," she said.

Jezebel let her knucklebones trickle between her fingers onto the table top, heedless of where they fell.

"Someone is coming," she said.

Annabel peered intently into her cup, trying to make some sense out of the little bits of pumice floating there, and merely repeated, "Ooh."

"Someone?" said Salome.

"*He* is coming," said Jezebel. "It can be no other."

"Oh dear," said Salome.

"Ooh, golly," said Annabel.

The other two winced. What kind of a witch says "*Golly*"?

"Go, child," said Jezebel. "Go and see."

"Me?" said Annabel.

"Yes, *you*."

Jezebel picked up a cluster of grapes covered with glazed molasses with small, live insects set artistically onto each one (another witches' acquired taste) and began to devour them rather messily, apparently oblivious of Annabel, but the order had been given, and Annabel rose and went. Barefoot and silent on the stairs, she descended into the depths of the house. She conjured a cigarette in a long-stemmed holder out of the air, and trailed smoke behind her.

Down she went, into the labyrinthine bowels of the house, into the mass of stone and wood and strangely colored, warped glass that shifted as she passed, rooms popping into and out of existence like bubbles, doorways to whole worlds and dimensions opening and closing like mouths. She came to a vast, high hall where hundreds of other witches had gathered alongside the occasional visiting warlock. Wriggling, upright serpents circulated among them with trays of drinks and hors d'oeuvres, but few paid attention to them. There was palpable excitement, tension rising in the whispering susurrus of conversation. The house itself seemed to be come awake, aware, intent on what was about to happen.

Annabel made her way through the crowd, scarcely noticed, muttering no more than the occasional, "Excuse me," until she reached the opening of another stairway, and ascended, or descended, or moved through angles that human (or even witchy) senses could not quite follow, until she emerged on another balcony, like and yet the opposite to the one from which she had come, for here she did not gaze down on the distant fires of Hell, but on the starry Abyss, and galaxies splashing and swirling like foam in tidal pools.

She leaned over and studied the stars as she had the floating lumps in her cup. Yes, she saw a comet disturbed from its path. A constellation rippled, then another.

Someone was indeed coming.

But before she could even report back to the others, as she was pitter-pattering softly up a stairway filled with portraits of the famously damned, the whole house shook with a tread louder than thunder. She was thrown against the wall, hard, and one of her flailing hands went right through one of the paintings and the painting yelled, "Hey! Watch it, girl!" But she couldn't help herself. The whole place tilted as if an elephant had just stepped into one end of a rowboat. She found herself trying to crawl up the stairs on hands and knees, which was very undignified, particularly in the filmy, see-through dress she was wearing. The other figures in the portraits seemed clearly agitated as they brushed their shoulders or straightened their ties or polished their medals, making themselves ready to greet some *major* dignitary. A full-length painting of Faust at the top of the stairs said "Ahem!" in a soft voice as she almost touched it, before she regained her balance and managed to make her way past.

By the time she was able to say, "Yep, somebody's really coming, all right," Jezebel merely replied with a deep and rumbling sigh, "No, *He* is already here."

"Oh my G —!" said Salome.

"Don't say it! Quite the opposite, actually."

"*The* Him himself?" said Annabel.

But Jezebel just waved her right back down again, into the depths of the house. This time, all the figures in the portraits had left their frames. She encountered some of them among the milling multitudes in the great hall, along with quite a bit else: several giants, a Cyclops, a horde shambling and rotting corpses, assorted vampires, and a three-headed dog, not to mention witches of every possible size, shape and description.

By the time she reported back this time, the dragons that slept beneath the eaves of the towers were uncoiling with fiery yawns, and outside every window she saw flocks of bat-winged demons blotting out the stars. The whole house tilted ever more precariously beneath the weight of their massive, distinguished visitor, who stood so high above the others that when he straightened himself he took out the ceiling and stretched his wings out to brush the clouds of demons aside and touch the stars.

His face was all of fire, his eyes too bright to look upon. Yes, it was definitely him, the Big Mahoff, the Boss, the Chief, the Father of Lies, Lord of the Flies; the one they'd all kissed in a curious place when they'd signed his book, Satan himself, the Fallen Prince of Angels. When he spoke the air seemed to explode. Glass windows blew out into splinters.

Now was the time, he told them. *Now* the season had come at last for vengeance, for storming the very bastions of the enemy, for setting the whole universe to right (or more properly, to wrong), for soaring up out of the abysmal depths and smashing countless worlds, until they, all of them, all the witches and warlocks and dark demons and minions of every sort, the countless, unimaginable dark legions of Sin, burst through the unguarded gates of the Other Place and took the Throne of Creation for themselves—or for him, their leader, to be precise—that He might rule the universe for time without ending. For who said anything about time having an ending? Who said anything *at all* now that the word was out, as even the lowly humans had begun to suspect, that the Other Chap, the Master of Light, the feared and eternal Master had proven less than eternal after all and was in fact *absent*, either absconded or dead, definitely not doing miracles anymore or sending forth sword-wielding, winged hosts, consistently failing to answer prayers, and not even smiting with wrath those skeptical philosophers who doubted his very existence.

"*Now* is the time for the final war and the final triumph!" spoke the Lord of Darkness. "Now let us make all of creation tremble!"

There were considerably more words to that effect. Whatever else Satan's presentation may have been, mind-searing, capable of shaking the stars from their courses, it was definitely not brief.

And though such a discourse would never have descended to such trivialities of phrasing as *when the cat's away, the mice will play*, that was how Annabel summed it up in her own mind as she struggled to make her way back to tell Jezebel and Salome what was happening. She was somewhat the worse for wear, bedraggled, tattered, and buffeted about like a leaf on a roaring wind. By the time she got there, the House was well on its way to transforming itself from a conglomeration of stone and wood and charmingly-cut gingerbread trim into a thing of living metal, covered with scales, blazing fire out of thousands of windows like a multitude of eyes, spreading its wings from one end of the cosmos to the other as it made ready to leap from its stony perch and crash over the very battlements of Heaven; by that time Annabel, who was not the most articulate of witches under the best of circumstances, had scarcely managed a "Jeepers," much less any further ineffectual clichés, and no further summation was necessary. It was all too obvious what was going on.

Once more the House shook and heaved, and Jezebel actually slid forward like a fleshy avalanche onto the floor, making inappreciative noises before she finally managed to mutter, "You know, this is going to be a *lot* of bother!"

"Oh dear," said Salome plaintively. "I liked things the way they were."

Annabel managed one last "Gee—"

Jezebel raised herself up with all her strength, caught hold of the couch with one hand, and paused, gasping. Sloth and Gluttony were fine Sins, she knew, but there could be times when they were *damned* inconvenient. Nevertheless, she was the one who was going to have to *do* something. The other two could only flutter and say, "Oh dear! Oh dear!" Annabel's cocoa cup fell from the table onto floor and shattered, making a mess. Knucklebones scattered everywhere. A dish of some kind of sauce splashed onto the floor, making a hideous mess. Salome clung to a drapery hanging for dear life. Annabel managed to flop down on her rump, her legs spread apart, her slinky dress ripping all the way up the side as she did.

"Oops," she said.

It was Jezebel who kept her presence of mind, as she always did. She nodded to Annabel and then jerked her head toward the stairway.

"What you can do, Dearie, is ask our guest to come up and have a chat."

"*Him?* Ask *him* to come to you?"

"That's what I said. Go!"

So she went, yet again, but not very far, because soon she found herself face to face with Satan, who came roiling at her up the stairwell like an explosion of fire up a chimney. It was all she could do to scramble back the way she came, and get out of the way before the immense face floated in the air before Jezebel.

The eyes were indeed too bright to look upon. Even Jezebel held up a hand to shield herself.

"You'll pardon me if I don't get up," she said.

"*You* did not attend when I summoned *all* before me!"

Salome whimpered. Annabel cringed. But Jezebel merely said, "I'm not *all*. I'm a special case. A specialist. In my two particular sins, you must admit, I am exemplary. I was *so* hoping you would stop by so we could have this chat, before you did anything rash."

"*What?*"

"Dreadful One, it is only out of the deep devotion I hold for you in the depths of my blackened soul and corrupted heart that I am able to bring myself to tell you that maybe your present enterprise needs a few finishing touches—"

"*What?*"

"It's your image, Sir. A bit old-fashioned. Sure, you *can* rule the universe through sheer monstrosity and terror, but wouldn't it be more elegant to *allure*? Maybe I'd have to ask the young girls, the under-a-hundred set like Annabel over there, but I am pretty certain that we witches don't go into for the winged, clawed horrors anymore. And if you will pardon my saying so, you reek, of sulfur and goatiness and I don't know what all else. Were you not *beautiful* once? How about that again?"

"What do you suggest?" said Satan, his vanity piqued.

Jezebel snapped her fingers. The shattered cup miraculously repaired itself. It sat on the table top, steaming, not with hot cocoa, but with something white and bubbly which dribbled smoke over the rim.

"I've prepared a special potion. Drink up," he said. "By my wickedness, it's just the thing."

An immense claw materialized. Satan took up the cup delicately, doubtfully.

Jezebel winked at him.

He drank, throwing back the contents like a shot of whiskey.

The transformation began at once. His whole outline shimmered. Before long he towered only three or four feet above than Annabel, and *all* of him fit onto the balcony, no longer goatlike or serpentine or resembling a winged, bipedal dinosaur, lacking scales at all or even horns other than a faint hint of a pair of bumps at his hairline, entirely sans forked tail and without his sulfurous stench. If anything he seemed to be wearing cologne. He had assumed a far more human aspect, immense, but otherwise the extreme archetype and composite of tens of thousands of movie idols and rock stars, the perfect lust object in tight leather pants and a white, silken shirt split open in the middle to reveal a muscular, gleaming chest and a neck draped with jewelry.

And, decidedly, without wings.

Very much to the point, without wings.

Now it was Annabel's job to lean on the balcony in the tattered remains of her slinky dress, a condition of near nudity never being inappropriate for a witch even under ordinary circumstances, much less when she was heaving her assets and murmuring breathlessly, "Hey there, big boy…"

Satan turned, leering. He stepped toward the balcony. Below, there glowed no mere stars and galaxies, but the fires of Hell.

And it was Salome's job to give him a firm shove, precisely as Jezebel, shifting her position with more vigor than might have seemed possible, reached out with a cane she had not used in centuries and deliberately *tripped* him.

Then all Annabel had to do was get out of the way, as he let out a yell and was gone, very quick but not quick enough to work out the implications of not having any wings.

Annabel looked down. She thought she saw the Hell fires flicker.

"Oops," she said.

* * * *

To no one in particular, Jezebel said, "The problem with corrupted souls and blackened hearts is that they tend to think of themselves first. Selfish and lazy, the lot of them."

"Even our vices have vices," said Salome.

"Like fleas having fleas," said Annabel.

"That's right, girls. Now help me up."

They helped her up, and she said, "We three actually do make a pretty good team, you know. Here, have a grape."

Around them, the House of the Witches settled back into its old, ramshackle, infinitely changing, shuddering self, with countless comfortable verandas and porches and balconies decorated with gingerbread trim, perched precariously on its basalt spire amid stars and galaxies, always about to topple off but never quite doing so.

Annabel sipped her brimstone cocoa. Jezebel and Salome played at knucklebones, trifling with the destinies of worlds, but no more than that; and if the gates of Heaven were ajar and the throne of God empty, they must have remained so, because none of the witches ever bothered to check them out.

For the two Sins to which Jezebel was especially devoted are as Deadly as any of the others, but they have the one self-limiting feature that they do not inspire ambition.

Such are the ways of wickedness.

THE BONES
by Erica Ruppert

The bones lay like a mosaic on the damp dirt floor, so old they no longer smelled of death. Toni had no idea how they had gone undisturbed so long. The debris in the basement's corners spoke of other break-ins, other explorations. She kicked crushed cans out of her way as she made her way closer to the bare brown skeleton. A faint thrill of fear fluttered under her heart, but it was distant. She had sought it out so often that it had dulled.

Light from the high broken windows reached into the room like a mist. Toni played her flashlight beam over the curved ribs, fleshing them out with their own shadows. The skeleton was on its back, looking as if it had fallen there. It looked complete, from what Toni could tell.

Between the long fragile bones of the skeleton's hand stood a flat rectangle the size of a postcard. Toni reached for it gingerly, pinching a corner between her fingers. It was an old sandwich bag folded over on itself, and it tore as she lifted it free. What the decayed plastic protected was still intact.

She moved closer to the windows to let the thin sunlight drift over her shoulder. The filthy plastic crumbled as she opened it. She let the tatters drop and unfolded the brittle paper inside.

The pencil drawing had blurred as the paper aged, but it was still a recognizable portrait. Toni glanced over the paper's edge to the skeleton sprawled at the edge of the light. The angle was right, the skull's tilt, the bend of the leg. On the paper, a woman's breasts lolled, her hair spread out across the dirt, her eyes shut as in sleep. Whoever had drawn this had included the bruises around her throat.

Now Toni felt the fear as more than the weak beating of wings in her throat. She shifted her feet, felt grit roll under her soles. Now. Here. This was where the artist had stood. She looked back down at the paper. The woman had been pretty enough, her nose a little pugged but a sweet face.

She folded the paper carefully along its old creases and slid it into her back pocket. Then she hitched herself out through the broken window she had used to get in.

The street was quiet, even for this early in the day. The neighborhood was fading out slowly, its inhabitants shifting further east in the city. Too many of these buildings were empty, now, except for the squatters. Toni walked the two blocks back to her car. She'd left it parked in a neighborhood where people still lived.

Her hand left a smear of blood where she gripped the wheel. She'd cut it getting out of the basement, she thought. Cocooned in her car the fear she dragged out with her eased. She realized she had forgotten to take any pictures of the body, of the lonely cellar, of the garbage.

As she drove out she thought the streets seemed emptier than they had when she had come in. She headed back over the highway to familiar territory.

* * * *

At home she opened up the drawing again, smoothed it out gently and pinned it to the board above her desk. The paper had taken on a pale ivory tint from age. Toni stared at it for long minutes, memorizing the smudged pencil shadows of the woman's face, the dark pool of her hair, the curve of her thighs. The detail in the drawing gave her a strange impression, as if the artist had traced over a photograph to make this.

She took the drawing down long enough to scan it and open it with the freeware modeling program she had downloaded. Her shoulders already tight, she leaned in to her screen and got to work.

Willa came in with a clatter of keys as she dropped them on the entryway table. She was never quiet. Toni's eyes flickered to her and then back to the screen.

"So, did you find some inspiration?" Willa said.

"Yeah," Toni said. Her hand hovered over the mouse as she studied what she had done so far. "Up on the other side of the Forty Three. The neighborhood up there is emptying out."

Willa walked past Toni and into the kitchen. She opened the refrigerator, closed it again. A drawer clattered open. Silverware clicked. Toni shut her eyes, wishing the distractions away.

"Everyone's moving away from that end of town," Willa said, loud enough to be heard across the apartment. "I hear it's not safe up there anymore."

"I know," Toni said, pressing her fingers to her temples. "It's pretty creepy with hardly anyone around."

Willa came back into the living room with a sandwich in her hand. Toni opened her eyes to refocus on the screen.

"Look, Toni," Willa said. "Let me go up there with you if you go again. Safety in numbers and all that."

"Alright," Toni said, not turning around. "Now I gotta work."

Willa came up behind her and leaned over her shoulder to look. Toni tensed at the intrusion. At first Willa said nothing, only breathed into Toni's hair.

"Well," she said after a moment. "That's a pretty messed up self-portrait you've got going on."

Toni brushed her away.

"Shut up. It's a drawing I found today."

"Where was it? It looks like you. Or is that what you're trying to do?"

Toni didn't answer.

* * * *

It was closer to morning than night when Toni finally shut down and went to bed.

The night outside the window was too quiet, without even a distant rumble of traffic. Toni curved herself around Willa's warm back for comfort and reached up to stroke her face. Her hair had fallen over it, and Toni brushed it away. Willa's hair felt thick and wavy under her hands, and the curls tangled in her fingers. Toni pulled her hand back. That wasn't Willa's hair. Who she held didn't smell like Willa, was too tall and too muscular. Toni screamed in the dark, awake.

The bedsheets fell in a tidal wave as Willa threw them up and back and rolled to grab at Toni's shoulders, shaking her out of nightmare. In the dim glint of streetlights through the window Toni could see it was the right Willa. Toni stopped screaming and clutched at her, still caught between.

* * * *

Over the next few days Toni built up the face in clay, copying the model she had made of the sketch. She pressed her thumbs into the soft clay, smoothing out the curve of the cheeks, the pinch of the chin, the wide-set eyes.

It looked like the drawing and her 3D model of the drawing. But any initial sweetness Toni had seen in the face was gone. It was still pretty, and recognizable from the pencil sketch. But Toni didn't like looking at it any more. There was a cast to it now that cooled her blood.

She took a picture of her sculpture before she mashed the clay back into a featureless mass and rewrapped it in plastic bags for storage. She didn't want to see it any longer, not as a physical presence in her world. The woman's sketched features already followed her, living through her eyes.

Toni imagined the woman in many faces, now, reflected in windows, caught in profile in a moving crowd of pedestrians, in the background of videos. One morning Toni thought she saw the woman turn the corner in her hallway just as she stepped out of her apartment. Toni took to staying in more than she went out. She worked on the computer model she had made, changing the angles, altering the features, trying to find something familiar in it. It looked more and more like her as she tweaked it. She didn't dare erase it. It had gone too far.

* * * *

Toni thought she could perform an exorcism of sorts if she went back, if she returned the pencil sketch to its keeper. Maybe if she stood the folded drawing back between those dry fingers she would be rid of its power over her imagination. She knew it was magical thinking. She didn't care.

She parked on the block she had used the first time, but now even this area was becoming depopulated. At this rate, she and Willa would need to start looking for a new place soon. She walked quickly, head down, hands clenched in her jacket pockets, waiting for a threat that didn't come. She had trouble finding the building again. It seemed as if the neighborhood had fallen to ruin in the few weeks since she had found it. The street sign was down, and more than one apartment house on the block had burned and fallen and left a jagged gap behind.

She walked up and down the block, aware of how alone she was. Finally, one shabby building seemed familiar, and Toni thought she recognized the unbarred broken window she had used before. She bent low to peer into darkness, holding her phone up for its fragile light. Shadows hung in the air like a haze of smoke. There were shapes on the floor that might be a narrow figure, a sheen that could be long, bare teeth. Toni wriggled down and put her head through the window. She thought something moved in the depths of the room, scratching the floor. It could have been her own shadow, her own sounds. She could not be sure. She stood free of the window, quickly, her heart beating fast.

Every window was an empty eye on her. Toni wished she had parked closer. She drew her shoulders up against the solitude and walked to her car without looking back.

* * * *

Toni stared when Willa pulled open the apartment door for her before she could turn the key. She thought Willa would still be at work. Toni walked past her with a scant shrug and started her laptop. Behind her she heard the door click shut, light footsteps, the creak of furniture. Toni tried to keep her eyes on the screen, but Willa coughed for attention. Toni turned half-around, just enough to see her.

"Where did you get to today?" Willa asked, lounging in a sloppy heap on the sprung sofa.

"Other side of the Forty Three."

She swung back to her laptop. Toni knew better than to open up the modeling program and look at that face again, but she still did. Willa sighed behind her, getting up.

"I wish you'd have let me know."

Toni saved the project and logged off. She couldn't gauge how upset Willa was. "I wasn't sure I could find it again."

"Did you?"

Willa stood over her. Toni looked up. "Yes."

"And?"

Willa's face shifted as uncast shadows moved across it. Toni blinked and rubbed at her eyes. She turned away.

"It was empty. Just empty."

* * * *

Toni spent the night in the living room, lonely from Willa's anger. She set her alarm for too early, hoping to escape the apartment's confines before Willa woke. But the silence of the building around her kept her restless and half-awake, waiting for some human sound to come. The emptiness had followed her back. Shadows coiled through the lace curtains like strands of hair, and she dreamed the face behind them.

Toni finally stopped dreaming with the morning, and slept through the alarm's bright buzz. When she got up Willa was in the kitchen, and it was too late to leave without a fight. She didn't have the energy for it. She tried to walk out before it could happen.

"Where are you going?" Willa asked, stopping her at the door.

Toni looked away. Willa stood her ground. She took Toni's chin in her hand and made her look at her.

"You have someone."

Toni pulled her head free. "Don't be stupid."

"I'm coming with you," Willa said. Toni squirmed like an embarrassed teen.

"I'll wait for you downstairs," Toni said then, guilty and impatient, and she headed down the hall to the elevator while Willa was finding her shoes.

Toni walked out of the building and saw that the desolation had come to her. The steps of their building were cracked, the façade caked with graffiti. The only cars on the street were stripped-out shells. The one in front of her building still had faded memorial poppies hanging from the rear-view mirror. She realized it was hers.

Willa should have been right behind her. Toni turned, frightened.

"Willa?" she called. Her voice fell flat in the empty street. She turned back, up the steps and back through the peeling door.

"Willa? Where are you?"

The foyer was filthy, littered like an animal's den. Had it been like that when she came down? Toni couldn't remember. The elevator door was jammed halfway open, now. She was sure it was working a minute ago.

She noticed that the basement door was chocked open. It was never left open. That was one of the superintendent's pet peeves, and he enforced it. She peered into the shadows of the ugly stairwell. "Willa!" she called again. A voice came back to her. She wasn't sure it wasn't her own. Wishing for stronger light, Toni started down.

The same decay in the streets had ruined the basement. The elevator doors were blocked with old furniture. The storage lockers were opened and looted. Hook-ups from the washers and dryers dangled against the unfinished brick wall, the machines gone. Toni remembered a tiled floor down here, but now there was nothing but dirt.

Pale light came in through the narrow windows at the front of the building. Toni turned toward them. She walked forward, gauging the lay of the room. She knew where she was. Then her feet tangled in the ribcage hidden by shadows and she stuttered in place, fighting gravity and trying not to break the fragile bones with her clumsy feet. She found her balance, bent and moved the bones away. It felt wrong to disturb them after they had lain so patiently for so long. Under her fingers the long ribs were smooth and warm.

Toni looked down at what her hands did, disturbed by the sensation of heat. Her hands were empty, her fingers closed on air. She squatted at the edge of the light, where the bones should be. They were gone, and she crouched in a swept-clean circle on the hard dirt floor.

She stood and looked around her for evidence of the body. There was nothing. She walked to the broken window. There was blood on the frame where she had cut herself getting out. She turned around, recreating her first sight of the dry brown bones. Shadows bent into familiar, suggestive shapes, but the hard skeleton was gone.

Toni walked slowly back to where it had been, where it should have been. She tilted her head, at certain angles catching the distant curve of the skull and the web of the tapering finger bones. The dim light tricked her eyes. The ground beneath her seemed to ripple and fade. She knelt down, feeling heat beneath her knees. It was beneath her. Waiting.

She dug into the packed dirt with a broken chunk of brick, scraping up the hard surface enough to get her fingers into it. She felt her nails tear as she dug, but the pain didn't matter. The hole grew. A hand's-span down her fingers scraped on something smooth and hollow. When she pried it loose she saw it was a small plastic box, faded into a milky pink from its long burial. The brittle catch snapped off as she opened it.

Blood smeared the box as she lifted a dull pencil out. Beneath it was a washed-out photograph, curled from being pressed into the narrow box. Toni held it up to the light. It was the woman from the drawing. In the square image she stood in front of the basement window with a pad in the crook of her arm. Her dark hair hung over her shoulders. She was looking down and smiling.

Toni turned on her knees to face the empty window. The picture had been taken from where she crouched now. Where the body lay in the drawing. Her scalp prickled with sudden sweat. Behind her, where the light didn't reach, lead scratched on paper. Sketching her.

TWIN HUNGERS
by Scott J. Couturier

My neck shows the scars—
two toothsome, pearlescent punctures.
Now, sealed behind iron bars
I am kept from satiating sanguine hungers.

I crave hot blood—
but more, I desire the rapturous bite!
My own ichor in bright flood
gorging that lovely revenant of the night—

Oh, it pains me terribly
to be so hale & flushed with life!
My passions wax unbearably—
from secreted metal I hone a razor knife.

The orderlies mock me—
call me mad, dump pig's blood in my bowl.
I lap it up with a ghoulish glee,
mind fixated on my final, fatal goal.

The knife, now keen,
I save until late one mournful winter's eve;
He comes to me in a dream
re-enacting our delicious, deleterious cleave.

The yearning is too great!
Slitting down my wrists with nary a cry
I seek my twin hungers to sate
until I collapse dead, drained blissfully dry.

THE IDOLS OF XAN
by Steve Dilks

1.

The thunderous roar of the turbine ships filled the sky as they continued their relentless search and pursuit of survivors.

In the shadows of the desert canyon below, Matt Randall clung to the rocks like a cornered beast. His eyes, desperate and feral, swept the skyline. No movement or sound did he make though his leather combat armour was ripped to shreds and he bled from a score of dripping wounds. Only the heavy steel of the gun in his hand wavered slightly to betray the tension etched on a bronzed and scarred face.

The sun blazed down from the pale sky- a red fiery eye of death.

Then he heard it. From up the valley, the hiss and crackle of company issue radios. The soldiers were on the ground and coming his way.

Randall snarled and braced his back to the wall again, one hand outflung and gripping a jagged piece of rock, the other raising and lifting the heavy snouted heat-gun in a knotted fist. He licked dry lips, finding himself wishing for a drink of water before he died.

He thought of the shade of the marble palace walls in Yarissha and the easy company of the tawny eyed women living there. He wondered if they would miss him. He shook his head and, bending his lips in a grim smile, shrugged. After all, today was a fine day to die- and this fine day he would not die alone.

The echoing tread of the soldiers drew nearer, setting his heart to thudding until he thought it would burst through what was left of his armour. He craned his head round an outcropping and saw them fanning out toward him, rifles held pressed against their shoulders and moving in full tactical maneuver. He noted their full plated body armour and close set visor helmets.

Randall crouched low, still gripping the wall with one hand for support. He stood on a hard pile of granite forming a depression in the valley wall. They would not see him until it was too late. In the shadows his eyes narrowed to slits of feline fire.

The first scout rounded the bend, skirting the foot of his rocky perch without seeing him. A second swept into view, ranging further out, his helmet moving to and fro as he went. The rest came by in a successive wave of ones and twos.

Suddenly, there was a roar overhead as a turbine ship flashed across the skyline. In that moment a soldier jerked his head up and saw him.

Without thought, the heat-gun bucked in Matt's hand and the soldier somersaulted into the air, spraying misted blood and brains from a broken helm. His rifle spun, hitting another soldier and for a moment confusion reigned. Randall leaped and, landing in a crouch, came up running. His heavy boots churned the gravel as he charged them- a detached shadow coming out of hell; the heat-gun hissing death in his hand.

One soldier spun and hit the ground, an arm blown completely off at the shoulder.

Another screamed and crashed to his knees as he was blasted through the chest, his armour useless at close quarters as the collapsed metal fused to his melting innards.

He came in so low and fast, they could not bring their rifles into play. He hit a man hard in the thighs with his shoulders and, as they crashed to the ground, he rolled up- heat-gun poised.

But he had not reckoned with the quick thinking reactions of the company.

From out of nowhere, a lithe figure moved in. There was a snapping hiss and a baton darted out, caressing his elbow like the tongue of a viper. Pain exploded in exquisite waves along Randall's arm and the gun flew from his nerveless fingers. He yelled in agony and rolled away, his left hand darting to his boot. He came up with a long knife held in a reverse angled grip. The soldiers moved in a step and stood, rifles levelled.

The frozen tableau held; Randall bloodied and snarling, crouching in the dust ready for death- the soldiers statue poised, ready to take his life. Then the lithe figure held up an armoured fist and, stepping forward, indicated his chest with the baton; "Surrender."

Randall sneered back at his own image reflected in the dark visored helm.

"Die!" he growled and sprang. The baton lashed out, striking him across the temple.

He collapsed in a heap and lay very still.

The tall soldier, moving forward, prodded his form with a booted toe. Reaching up, they removed their helmet and shook out a cascade of long dark hair.

"Bind him." she said.

2.

When Matt Randall finally came to, a vagrant moon was riding high up over the valley ramparts. He found himself propped against a boulder, hands bound tightly behind him. A canteen was thrust rudely to his lips and he slurped from it greedily until it was snatched away again. Close and near by, black armoured figures crouched in the dust. The occasional crack of their radios and mumbled reply was the only sound. Otherwise they were quiet and motionless as statues these men, carved seemingly from the rock around them.

The soldier that had given him the water stood and motioned to another crouching someway off. That figure rose and came toward them in long easy strides, helmet tucked under one arm. Randall noted it was a woman. A strikingly beautiful woman. She nodded as she came up.

"You are not of Mangala." she said bluntly. "What brings you here?"

Randall stared and grunted, "Money, what else?"

"Do you know what the penalty is for off-worlders who interfere with the politics of our planet?"

Randall said nothing. The big soldier beside her muttered something in a guttural tongue and fingered the hilt of a combat knife strapped to his thigh. He had bleak eyes and a fierce emblem tattooed down one side of his face. He stared at Randall with the old primeval hatred for the outsider. The off-worlder grinned at him. Then, staring directly back at the woman, he said; "Listen, I'm flattered- truly. But war is money, lady and I'm paid to fight. I don't give a damn for politics. Of your world or any other."

"The courts at Nygol will be the judge of that," she replied, "not me. That's if Kurghuz, here, doesn't get to you and carve you a new face first."

Randall laughed. "So the grunt has a name, does he? Well, I'm Matt Randall- and you?"

"Lieutenant Arealla of the second core recon division."

"Well, Lieutenant, seems like you've gone to a hell of a lot of trouble today."

"We were sent to track down you desert raiders after that last caravan heading out of Zavoskol was attacked. Some of the recon crew are scouring the valley. We have reason to believe there is a hideout down here. It's rumored Borquha, the Bloodhawk, chieftain of the Zuethii raiders, is hiding somewhere here with his men. Perhaps you know something about it and were even making for his camp when we ambushed you?"

Her large dark eyes narrowed as she spoke.

Randall shrugged. "If there is a camp down here you'd never find it. These valleys are honeycombed with caves and tunnels. It'd take ten squadrons a thousand years to sweep this place. What have you got- twenty men?" He shook his head in mock derision and leaned back.

"Best go home and face the music, lady. Trust me. This is a dead end. Even if there were raiders down here they would tear you to pieces. They were born and bred to this land. I may be a stranger to your world but you are just as much a stranger to them. You don't understand them."

Arealla laughed, eyes glinting hard in the reflected starlight. "And you do, I suppose?"

Randall looked at her. There was no mockery in his voice when he replied; "I am an outcast like them. Their cause speaks to something inside me."

"What could an earthman know of a cause beyond his own greed?" snarled Kurghuz.

"Have I said I was an earthman?" Randall said, his head jerking up.

They looked again at him, noting the lambent fires burning deep in his eyes, the hard angled planes of his features.

"My mother was of earth, my father a full bloodied warrior of the Baerri."

The Baerri were space farers. Nomads of the stars. They came of a restless, violent breed. They knew no homeworld and were outlaws- pariahs of the universe. Wherever their ships plied the systems, they were feared and despised. There was no love lost between them and the planets pledged to the imperial union.

Kurghuz grumbled and, spitting in the dust, turned away. As he did, a soldier came running up and saluted Arealla.

"Trouble, Lieutenant," he said breathlessly, "Faymun and Sindor haven't checked in. Both their radios are dead."

Arealla swore feelingly. "What was their last location?"

"North and east; approximately five pargon from here, sir."

She turned to Kurghuz. "Round up the men. We'll take off on that course then split into two divisions closer to the rendezvous point. If there's someone out there, we'll give them a nasty surprise."

Kurghuz nodded. "What about him?" He jerked a thumb at Randall.

"He comes with us. Put a collar on him and place him at the rear of the column guard."

3.

Dark fingers of rock thrust up against the stars, bathing the valley in soft shadow. In these shadows the company clung, skirting boulders as they went, silent and methodical in their advance. Randall stumbled along behind, the leash of his collar secured in the grip of a rear guard soldier. He made no complaint when he fell and a curse and well aimed rifle butt drove him to his feet again. His body was bruised and numb, but his mind absorbed the pain. Years of living at the edges of the universe, surviving in impossible terrains, had hardened him to a life that would have broken a lesser man.

Arealla cursed her luck. She had already lost three men. Losing two of her scouts was something she could ill afford. It was still some six hours before rendezvous at the pick up point. She wanted the rest of her crew intact and stable until then.

Up ahead Kurghuz, reaching a plinth of granite, began climbing dexterously. At the summit he crouched suddenly and, turning, held up a fist. As one the unit melted into the dense shadows, rifles ready.

There was an eerie silence.

Arealla, squinting down the sight of her own rifle, counted to twenty. She could see Kurghuz, his broad shoulders outlined against the stars.

Then, quiet as a sand cat, she crept along the broken trail. Slinging her automatic under one arm, she raced up the incline to join him at the top. He did not look as she came up but pointed downwards with his free hand, his weapon still primed. Arealla, following to where he indicated, stifled a gasp.

Below, washed in the cold light of the moon, stood a ring of columns. Black carved, asymmetrically lined with strange runes, they seemed to draw in the light from everywhere around them until they radiated with their own luminescence. Even from where they sat, crouched high up on the precipice, they could feel their power. But that was not all. Just inside that ring lay two black armoured figures.

Arealla felt the icy hand of fear clutch her heart. She bit down an irresistible urge to run screaming. "Bring that earth bastard up here." she choked into her helmet mic.

Presently, Randall was brought up and hauled onto the ledge.

"Two of my men are lying down there. What is that? Some sort of trap?"

Arealla stabbed an accusing finger at the ebon columns.

The soldier holding Randall's leash grabbed him by the roots of his lion like mane of hair and forced his head back. Randall grit his teeth but made no outcry.

"I don't know what that is," he growled, "and yet..."

"And yet, what?"

"I don't know, it seems... familiar somehow. As if I've seen a place like it somewhere before. In a dream perhaps, or a nightmare."

Arealla frowned and nodded to the soldier who let him go with a curse and a well aimed kick to the ribs. Kurghuz looked to her. "He's telling the truth, I think." she sighed, "Or, at the very least, he's not lying. Do you know where we are?"

"According to these survey readouts, a place known only as Xan. An old place. No data about it. Maybe it's shunned for some reason. There are certain places in the Jakor desert that are taboo to the tribesmen. This could be one of them. I've heard stories among my own people about the ancient ones and the stones they left behind. The shamans say that the ancients were terrible beings. More ghosts than men, it is said that they still haunt the old canal ways of Tiu-Maris, worshipping and awaiting the return of the black gods."

Arealla grabbed him by the shoulder and, staring hard into his eyes, whispered; "None of this talk in front of the men, Kurghuz. You're a soldier of the core now."

Kurghuz nodded but his face was a grim, taut mask.

"Whatever that is," she continued, "we have to investigate. Prepare the men. We'll make a parameter sweep and come in from all sides."

4.

As they moved in they fanned into a semi-circle. The columns reared above them. Inside the ring they could see their two fallen comrades, lying spread eagled in the dust. Where the valley was a composite of dark grey rock, inside the circle there was only ash- barren and lifeless as the surface of a dead moon.

They held their positions a few paces off.

"What now, sir?" whispered a soldier through his helmet mic.

"Send in the prisoner." Arealla replied.

Randall cursed as he was pushed forward. The collar was taken from his throat and the manacles unsnapped from his wrists. He looked at the blank faced visors around him, searching for Arealla. "Well, you might at least give me a drink of water before I die."

A soldier unclipped a canteen from his belt and handed it to him. Randall took it, downed two swallows then upended the rest of the contents on the ground. Dropping the flask, he kicked it clattering into the columns.

"Thanks." he said and stalked forward. The cold touch of fear played down his spine but he forced himself on. He passed through the ring and, as he did, a change came over him.

It was as if he were suddenly wading through heavy water. Every hair on his body stood up on end. Then it passed and he was through and standing inside the ring.

He looked at what was left of Faymun and Sindor and shuddered. Of their corpses only bleached bones remained. Empty eye sockets stared at him in hollow mockery. Grinning jaws gaped in eternal silent screaming. It was as if they had lain there for centuries. Only their armour and equipment, perfectly preserved, betrayed the fact they had only gone missing a few hours before.

Randall turned to stare outside the ring. His brow furrowed. He could see the soldiers but it was as if he was looking at them from the bottom of a pool. The air between him and the columns contracted with some unseen force or energy.

Dimly at first, then with dawning realization, he began to understand.

He now knew why Faymun and Sindor had not checked in and why their radios had gone dead. He now knew what strange sensation it was he had felt when he had first stepped between those ebon columns. They were protected by a magnetic force field. By some strange token he also began to understand that the natural laws of time and space did not apply here. That last was the most uncanny realization of all. Indeed, it was then, at last, that he truly began to fear…

The air around the columns rippled like the surface of a pool disturbed by a thrown pebble. Kurghuz, leading the first of the soldiers, had passed through the barrier. Another wave, led by Arealla, came in from the rear. They closed in to where Randall stood over the bodies.

Arealla, eyeing the corpses at his feet, was first to speak; "What is this place?" she murmured. Her voice trembled in a mixture of awe and fear as she wrenched off her helmet.

Randall shrugged. "I think you'll find your radios are dead. We passed through a magnetic field back there."

"He's right," said Kurghuz, "there's no signal."

"What's this?" Arealla, moving past the bodies, made her way over to the centre of the ring. Standing there was a colossal rock carved from obsidian. Chiseled into its surface was a symbol; stark and bold, pregnant with unknown meaning.

When Randall beheld that symbol he flinched. An icy sweat formed on his brow. It was as if his DNA recoiled screaming from it. He turned. When he looked, his hands were trembling.

"Frightened, earth boy?" Kurghuz sneered. Randall looked at him. "There's something wrong here. Something we don't understand. Something… alien."

Just then a soldier yelled out and Randall whirled. The symbol on the rock had begun to glow. A dull pulsing, deep veined red, it fanned into a searing white hot flame. Soldiers fell back from it, throwing up their arms and shielding their eyes.

As if that was the prelude to something more sinister, ominous clouds began billowing up over the tops of the columns, blotting out the stars. They drifted in heavy misty wreaths. Then, slowly as they watched, they began to fall in a descending mist, clinging to those columns in white slumbering folds.

Then—madness!

5.

Inside those billowing clouds, something began to stir and take shape. It formed in the air above the obsidian rock, huge as a shield, emanating a cold, impersonal evil.

Then it opened.

A gigantic malefic eye.

A soldier fell back screaming, opening fire with his rifle. The deafening sound of the heat blasts made no impact. The mists were all about them and suddenly, from the very ether, a colossal tentacle whipped downward. It coiled itself around the waist of the soldier, a hideous pulpy mass of translucent flesh. Before he had a chance to scream, the loathsome appendage had whipped back into the mists again and vanished, bearing away its horrified victim with it. All hell broke loose. Soldiers began firing into the mist, falling over themselves in panic to get away from the blaze of the supernatural orb glaring above them. Kurghuz, charging like a bull, hurled himself forward, roaring for Arealla. Tentacles began lashing out in all directions. Every strike ensnared an armoured soldier in a clammy embrace. Kurghuz avoided those whipping coils, skidding and diving in the dust to where Arealla crouched, her back against the rock, blasting away with her rifle. Above her the symbol in the black stone burned with a fierce light.

Unarmed, Randall staggered back toward the columns. Behind him he could hear the screams of dying men, the chooming blasts of their rifles as he groped for the magnetic barrier. The coiling mists grew denser. All around, the columns outthrust at bizarre angles like constructs from a nightmare. His boot snagged in something on the ground and, as he fell, his hand closed on something familiar.

Squinting through the mist, he made out the remains of one of the missing soldiers. He rose, slinging the dead man's rifle over his shoulder. Clambering over the corpse, he made for the columns. It seemed as if they loomed gigantically now. He groped his way onward - down an impossible lined avenue of pillars that opened up to let him pass. They stretched on into a fevered eternity. Above, there were no stars, just a tumultuous sky. His feet carried him on, though it seemed he was drowning forever in mist.

Ahead something began to glow in the darkness. The mists evaporated before a cold light- white and ethereal. It was the symbol- the rune carved on the black stone. He stopped, looking behind him.

There was nothing. An avenue of titanic pillars stretching into infinity. Before him he saw a carved set of ebon steps. At the top stood a hideous idol hewn from the same black volcanic rock. A blasphemous effigy of monstrous dimensions, it stared at him from a huge cyclopean eye. It squatted on a dais high again as he was tall.

In the centre of that dais burned the symbol - a forgotten rune of the gods.

Before it, Randall's soul shriveled in fear. He would have turned and fled but there was nowhere to go. That this was somehow ordained he was resigned.

Mechanically, he began walking up the stone steps of the dais.

6.

Behind him a lost wind moaned, crying an anguish of the damned.

He lifted his head. Above him the statue towered into the sky. His narrowed gaze focused on the symbol on the dais. As it did, memories flashed deep inside his mind's eye. He saw a dust shrouded world, a stinking hell hole of a planet where volcanoes reared and the sun beat down from a dirty yellow sky. Ninurta IV. He had been lured there by the mining corps with the promise of a precious ore that made men rich. Instead, all he had found was hunger and death. Working in the heat and dust, he saw again a line of hooded robed priests as they filed out of their black carved temple, swinging their censers. One word they chanted.... over and over again... a mantra that drove like a red hot needle into his brain. Despite the warnings of the natives not to, he remembered staring into the hood of an acolyte that passed nearest him. The darkness of that hood turned toward him and he drew back- unnerved by what he saw. Then they had passed and he shouldered his way out of the throng that had gathered to watch on the shores of that nameless town. That night he drank more than usual in the saloons as if to wash away the very memory of those strange priests. Still later, he dreamed.... dreamed that he stood inside their temple as it squatted in the shadow of the volcanoes under a black moon. He saw again the hooded figure of the acolyte. This time he stepped up to Randall who stood shackled by invisible bonds against a black pillar. He watched frozen, unable to move limb or tongue. He could only look in horror as the acolyte slowly reached up his hand toward him. On his palm, carved into the grey flesh, was a symbol. A voice issued from the hood, soft and sibilant, speaking an alien tongue that he somehow understood. "The centre of the universe is not a place... it is a vibration, a sound. Learn that sound. Embrace it and be at one with all things." The priest then reached up and clamped his hand onto his forehead- pressing the symbol deep between his eyes. He spoke a word and the might of it struck Randall like a thunderbolt. He screamed in mute understanding but his voice made no sound. It was the same word he had heard the priests chanting that very afternoon. It became a part of him. Then the hooded figure stepped away and Matt fell to his knees, freed from the invisible bonds that shackled him. He looked up but the strange priest had gone, melted silently into the shadows. Somehow he knew that he had been given a terrible knowledge and that gift was old, perhaps as old as time itself. He awoke then, as if from a fever, and lay there staring out of his cabin window into the dusky, sweating night beyond. The dream ebbed away and he had slept, never to be troubled by it again.

Until now.

Now that dream seemed very real. Understanding washed over him. There was great conflict in the universe. Things lurking unseen which man had little comprehension of. There were those that tapped into the very fabric of the universe, those who reached out among the cold indifference of the stars where thought and consciousness did not exist and only a dark and cosmic evil reigned. That nameless priest on Ninurta IV had understood and chosen to unlock within him a great power. Why? Because he had mocked their customs? Or because he had dared stare into the abyss? He could not say. Perhaps he had always been marked. Perhaps it was always ordained that he should be standing here on the edge of a cold and distant world facing a nameless horror born of the stars. For he knew now what he must do. He must give himself over to the will of that which had been unlocked within him. He lifted his head. Staring up at the great statue above, he began climbing the stairway.

As if sensing his intent, dark winds screamed, seeking to tear him back. Deep rooted memory surged through Matt Randall now, thrummed coursing through his veins. His will would not be denied. As he stared at the rune on the dais, a key began to turn inside his mind. From it, a word was released and given power. An unvoiceable word. Randall mounted the final step and, as he did, that word surged up from within him and filled the core of his being. He knew now that the word and the symbol were one…

The cyclopean god stared down.

Matt Randall spoke the word.

Time slowed to a heartbeat.

The horizon receded.

And the universe—*screamed!*

For a brief instant Matt Randall ceased to exist. His corporeal form was torn to atoms as he became the word. Then time came crashing in again on the fractured shores of reality. Black pillars swayed and cracked. The effigy of the ebon god reeled as the ground beneath it trembled and shook. Stone cracked and fissures opened up, swallowing columns whole.

The dais crumbled and Randall leaped back in a cat like bound, hitting and landing on the stairway half way down. Another tremor split those steps in two and, as he fell, his left hand reached out, his fingers grasping the step above. For an instant he held there, dangling over an impossible abyss. Then the whole stairway collapsed and, he too, dropped plummeting downward into an unfathomable darkness…

7.

Awareness was a throbbing pain that beat a hammered rhythm in Randall's brain.

Before consciousness had fully returned he had made a solemn vow to the seventeen gods of Unar never to touch Varn wine again. Then slowly, as that dull throbbing gave way to an all out war, he opened his eyes a crack. As he did, memory came flooding back and he rolled over, scanning his surroundings.

Everywhere dust. Plumes of chalky dust billowing in a light breeze.

Overhead the last stars were paling as the sun began edging up over the horizon. With a groan he sat upright. The rifle he had picked up fell into his lap. It was covered, as he was, in a thin layer of chalk.

What had happened?

Surely he had blacked out, suffered an hallucination born of excitement. Even now, when he tried to recall the events of what had occurred before the dais of that hideous god, they ebbed and became hazy. In his tattered armour he shivered.

A coughing curse jerked his mind back to the realities of the present. Through the dust he could see the swaying silhouettes of two figures moving toward him. As it began to clear he recognized Kurghuz and Arealla.

Reeling dizzily to his feet he lifted the rifle and grinned.

"Well, at these odds, I think I'll take my chances. They seem to have dropped in my favour."

Open mouthed, the two soldiers stopped short. Then Kurghuz laughed; a short, mirthless bark of admiration. Arealla threw her helmet into the dust at his feet.

"Put up that weapon, you fool." she spat venomously.

Slowly, Randall lowered the gun. "Are we all that are left?"

Arealla nodded. She was caked in dust and, as she stared around, a wild look was in her eye. Kurghuz held her arm, steadying her.

"Let's get the hell out of here." Randall growled and together they moved off.

The ring of columns lay in shattered ruins. Some were broken stumps, others were toppled and lay on the ground. Shards of ebony lay all around. The magnetic barrier had gone and, as they crossed over where its boundary once stood, Randall looked back. Armoured bodies lay everywhere, stripped to gleaming bone. His skin crawled in revulsion.

When they were far enough away, they collapsed in exhaustion.

The sun began spreading its warmth over the valley. In silence they stared as it rose over the grim peaks and the shattered ring of columns before it.

When they had drunk of their canteens and eaten enough from their dried food rations, Kurghuz sat back. "Two hours to pick up. What now? We won't make the rendezvous."

Arealla looked at him; "I've already punched a distress signal to our coordinates. A ship will be here soon."

Kurghuz glanced sideways at Randall. "I don't know what happened back there, boy, but I have a feeling you had something to do with the reason we're still alive."

Randall's face became somber. He lowered his head. "The universe is a vast place. There are things out there we can't hope to understand. There are some things we're not supposed to know. So don't ask me any questions."

He looked at Kurghuz with a strange expression and the soldier drew back from him.

Arealla frowned. "Well, it seems you did do something to save us and that puts me in a dilemma. Do I let you go and report back with nothing to show my superiors… or take you in and at least have something to show for the loss of twenty men?"

In the distance the low ominous growl of a war-ship, approaching from over the Uular mountains, began to shake the valley floor.

Sat between them, Randall smiled. Looking up, he said; "Maybe fate has already decided for you."

With that he stood and, looking out across the valley, lifted his rifle into the morning sky.

Across the canyon, on an out ridge of broken rock, a salute was raised in reply.

Out of the shadows of the early dawn, a file of warriors came riding down into the narrow defile. They were fierce looking individuals, dressed in burnooses and long robes with swords tied to their saddle pommels. The white underbellies of their sleek, long tailed reptiles slithered over the ground. On thick nailed paws, driven by squat powerful legs, they glided silently toward them. As they came up, the warriors shouted with unfeigned joy.

"Aiiee! *Sabihb!* Borquha—you live!"

"Borquha?!" Arealla exclaimed, leaping quickly to her feet, "*You?* You are the leader of the Zuethii nomads?"

Turning, Randall grinned at her. "How else do you think these war dogs got organized so quickly? It takes an off worlder to see through the deceits of this world in order to reap its rewards."

The great reptiles whipped around them now, hissing and stamping in the dust. The warriors, proud and fierce eyed, looked down on the two company soldiers with ill disguised contempt. Randall, swinging into the saddle of a spare mount led by a tall nomad woman, looked out across the valley. He could not suppress a laugh.

"Here comes your ship. Don't worry, we'll be long gone before it arrives. As I said earlier, it will take a thousand years to sweep these canyons, so don't bother coming to look for us just yet."

He turned the head of his reptile and gave an ironic salute.

"*Shabhala!,*" he cried, in the traditional Mangalan farewell reserved for warriors, "until we meet again!"

Then, with a wild tribal shout, he and his warriors were racing down the valley to be lost in the darkness of the ridges beyond.

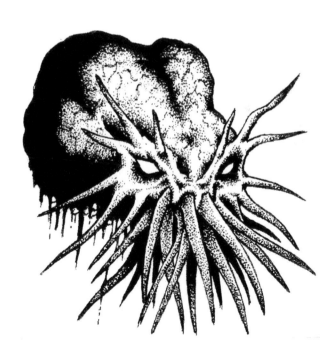

CONJURINGS
by Marlane Quade Cook

Shadows played an eerie dance over the stooped form of the woman beside the fire. Her fingers drummed with faint irritation as she watched another, slightly less hunched figure, hovering over the pot on the hearth.

"Stir it again," she intoned, her voice rasping with age.

"I have stirred it," the other retorted. "If I stir it again it may slosh."

"I swear you will be the death of me," grated the elder. "Stir."

Muttering, head shaking, the second figure, almost as hag-like, stirred again. A scratching at the door took the scrutiny from her as the first crone hobbled laboriously to the entry of the small hut. She threw back the bolt and rain spattered through the gap made by the night air. A third form, swathed in ragged black, entered.

"Have you collected everything?" she was challenged upon entry.

"Everything on the sodding list," was the arch reply.

"Come, show me." Demanded the eldest, who was clearly in charge of the proceedings. The newcomer held out a damp sack. Perusal of the contents by the head of the little coven brought forth a peal of raucous laughter.

"Ah, vengeance," she chortled, greedily clutching the sack to her chest and scuttling to the hearth. The youngest of the three, stirring resentfully, spared the others a baleful glare.

"Hah," spat the newly arrived member of the coven, "our young friend thinks it hard to sit and mind the mix, does she? *I* have traveled through a tempest to do our work!" She seemed to expand with indignation as she rolled her head and attempted to stretch her arms, hands reaching in a claw-like grasp. Her shadow grew menacing behind her, and the feeble lights in the tiny dwelling appeared to grow dim in the onslaught of a malevolent force.

"Peace, be still," the eldest rattled in her throat, "it is nearly done. We must begin the chant."

The three huddled around the small cauldron, muttering and swaying, their voices joining in a rhythmic murmur. Slowly the sound grew louder, more fierce, more keening. Then it abruptly stopped.

"The charm is done," spoke the eldest in a hoarse whisper. The others poised over the caulron in anticipation.

"…And that'll do," interrupted a man's voice. The three women, jolted from the trance of their chant stared for a moment: silent, blinking. Then, the spell broken, they moved apart.

"By God, Will, you couldn't let us finish the scene?" The eldest demanded, dissolving into a fit of coughing. She straightened her back painfully and stretched her talon-like nails.

The youngest sighed irritably, leaning on the rough stone mantle. The middle woman shook off her cloak with some impatience, draping it over a chair to dry and revealing a very un-crone like figure: all corseted curves and wild, but lustrous hair. "Well, I'm not going out again, you can forget it." She flopped languidly into a wooden chair and her eyes smoldered as she gazed toward the man seated at a low wooden desk on the other side of the hut.

Her coughing fit over, the eldest removed her wig and tattered shawl, also revealing a surprisingly un-hag like appearance. The youngest of the three—not much younger than her companions—craned her head back, and lounged against the mantle. Immediately the guise of twisted age fell away to reveal her youthfulness. Her posture made the most of her ample bosom, and she appeared to be trying to catch the writer's eye. The now-youthful woman who had posed as the eldest crone glared at her.

"Oh, come on," the buxom one scoffed, "it's only Will."

"Will," added her reclining sister, twining a strand of wild hair around her finger, eyes kindling with a predatory gleam. "Will he or won't he?" She grinned wickedly, "the night's wearing on, Will. Home to the lady wife? Or the dark-haired mistress?" She rested one leg over the arm of her chair and swung her foot idly, revealing a length of ankle encased in tattered stocking.

He looked up with a frown, then back to his parchment, "Come now, girls, you know our arrangement. Strictly business collaboration. This is wonderful stuff, it really is! What would I do without my muses?" He paused for a moment to place a hand over his heart and gaze fondly at them, allowing his personal charm to do its work. Then, with a self-content expression, he continued writing.

"The question is," his tormentor persisted seductively, leaning toward him, "what would you do *with*—"

"Kate, hold your tongue!" her elder sister snapped, "Will is a great writer, and as he quite truly says, we have an arrangement. Why cheapen ourselves further when we're already making a morckery of our art?"

"Oh, Marianne," he said in a conciliatory tone, still writing, "don't say a mockery! A parody, perhaps, but…you wouldn't expect me to display witchcraft in all its glory for the masses? *That* would cheapen it. Let them have their superstitions, and us: the wealth, the glory!" He glanced up periodically, trying to sway them with his enthusiasm. Marianne cast a meaningful glance around their humble surroundings.

"What about….the power," dark-eyed Kate still eyed him with a ferocious smile. "Do you find our power intriguing, Will?"

He paused in his writing, then continued as if she hadn't spoken. "Of course, I'll need to work on MacBeth and Banquo. Nothing spectacular yet, Banquo is a stock "good guy," who dies unjustly, and MacBeth doesn't get interestingly bloodthirsty for some time yet."

"But I don't understand," the youngest sister protested. "why make us ugly? Why evil? Why—bearded, for God's sake?" Murmurs of perplexed assent from her sisters followed this interrogative.

"It's fiction, Bianca!" he protested, laying down his quill and stepping out from behind the writing table. "I have to give the crowds what they want—this is masterful stuff, and they'll eat it up!" His enthusiasm grew with every word. "And you girls," he slid his hands around Bianca's corseted waist, "Oh, if I could only put you girls on the stage…but the London of our times isn't ready for that. You'd stun then, blind them," he leaned in close for a teasing whisper, "scandalize them," Bianca giggled throatily and Will nestled his bearded face into her tangled red locks in an un-businesslike manner. "No, sadly they expect ugly old hags played by uglier old men." he sighed dejectedly, "I have to work within the scope of my trade."

Kate and Marianne exchanged a skeptical glance as he stepped away from Bianca, withdrew his hands, and rubbed them together eagerly. "In any case, this is all we have time for at present, girls. A thousand thanks!" He breezed between Marianne and Kate, stepping lightly to retrieve his manuscript.

"You won't stay for dinner?" Bianca peered into the cauldron with a pout. "I've stirred it enough to drown a cat."

"Uhhhh…tempting, but I'm afraid I have to keep at work on this." he handled the drying parchment with great care. "But there's more, much more! I will be back. There is the conjuring scene, and you three bring the images to my mind like nothing else can."

"Not your wife?" Asked Bianca, with a seductive pout and a raised eyebrow.

"Not your mistress?" asked Marianne, tossing her sandy-colored hair with a trace of scorn.

"Not your golden apprentice?" Kate bit off the question with a playful snap of her smiling jaws.

Will cleared his throat loudly, and drew on a cloak, tucking the parchment carefully under it. "Fare you well, girls, until next time." and abruptly, he was gone.

Bianca and Kate laughed wickedly to themselves at his discomfiture.

"That was a bit much," Marianne said quietly, "you know he's sensitive about his personal life."

"Oh, come on!" Kate threw her head back with wanton humor, "it's just Will. It's just a bit of fun!"

"You shouldn't toy with him." Marianne said thoughtfully. "He's going to be great, you know."

"Great at the Globe?" said Bianca with a smirk.

"Great at the Rose?" asked Kate, toying with her unkempt hair again.

"Great," replied Marianne, her hazel eyes far away, "Immortal."

Her sisters laughed merrily, "well, I am starving," announced Kate. "I hope you haven't overcooked it. Bia, do you have to stir so obsessively?" she gave her younger sister a playful shove, and they bickered good-naturedly as Marianne stood by the window staring out into the darkness. Her gaze was so deep and intent she might have been staring into eternity, weaving the threads of time.

✗

THE JACKAL
by Ashley Dioses

The jackal suckles from the teat
Of daemon's mistress fair.
The jackal grows to hold a seat;
The left-hand of His chair.

The jackal bears the seed of Scratch,
And waits forever-long
For Son of Hell to rise and match
His Father and grow strong.

The jackal to her true love calls,
Yet Scratch has done his deed.
The jackal calls her son, yet falls
From grace; none hear her plead.

The jackal lies among the dead,
Beneath a graveyard mound.
No little headstone marks the head
Where rests she in the ground.

MATRIARCH UNBOUND
by Glynn Owen Barrass

The night-shrouded town was a place of chaos and death. Half-collapsed from decades old bombings and assaults from alien giants, the area remaining, a few dozen buildings with boarded up windows and doors, housed the human vermin Zero despised so much. Upon her dropships' arrival, the vermin had poured from their hovels and begun to defend themselves. Men and women dressed in raggedy body armour and patched rubber gasmasks, they fought from behind the rusted hulks of cars, the crumbled walls flanking the buildings. They used single shot weapons for the most part, rifles and pistols, whereas Zero's soldiers retaliated with automatic weaponry, riddling their defences and picking them off, one by one.

Her soldiers wore head to foot metallic blue ceramic armour, some crouched behind defences like the humans, others returning fire unperturbed by the bullets bouncing off their bodies and bug-eyed, oval helmets.

It was a losing battle, for not only did she have heavily armed and armoured troops at her disposal, but half a dozen champions, beings enhanced beyond the capabilities of the enemy humans and her synthetic forces alike. The champions leapt and ducked, swinging swords and cutting through their foes. Many didn't bother with armour, and some stood naked, like her.

Zero's small, slim form stood bare to the elements, her hands pressed against her hips as she watched the scene untroubled by flying bullets.

The battle appeared to be subsiding, the silence between the gunfire increasing, the screams of the captured and dying trailing off to be replaced by numbed moans.

Zero smiled. Her soldiers had performed adequately, as always. She surveyed the scene and saw humans on their knees, arms shackled behind their backs. Humans dead, prostrate upon the ground. Already, her soldiers were retrieving the dead to carry them to the dropships. They were of use, as much as the living prisoners, for their bones and ligaments could be utilized in the creation of future soldiers, or the repair of injured ones.

"Matriarch Zero," a voice said from her left, and she turned to see her champion, Elvira, approaching. A redhead, with opaque blue eyes, Elvira stood naked but for a scarlet domino mask and a pair of frayed, tan stockings. She held a bloodied Katana in her left hand, the gleaming white flesh of her arm and chest spattered with red.

She paused before Zero, said, "Ma'am," and performed a quick bow. "There are thirty-seven humans in custody, eighteen dead, and seven of low functional ability," she continued. "What are your orders?"

Zero eyed up Elvira and noticed some bullet holes in her chest. The synthetic woman's resin-like blood had already begun sealing up the injuries.

"Try and sustain the dying humans lives for as long as possible, especially any females, and return them all the compound." She bit her lower lip and looked to the sky, examining the black clouds hovering within the purple starry firmament. This zone was prone to heavy, toxic storms, she knew from satellite maps. She returned her gaze to Elvira. "Have one dropship remain, search the buildings and remove any stragglers. If the weather looks set to turn, have everyone return immediately."

"Would you like me to supervise Ma'am?" Elvira said with eagerness in her voice.

"Yes, do that. You and another. Ténèbres I think," Zero replied.

Elvira grinned, revealing perfect white teeth. "I can and shall obey." She bowed and turned, heading towards the group of soldiers to Zero's right.

Zero watched her stride away with a smile. The champion walking proudly, her head held high. The smile disappeared as she recalled the servants who hadn't proven so faithful.

"Glass half full," she said, and turning, stepped between the two rows of soldiers guarding her, towards the ramp to her dropship.

The synthetics saluted as she passed.

The ramp's steps were illuminated blue, the hatchway above dark but for the ghosts of flickering instrument lights. Her guards fell in behind her as she ascended, and soon she was stepping across steel plates, between the spacious cargo area's bulkheads. As she reached the far wall, a massive steel door rolled open in two parts, revealing darkness beyond. Strong odours issued from within: ammonia mixed with thick animal scents.

A large, circular green light appeared near the unseen ceiling. It blinked, then six more, three to a side, joined it.

Her eyes, adjusting to the darkness, saw the shadowy movements of hundreds of tentacles, huge wings stretched out to the edges of the walls and ceiling.

The eyes attached to the bulk blinked as one, and a tentacle whipped out from the being, thrashing around the darkness until it found Zero. She raised her arms, allowing the tentacle to embrace her chest, the end of which probed then speared a small hole at the top of her spine.

Zero slumped, an empty puppet.

* * * *

Infectious little thing.

Matriarch closed her eyes, absorbing the facet of mind she had loaned the synthetic.

The facet danced with glee in her psyche. The proxy's brain capacity had been so tiny, so constraining. Matriarch relived the facet's experiences in a thousandth of a second, splitting thoughts and sensations and feelings apart, destroying some, archiving others. She relived the cold against Zero's skin, the wind in her hair, the stink of battle and death.

The floor plates rumbled beneath her, the dropship taking off to return them to the compound.

These emotions, so addictive.

Zero's pleasure as the soldiers destroyed the human vermin.

Fear, as a stray bullet whizzed past her ear.

As she replayed the emotions, her gigantic form rippled with gratification.

* * * *

In stockinged feet, Concubine rushed down metal corridors, amber ceiling lights illuminating her hurried progress.

Other Concubine units passed her, their naked, nimble forms hurrying as urgently as she was. A few minutes earlier, a message had arrived from the dropships, relaying that humans had been captured and harvesting was to begin at their return. Hence the compound was in chaos, giving Concubine an opportunity to escape her guards.

Of all the female Concubine synthetics, she was the only one wearing clothing.

It was a punishment, the white, silver flecked frock trailing the floor as she ran. Her white hair was braided, styled in a topknot, her cheeks rouged red, her lips scarlet and her eyes thick with purple mascara.

Being forced to look like this... doll, a humiliation that set her apart from the other synthetics, was almost as degrading as the acts her mistress made her perform with her proxy, the grinning synthetic sadist Zero.

Almost.

The route she took ended in a circular room with doorways at each cardinal point. From memory, she knew the exits before her and to her right held descending stairs, the one to her left, ascending.

"You. Hold up!" Stamping footsteps appeared behind her, the noise of her guards catching up.

Damn it! Matriarch's Hunter models had found her

She took the right-hand exit, descending deeper into the compound. At the last six steps she jumped, landing heavily on the grilled metal catwalk at their termination. Before her, the catwalk extended hundreds of feet across a chasm-like space filled with machinery: the factory for synthetic production.

Footsteps pounded down the stairs as she stepped towards the catwalk's handhold. Far below, powerful flood lamps on distant walls illuminated the silent factory starkly. There were lots of places to hide, and the residual heat from the deactivated, broken synthetics spotting the factory floor would act as camouflage from the Hunters' infrared.

With the sounds of pursuit growing dangerously near, Concubine pulled herself over the guardrail. The air rushed past as she plummeted to the factory floor, ruffling her dress. The area she aimed for, a row of large metal tubs filled with spare parts, would offer a painful landing, but not crippling or deadly, unless her aim was off and she hit one of the rims. She curled her body into a white cloth ball, then closed her eyes.

The impact winded her, sharp edges lacerated her flesh. Concubine dug deeper into the tub until she hoped she was completely concealed. Now, all she had to do was wait within the pile of her unborn, unassembled siblings. She opened her eyes and found another face staring back. Thankfully, it was not connected to a power core, and remained unmoving.

No discovery came as the minutes passed. Her pursuers were crafty though: Concubine knew this from previous escape attempts. She bided her time for a while longer, then pushed herself upwards to poke her head from the pile.

Silence, after the parts settled down around her, and nothing visible beyond the tubs but unmoving factory machines. She looked at the balcony, and finding it empty, released a breath she hadn't realized she was holding.

Still, moving as quietly as possibly, she waded through the parts to the edge of the tub and then pulled herself over onto the concrete factory floor. Her dress she found was in ruined tatters, and with no little pleasure, she unzipped the rear and shrugged it to the floor. She next undid the hair knot, letting her hair fall loose around her neck.

Naked now but for her tan stockings, she considered removing them, then decided they might provide insulation from noise. She looked around, seeing the many limbed formed of factory robots, limp and deactivated red metal hulks that on activation would be hovering around, picking parts from the tubs with claw-handed, spindly limbs. She walked between a pair of these and found rows of sponge-covered beds beyond, hundreds to a side disappearing into the distance. Each bed held an array of white robot arms and a computer bank at its head—constructor units for the synthetics. A glance at the nearest informed her the banks were of no use for mainframe access, and walking quickly, she strode between the beds, scanning the areas beyond for a console.

Concubine cursed herself for never having mapped the factory, for in its inactive state it would have proven the perfect place to work in. *Might still be*, she thought, *there must be an accessible console here*. She continued between the beds, passing some that held broken synthetics. A few held Concubine models—the wrecks of those that came before her, slaves destroyed servicing Matriarch's lusts.

Come on, where are you? There must be a console here, surely.

The far wall was visible now, flanked by a row of flood lamps high upon a grid of yellow scaffolding. She saw lights within the framework, and hoped, as she increased her speed, that this indicated consoles. Her nose wrinkled as something sour and organic reached her nostrils. Except for Matriarch's sour, gamy scent, the compound usually smelled of nothing but machine lubricants and dust, but this…

Oh… Concubine paused when she saw human forms within the scaffolding.

Female humans, hundred of them, were cocooned tightly in clear plastic, transparent tubes plugged into their mouths, nostrils and nether regions. The women had bulging bellies, all in various stages of pregnancy. Not all the tubes for waste were sealed properly, and she gagged at the sight of faecal matter dripping down the prisoners' legs. Inactive machines dangled above the rows, their limp white spider limbs holding various surgical tools. Some were dark with recent bloodstains, and searching the rows, Concubine found some empty, nothing remaining but ripped plastic and unattached tubes.

She knew Matriarch had been collecting humans, experimenting with their skeletons and nerve structures to hybridise synthetics. Pregnant women though? Concubine considered this for a few moments, wondering what use Matriarch would have for a foetus. *Embryonic stem cells? Quite probably.*

With hesitancy, she stepped towards the lower scaffolding. Between two pregnant forms the same dull lights flickered she had seen from a distance.

The ugly smell grew, but in the darkness she spied the familiar screen and keyboard of an interface console. The stink from beneath the plastic-wrapped flesh increased as she approached, and she noticed gentle movements on the women's faces, breathing apparatus beneath the cocoons. Concubine sighed, shook her head, and reaching the rectangular, yellowing white plastic console, stared at the blue screen a moment before touching the plastic to the right of the keypad. Her questing fingers quickly discovered four indentations in the plastic, and pressing them in, found a needle-tip within each one. She braced herself, shoving her hand forward so the needles pierced her flesh. Then, she was somewhere else.

* * * *

Ramps descended from the three dark grey, egg-shaped dropships to pour troops onto the compound's pentagonal rooftop. The cone-shaped antigravity modules around their bases hummed as their power dissipated, quickly replaced by the noise of boots on tarmac. Matriarch's soldiers exited the ramps in orderly rows, heading towards the concrete, pillbox-shaped stairwells spotting the roof.

The roof held other vehicles, including a dozen rusted old attack helicopters and a crash-landed civilian transport plane.

As she descended the ramp, Matriarch wondered if any technology could be salvaged from the helicopters. Possibly there were even viable skeletal structures in the plane.

The last to leave the ship, as her tentacles touched the rooftop the sight of two soldiers heading towards her interrupted her thoughts. No not soldiers, she saw, but a pair of Hunter-models dressed in grey body armour. Each one was pale skinned, with short white hair, and the sight of the production line numbers tattooed on their left cheeks, Seventy-Nine for the female and Eighty-Seven for the male, made her shudder in anger.

"Ma'am," Seventy-Nine said.

"We've lost her," Eighty-Seven continued, and lowered his head.

Matriarch hissed from hidden mouths, then opened the lower part of her chest to reveal the Zero proxy. No exchange of consciousness this time, just a direct link from her mind to the synthetic's mouthpiece. She lowered Zero to the tarmac, and opened her eyes.

The Hunters stared at the tarmac floor.

"Look at me!" she ordered.

They raised their heads with subdued, frightened expressions on their faces.

"Ma'am, she escaped us when news of your return reached the compound," Seventy-Nine said.

"We searched for a long time," Eighty-Seven added, as if this made up for their failure.

Matriarch growled, low and deep, the sound making the Hunters step back in fear.

"You idiots," Zero said through gritted teeth, "she'll be looking for mainframe access again." She strode forward, Matriarch lumbering heavily behind.

"We need to get to a console. I'll find out where she is and assemble a team to catch her." She strode purposefully towards a circular area surrounded by lights, a rooftop elevator large enough to fit Matriarch's bulk. The Hunters fell in to either side of her.

"You'll be punished for this," she said, and the creature behind her snarled.

"Yes Ma'am," the Hunters said in unison.

What has you so obsessed with my mainframe? Matriarch wondered. *It's time to put an end to your subordination permanently.*

Zero sighed. *What a waste of such a pleasing toy.*

As they stepped upon the elevator, a roar from the east made Zero turn. She saw the final dropship floating through the sky, moving into a descent towards the compound.

*   *   *   *

The console and factory disappeared, replaced by the mainframe's virtual environment. Surrounded by a purple sky and abyss, the cyclopean skyscraper-like structures around Concubine stretched off in every direction. Their gigantic shapes shuddered as she watched, extending and retracting pseudopods, data bridges encoding, storing, and retrieving information between their virtual memory banks.

Chaotic movement filled the spaces between them. Multicoloured streams of data, represented by tiny spheres, swam around and through the structures. Miles below, upended basaltic ziggurats and revolving, iridescent congeries of cubes filled the abyss with constant motion.

The virtual world was massive, a labyrinth like no other. On her first visit, Concubine had been overwhelmed by its immensity, but now, what overwhelmed her was the absolute sense of freedom.

She smiled, then flew down, her speed giddying as she rushed between the structures. Millions of alternating skill sets and emotions were stored within the memory banks, updated constantly as Matriarch's synthetics learned new things. This meant when a new synthetic was created, a fully functioning, highly advanced mind could be installed. Matriarch's soldiers were linked to and frequently upgraded by the mainframe. Her lesser servants, such as the Concubine models, were rarely if ever given access beyond their initial creation.

But Concubine had invaded the mainframe, stealing skills that had once helped her escape the compound, skills that just recently helped her elude her guards.

She passed below the towers bases, swooping forward to brush the top of a revolving ziggurat. She whooped in exhilaration, a virtual representation of the sound filling the void.

A rumbling crack of thunder answered her from below.

She paused, examined the area, and saw a cube cluster rearranging its configurations into a circular, darkness filled portal. A moment later, a pair of silver, shark-like entities emerged from its depths and began homing in on her.

Damn, they've found me.

She escaped at speed, darting between and through ziggurats with manoeuvring skills she hoped the Hunters, less experienced with this environment, weren't capable of.

Each time she entered a ziggurat, an AI core assailed her, hungry for memories and upgrades. She pushed them away as she concentrated on her escape, and after uncounted ziggurats, dared to pause and look back. Some hundreds of virtual feet away, she found the sharks, floundering, searching in confusion.

She continued, heading lower now, the topography changing to include polyhedrons and cube-and-plane clusters. The space here was even more manic with movement, data streams whizzing like bullets between the dancing structures. At her approach, four pink polyhedrons stopped rotating to zoom towards her, transforming as they did into angry faced, luminous green Fu Dogs.

Concubine pushed away her sudden fear, concentrated, and altered her outer form to resemble an innocuous data packet.

It worked, the Fu Dogs halted in their tracks, and feeling ingenious, she warned them of the invaders pursuing her.

One refreshed its form, becoming a floating red Sphinx that sped off to intercept the sharks. The other three returned to polyhedrons and rejoined the other dancing shapes.

Concubine surveyed this system of mad yet synchronized movement until she found a shuddering, blue-tinged cluster of cubes.

This was what the Fu Dogs guarded, the cluster holding the core controls for Matriarch's soldiers and slaves. Her previous visit was interrupted when she had been discovered accessing the mainframe. But this time…

"Slave no more," she said, and descended towards the cluster.

* * * *

Matriarch was inside the synthetic doll again. It couldn't be helped. After descending into the compound, she ordered the Hunters to go find Concubine in the mainframe, and the nearest room with console access was not built for alien dimensions. Hence she stood, arms folded, watching impatiently as the Hunters sat connected to the console array upon the north wall. The room was large, with a high ceiling flanked with steel girders, but the door in the south wall was sized exclusively for human-sized occupants. Damp, dirty, the metal-plated walls were riddled in rust, as was the dented floor. Two lights, dangling from the girders, flickered above, clicking loudly. The blue metal console array had also suffered from the damp. Nine of the sixteen monitors were dead while the others buzzed with static.

The Hunters sat side by side in two of four rotted black leather seats. Their heads slumped, their hands were pressed against the interface mats to the touchscreen keyboards sides.

Seventy-Nine's head twitched, the only movement from either of them. Zero had been tempted to insert herself into the mainframe, but no, the moment the Hunter's came out with Concubine's location, she would rush there herself and put an end to her rebellious slave's troublesome attitude.

The female Hunter's head shook, and then, her whole body spasmed. Zero stepped towards her, wondering what was wrong. Eighty-Seven moaned, began shaking like his companion. A moment later they were removing their hands from the mats.

Seventy-Nine cricked her neck, blinked and turned to Zero. Eighty-Seven lifted himself sluggishly from his seat.

"She got us, Ma'am," Seventy-Nine said and stood. "First she outraced us and then she sent antibodies to kick us out."

Zero scowled at the Hunter.

"We can go back in. Just—"

"Shut up, just shut up!" Zero interrupted Eighty-Seven, and the Hunter shrank from her.

"You!" she addressed Seventy-Nine with venom in her voice. "Where in the mainframe is she?"

"Uh…" Seventy-Nine stood and swayed uneasily. "It was low down, around the core kernels."

Zero frowned. That was a sensitive area of the system, if…

"Ack…" Seventy-Nine flinched, reached for her head and froze.

Eighty-Seven's head snapped back and remained in that unlikely position.

The kernel, the central core, holding complete control over everything in the system. Everything, including my soldiers.

In a flash of movement, Seventy-Nine reached for the machine pistol holstered at her right hip. She sprayed bullets in a thunderous rattle, but Zero was already on the floor, moving swiftly on all fours, her teeth gritted into a snarl. The moment the gunfire stopped she leapt upwards, climbing between the steel girders on the ceiling. The Hunters charged forward, Seventy-Nine reloading her weapon while Eighty-Seven began firing wildly into the ceiling.

The bullets spat and ricocheted around her. She hissed as one sliced through her leg. Zero leapt across the girders and dropped between them, landing on Eighty-Seven's shoulders. She gripped his neck and twisted, forcing it round with an audible 'snap'. He collapsed, dead, and before he touched the floor she was holding his machine pistol two-handed, discharging it into Seventy-Nine's back. It tore through her body armour and flesh, the Hunter shaking spastically before falling to the floor with smoke gushing from her ruined insides.

The machine pistol clicked empty.

"Fuck," Zero said, and dropping the pistol bent to remove the combat knife from Eighty-Seven's boot.

Footsteps appeared from the corridor beyond the door. She braced herself and found Elvira charging towards her, a murderous expression on her face. Zero leapt forward, avoiding the swinging katana to tackle Elvira to the floor. The brash attack stunned the champion, giving her the time she needed to get up and escape the skilled and deadly synthetic.

She turned and ran left down the corridor. More footsteps issued from the T-Junction before her. Four bug-masked soldiers appeared at the intersection, and she dove forward, bowling them over. Entangled in a mess of arms and legs, a gloved hand clamped around her throat. A savage stab with her knife made the hand go slack, then she was up again, running down the corridor with the bloodstained blade in her left hand, a machine pistol in the other.

She turned a corner, barrelled down a flight of stairs in the direction of Matriarch's sanctum.

The sounds of automatic gunfire followed by chilling, alien howls increased her panic a thousandfold. She continued down a corridor then stairs towards a green-lit doorway filled with flashes and noise. A moment later she was past the threshold and froze in horror at the sight facing her.

The cavernous room was built to an alien aesthetic, the walls and ceiling covered in resinous knobs of sparkling black matter. Green lights built into the resin floor and ceiling gave it an undersea look, illuminating the six soldiers firing on Matriarch's huge tentacled form. Bullets peppered her shuddering, screaming body as she batted with tentacles at the champion going at her with a sword.

Ténèbres, my head champion. He looked at Zero and his naked, brown-skinned body was hooked up and lifted by a silver tentacle.

Zero opened fire, spraying the soldiers from left to right. Five went down, and one spun on his heels to fill her chest with holes.

The impact sent her staggering backwards. She dropped the gun and knife as intense pain wracked her body. Her attacker turned his gunfire on Matriarch until his clip ran empty. A tentacle shot out, snapping his head backwards and sending him to the floor.

Zero coughed blood, staggered and fell to her knees beside the dead soldier. Matriarch swayed before her, most of her tentacles gone limp. The being breathed loudly with struggling, titanic breaths.

The champion, wriggling in the tentacle's grip, thrust with his sword, right through Matriarch's centre eye.

Zero went to scream, but her blood-clogged throat only managed a gargling croak. The tentacle holding Ténèbres snapped him in two, the pieces falling to the floor. Matriarch's large eye, the sword still jammed in it, dripped black fluids as it, and those surrounding it, started to dim.

No. With painful movements, Zero dragged herself towards Matriarch.

Matriarch lowered her body towards her, ripped, bleeding tentacles reaching out to embrace her proxy.

As their eyes met, Zero's vision blurred, filling with tiny black spots. A grim silence filled the room. She raised her left arm towards Matriarch, dead weight that it was. Fingers touched tentacle, and darkness followed.

* * * *

It's mine now, this room, the compound, everything, Concubine thought with no little satisfaction. Matriarch's Sanctum had been mostly cleared, Zero, Ténèbres and the other corpses taken away for recycling. The alien and synthetic bloodstains remained, black in the green light. She watched as eleven soldiers, each holding a large hook, tried to drag Matriarch's corpse towards the oversized doorway at its rear. The synths were struggling, the stinking, alien body barely moving from their combined efforts. They stopped, and one of them turned and approached Concubine.

"Ma'am," the female soldier's green-tinged face showed consternation. "I think… I think we may be better cutting it up into smaller segments. What do you say?"

Concubine blanched at the thought of cutting it up, but what other option was there? If she brought in more workers there wouldn't be enough space on the corpse to accommodate them.

"Do it. Cut the damned thing to shreds," she said.

The soldier nodded and walked away.

"Hey," Concubine said to her retreating back. "Contact the armoury, order chainsaws."

The soldier looked at her, nodded, and pressing her hand to her left ear, began talking quietly.

The corpse smelled bad enough whole. Concubine didn't want to be around when it was dissected, so she turned and headed for the doorway behind her. She exited the room then stopped, pressing a finger to her left ear. There was a click and a beep, and she said, "Acquisitions. What is the status of the humans we have in storage?"

There was a brief silence, then a male voice replied, "Harvested or sedated, Ma'am."

"Hmmm. Are any fit to be freed?"

Another, longer pause, then, "Sorry Ma'am, their brains have been shunted."

Concubine grimaced, said, "Okay," then lowered her hand.

Her intention had been to release the human prisoners and abandon the embryonic harvesting program. Neither was possible. The latter, especially, she now knew was necessary for repairs and future synthetic creation. She sighed and stepped down the corridor. Benevolence was proving more difficult than she had envisioned.

"Glass half full," she said.

THE MOUTH AT THE EDGE OF THE WORLD
by Luke Walker

The walk to the edge of the world took us about an hour—a few miles of nothing but unploughed fields, overgrown grassland and a road that was barely a line covered in cracks and weeds. We didn't speak much on the way; there'd been plenty of talking in low voices before we left the house where my brother and I lived with our mum. Plenty of angry whispers from Marcus about how there was no way I was coming, how he'd beat me up later if I didn't leave them alone. The thing was I knew he couldn't threaten me too much. Not with his girlfriend Jane there. If I hadn't overheard them talking, none of it would have happened. I think about that now and I weep.

Marcus let go of Jane's hand as we crossed the road. He jogged to the opposite pavement and stood at the opening of the pathway that led to the edge, peering down into the gloom cast by the spindly branches heavy with summer leaves. Jane spoke in a low voice.

"Are you okay?"

I nodded, not wanting her to think of me as a kid even though at eleven, I was four years younger than my brother and Jane. They were almost old enough to remember life *before* while I had no idea about that beyond the stories my mum told me or the rumours I heard from the other kids in the village.

"Yeah." I tried to make my pre-adolescent voice a little deeper and failed. "You?"

She smiled, as pretty as always. She'd tied her thick hair back with an elastic band. The heavy weight of hair pulled away from her face, the light in her eyes: I loved Jane. Not in any complicated or teenage fashion, but as a sister. She and Marcus had been friends most of my life and a couple for two years. Like all young people in our village down in Devon, they were expected to marry at sixteen and have child after child if only to get the population back up towards the levels of previous decades—before all the people had died from the floods and earthquakes.

"I have no idea," she whispered and jogged ahead of me to join Marcus. I slowed, giving him a second to slide a hand around her narrow waist. The red sunset burned the expanse of land already growing wild despite the relative lack of time since our village had been a small town. A mile beyond the uneven land beside the path and above a massive woodland, the sky was as full of its spinning, rolling colours as always. The sight was a silent storm: red and orange streaks dancing with blue flashes, then purple sheets. My mum and the older people still didn't like to look at it or speak of it, but it was no more unusual for me than sunshine. Where field met road, the remnants of an old fence were almost lost behind weeds and vines. Twelve years of summers and winters had cracked the wood, split the posts and sent it tilting towards the ground. It probably had another year or two of life before it came down: a thought I found oddly sad.

But the fence wasn't why we'd come out to the empty land beyond Thistlemoor Wood and the unused meadows. We'd come for the edge of everything, come to see what was beyond it.

Marcus glanced around as I approached. He kept his arm around Jane. The sleeve of his t-shirt had ridden up, exposing the heavy muscle of his bicep. Not even sixteen and he stood taller than most of the other kids and almost reached level with our teacher, Mr Pateman. Our mum said he'd make a big, strapping man if he carried on working so much on the farms around the village. She didn't say that about me.

"I meant what I said at the house," he muttered. "You tell anyone, Willy, and you're in big shit."

I think the swearword was supposed to intimidate me. Our mother often said if she caught either of us swearing, we'd be in trouble. Jane's dad, the village's vicar, said the same to her as well as more. I'd spied on Jane and Marcus one night a month before our walk to the edge. They'd been talking about *it* and how Jane's dad said if they did *it* before marriage, he'd banish them. I knew what the *it* was. What I didn't understand was the look of fear and frustration on Marcus's face. It took me another two years to reach the point of a teenage boy's life where sex controls almost everything.

"I know," I said. "Don't worry. I won't say anything."

He nodded without speaking and studied the path, again. The trees grew much thicker than I'd expected. Their branches met like frail arms, forming a roof over the ground and keeping any warmth and red light out. A short way in, the path took a sharp turn to the right. Anything beyond that was imagination. And imagination was beginning to send skinny fingers creeping up and down my narrow back. Even though the evening remained warm, a slight edge to the air sank below my thin jeans and the holes at the knees. My itchy woollen fleece—a hand-me-down from Marcus, naturally—had a few holes in the back; the air crept in through those holes, caressing my skin and bringing promises of an early autumn when thick morning fog would cover the moorland around the village and warmth would be a memory and my home would feel as dead as most of the rest of the country.

"What do we do?" I whispered and hated myself for not speaking at a normal volume as Marcus would have done.

He wouldn't be asking that question, I thought and again felt like a much younger child than my brother and his girlfriend. All at once, I didn't want to be there. Not because of what might be at the other end of the pathway, but because the area was for older kids. I was four years too early.

I have no way of knowing, but it's possible Jane understood some of that or maybe she just didn't want to be there, either. Everything we knew was a few miles away; night would be on us by the time we got home, and the silence of the wide fields seemed to have its own ears and was listening to us.

"Maybe this isn't a good idea," she said. The sunset shone on her glasses.

"Come on." Marcus tried to smile and maybe only I saw how fake it really was. Maybe it was a brother thing. "We're here now. I know we're not supposed to be. I know someone might come along to…you know… offer themselves, but if they do, we run. I bet we can run faster than anyone who's going to jump over."

I thought I understood him. The solid burden of despair strong enough to lead to suicide was an alien thought to the boy I was, but I knew life was hard and I knew some people thought there was only one way of escaping that hardship. I'd seen a few people get to that state and pass through the village on their way out there. Not many but enough to spot the signs: the unwillingness to speak or wash their stinking bodies; the closing away from human contact. Maybe half a dozen people in four or five years. They came out to the edge of the world and they *offered themselves* to whatever existed on the other side. My mum told me it all one night when she'd been smoking something funny. She said she didn't know what was at the edge of the world; she didn't want to know. She told me it hadn't always been there, that it came from where the stars live in the sky. Out of the black, she said. It came and bit off half the world. Ate it like I ate carrots or potatoes. And now here we were: a world broken in two and kept alive by a thing that didn't have a name or a face anyone had seen. It wrapped its arms around us, she said. Kept the wind blowing and the sun rising and the rain falling, somehow. Kept us in our little bit of space and everyone thought it would carry on doing so as long as we didn't try to hurt it and as long as those who wanted to were allowed to jump over the edge of the world. I'd asked her what would happen if people stopped wanting to do that and her face, usually tanned from working outside, turned white like milk from our cows. She'd tucked me into my old, creaky bed, said goodnight and blown out my candle.

Marcus spoke to Jane, not me. "Think about it. We go down there. We see and we come back. We don't need to tell anyone. It's not about that. I don't want any of our friends thinking that we did it to impress them. We're doing it because…" He struggled to complete his thought and I understood that. The attraction wasn't down to being brave or being better than anyone who hadn't come out to the edge. It was because we wanted to see the unknown. We wanted to look right at it and know we'd done so.

"Because we have to," he finished and pulled away a little from her. "Come on."

Jane chewed her lip. I stood, probably forgotten by both of them. My head ached; my vision danced. *Home.* That's what I wanted more than anything.

"Okay." Marcus nodded as if Jane had spoken. "It's fine. I don't mind." He backed away.

"Marcus—"

"You stay here." There was no anger. I remember that. I hold on to it. "I'll be back soon."

In one motion, he spun and ran straight into the murky half-light filling the gap between the trees. Before either of us could react, the turn in the path took him out of sight.

Jane and I stood in silence while the red light stained grass and road and us.

* * * *

Jane's hand was in mine. Her sweat mixed with mine. Her fingers joined with mine tightly enough to feel as if they were part of my body.

We walked side by side, close enough for my hip to brush her leg and the whisper of our clothes rubbing together to seem much too loud.

Visibility was almost nothing. Above, the tiny gaps between leaves let a little of the evening light rain on us but it made our vision simply flicker rather than showing the route ahead. When Marcus ran, Jane said we'd wait but after long minutes of nothing and the shadows creeping closer, she whispered we had to follow him. Any argument stuck in my throat because there was no choice.

So we'd linked hands and set out, the dark swallowing us as it had eaten my brother. We'd both heard stories of how the rest the world was: empty for the most part, the populated parts full of dangerous people who'd kill anyone for any little bit of food. We were safe from them, the adults said, if we stayed in our village and left the towns to the rubble they'd become. Walking down that pathway and moving further away from the known world with every step felt like we were heading straight into the places destroyed by violence after everything changed. And I can honestly say the only reason I kept going was because Marcus was at the other end of the path. I didn't have many friends, but I'd have happily left any of them at whatever sat at the edge of the world if it meant being far away from it.

"It's all right," Jane whispered and I cringed at the sound of her voice. Replying was impossible; my throat had never been so dry. Not even during the hot days of the summer when we worked on the farmland. All I could do was offer her was a squeeze between our hands.

We walked on, straining to hear anything from Marcus. There was nothing but the occasional snatch of sunset light above and the soft tread of our battered shoes. We walked; I kept one eye on the trees closest to me. They bunched together like old men, their high branches reaching down to grab my head and yank me into the air and keep me prisoner as night fell and—

Stop it.

I cut the thought and the fear in half. But I still watched the old trees as we walked, quietly convinced something walked beside us in the gloom, watching, curious how far we'd dare to go.

"I knew we shouldn't have come," Jane breathed. "Marcus said it would be okay, but I *knew* it wouldn't be."

Again, all I could do was squeeze her hand. We passed under a slightly larger gap in the branches and enough light touched Jane's face for me to see her as the child she was. She and my brother might have seemed bigger, older, stronger and much more adult than I could have ever been, but it was all in my head. We were kids, playing with something that went far beyond adulthood.

"We find him and we run, okay?" She said it more to herself than me. Even so, I somehow found a little of my voice.

"Okay."

Ahead, the path ran in a series of curves, left, then right, then straight, then headed into a sharp right. Thankfully, there was only one line and the grouped trees parted a little more the further we walked, letting more of the dying sunset fall in. I tried not to think about how much time we had left before night came and what would happen if we were still looking for Marcus when it did. Silently, Jane and I took the curving path, my mouth a dry hole and the stink of the sweat that covered me from head to foot clinging to my nose.

Jane jerked to a stop. I stumbled and stayed standing thanks to her hand in mine.

"I think I heard him," she muttered.

I listened past the thud of my heart and heard a wail that sounded like a dying animal. Not for a second did I believe it was Marcus. But then:

"Help me. Oh, God. Help me."

It was Marcus.

Without any conscious thought, my hand fell from Jane's to flap against my thigh like an injured bird. I backed away and the murk behind was a growing sheet closing in at the corners of my vision.

"Jane," I croaked.

She stared at me, helpless, a child like me, and again, I wished with all my strength to be faraway.

"Help me. It's coming."

It was coming. I had no idea what *it* might be and I didn't want to know.

"Jane, help me. Help me."

She shook, tears running freely down her cheeks. Perhaps moving before she could stop herself, Jane grabbed me, pulled and we sprinted the last section of the path. Trees raced with us; the red light danced and waved madly and the path spat us out to the wide slope of dead grass.

Both of us fell together, hitting the cold grass and knocking the air from our lungs. I coughed, pain lighting its way through me, and drew in a sharp breath. No July warmth; only the miserable chill of winter. We'd jumped forward six months in the space of a few feet.

"Marcus. Where are you?" Jane shouted and coughed. Her breath fogged like smoke.

"Jane? Help me. Oh, God. Get me off this."

What I saw registered but not all the way down. I don't think it could fully. My eyes took in the sight of stunted, brown grass and the steep slope that went in both directions for miles; my nose and mouth tasted the freezing air; my brain refused to process any of it. Memory, though; memory was ready to store all of it and torture me later.

Above, the streaming colours had vanished. So had the sun. Light was a long-ago dream. *Black* lived above, but a black thicker and weightier than any midnight. It was the black of a hole that led all the way down to the other end of the world.

Jane sank to her knees. Marcus was still calling for us, screeching both our names, and the emptiness storming across the ceiling of the world would drop at any second to turn us into shadows on the dead grass.

"Marcus," I whispered to Jane.

She shook her head, shaking, sobbing.

"We have to find him."

All I got in answer was Jane's mewling cry.

Something in my head clicked off. I don't know if it was fear or considering the potential we all might never find our way home. Whatever closed away inside, it let me move.

I staggered up the slope, shouting in a high-pitched, childish yelp for my brother. He answered at once.

"Willy? I'm here. Get me up, quick."

I ran on, panting for breath, mouth and throat full of the taste of blood, my eyes unable to close and black filling my peripheral vision. Abruptly, that black wasn't just at the sides; it was right in front and closing in fast.

Screaming, I windmilled my arms to keep from pitching forward because *nothing* was forward. I'd hit the top of the slope and reached the edge of the world without realising it.

Looking down, I saw several small outcrops of rock jutting from the exposed earth. Marcus stood on a narrow ledge, barely big enough for his feet. He clung to the weeds and roots growing from the open wound of the earth; dirt streaked on his face, tears cutting a clean line through the muck.

"Willy," he whispered.

"Marcus."

I was crying, as well, lying flat to tip my arms over the edge and convinced that the top of the slope would break free at any second.

Below Marcus's ledge, a sea of nothing pitched and waved. It reduced me to a fly, a speck of dust. I was looking at everything that lived outside the world and it was all within touching distance. While I'd never known the other half of our planet, I saw at once how obscene the lack of it was. We should have been a whole world, a smooth rock floating through space and warmed by our sun. Instead, we were a broken chunk of wasteland with this forever night staining our side like a terrible growth.

"Willy. Reach down. It's coming."

I didn't want to look again, but I did.

The sea's movement had changed slightly. The waves parted; two lines hundreds of miles long parted from each other and something moved between them, something uncoiling; a purple line *stretching* far beyond anything I could measure as a distance.

The voice of simple horror spoke to me.

It's a tongue.

Marcus looked down, then stared straight at me. He shoved his hands up and spoke his last complete sentence.

"Willy, reach for me."

I reached. Oh, God, I reached.

My hands touched nothing but the freezing air of the void because I was simply too small to reach him. Even sliding forward so my belly rested on the edge did no good. He'd fallen too far and I was too little. Marcus saw this; his arms dropped to hang limply. Without a word, he crouched and tried to curl into a ball on his tiny ledge while the sea pitched and shook and the giant mouth rose.

I screamed. I raged. I shrieked for it to leave my brother alone and my only answer was the mouth opening further and further.

For one last time, I howled my brother's name and kicked backwards, propelling myself an inch further over the edge. My dancing fingers touched air; my belly rested, then slid forward, pitching me over the edge. For a tiny breath of time, I was sure the purple tongue flicked a degree in my direction as if already tasting me. Then a hand slammed down on my back and yanked.

It was Jane.

I crashed into her; we fell together, the world turning up and down and the cold grass welcoming us. Marcus screamed once before the noise was cut in half, then died.

* * * *

That happened fifty years ago, I think. It's hard to be sure these days. My memory of the last few years isn't what it used to be, but the evening in the sunset at the edge of the world is right with me as if it happened minutes ago. Sometimes in the summers when the sky burns and the sun goes down in a fiery ball, I'm eleven again, reaching for Marcus and not coming close to finding his fingers with mine. Sometimes, I feel Jane's hand on my back and I try to fight her off so I can have one more attempt at stretching over the edge for Marcus. I never make it, though. She saved my life and carried me home and all it cost me was my brother.

There is little left to write about. It'll be dark soon and I don't have many candles so it's best to put down this feather and yellowing piece of paper I've covered in my tiny scrawl. The cuts I've made on my arm are sore and tacky with blood. They'll heal, though. Wounds heal.

We walked back to the road without talking, Jane carrying me. Full dark had come by the time we made it to the main road of the village. We stopped outside my house and she told me to go in and not say anything. She said we'd talk in the morning but I never saw her again. The next day, while my parents searched desperately for my brother, I heard she'd left her parents a note to say she and Marcus were running away together. Where she went, I don't know. I think she simply ran from our village much as I did on my fifteenth birthday. My promise to my parents to return one day soon must have been some comfort, but they were a lie. I haven't been back there in decades. The state of constant terror I lived inside for four years powered me, made me run as fast I could into the fields, hills and what was left of the towns. I've barely stopped running since.

Now I sit in my cottage with the wind blowing off the loch, and the animals from the mountains sometimes sneaking down in the middle of the night to try and kill my chickens; I sit here with the cold air whistling through the holes in the stone walls; I wrap myself in as many layers as possible and I think about my brother screaming for help and my hands close and still too far from his.

I think about the mouth opening in the black sea and I think about what it must see all of us as: offerings. And I think about how it must see those offerings when one comes and tries to escape.

I think about another curious child going to the edge of the world, seeing what lives below it and pulling back, pulling away, running for his life.

I see the mouth rising from the sea, rising to the edge of the world and slithering over it as it hunts for its offering.

I see the purple tongue darting towards me as I begin to slide over the top of the slope.

I think that and I try not to scream.

My candle is going out. My hand and arm are sore. My blood is drying. Goodnight, Marcus.

I am sorry.

"AN AUTUMN SETTLING"
by Alistair Rey

She was a fastidious woman. Veronique had been able to tell from the minute they met. It was the way she pronounced "fifth-floor walkup," as though the phrase left a bad taste in her mouth. An air of habitual defeat loomed over her husband whose quiet deference spoke volumes. Veronique could vividly imagine the years of disapproving glances and verbal lashings that had emasculated a once proud and maybe even ambitious man. And now, as the woman held out her child's arm to her, Veronique realized over-protective mother could be added to this list.

"*What* is this?" the woman asked, tugging sternly at her daughter's wrist in an effort to extend the slack limb. From palm to bicep, the girl's arm was riddled with small red inflammations. Dried blotches of calamine lotion dotted her face, although the girl had clearly been picking at the bites on her cheeks. "For the price we pay, you would think the apartment would be free of vermin."

Veronique looked at the girl, puzzled. "They look like mosquito bites," she said.

"That's exactly what they are," the mother replied.

Veronique was fairly certain that mosquitoes were non-existent in Paris during the winter months. Moreover, the number of bites suggested that the girl was attacked by a veritable swarm.

"Did you see any in the apartment?" she asked, turning to the deferential husband whose name she had since forgotten.

He looked to his wife and emitted a meek, "not exactly, no."

"Did you sleep with the windows open?"

"It's January!" the woman said. "Who would leave the windows open at night?"

"I don't understand then. Is it some type of allergy?"

This remark clearly did not sit well with the mother. "My daughter doesn't have allergies," she replied tersely, turning the conversation back to the price they paid for the rental and the complications that *her* mosquitos posed for their vacation.

Having dealt with short-term renters on a more or less consistent basis over the past four years, Veronique knew when to defend herself and when to concede. Here, the choice was obvious. As the woman ran through her litany of grievances, Veronique mentally formulated the terms of her apology. It would be courteous, anodyne and, most importantly, insincere.

* * * *

Veronique liked to think of herself as an understanding person. Her venture into the real estate business, however, had severely tested this assumption.

When her father died, Veronique inherited a modest sum of money. Rather than squander it, she opted to invest. The market for tourist rentals in Paris was secure and seemed a safe bet. She became a *rentier*, living in Poissy and augmenting her income with prime urban real estate. Her father—a dyed-in-the-wool communist like most French intellectuals of his generation—would have probably been disappointed, but then again he may have been happy to know that his daughter was financially secure. At least this is what Veronique told herself.

She purchased the apartment with the tourist market in mind. It was located in a nineteenth-century building in the center of the city. The old spiral staircase winding itself around five floors to reach the apartment might have been slightly inconvenient, but a two-bedroom flat was practically unheard of in Paris these days. The large windows in the master bedroom looked out onto an enclosed courtyard with a cobblestoned patio and well-kept garden. She found it slightly amusing that the top floor offered a panoramic view of the other apartments in the building and hence momentary glimpses into the daily lives of the occupants.

Finding the place should have been the difficult part, but serving as a landlord proved exceedingly more burdensome. Property taxes and insurance—both of which Veronique had not accurately accounted for—were exacting. She also quickly learned that short-term renters were a demanding and inconsiderate breed. They complained about amenities, called at all hours of the night and frequently left the property in a state of disarray. Veronique began questioning her decision the first time she had to clean semen stained linens and unclog large balls of hair from the bathroom drains. A year into her venture, she let the place to an American who was staying in Paris for six months on business. The man insisted he was "the bookish sort," and for the next six months the only contact Veronique had with him was the rent check wired directly to her account each month. The peace of mind was welcomed and she congratulated herself on having finally let the place to a responsible tenant. That is until the lease expired.

On the day she showed up to collect the keys and inspect the premises the American was nowhere to be found. Nothing seemed out of place; the man's coat and clothes still hung in the hall closet. Yet a putrid odor wafted through every room. Stepping into the kitchen, she discovered a mound of rotting fruit piled on the counter. It was more fruit than any one person could possibly eat. The assortment of plumbs, apples, pears and melons had liquefied to a pulpy black color. Moving closer, she heard a disturbing buzzing sound and watched in horror as a blanket of flies erupted into the air and dispersed across the walls and ceiling.

Veronique filed a police report but nothing ever came of the matter. The American had left Paris earlier that month, a fact confirmed by the other residents of the building. They described him as being a reserved and polite individual, unremarkable in almost every respect. He never contacted Veronique to claim his belongings or demand the return of his hefty deposit, a significant portion of which went to paying for an exterminator. Tossing the abandoned shoes and suits into the trash bin, Veronique helplessly anticipated the next renter who would no doubt find some way of violating her trust in humanity. She balled her fists and bit her lip. It was the only thing preventing her from screaming.

Now, three years down the line, she was once again fighting back the urge to scream. The woman had stormed out of the apartment with her browbeaten husband in tow. Even before the door slammed, Veronique had made the decision: she was going to cut her losses and sell the apartment.

* * * *

The property was in a good part of town, the real-estate agent assured her. It would not be difficult to find an interested buyer within a month. He was confounded as to why she would want to sell such a place given its potential market value over the next ten years. Veronique did not have the patience to explain that ten years of peevish tenants, clogged drains and meticulously itemized insurance claims seemed like an eternity. The entire situation had the feel of a bad marriage in which divorce now seemed the only sensible option.

Despite the agent's optimism, though, the apartment didn't sell. Viewing appointments came and went. The agent phoned on a weekly basis providing updates. They were close, he said. The latest couple that viewed the property always showed "serious interest" in the property. Yet none of these promising signs ever translated into an offer. By the summer, the viewing schedules became irregular and the phone calls more sporadic. Veronique lowered the asking price, and when that did nothing she registered the apartment with a second real-estate agent for good measure. The process repeated itself: initial confidence in a quick sale, followed by puzzlement and finally resignation. As September rolled around, Veronique began to worry about the financial impact of her decision. Five months without rentals had thinned her assets considerably.

"Should I just give up and start renting again?" she asked the agent one afternoon. She tried to mask the defeat in her voice, but it came off badly.

"That is an option," he replied pragmatically.

"I don't understand. Why isn't it selling?"

The agent didn't have a good explanation. He just shrugged and chalked it up to fluctuations in the housing the market.

Veronique knew a bullshit excuse when she heard one.

* * * *

What was it about the elevation, the way it induced a sense of falling? Not a terrifying feeling of plunging to the earth, but a pleasant and dream-like one akin to floating. Was it the way the windows appeared to cascade into the courtyard? Or how they seemed to enfold the walls of the building in a honey-combed pattern of mortar and glass? She diverted her eyes away from the walls to the rooftops and autumn sky. The ground felt solid once more, her bearing restored.

Veronique returned to unpacking her duffle bag wondering why she had not packed more practical clothing. Realistically, Poissy was not far away. Should she desire a change of clothes she could easily hop on a train and be there within an hour. And yet, this was not the impression she had entering the building. Pushing back the heavy carriage doors, home suddenly felt very distant.

Stepping into the shaded corridor she saw a man standing in the courtyard. He was elderly-looking, and the tweed jacket he wore seemed purposely old-fashioned. It reminded her of the attire prominent in her parents' photo albums where time was frozen and two-tone plaid and pillbox hats never went out of style. The man did not stir or even move as the door closed behind her. He remained still, his head angled toward one of the flowers in the garden. Veronique could not say that he was smelling the flower so much as had his nose pressed directly against it so that the pedals covered his lips and cheeks.

"Hello?" she called.

The man jerked. Specks of pollen dotted his nose.

"Hello," he said after a moment. It sounded more like a question the way he said it, as though he were trying to decipher the meaning of a strange word.

"Are you a vacationer?" he asked, eyeing the duffle bag in her hand. "It's up the flight of stairs just there."

Veronique smiled awkwardly. "How do you know that?"

The old man pulled a handkerchief from his pocket and began dabbing at his nose. There was something unsettling about his gaze. He was looking at her and not looking at her at the same time. "That's where they all go, and you don't live here," he said absently.

She was about to correct him but reconsidered. It was true. She owned the property. It was hers. But she did not live here. She was just as much a stranger to this man as any of the tourists she rented to.

The man swatted in the air at a gnat. "It's warm for this time of year," he offered. "They always come when it's warm."

Veronique just nodded and continued on her way across the courtyard to the stairwell. She couldn't help thinking that half-senile neighbors were hardly a selling point.

Now, sitting on the bed, she could admit to herself why she was here. It wasn't because a break from Poissy felt needed or the fact that she had a vacant apartment in Paris at her disposal that had motivated the stay. It was to understand what precisely was so disagreeable about *this* apartment in one of the world's most frequently visited tourist destinations. Had her instincts been so completely wrong? What had she seen that others did not? These were the types of nagging questions that haunted Veronique as she unpacked her clothes, pulled clean sheets from the armoire and set to work preparing a modest dinner.

Before bed, she performed a quick inspection of the apartment, checking that all the faucets and electrical outlets worked correctly. She even got down on her hands and knees to inspect the baseboards for signs of decay or dry rot. Nothing seemed out of the ordinary. If anything, the place had a hygienic quality that one wouldn't expect in an old building.

Lying in bed, she listened to the water moving through the pipes and the silent hum of the electricity behind the walls. The sounds of the building were soothing, Veronique thought as she began to doze. She concentrated on them, allowing herself to be lulled to the edge of sleep. The more she concentrated, the clearer they became. The soft electric hum filled her ears and progressively seemed to fill the room. She turned her mind to other things expecting the sound to dissipate but the warm buzz lingered, a slight hum just above the silence.

It had transformed so slowly she had barely noticed it, but the sound was now different, alien even. Rising and approaching the windows, she felt the latches vibrating ever so slightly beneath her fingertips. When she opened them the sound enveloped the room. Outside, the courtyard was welled in impenetrable shadow, creating the illusion of a vacuous pit. The hum resonated from all sides and in the garden below Veronique perceived a series of incandescent flickers similar to the light of fireflies. They burned in the darkness, each nimbus emitting a hypnotic glow. Had she detected her body listing slightly forward or felt the metal guardrail press against her stomach? She could not recall. By the time she realized the dangerous angle of her body her mind had seized upon a more menacing detail: buried within the drone was a low chorus of sibilant voices.

* * * *

The unseasonable warmth persisted, even as Paris turned wet and rainy. On most days she sat for a long period of time listening to the rain against the windowpanes with no desire to do anything in particular. The only person she knew in the city was a former boyfriend with whom she had no wish to reestablish contact. The d'Orsay had an exhibit on Cezanne, but she had always found his work boring. Under the circumstances, Veronique was perfectly content to remain indoors and even entertained the possibility of exploring the building in greater depth. Four years previously, she had accompanied an inspector through the premises prior to buying the place. He had pointed out the old drainage system as they walked through the utility corridor, informing her that it predated Haussmann's urbanization projects of the mid-nineteenth century. The labyrinthine passages lined with piping and modern fiber optic cables were oddly fascinating. They coiled and fed back on one another like the streets of an old oriental medina. In some places, the walls were clammy and rough as though hewn from raw stone.

On the third day, she met the tenant in the apartment opposite hers. Veronique was in the process of examining some scratches on the wood paneling in the hall when she heard him coming up the stairs, two bulging grocery bags in each hand.

"Hello," he said cordially.

As he lowered the bags to extend a hand, a stream of avocados and kiwis rolled across the floor. Veronique picked up the pieces of fruit that accumulated around her feet and politely handed them back. One of those people who followed fad diets, she speculated. It seemed typically Parisian.

"I suppose you're on holiday?" he asked, returning the articles to the bag.

When Veronique corrected him a smile spread across his face. "Then I suppose that makes us neighbors. I'm 5B."

The man was well-dressed, possibly a mid-level executive at a firm from the look of his suit and shoes. He spoke French with an accent, but one Veronique could not immediately place. "Something like that," Veronique replied.

The man asked if she had been looking for something, and Veronique laughed.

"No, I noticed some marks on the wood," she explained, adding, "Have you noticed anything out of sorts with the building? I have heard some stories about the property management here."

If the man realized she was trying to coax an answer out of him, he didn't show it.

"No," was all he said. As far as he knew, the property management was adequate.

Over the next week, her encounters with the man from 5B acquired what she came to think of as an "asymmetrical routine." They bumped into each other in the hall, engaged in light conversation or simply nodded in passing. It felt neighborly enough in that informal urban way. Contrary to Veronique's initial hypothesis, it did not appear the man worked in the financial sector. His hours were too irregular. She would hear his footsteps in the hall during the late mornings or catch him whistling some tune in the evenings. Once or twice she spotted him in the courtyard on his way to the communal trash bins where he always deposited exactly two black bags in the compost bin. She never learned his name and referred to him only as 5B. Something about the label felt appropriate. It smacked of the anonymity and ordinariness that characterized modern city life.

One afternoon (Veronique thought it was a Thursday) there was a commotion in the courtyard. A vagrant had somehow found his way into the building and been camping out in the utility corridor. Nobody was certain how long he had been living on the premises, but a child had found his body that morning in one of the passageways. Tenants gathered in the courtyard despite the drizzling rain, their necks craned in the direction of the police and paramedics walking in and out of the corridor entrance. Veronique kept her distance, observing the scene from her window. The throng below traded glances and whispered amongst themselves in small circles.

Even before the paramedics emerged from the corridor bearing the body on a gurney, Veronique knew it was bad. A fetid smell filled the air. The man's skin was black and mottled with flies. When the paramedics hoisted the body into the standard-issue coroner's bag, it landed with a soft thud that sent a frenetic black cloud of insects whizzing into the air. A few of the spectators in the front rows scampered for cover, but most refused to give up their privileged viewing positions. In the midst of the commotion, Veronique saw the old man who had greeted her upon arrival. Although she was not positive, it appeared that he was looking over his shoulder directly at her window. If their eyes met, neither of them acknowledged the silent exchange.

Watching the paramedics haul away the body brought to mind a childhood memory. In an effort to teach her daughter English, Veronique's mother had sung an old English nursery rhyme to her each night before bed. While she could no longer recall the entire rhyme, the final refrain had stuck with her.

The king counts days
The queen's in delight
The princess is waiting
For her prince to alight.

With her rudimentary understanding of English at the time, Veronique always heard "prince of flies" rather than the alien Anglo-Saxon word "alight." The phrase conjured up visions of a man dressed in splendid court attire with a mass of ravenous flies feeding on the spoilt flesh concealed within the garments. This creature wove its way into her childhood nightmares. When Veronique, on the verge of tears, told her mother that she didn't want to marry the prince of flies, she laughed. "Whatever gave you such an idea?" she asked, never making the connection between the rhyme and her daughter's active imagination.

The wheels of the gurney made a rickety sound as they rolled across the convex stones of the courtyard. She knew it was inappropriate to think such things, but she imagined the vagrant wandering through the maze-like passages that stretched out beneath the building. Had he first experience amazement at their vastness? Had this wonder soon converted to terror when he realized that he had completely lost himself in the winding passageways? This was, of course, pure fantasy because the child had discovered the body near the entrance to the corridor. Nonetheless, she could not let go of the idea.

Throughout the afternoon, Veronique caught herself humming the childish melody of the rhyme. It had been ages since she had last thought of it. The dulcet sound of her mother's voice had been stowed away somewhere in the back of her mind for years, buried but not forgotten. It brought back memories of her childhood in Crécy-la-Chapelle where her father had taught at the local collège. By the time they moved closer to Paris, Veronique had all but forgotten about the prince of flies and the nightmares.

She was still humming the melody when she extinguished the lights and crawled into bed. Closing her eyes, she imagined the prince of flies hovering above her. His face was different now as he smiled and exposed his white teeth through a beard of frenzied insects. Veronique reached out to take his hand and felt a formicating sensation envelope her entire arm. He was drawing her closer, wrapping her in his churning embrace. When he pressed his lips to hers she could feel him inside her mouth, filling her entire body with moiling, writhing life.

At this thought she began gasping for air. The room was silent and she was alone. Pale light trickled in through the blinds casting a striated pattern across the expanse of the floor. Inserting her thumb and index fingers between the venetian blinds, she noted the source of the light. A single window was illuminated two floors down on the opposite side of the courtyard. The kitchen of the opposing apartment was visible from her vantage point. It belonged to the old man who was sitting alone at a table drizzling honey over a bowl of pears. Veronique was about to check the time when she noticed the man begin to convulse soundlessly. His eyes rolled back and his mouth stretched and distended in an unnatural movement. Veronique could not believe her eyes as the lower portion of man's jaw appeared to dislocate, forcing the top portion of his head back at an impossible angle. A long conical tongue sprouted from the gaping mouth and flailed wildly in the air before slithering toward the pears. All the while the man sat perfectly still, his body catatonic.

Naturally, she was still dreaming as she watched the pulsating tongue borrow into the fruit. She was still dreaming when the pears liquefied and the proboscis-like tongue retracted back into the man's throat. She was still dreaming when she slunk back into bed and buried her face deep in the pillow. Perhaps she was even still dreaming when she noticed the first traces of dawn light bleed across sky.

* * * *

5B found her crouching in the hall with her nose pressed to the ground.

"Something interesting?" he asked, clearly uninterested in whatever it was she was doing.

She pointed at a desiccated fly carcass lying on the parquet in the hall. It had been sitting there on its back motionless when she opened the door.

"Dead fly," she said.

"There are more of those in the courtyard if you fancy them."

"Yes, terrible what happened the other day," she said, rising to her feet. It seemed the only appropriate thing to say.

A troubled look passed over his face. "You know they believe you're responsible," he finally said.

Veronique furrowed her brow. "They don't think that I…"

He shook his head. Talk among the tenants had led some to speculate that Veronique had left the front doors open allowing the vagrant access to the building. Looking at it from their perspective, it was not an implausible scenario: a new person in the building followed by an episode involving a death and the police. A majority of the tenants appeared to be older and had probably lived in the building for years without incident.

"Should I speak with them?" she asked after he had finished. "I certainly don't think I'm responsible for this."

5B shook his head again. "No. They'll summon you once they hold a meeting," he said. "It normally works that way."

Veronique doubted she would be sticking around for some building council meeting to decide her fate. She was uncomfortable with how the place was affecting her behavior and she was pretty certain that the problem with the apartment had little to do with the actual state of the property. Her plan was to spend the day out and return to Poissy in the morning on the first train.

She found a quiet café to pass the afternoon reading the newspaper. Out of habit, she scanned the property values listed in the real-estate section. A left bank cinema house was showing The Third Man, finalizing her plans for the night. She spent the evening watching Joseph Cotton and Orson Welles meander around postwar Vienna. It occurred to her that she had only attended a movie alone once before in her life. Some weeks after her father's death, she had sat through a Claude Charbol retrospective in Archère. Her days then had been filled with sad looks and tepid condolences, and the thought of being surrounded by complete strangers in a dark room felt comforting. There would be no sad looks, no obligatory expressions of sorrow. When the credits opened, Veronique had begun crying. It was the first time she had cried since the funeral. At that moment, with everyone's attention fixed on the screen, it felt permissible.

These thoughts slowly rolled over in her mind as she sat watching The Third Man. She found it difficult to concentrate on the film. Her attention continually trailed off and the story seemed hard to follow. More than once she got the impression that something was lurking there in the expansive darkness of the theater, waiting for her. If she listened closely, the faint drone emitted by the old projector sounded eerily like insect noises. Half way through the movie, she got up and left. Her thoughts were now on packing and catching the first train from Saint Lazare at six.

She pushed back the large front carriage doors with the certainty that tomorrow would be the last time she would ever set foot in this building. The corridor was dark, although she could just barely make out the garden in the ethereal moonlight as she stepped into the courtyard. Her fingers trailed along the wall for the switch to trip the courtyard lights. She located it, pressed the button and screamed.

As the lights illuminated the courtyard, she saw a collection of bodies making their way through the garden. They were hunched on all fours and moved with a predatory silence. Disjointed limbs thrashed in the air and bent at abnormal angles like the legs of spiders. When they laid eyes on Veronique, a ferocious buzz filled the courtyard. Their faces contorted to expose long tubular tongue that dragged on the ground. A familiar iridescent glow began to pulse in their abdomens. She turned to run but realized that there was nowhere to go. On all sides, tenants were now spilling out of the windows and crawling down the sides of the building on their bellies like beetles. There must have been fifty of them swarming towards the courtyard, converging from every direction. The insectile drone echoed in the air, eclipsing her screams.

The horde fell upon her and everything went dark. She felt her body being forced to the ground and then raised up into the night. When she opened her eyes she was staring directly at the moon. The contours of the surrounding courtyard walls now framed the night sky and from this position she could clearly see how the enclosure resembled a giant combed hive teeming with gangly bodies scrambling from every window. She felt the creatures roiling beneath her and experienced the sudden sensation of movement. Despite her resistance, she was transferred from hand to hand, inched closer to the gaping black opening of the utility corridor at the far end of the courtyard. She understood now where she was going and attempted to cry out one last time over the shrill drone. Her voice, hoarse from screaming, came out in a disconsolate whimper.

"I don't want to marry the prince of flies," she puled. "I don't want to marry him."

I KNOW HOW YOU'LL DIE
by K.G. Anderson

I know how you'll die.

Not when, or why, or even where—though I could make a good guess. Based on what I can see. Because what I can see is what *you'll* see—in the final moments before you die.

I call it the Vision, and I've had it since I was a child.

No one knows about the Vision—though I've been tempted to tell my uncle Manny. Poor old guy, estranged from his kids. Yet my Vision shows him surrounded by children and grandchildren. A grey-haired woman holds his hand. I wish I could tell Manny that at the end, all will have been forgiven.

It won't be forgiven for you. I can tell you that.

For the Vision to work, I need time to get into the person's head. I need a sort of *permission* from them.

We'll be having coffee—you remember *our* coffee?—or arguing over a project at work, and there comes that moment: The eye contact. The moment when we both know the relationship could go deeper. There's a door, and we could decide to walk through it. Or not. Whether or not we act, the door is open. With the Vision, I can see in. And what I glimpse is the final moments before that person dies.

People might wonder why I sudden busy myself with the paperwork. Or gasp. Or bite my lip. Or shake my head. Or change the subject. Do you remember how, after our eyes met, I jumped up from the table in the coffeehouse? I was terrified.

You bet the Vision plays havoc with friendships. It's why I won't go with my cousin Patricia to the beach. I always turn down those invitations.

"Vampire Sara," she calls me. But it isn't any fear of the sun or the outdoors that scares me. It's what I know about Patricia's final seconds on earth: she'll see the sun, through rippling green water. Then the water grows darker, the light grows fainter and…

I refuse to be there when the water takes her.

Having the Vision isn't always that bad. There's Margot, my boss. I don't trust the bitch. And she doesn't trust me. It's possible that she senses what I know: that she'll die seeing the blur of bodies through a windshield and her ring-choked fingers grasping the leather-wrapped steering wheel of her Mercedes. Poor Margot.

Well of course the Vision is hell on my love life. Sex is best in the dark, with strangers; no eye contact required or wanted. No sight means no Vision.

It's only when I start to get close to someone that the problems begin. I run from the ones whose final moments appear violent, self-induced, or seem likely to be soon. When the Vision shows me pleasant surroundings or the face of a loving companion, that's when I make an effort. I give it a try with that person. But sooner or later the relationship sinks under the weight of my undeserved and unwanted foreknowledge.

But you. Oh yes, you were different. When the Vision came, I jumped up from my chair, jarring the table and sending cappuccino gushing across the white tablecloth. A flash of annoyance crossed your face before you put on your mask of concern.

"Sara?" you asked.

The waiter hovered over me.

"I'm sorry, I'm sorry, I'm sorry," I mumbled. "Not well. I have to go home. No! Please don't come with me. Fine. I'll be fine. I'll call a friend."

I stumbled out the door of the restaurant, into a cab, and babbled the address of my apartment building. I know now that you overheard.

At home, I poured myself a glass of whisky, hands shaking, and stood at the kitchen counter, trying to rewrite my Vision of your death. Because how could your final sight be of me, pointing a small black gun at you and firing? *Insane*, I told myself. *I don't even own a gun.* Well, I didn't at the time.

But then you texted. You called. You emailed. You appeared in the lobby of my office building. *No*, I told you. Again, and again. *No.*

Embarrassed, I finally talked to my friends. Frightened, I went to the police. When you stalked me on social media, I hired a lawyer. But of course, I couldn't tell anyone I knew I was going to kill you.

I'd quit my job and was packing to move to another city when Patricia brought me the Ruger pistol. She meant well. She showed me how to load it and how to aim it and how to squeeze—not jerk—the trigger. She told me not to be timid.

"You never know, Sara," she said.

But I do. So when the sound of shattering glass wakes me at 3 a.m., I know it's you. I take the black gun from my bedside table. Feeling my way through the stacks of packing boxes, I creep down the hallway toward the living room.

A light from the parking lot illuminates the room. Shards of glass glitter on the wall-to-wall carpet. I see your gloved hand reaching in, turning the handle. The door from the patio swings open. Glass crunches softly as you step into my apartment, at last. I move out of the darkness holding Patricia's gun cocked.

"Sit down." I point with the muzzle to indicate your seat. I tell you about the Vision, what I've never told a soul.

And then I squeeze the trigger.

OUR FAMILY GHOST
by Joshua Gage

We never see her ghost, but she is home.
We know from sudden chills and the smell of smoke.
We never see her, but feel her in our bones.

Mornings are rich with coffee, sunlight sewn
in slants across the eggs' erupting yolks.
We never see her ghost, but she is home

in the cracks of the porch steps, the footpath overgrown
with moss and weeds, the bent spine of the oak.
We never see her, but feel her in our bones.

The neighbors never asked, and never phoned,
as though her name would kill them if they spoke.
We never see her ghost, but she is home.

Mother rocks in granny's chair, alone,
burnt quilt wrapped about her like a cloak.
We never see her, but feel her in our bones.

Father keeps time with his axe. "No one
would ever want a half-blackened crib," he chokes.
We never see her, but feel her in our bones.
We never see her ghost, but she is home.

FAIR SHOPPING
by Jack Lee Taylor

It starts when Nora and I see the black-and-white flyer on one of Ember's Grocery tack boards by aisle 7.

24th ANNUAL EMBER COMMERCE STREET FAIR

SATURDAY JUNE 28

FOOD CRAFT MUSIC FUN!

We turn on aisle 8 and I stiffen, rubbing the back of my neck.

"Why do you keep doing that?" Nora says. My wife looks at me, her eyes luminous and accusing.

"Do what?" I reply.

"This." Nora stoops forward in the cold air of the grocery store and rubs the back of her neck briskly with her left hand, her arm bracelets jangling. "Always when we get to the baby aisle."

"I'm just walking, Nora," I say, knowing where this is heading.

I see her let several weeks of pent up frustration go as she slaps both hands to the sides of her white summer dress in frustration. She studies my face and then says, "Stop pretending, Alan. It's not just the damn grocery store anymore. It's everything. You go all stiff and start rubbing your neck like that. It drives me crazy!"

"What are you talking about?" I say and see a grocery stock boy walk by us, eyeing us briefly to catch our little soap-opera. I stare back at his preadolescent face and he looks away, walking past the rows of stacked *Huggies*.

I take a patient breath. "Do you really want to do this here?"

"Why not?" she says. "Why do you think I cut through here all the time?"

I close my eyes, letting out a long tired sigh. I then look at her and try to smile a degree below patronizing.

"Nora, all I want to do is pay for our stuff and get out of here. We're going to the street fair. Right?"

She stares at me for a moment and then says in a gritted hiss, "Just take me home." She drops the grocery basket full of comestibles we planned on smuggling into the town fair and storms off, tucking her purse hard to her side. I watch her leave, her thin dress flowing wildly behind her.

The miscarriage was three months ago and ended Nora's chance of ever carrying again. After her surgery, my attempts to support seemed hollow and pretentious to her, angering instead of comforting. So I left her to herself and waited for the normality of our three years together to resume. I'm still waiting.

I run after Nora, catching her near the exit. People stare when I turn her around and hug her tight. She goes rigid and then shudders. I raise her head to look at me, seeing tears fall on her pleading eyes and knowing what we both want. We want the pain to go away.

Nora smiles slightly and skirts her eyes to see our audience. She then looks at me and crunches her brows together as if in pain.

"What is it?" I say. She goes slack, dropping her purse. Her eyes become chalky stones in their sockets. I hold her tighter in my panic when I see her mouth droop open to an impossible length, her howls of pain cut short when the lower half of her face suddenly falls off and splatters to the ground. I hear my own screaming when I see the rest of her fold inward, her skin becoming diaphanous, revealing the dark meat inside. Her bones crackle and her coppery smell ripens the air. She becomes slippery in my grasp, like a giant gleaming internal organ. She squirts out of my arms and drops to the ground in a splash and I stare in horror at the bloody dress and the clump of flesh on the tile floor, a ruined mass looking nothing like Nora or anything remotely human.

I move my head up slowly, my wide eyes searching through a haze of blood-pounding shock.

Someone has to come to me.

Touch me.

Move me.

No one does. I walk slowly in a mindless stupor. When I bump into an ice bin near the wall, I come to and see the other bodies. Bloody messes spot the grocery store like droppings from some large animal. I see the crimson-drenched garments on the floor in loose piles and I reconstruct the image of their former wearers: an overweight man in jeans, a young girl in a *Hello Kitty* shirt, a cashier lady in a beige *Ember's Grocery* work shirt. All of them reduced to what looks like slabs of mangled butcher meat.

A car crashes through the face of the store. Brilliant shards of glass scatter. The sound of it brings me above the numbing cotton of disbelief and I start to run. The car, a pearl-like Cadillac, plows into rows of checkout counters, catapulting candy bars and magazine stands toward me. I watch the car teeter to stillness and can see through the gloom of the passenger window the writhing things that splatter dark-red into the windshield. Outside air rushes through the gaping hole in the wall the car left in its path. Several dead birds line the sidewalk leading to the parking lot.

I run around the car and head back toward the exit where Nora is. There are sounds of collision and destruction outside; a chorus of car alarms screech endlessly in the distance. I look through the automatic sliding doors, pulled instinctively to exit this place. I pause to look back down at Nora's ruined remains. I kneel down, feeling the loss of her strike cold and hard inside my chest.

I pick up Nora and cradle her slick form into my chest, holding her like a baby. Like our baby, the child that defied us its life and struck Nora barren before it died. I whisper the song. Hush little baby...

The car alarms continue their crying outside, blocking out my toneless singing. Nora begins to stick to me, the glistening coat of blood of her gluing against my forearms and neck.

The pain is slow, a kindling heat deep in my stomach. I cough the foaming blood up from my mouth, letting it spew onto Nora.

My eyes go dark, dissolving into mucus-like tears down my cheeks. The unseen takes me. Consumes me.

One trickling afterimage.

A parting thought.

Aisle 8.

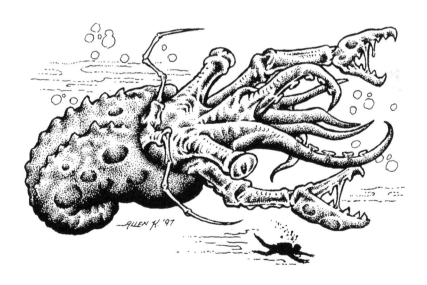

BLACK AGGIE
by Marina Favila

Caroline had never heard of an urban 'Christmas' myth. Nor would she be inclined to believe one had her ten-year-old daughter not promised that this one was true, cross-your-heart true, and Bethel had never lied to her before, save once. That was thirteen years ago, on Christmas Eve, when Bethel's best friend had coaxed Caroline's little girl to sneak out of her house at midnight to see Black Aggie caress the baby Jesus. Of course, none of it made sense. The girls had conflated two local legends: one, of a graveyard memorial just outside of Baltimore, the stone figure of Grief, worn dark with time and nicknamed Black Aggie. The statue was haunted by an evil spirit, and moved on Halloween night, so said the locals and the local papers, at the witching hour, no less. The second—that was a statue, too, of a towering black workingwoman on Pier 33, another Black Aggie, in Bethel's mind. Commissioned thirty years ago, the statue was supposed to commemorate contributions of African-American women in the South; but the nine-foot monstrosity at the edge of a dock, with her arms out-stretched to the sea, looked suspiciously like a southern mammy, with her long skirt and sweeping apron, and that terrible look of weariness carved into her broad-shaped face. Liberal groups saw a slavery icon; conserva-tive groups called PC foul. Petitions to the state to tear Black Aggie down rolled in on a regular basis.

The mammoth statue gained so much notoriety that high school and college kids started hanging out on the pier after midnight, and Aggie's leg-end grew. Her eyes glowed in the dark, said your best friend's best friend, and her arms moved up to her chest as if to caress an infant at the stroke of midnight. When Caroline was in school the favorite dare was to climb up in those giant arms to prove the myth true, and Caroline had heard more than one story of somebody's somebody's cousin's ribs bruised or broken after a night in Black Aggie's embrace.

Caroline had never seen the statue herself, built on the far end of Fells Point and in none too great a part of town. Caroline's mother had forbidden her own little girl from seeking such worthless thrills with her best friends and later beaus, and Caroline had faithfully obeyed. But not her little girl. Bethel had been afraid of nothing, and she would see this midnight-moving statue, now moldy with salt wind and sea fog, facing east and raising her muscular arms to her bosom, as if to embrace a child. Or in Bethel's mind, the baby Jesus. It was a ridiculous story.

But Bethel stuck to it for years. And told her mother in great detail how she and Bunny Wooster, and Bunny's older sister Madge and Madge's older boyfriend Max (all of fourteen) had decided this was the bitchin' year to prove once and for all if Black Aggie would move on Christmas Eve. At first, Caroline hadn't believed Bethel at all, for neither she nor Ted had heard the girl sneak out, though they had stayed up all hours, putting together that damn dirt bike with the silver streamers, the one Bethel begged for, for months. It was 3:00am before they finished; and after that, they made love, as they always did on Christmas Eve, in the den with only the Christmas lights on. When Caroline checked on her little girl, she was dug deep in the covers and snoring.

But Bethel's story was so detailed, the bumpy ride on the bus, ten blocks down Charles and five blocks on Pratt; the lights in the harbor for Christmas, all white and outlining the bay, the two pavilions, and the tall ship from Prague; and then the long snowy walk past the shipyard, all the way to the end pier where the statue of Black Aggie faced the black harbor, black on black. Bethel claimed she cried when she saw the statue, for the woman had such a sad look on her face, and the foam flung up to her cheeks from the bay made it look like she was crying. And Madge's boyfriend said she was crying for the baby Jesus, though he didn't explain why. And then Bethel said she got cold, cold to the bone (and Caroline was sure this was not her little girl talking, but some phrasing from the older Madge); and then, then the statue's arms moved, Bethel swore it, folding up to her chest, and maybe lightning struck, for Bethel remembered something dramatic happening, though she wasn't sure what, and they all ran down the lengthening pier, laughing and screaming, all the way to the bus, which came chugging along just as they got there. And then home, and then bed, and then fast asleep in her Star Wars-Princess Leia quilt, with her two parents none the wiser—and was she mad? Don't be mad, Mommy. Daddy'll be proud.

And Ted was. He scolded Bethel, then scooped her up in his long, lean arms, looking at her with laughing pride, and said, "Bethel, my dear, what would I do without you?"

But Caroline had been horrified and rightly so, and she worried for years that something had happened that night, some horrible thing that Bethel had repressed, but nothing seemed changed: her little girl still sang each day in her high falsetto voice, and hiccupped when she laughed, and skipped rope in the hall, despite always scuffing the mirror, and even slid down the banister when her mother wasn't looking. Ted encouraged this, of course, as he always encouraged her to rebel, to ride dirt bikes and read boy books, thinking he was raising a feminist like his own dear mom. But Caroline worried about everything, until Bethel died of a fever that no one knew how to explain, and didn't explain, just something that happened when she was twenty-two years old. That was last year, on Christmas Eve. And now she and Ted were getting a divorce because she couldn't move on, he said, and because, she said, he could.

Caroline looked up at the clock on her wall, festooned in holly, real holly from the Martha Stewart store, courtesy of her mother. How she hated the shiny curlicue leaf, sharp as a pin and able to draw blood if you didn't handle it the right way. No one ever talked about that, only its cheerful waxy evergreen-green, and never its poisonous bright-red berry. But Caroline agreed to the wreath, to all the decorations, just to get her mother out the door, with her bag of tinsel and good-will nagging that she needed to move on. Move on, they all kept saying it, as if you can move away from the part of yourself that is missing.

Tonight was Christmas Eve. Ted would be with his new girlfriend, the one he thought she didn't know about, and her mother would be with Caroline's other siblings, at Hanover's for the holiday feast, where they would toast God and pray for her daughter. It was only by promising to meet them at midnight mass that she got out of dinner, though she had no intention of going there either. The one positive thing to come out of all this was her ability to lie, without thought, without guilt. Only one place she wanted to be tonight. She would be there before midnight.

* * * *

No snow. Caroline rested her head on the bus's wet window. Moisture from the grimy vent above, emitting its germy heat in spits and bursts, collected on the pane in miniscule beads and jumped erratically with each pothole slump. Everything inside and outside the bus seemed dirty and second-rate in Caroline's eyes. Even the Christmas decorations, ten or so blocks from the chichi Inner Harbor, were obviously made decades ago, used and reused, and stored without proper care. Most of the red light Rudolphs had busted noses, and the corner snowmen were smeared with years of pollution. Still, the coolness of the window felt nice, and Caroline thought she might be running a fever. She leaned in. Think nothing, she said in her mind. Just get there.

Outside few late-night shoppers were hurrying along the sidewalk. They all have places to go, she thought, places that are warm and filled with light. Caroline corrected herself. Holidays are hard; it's a myth they're anything but. Some have lost husbands, daughters, hate their jobs, their lives, themselves. These thoughts did not comfort her; that was a surprise. Misery doesn't love company. It loves nothing.

When the bus approached the last light, a yellow blinking one, strung up over a deserted street, Caroline pulled the lever to get off. A light snow swirled above her as she exited the back of the bus. Wisps of crisp white lace, bright in the ice blue of the street lamps and the midnight blue beyond, circled high in the air, refusing to land. "This would have drawn me once," she said aloud to no one. The bus rambled on.

Caroline turned right. The statue was supposed to be three blocks from the bus stop, just east of the city. The dock was near empty. Did she expect someone? Maybe a homeless man or two, with their hunkering shadows, bullying a doorway. Of course, had Bethel been here, she would have insisted on going home to get blankets and cans of coke, even bagging up her mother's famous holiday cookies. And though Caroline would have forbidden such nonsense, Bethel would have charmed her father to her side; and Ted would have said yes, in less than a minute, for he loved the chance to rescue anyone with his baby girl by his side. And Caroline would have finally agreed, complaining and laughing at the same time, calling them both a couple of nuts, but also calling the police for drive-by support, and then thanking God under her breath that she'd sent in those holiday checks to the City Police Fund. This loving memory never happened, but Caroline imagined them all rushing around, supplies in their arms, laughing and late for the Hanover family dinner, and not caring a bit if they were. Now Caroline didn't care. She was ice cold in.

By the time she was halfway down the second block, Caroline saw the statue rising out of darkness. It was huge, much larger than she had imagined, a deep mahogany-black, the same color as the bay. The line and sweep of the statue's form was fluid, round; but the posture of the workingwoman was straight as an arrow, her head tilted slightly to the sky and her muscular arms outstretched, palms up and open, as if she were asking for something or expecting something to be delivered into her arms. The statue's eyes were vacant, in the old Greek style, large and wide, but without an iris to focus her glance. She appeared wise and blind at the same time, and faithful—how could she be otherwise? A statue waiting forever for that which would never be given.

As Caroline came closer, the statue loomed above her own small frame, for she was barely five foot four and thinner than she'd been in college. She ran her fingers up the giant folds of the statue's apron, bunched to the side as if a sea wind had swept the skirt up and over the ankle. Caroline marveled at the detail of the jumbled laces carved into the workingwoman's shoe, for the statue was made of wood. She had always assumed it would be stone or some cement mixture, but she could feel the ridges beneath the fine sanding and polish and paint. The scent of wet pine filled her nostrils, or so she imagined.

Balancing on the two-step pedestal, she reached up to touch Black Aggie's arms. They were rock solid and would easily hold her weight. Using the skirt as a makeshift step, she hoisted herself to the statue's hips, locking her legs around the waist, like a child riding piggyback. Over the statue's shoulder she could now look out to sea. Blackness stared back and the occasional line of harbor light hitting a lapping wave.

Reaching her arms around the statue's shoulders in a clumsy embrace, she felt snowflakes coating her hands in a fine wash. That beautiful crystalline snow was finally descending and turning to rain. No matter. *I wasn't looking for beauty tonight, or warmth, or comfort, or even an answered prayer. I have no prayers, and no answer is acceptable.*

Placing her feet on the splayed bow on the back of Aggie's apron, Caroline rose up to a near-standing position, her form hovering over the statue's head. If she spread her arms wide, she would look like that silly girl in *Titanic*. She was sure other silly girls had done the same thing before her, their boyfriends holding on to their hips, copping a quick feel, perhaps, as their Friday night dates surveyed the harbor below. Even Bethel might have held this same position a hundred times before. It would be like her, too, to spread her arms wide, straight out to the side, like a gibbet or cross, her hands surfing the air in an attitude of flight. Caroline held fast to the statue's head, and again peered into darkness.

You came looking for nothing, she reminded herself. *And nothing is here for you. Reach out. Spread your arms wide. Hold on—to nothing.*

But Caroline did not do that. Instead she felt herself crumble, like a building destroyed from the inside out and falling in perfect precision. Her body folded in, and tumbled over the shoulder of the wooden Aggie, where she curled up in her arms, like a sleeping child.

* * * *

Several BT Skulls, with nowhere to go, looked on, as a woman walked down the pier alone. She looked prosperous, though disheveled; and perhaps due to the late hour, she walked quickly past them—some thought, wildly. Even so, they were irritated, for the woman took no notice, and they were wearing their colors and standing with authority on their corner of turf. Pier 33 was theirs, and the black mammy statue, with its towering shadow, a good place to sell crack and settle disputes.

The earlier promise of snow had turned to a thick, wet mist, and the crew had taken refuge across the street, under the Little Buddha Bridge with the red lantern, a faux lacquer entranceway to a popular Chinese dive. The boys felt safe there, for Old Rummy Chang had a nephew with the BT Skulls, and liked the prestige of being protected by a black gang.

Most of the boys were hungry this time of night, well after dinner but before their nightly cruise around the Point. Little interest was paid to the small woman rushing by, until she stopped to peruse the statue. Hesitant, seemingly in wonder, she fingered the wooden monument, as if trying to measure it. And then she began to climb, like a bear shimmying up a trunk, arms and legs wrapped round the accordion folds of the statue's wooden skirt.

The woman was neither young nor graceful, but a certain diligence and care governed her movements. Despite the rain, wet clothes, and dripping hair, she made it past the statue's waist, her feet and hands placed just so, until she could stand—straight, almost straight, seeming, for a moment, to hover in the air. The crew of boys began to applaud this unexpected feat, but then the woman began to shake, a horrible near-violent eruption, like a puppet dancing at the mercy of a child's unfirm grasp. Dropping over herself and under herself, she collapsed into the statue's arms.

The boys' focus shifted, back and forth, between the still woman caught midair and the pungent smell of sweet and sour pork, calling from the Little Buddha. Some counseled food, before it was too late, while others wondered what fun might be had should they wait for the woman's descent, and make a quick grab for her purse, or jewelry, or worse.

But then she disappeared, in a second it seemed, like a night switch in the night turned off. "Where the hell… " the leader swore at his unobservant crew. "Bitch tripped while we was joking," said his second-in-command. "Or smoking," another added. "Broke camp while we be lampin'… wait dawn, she'll be loooong gooooone." Two of his boys did a quick shuffle tap and clapped their hands in unison. The leader chuckled softly, raising their play of rhyme to the level of wit. Leaders can do that. He passed his cigarette around the group, its tiny lit end streaking neon-red, from his mouth to the next and the next, lighting up the darkness between them.

"Maybe she's hiding in the shadow," someone offered between puffs. "Or fell into the smelly bay…"

One recruit knew better. He had watched the woman keenly, from the moment she arrived, rushing down the pier, in her open flapping coat. He was new, the youngest in the crew. And it was Christmas Eve. Not long ago he had believed in magic on this night. But the boy was no fool. So when the statue's arms began to rise, folding over that spacious chest, and the City Clock began to chime the midnight hour of Christmas Day, the boy said nothing. Nor did he speak when those wooden arms lowered seconds later, revealing their empty embrace. He knew without doubt the woman had not slipped away unnoticed, or fallen from the dock, or stood shivering within the statue's shadow. She simply vanished.

AFTERWORD: The first Black Aggie in the story is a real statue, a graveyard monument outside of Baltimore. I grew up on urban myths about Black Aggie, which included moving arms to crush anyone sitting on the statue's lap. It was later moved after so many tourists and young people came looking for the legends the statue inspired. The second Black Aggie in the story is fiction (as is the gang of the BT Skulls). Some liberties were taken with the map of the dock and city, though I hope I did credit to the magic of Charm City. I grew up running around the dock before Inner Harbor was in place. For a girl on the verge of adulthood, freedom seemed unlocked by its darkness.

THE CHROMA OF HOME
by Arasibo Campeche

Kromel found small, chewed bones scattered around the extinguished fire pit. He bent to one knee and saw pulverized cinders sprinkled in the ash. The traitor Marko had built a fire here recently and made no effort, or was too sloppy, to hide the fact. Kromel looked at the bones again. Some were hollow, suggesting they belonged to a creature capable of flight. He attempted to reassemble the broken skeleton in his mind.

Pale blue light covered the ground around him. A blue iridescent bird flew over his head, squawked, and landed across the fire pit. The bird, thrice his size, spread its wings, changing the color of its feathers from aqua to violet. Kromel recognized the species but had forgotten its name.

"I am not your enemy," Kromel said. There was no chance the creature understood him but talking in a soothing voice might calm it.

The bird lowered its head, pecked the moist soil, and straightened again, changing its feathers into a fiery red. The bones must have belonged to one of its chicks.

"I swear this was not me," Kromel whispered. Sweat ran down his back.

The animal's long neck whipped forward. Kromel sidestepped, avoiding the sharp, wide beak. He grabbed a dagger from his belt. The bird jumped over the fire pit and attacked with great speed, but Kromel was ready. He grabbed the bird's neck and rapped its skull with the hilt of his dagger until the wings went limp.

Kromel pulled a leather-bound notebook the size of his palm, along with his blood pen, from the rucksack that hung from his shoulder. He laid the unconscious bird flat on the ground and measured its dimensions with his dagger. Its body was five times the length of the head. The feathers on both wings, half the length of the head. The feet, including the talons, were the same length as the feathers. Kromel opened his notebook, then poked his fingertip with the blood pen. While occasionally consulting the measurements he made, he drew a flawless diagram of the bird in his notebook. He blew on the page and recited the shapeshifter's prayer: *From your body to my page...* The drawing filled with vibrant color.

He puzzled the chick's bones into what seemed like their original arrangement, then pushed them into the soft earth and drew them on a separate page. Instead of keeping this page for himself, he filled in the color with paint from his bag, then laid the portrait beside the bird, leaving a small memento for a parent who lost their offspring, a last show of respect to the creature Marko had slain. Kromel had relied on his mediocre painting skills, and not the use of magic to fill in the color, since art achieved by magic was sterilized of all emotion.

Kromel searched until he saw Marko's tracks leading away from the campsite, into the mountainous region of Dunke, in the direction of a large volcano. From a distance, it looked as if the flowing lava formed a static, orange web on the volcano's gray surface. He had some distance to travel, but he'd make it before dusk.

Kromel rubbed the thin paper that made up the pages of his notebook, eager to be free of military service. He leafed through magically created paintings, a collection of every known creature for many thousands of miles, which he could transform into at will. Part of the notebook's magic was to give it a slim look despite the countless images it contained. He reached the last few pages, where names were written. Names of people Kromel couldn't remember anymore, but that had once posed a threat to the stability of the kingdom. A list of traitors and political insurgents he had recovered throughout his career as tracker. There was space for only one more name. Although he had written down all the names of his prey, he'd only written the details of the pursuit during the first few years, then abandoned the practice. It became evident that the criminals he tracked were variations of the same thing: a rogue element that thought he could run the kingdom better than the current king and ran towards hiring their own army or away from a tracker.

After capturing Marko, he'd be able to retire from the king's service and move his family near the ocean. If he failed he'd retire in shame and be left to live in the streets as a beggar, forbidden to receive aid from family and friends. The space for listing names was either complete or worthless. The kingdom's laws were harsh, but it remained unconquered throughout all its history. Absoluteness begat strength.

After retiring with his honor intact, a cool breeze blowing from the shoreline awaited him. Unlike some of his companions in the service, Kromel's mind would remain intact and free of the demons of his past. Kromel was the only soldier he knew that had never killed anyone.

* * * *

All the structures in Dunke looked the same: flat-roofed and the color of brown clay. The buildings flanked a long walking path that lead to the volcano, the heart of Dunke. Thin cloth veiled the squared windows on the buildings. Kromel's boots crunched black, grainy soot. Goblins peered from their windows as he walked by. Their spherical heads barely fitting through the windows. Sweat ran down their green lathery skin. A few shops, selling all sorts of trinkets and products, were strewed along his path. The shops varied in shape and size, but all consisted of wooden boxes covered in merchandise. Goblins climbed in and out of other shops around him, carrying items too big to fit in the boxes.

A foul stench, reminiscent of rotten flesh, forced Kromel to breathe through his mouth. A few goblins ran from shop to shop, the top of their heads barely reaching knee level. One bumped into him, then changed direction while glaring up. The ratio between their orb-like eyes and heads were replicated to perfection in several pages of his notebook. *One head, the length of five eyeballs.*

A goblin yelled from a shop. "Human." He waved. "Yes. You with the fancy boots. Come here."

The goblins of Dunke never wore shoes but calling him human would have sufficed; there were no other non-goblins around. Kromel's stomach was grumbling, and Marko's trail had disappeared, so he decided to walk over to the goblin.

"Do you sell any food?" Kromel asked, pulling a gold coin from his bag. He was famished and out of rations, but he'd be careful what he ate in Dunke. Goblins were immune to diseases that could kill human villages in days.

"Hello to you too human, I'm Tarc." The goblin grunted. "I sell something you'll like." Tarc knelt and removed a wooden panel from his side of the box-shaped shop and climbed in. Heat rose in visible waves. Volcanic fumes mixed in with the heat made Kromel's eyes water. The door led underground.

"Here we have it." Tarc lifted an oval plate out from his underground inventory and placed it on the box. A rodent-like creature with its legs stretched out lay on its back. Its teeth were mostly charred, but Kromel saw white spots here and there. The rest of its body was black with burnt skin. The spoor of decay was now stronger than before.

"It's not very colorful, and it smells awful," Kromel said and grimaced.

"What?"

Kromel sighed. "It's not pleasant to look at." Kromel's stomach grumbled again. "And I don't eat meat. Do you have anything else?"

Tarc scrunched his face in annoyance. "I thought earlier you said that humans eat whatever keeps them alive."

"I never said that."

Tarc looked down and brushed a finger over his lip. "I apologize. You all look the same to me."

Kromel leaned closer to the goblin. "Another human came through here recently? What did he look like?"

"I just said. Like you." Tarc tapped his chin. "He might have had longer hair. A female then? It's hard to tell when you're clothed."

"He betrayed my people," Kromel said.

Tarc blinked, tilted his head, and shrugged. "What's your question?"

"Do you know where I can find him? I'll pay you five gold coins." He shook his bag, and it clinked.

"You seem like a soldier-type. I know that, because you lack a personality." Tarc nodded as if agreeing with himself. "I'm in the business of making gold without making enemies."

"It's hard to make one and leave the other out," Kromel said.

"A soldier and a philosopher. No wonder the other human is running from you." Tarc chuckled.

Kromel felt Tarc was challenging him, letting him know he wasn't afraid of a much taller being. Kromel had prohibited himself from killing, yet he was still a soldier. Violence and intimidation were tools of his trade. He grabbed the oval plate with the rat on it, brought it to in front of his eyes, dropped it, then spun in place, and caught the plate near waist level with his other hand.

"I know soldiers get poor pay. But you're too ugly to dance for a living." Tarc cracked a half smile revealing yellow jagged teeth with red stains on them.

Kromel grinned. "Look between your legs."

Tarc looked down and his eyes bulged as they registered the dagger buried between his feet. The surprise on his face told Kromel he hadn't seen him grab the weapon, much less throw it. The goblin attempted to regain his composure, though his trembling lips gave him away.

"Goblins are weak but fast. I might tell my friend standing behind you to climb up your back and bite your neck off." Tarc placed both hands on the box, then fully exposed his teeth.

Kromel hesitated. Of course, Tarc was probably bluffing and there was no such friend. Kromel considered walking away, and tracking down Marko on his own, but he'd be sitting on the beach, painting a beautiful landscape while enjoying his retirement much sooner with Tarc's aid.

"I'll give you all the gold I have," Kromel said.

Tarc licked his lips. "How much? I need to make a few bribes and you're paying for them, but if that's all you have, I still want the bag to be heavy after we're done."

After Kromel emptied the leather pouch on the table, Tarc gave a cursory glance and nodded.

"Deal. You're going to pose as a customer and come to my house, because I want to remain anonymous in all of this. So, walk behind me and look as stupid as you do now."

Kromel considered Marko had set an elaborate trap, but even if ambushed, Kromel was more than capable at defending himself. The buildings on both sides grew larger as they travelled deeper into Dunke. Some structures were merely wider, but occasionally, a few had several levels, the color still that of brown clay. The viscous lava that looked like static orange webbing on the volcano's surface from afar now flowed like liquid fire. Tarc stopped frequently during their trip to approach lone goblins, whispered in their ears, and slipped each a few gold coins. Immediately after earning his pay, a shabby goblin ran to a nearby shop and purchased a rodent like the one Tarc offered Kromel, except this one was still alive.

The number of beggars on the path decreased as they walked deeper into Dunke. "How far are we?" Kromel asked, his forehead dripping with sweat.

"My house is close." Tarc snickered. "If you're hot now, wait 'till you have to go on your hunt."

They entered a circular plaza. The gravel on the ground was grainier than before. All the buildings on the plaza's perimeter were two or three stories high and had colored banners hanging in front. Kromel had never been this close to the volcano and was convinced that he'd entered the living space of Dunke's aristocracy.

"It seems you're better off than I thought," Kromel said.

"Maybe more than the filth that live on the street." Tarc looked over his shoulder. "But not enough to retire from the noble profession of swindling tourists. Not even a goblin dying of starvation would eat a dead rat."

Tarc stopped and entered one of the buildings. Kromel hunched low to fit through the threshold into Tarc's house. Rich, colorful tapestries hung from the walls inside. Most depicted the volcano flowing with lava. Delicate care had been taken to give the reds and oranges a varying range of warmness. Gradually shifting from red to orange to yellow, the variety of blended hues gave the tapestries the feel of living things, the lava ran like tears down the face of a great beast. The goblins, Kromel knew, worshipped the volcano as a living god.

It was rare to encounter art of this quality on his missions and part of him grew jealous. Soon, he'd have time to train under the best artists of his kingdom. His drawings equaled that of the masters, but his painting skills were lacking, and he needed both to call himself an artist. Eventually, he'd use his own hands, not spells, to produce work that would awe every aristocrat who visited his home.

"I see you're impressed," Tarc said, seemingly satisfied with Kromel's perusal. "Have you ever seen such skillful art?"

"I've seen even better."

Tarc exhaled, fluttering his lips. "Of course, you have." He walked deeper into his home and sat at a squared shaped table near the far wall. "Come and sit." The table was barely taller than Kromel's ankles.

To the left stood a box like the one Tarc used as a shop. It moved to the side, and a female goblin climbed out of the hole, carrying several trays. Luckily, these held a mixture of vegetables, and not charred rats.

"A customer," she said and sat near them. "Welcome. The one near the end is my favorite. Fairly priced too." She pointed to the tapestry with the most lava on it.

"This is my wife, Senia. And this is…"

"Kromel."

"I'm sure he would love to take some home," Tarc said, then lowered his head and stared at Kromel.

"I'm just looking around for now. My purse became a bit light after I arrived at Dunke." Kromel smiled and ate some of the vegetables off his plate. Their color and texture reminded him of sandpaper.

"In any case, I'll set up a bed roll. In the morning, I'm sure you'll feel different. Art becomes a part of you the more time you spend around it," Senia said.

Kromel knew this too well.

* * * *

Several hours after nightfall, when the goblins of Dunke slept, Kromel prepared himself. Tarc had learned that Marko was an invited guest in General Arel's manor. Kromel didn't know what a manor's security level was in Dunke, but he didn't worry.

Kromel removed the box from where Senia brought out the food earlier and looked down into what looked like a dark cave. The rising fumes made him squint. He grabbed his notebook from his bag and flipped through a section filled with goblin paintings. There was one he remembered well, not because the goblin had any outstanding physical traits, but because of how they met.

The goblin had attacked Kromel's squad while on a scouting mission many years ago. A lone goblin was no match for a group of human soldiers, but his ribs showed and some of his teeth were missing. Madness, and not common sense, drove him. The captured goblin begged to be buried near his mother in Dunke. *My mother is the queen, she'll protect me after death!* This was an odd request. Why not beg for your life? What did family matter after your body rotted and flies feasted on your eyeballs? One was either alive or not alive.

Kromel laughed off the goblin's request with the others and recorded his shape in his notebook. He made sure to leave camp before his friends killed the goblin as to not partake in the murder. This event occurred years after his training as a young man, when he'd seen the effect that killing had on the minds of many retired soldiers. Instead of happy retirement, these men only found nightmares waiting outside of military life. For some, peace only came by committing suicide.

There was an inherent risk in being recognized when in disguise. Indeed, he was more of a shape imitator than a shape shifter. Every other goblin in Kromel's notebook was well known in Dunke—most missions required influence and not anonymity. For this mission, he chose the wandering goblin that thought himself royalty.

Kromel ripped the page from his notebook and placed it on his tongue. *From your page to my shape.* Carefully, he stuck the page to the ceiling of his mouth. His body began to shrink. His shirt, dagger belt, and cloth pants fell to the ground. The skin on the back of his hands became dark green. He cupped his eyes in his palm and felt how large they'd grown. The rucksack was now the size of his torso. To compact his bag, he knotted it together until he could slip his arms through the makeshift straps and carry it on his back. He wore his dagger belt diagonally across his chest.

His night vision improved, but he felt as if he had walked into a goblin's mouth, given how loud the nearby snoring had become. With his equipment secured, Kromel jumped into the hole. A long rock tunnel stretched in front and behind him. The scorching heat now a comfortable warmth.

A rat jumped from a wall and bit his neck. He imagined the number of diseases that would've invaded his body if he was in human form. Another rodent scurried over and bit his feet. He grabbed both before they had a chance to escape, considered biting into them, tearing their heads off, and sucking they're luscious blood, but shook his head and threw them aside. They slammed against the wall and hurried away. *The shape is yours, but the spirit is mine.*

Kromel made a point of breathing through his mouth. The blaring wail of a windstorm accompanied every exhale, but Dunke's sickening smell had become a cause for sexual arousal in goblin form. The noise was an easier distraction to deal with than the need to mate.

Tarc's instructions led to a four-way intersection. In the center, a metal ladder led up into what looked like a well. He climbed and felt the temperature decrease significantly. The heat would be tolerable for a human. Kromel climbed out and stood in a marble-tiled hallway. Two iron doors at the far end of the hall separated him from what sounded like human laughter. That could be Marko. There were no guards. Kromel tiptoed over, placed his ear against the iron door, and heard the voices clearly. He found a loose edge on the papyrus stuck to the ceiling of his mouth and started to tug at it with his tongue. The fact that the tongue could only remove the page, and on top of that, only slowly, was the most inconvenient of shapeshifting laws. Once the painting was out of his mouth, Kromel would return to his normal form. With his human body, he'd be able to overpower Marko and any guards—goblin or otherwise—that might be inside.

A moment passed, and the double doors opened.

An elderly goblin stood in front of him. "I can hear your breath through the door, soldier. Close your mouth—" The goblin darted forward and hugged Kromel. "Khal. You're alive?"

Over the goblin's shoulders, Kromel saw a table in the middle of the circular chamber. Marko stood behind the table, wearing a bored look. To the left there was a floor to ceiling glass window. Brass handles were attached to the window's wooden frame at a height accessible to goblins. Several weapons that looked as if they've never been used hung from the walls.

"Can we finalize these plans, Arel? I want to still be young enough to enjoy the sweet caresses from the ladies when I take the throne," Marko called out.

"This is my son. We thought he was dead. It's been decades since I saw him last." Arel pulled Kromel into the chamber. He saw two female goblins holding infants in their arms.

"You have other sons." Marko waved his hand across the room.

"This is my oldest. And a great warrior. Tell him Khal." Arel looked Kromel up and down. "Why are you bleeding? These are animal scratches. Did you climb through the tunnels? My son doesn't need to hide!"

Kromel grunted. He had a goblin's body, but his voice was his own.

Marko looked over, squinting. Expressionless, he picked up a short sword that lay on the table. One of the goblin babies started to cry and wail.

"Why didn't you send word? Where were you?" Arel asked.

Kromel shook his head. He continued unrolling the papyrus on the ceiling of his mouth to transform back. Marko was a fat man, his body shaped by a career in politics and a sharp tongue, but even he'd best Kromel in a battle now—goblins fought in large numbers to compensate for their small, frail bodies.

"Is something wrong with your jaw? Are you in pain?" Arel placed his hands on Kromel's shoulders. "Let me take these daggers, you don't look well."

Kromel's eyes met Marko's. His disguise was shattered. His tongue whipped back and forth. He had to transform back.

"I'm going to kill you," Marko said, unsheathing his sword.

One of the female goblins stood in front of him, yelling, "I won't let you hurt my son."

Marko raised the blade.

"No!" Kromel shouted.

"No? Why do you care, shapeshifter? I am your prize." After several seconds Marko smiled. "I see now. The king must have at least some respect for me if they sent *you* to recover me." He yanked the baby from the goblin's arms and held it upside-down. The baby cried and wailed.

The female started to protest. Marko stabbed her in the chest.

"What are you doing?" Arel yelled, running over. Marko kicked the goblin general, slamming him against a stone wall. Arel lay still.

Marko pointed the bloodied blade at Kromel. "Don't transform back, Kromel. That would be a very unfair fight." He jiggled the baby, who was crying louder than before. Kromel knelt and shoved his fingers into his ears. "Trust me. The noise bothers me too. And I'm closer." Marko laid the baby on the table. "If I kill this baby, its blood will be on your hands." Marko scoffed. "A soldier known for not killing? You should trade those daggers for a skirt. The blood of the condemned is on your hands too, you idiot."

"Traitors condemn themselves and get what they deserve," Kromel answered.

Marko placed his sword hand on his chest and bellowed in laughter. "If I deserve death why don't you kill me now?" After a moment of silence Marko spoke again. "A coward and a hypocrite. I think its best that you die here, Kromel. You're much too confused." Marko grinned and showed a few places with missing teeth. "I heard a rumor about you shapeshifters and want to test it. Swallow the page in your mouth."

"I can't do that." Kromel hurried to the table but stopped halfway. Marko's blade was inches from the baby's neck.

"This creature doesn't even belong to your species. Do you draw the line anywhere? Your rules could use some leeway." Marko shook his head. "I'm not going to repeat myself. Swallow the page. This will help." He threw a filled water skin to Kromel's feet.

Kromel thought of his family living near the ocean without him. His daughter, resenting him for leaving her children without a grandfather. His wife and her plans to decorate the house with his paintings, to maybe try and have more children someday, dissolved. A future that would never be if he committed suicide now. The baby looked over at him with glossy eyes. He wouldn't enjoy a perfect future if he let the baby die. Others would find Marko and bring him back. His family would learn to move on, their pride intact knowing that Kromel died without violating his beliefs. He finished unrolling the page but instead of spitting it out, gulped some water, and swallowed.At first nothing happened.

Slowly, his skin became loose and his face sagged.

Marko giggled. "I can't believe you went through with it. When I am king, I'll disband the shapeshifters. My kingdom will rely on force instead of cheap illusions."

Kromel's limbs warped as if his bones were melting. He fell to his knees. His eyelids drooped over his eyes, blocking part of his vision. "Now that I see you, it makes perfect sense. Your stomach acid is burning the page and distorting the image. So much for the myster—" Kromel had to rotate his head to see Marko, who lay on the floor. Arel stood beside him, holding a long sword with both hands, the blade's tip buried in Marko's side. The goblin general took a deep breath and pushed until the hilt hit flesh.

"A surprise death is a traitor's death," Arel said.

Arel walked from the body and stood over Kromel. "You helped me make a profit without doing any of the work. I'll let you die in peace."

He looked over to the remaining female goblin, who was weeping over the body of the other female. "Come and bring the children."

The goblin general looked at Kromel again before closing the iron doors. "I hope death comes quickly."

Kromel's vision became fragmented, showing him multiple versions of the same object across his limited field of view. Nearing the end of his career, he'd imagined death coming in a soothing wave, sitting outside his perfect house by the water, alongside his loved ones. Instead, the smell of blood and metal filled his nostrils. His oblong shaped heart pounded in a staccato rhythm. The only desire he felt was the need to live.

He snaked out of his rucksack and fumbled with it until he opened the flap. As he pulled the notebook out, his fingers lost their tenacity and stretched like heated wax, still gripping the notebook, as it thumped against the floor. The notebook landed with the back cover facing him. He used his other hand to flip through the pages. Lists of names representing successful missions, which had given him a sense of completion, fevered his frustration as his body deformed further, approaching death. He turned pages, faster and faster, until he reached the section filled with paintings.The first image he stumbled upon was of the bird he encountered outside of Dunke. There was no record of a shapeshifter attempting to become two things simultaneously, but he had no choice. Kromel ripped the page of the majestic bird from the notebook and opened his mouth. His jaw fell to the floor as if unhinged from his face; his cheeks were long flabs the length of goblin arms. He placed the page on his tongue that dangled from his lower jaw on the floor, then brought his head down, trying to reassemble his skull. *From your page to my shape.*

The flesh on his hands hardened and feathers started to grow. His vision became clearer and everything looked green. When he stood he saw a great green bird glowing in the window's reflection. The skin on his face was still leathery like a goblin's.

He unhinged the window with his beak, grabbed Marko's body with his talons and flew out. The thoughts that had swirled in his mind when he was near death solidified. Marko had been right. Other soldiers tried to drink away or ignore the memories of the people they had killed. Kromel thought himself better than them, but he'd also hidden from the truth. Delivering a person to the executioner did not absolve Kromel of their deaths. A truth he spent a lifetime obscuring with complex lies. It was clear now that he always knew his fault and had chosen to remain blind, hiding behind a veil of naivety. The nightmares he spent his life trying to avoid would still haunt him.

Water droplets condensed on his feathers as he flew through humid clouds. A blue bird appeared flying beside him, holding the painting of a small bird grasped in its beak. The giant bird looked Kromel in the eye before flying away. There was no recognition in the bird's gaze and it had probably flown over out of curiosity. Kromel would have smiled had his beak allowed it. Because he was part avian himself, he sensed the blue bird was happy, a sense of serenity filled it despite losing its offspring less than a day before. The painting had surely helped mend the bird's spirit. He'd tried to prevent staining himself with the blood of others, accumulating bad memories, only to realize that he had failed. But there was another way to fight the madness that sets upon retired soldiers. He'd never killed anyone to advance a mission, leaving intact families that he might have broken. Not committing a bad deed was in itself a good deed. Throughout his career, he'd built good memories to fight the bad without realizing it. Kromel chose *this* to be his truth. His resolve had yielded the desired outcome, absolute in its purity, albeit misinterpreted. He had his entire retirement to imagine who he helped without noticing. And that was an adventure he looked forward to.

THE LAST RESORT
by Dean MacAllister

The bell at the counter rings loudly, echoing through the large foyer. Jimmy and his wife look around. The room is impressive, with gold and mahogany lining the walls and stairs. Three chandeliers brighten the empty room, the only sign that the hotel is even open. Jimmy wipes the sweat from his forehead with the back of his arm. The fans on the walls are set to their highest speeds, rotating from side to side, but they do little to give the new visitors relief.

Jimmy hits the bell twice. "Hello?" he yells out into the room, hoping someone upstairs might hear him. He leans back against the front desk and raises his eyebrows to his wife, who smiles a tired smile. "Hello?" he yells again.

"Hello," a calm voice says from behind the counter.

Jimmy spins around, startled.

"Jesus, don't sneak up on people like that!"

"Welcome to Frontera Hotel and Resort, my name is Michael," the concierge says, ignoring his outburst. "Names?"

Jimmy straightens out his Hawaiian shirt and clears his throat. He eyes up the toffee-skinned hotel worker.

"Jimmy and Molly Stone," he says. "I'm guessing you have our reservation."

Michael stares at him for a moment. His smoothly shaven head seems almost polished, like it has never had hair upon it and his surprising green eyes do not seem to blink. He looks down at his computer and begins typing.

"Here you are," he says, after a little while. He frowns. "We weren't expecting you so early."

Jimmy pulls out a piece of paper and slaps it on the desk.

"Our reservations are for today. I checked them myself," he says, defensively. "Now, the hotel we wanted to stay in was booked out. This is the only place we could find at this time of year. We've just had a rough plane ride and a choppy boat trip to get here. So don't go pretending you don't have a place for us to stay."

The concierge doesn't even bother looking at the piece of paper.

"Don't worry. We definitely have room for you," he says, his calm tone unwavering. "Luke!"

A door opens behind the counter and a bell-hop appears.

"Luke will take your bags to your room while we fill out the paperwork."

The bellhop lifts the divider up and exits from behind the counter. He grabs a large trolley and loads their bags onto it.

"Careful with the black case! It has my cameras inside it."

The bellhop nods and carefully loads up the last few bags before pushing the trolley over towards the elevator doors under the large staircase.

"Will anyone else be joining you here?" Michael asks, looking up from the screen.

Jimmy frowns. "No, why?"

Michael clicks with his mouse and the colour of the screen changes. His eyebrows rise.

"Wow! That many," he says to himself.

"That many what?"

"Hmm?" Michael says looking up at him again. "Oh, nothing. Never mind. So, it says here that you are American."

"Yeah, and? We are in the Caribbean aren't we?" Jimmy replies.

"Jimmy!" Molly says, disapprovingly. She smiles at the concierge. "It was a very rough trip."

Michael smiles back at her, a genuine smile.

"I apologise, but it seems that your room isn't ready just yet," he says. "Perhaps you would like to enjoy our facilities first. We have an indoor pool, spa, game room, prayer room, massage room. All the luxuries and comforts you would expect."

"Is there a quiet lounge where I could have a quick sleep while you get the room ready?" Molly asks. "I'm very tired."

"Absolutely!" Michael smiles again. "It is just up those stairs and to the left. We will come and get you as soon as your room is prepared."

Molly thanks him and slowly makes her way over to the stairs.

"ALL the luxuries and comforts?" Jimmy asks discreetly, when she is out of ear-shot.

Michael doesn't reply, he just stares at him with a blank expression.

"What types of massage do you offer here?" Jimmy asks, a sly grin on his face.

"We are not that kind of place," Michael says with a disapproving tone.

"Alright, alright. Calm down. I was just asking. Do you at least have a gambling room or something?"

"We are not that kind of place either. We have a modern gym, a cinema with a very large selection of films and a bar if you wish to pass the time. We also have a sauna, but it is not available at the moment."

"A hot box without heat is just a box, am I right?"

Michael opens his mouth to reply, but then pauses, as if thinking better of his initial response.

"I guess that you are right, sir," he concurs.

"Although it's already hot as hell in here."

"I assure you it is not," the concierge says bluntly.

"Excuse me?"

"This is not our hot season. Besides, all of our hotel rooms have air-conditioning."

"Sure, whatever. Look, the bar will do fine. Where can I find it?"

Michael gestures with his open hand toward the stairs. Under the stairs is a brass sign with the word BAR next to an arrow.

"Thanks pal. Let me know when that room is ready, yeah?"

"Of course."

Jimmy limps towards the sign and down the corridor to the bar. His back is playing up again. He had told his wife that he hurt it while golfing. She seemed to believe him, too.

* * * *

The bar is inside a dimly lit room. As he enters Jimmy can feel the impressive size of the room, but only the bar lights are turned on, creating a cosy atmosphere. The bartender is neatly dressed in a vest and a white bow-tie. His clean-shaven face and neatly parted hair give him a professional appearance. Standing at the far end of the bar, he is conversing with an attractive tanned lady in a dark red dress sitting across from him, nursing her drink. They are not leaning close to each other and, while they talk, the bartender wipes glasses with a white cloth and checks them in the light. If anything, they seem to be having a business conversation.

Jimmy approaches and sits at the middle of the bar. Their conversation ends and they both look over at him.

"Hey guys," he says, "Is it too late to get a drink around here?"

The bartender smiles in a polite fashion. "We are always open, for the pleasure of our guests. What can I get you?"

"Bourbon."

"Of course," the bartender says, "Any preferences?"

"Middle shelf will do."

The bartender nods and reaches up for a crystal bottle on the shelf.

"You work here too?" Jimmy asks the lady further down the bar.

"What is that supposed to mean?" she asks, pulling her long dark hair over to the side and playing with it.

"No offence!" he says, quickly.

"Some taken," a small smile curls the side of her mouth. "I am a resident here."

"Ah, ok. So, on holidays then?"

"Not me. I am always working."

The bartender clears his throat and puts a glass in front of him with two fingers of bourbon. He puts a small metal cup next to it with two ice cubes inside. He places a tiny set of tongs next to it, for the ice. The light coming up from the bar-top shines through his drink, which is the colour of honey. He ignores the tongs and tips the ice straight into his glass.

"Nice work, my man!" Jimmy says, taking a sip and nodding.

"Be careful of this one," the bartender says, nodding towards the woman. His serious face shows no hint of humour. "She has been the downfall of many a man at this bar before."

Jimmy opens his mouth, surprised. He looks over at her. She begins to laugh.

"Don't mind Barman," she says, "He is a wise man with a wicked sense of humour."

Jimmy smiles, confused. "You call him Barman? You guys friends or something?"

"My name *is* Barman," the bartender answers, again picking up and polishing some glasses. "It is a very old name."

"Well then, I guess you had no career choice then!" Jimmy jokes, cracking himself up. Neither of the other two smile. He clears his throat. "I guess you have heard that one before."

"Only a few hundred thousand times," Barman replies. "Would you like any snacks?"

Jimmy downs the rest of his drink. "No, but you can top this up."

"Sure, but take your time with this one. You don't want to get drunk tonight. You may regret it in the morning."

"Listen son, I have had my share of hangovers. Just keep my glass dark, ok?"

"As you like," Barman says, topping up his glass and putting more ice cubes into the cup.

"And what's your name sweet-heart?"

The lady smiles. "Rimmon. Pleased to meet you."

"Rimmon? That's nice. Never heard that name before," Jimmy says.

The smile disappears from Rimmon's face and seems to reappear on the face of Barman. Jimmy realises he must have missed something. Perhaps an inside joke. He ignores it.

"So, are you a local, Rimmon?"

She finishes her drink and places it on the counter.

"No. I actually work as an ambassador here," she says. "Tell me, am I going to have to pay for my next drink?"

"No, no!" Jimmy says, quickly. "Whatever the lady wants," he instructs Barman.

"Single-malt highland scotch, neat," she says to Barman. "Nothing under 30 years old."

"Wow! You sure have expensive tastes," Jimmy says, wiping the sweat from his forehead with a serviette. A ceiling fan spins slowly above their heads, barely creating a breeze.

"Well, money is just money. You can't take it with you when you go."

"I guess," he agrees. He turns to face Barman. "What about you? Where are you from? Let me guess, south-east Asia?"

Barman frowns, topping up Jimmy's glass. "Not at all. I am a local."

"Ah, ok. But I meant your background. When did you move here?"

"I have been here for a very long time. Excuse me." Barman walks around the back of the bar, behind the drink shelves, vanishing into the darkness.

Jimmy takes the opportunity and walks over to Rimmon with his drink. He sits next to her. She raises one eyebrow, but says nothing.

"Cheers," he says, raising his glass to her. She clinks her glass against his and takes a sip.

"So, what do you do for work Jimmy?" She asks.

"Wait, did I introduce myself?"

"We all know everyone who stays here. So?"

"Ah, yes. Well I guess you could say that I am a bit of an entrepreneur. I dabble in a lot of things, mostly pharmaceuticals. We aren't going to run out of sick people anytime soon, you know? It's a big business."

"Really?" she leans over, staring at him intensely with her deep, dark eyes. Her light-brown skin is flawless. He restrains himself from looking down her cleavage. "So, you must be doing very well for yourself."

"I do alright," he says, grinning. "I give a lot back, though. Through my charity."

She sits back upright, taking a gulp from her drink. He senses her losing interest.

"I didn't really take you for a bleeding-heart type," she says, her voice full of disappointment.

"I'm really not," he clarifies quickly. "It's just a tax write-off. I mean, what do I care about the starving kids in Syria or Australia? It's really my wife's thing."

Jimmy grimaces, wishing he hadn't mentioned his wife.

"Relax, Jimmy," Rimmon's smile returns. "I saw you take off your ring when you walked in. You weren't fooling anyone. It doesn't mean a thing to me anyway."

Before he can ask what she means Barman returns. He sees them sitting next to each other and sighs. Picking up the crystal bourbon bottle he walks over and tops up Jimmy's glass.

"Quiet night tonight, eh Barman?" Jimmy says.

"The hotel is full tonight," Barman says, matter-of-factly. "Not many choose to spend time at the bar, that's all. It's late. Many of our visitors are just asleep, in their rooms, with their loved ones."

Jimmy stares Barman in the eyes, wondering if he is subtly being attacked. He sees nothing in his bland expression. Their eyes remain locked.

"Well if it's too quiet in here we can go make some noise some-place else," Rimmon says, seductively.

Jimmy is surprised by her blunt remark and ignores the bartender, looking back at her. She has a cheeky look on her face.

"Well, aren't we forward?" he chuckles.

"Forward is the only way to travel," she replies.

"Your room is almost ready," Barman interrupts.

"My room can wait," Jimmy snaps. "One more for the road."

Barman pours him a drink and returns the bottle to the shelf.

"Now, just to make sure, you aren't for sale are you?" Jimmy whispers to her, his words starting to slur a little. "I mean, you aren't looking for any money are you? Cause I don't usually do that."

"Relax, Jimmy," she says, her hand rubbing his knee, "I just want you for a little fun, that's all. You're choice, though. You can always go wake up your wife if you like."

Barman returns with a small leather folder containing the bill.

Jimmy pulls out his wallet and counts out some notes and throws them down onto the bill.

"Are you sure you don't want me to charge these drinks to your room?" Barman asks.

"Don't be smart. You know what?" He takes back the note from the top. "There. Make another comment, see where it gets you."

Barman's face remains blank.

"Are we going?" Jimmy asks Rimmon.

She picks up her purse and walks out into the corridor, Jimmy following close behind. She turns out into the foyer, instead of walking straight to the lifts.

"Where are you going?" he whispers.

She walks past the front desk and he follows her, trying to act natural. Michael is standing there, but shows no interest in them. She walks to the far wall, a huge marble structure with gold beams. She touches a button on the wall and two golden doors part. She gets in and turns around.

"Coming?" she asks.

He enters the lift, standing next to her. Michael looks over to them and waves.

"Thank you for staying with us!" he calls out, as the doors close.

"No, I'll be back," Jimmy yells, but the doors cut him off.

The elevator is completely made of white marble, even the floor. There are only two buttons on the interior gold panel and Rimmon presses one of them. The down arrow.

The elevator descends.

"So where is your room?" Jimmy asks, scratching the side of his neck nervously.

"Rough flight?" she asks.

"What?" Jimmy replies.

"Did you have a rough flight?" She repeats.

"What are you…" Then it suddenly comes back to him. The screams. The pilot with fear in his voice. The oxygen masks. The weightlessness.

"Where are we?" Panic rises up inside him. The alcohol is wearing off quickly.

"You were on the border," she replies, pointing upwards. "You just had to choose which direction you were travelling."

"Wait. What? I'm dead?! How? My wife?" Jimmy stammers.

"It's a bit late to worry about her now, don't you think? Besides, she has other plans."

"And you? What are you?" he asks, tears running down his cheeks.

"Me?" She crosses her arms and leans with her back against the wall. She laughs, showing all of her teeth. "I guess you could say that I'm your tour guide."

The lights in the elevator slowly dim as the air grows hotter and hotter. And hotter.\

THE CRYPT BENEATH THE MANSE

by S. Subramanian

In January of 2017, a team of the Cambridgeshire branch of the Society for the Protection of Ancient Buildings was engaged in the restoration of the Church of St Andrew's in the village of Grisbury. One member of the team discovered a document that seems to have dropped unintendedly into the secret compartment of an old Elizabethan desk that was a part of the furniture in the decrepit manse adjoining the Church. The document purported to be a 'Statement of the Rev. Aubrey Melcroft'. Melcroft was a presbyter who had lived in the manse, and died in the year 1888. The 'Statement' is now in the possession of the Cambridgeshire Constabulary. A copy, leaked to a journalist, is reproduced below.

* * * *

Statement of the Rev. Aubrey Melcroft

Grisbury,
April 29, 1888.

In the remotest interior of Cambridgeshire, hidden from the prying eyes of even the most inquisitive (and intrepid) of tourists, is the village of Grisbury, not inaptly named, when one sees it in conjunction with the words 'grisly' and 'burial'. But I run ahead of myself in the telling of this strange but true story, and must make an effort to present a cogent account of those aspects of the recent history of Grisbury that I shall be dealing with, taking the time—despite the nearness of my own last extremity—to put things down in their proper place and in the right order.

For thirty years, from 1828 to 1858, I was the pastor in charge of St Andrew's, responsible for the upkeep of the Church, for the weekly conduct of prayer in the Chapel, and for the well-being of my parishioners, duties which I am told (if I may relay this opinion without fear of the accusation of self-aggrandisement) that I discharged with resolve and conscientiousness. I lived in the manse adjoining the Church, a privilege assigned to the presbyter in a tradition dating back to the tenth century when the Church of

St Andrew's was consecrated in the village of Grisbury. My modest needs were taken care of by the widow Henderson, an elderly lady of eccentric disposition whose roast beef was as underdone as her lamb chops were overdone, and whose standards of cleanliness and order for the manse left much to be desired, but whom I nevertheless tolerated in a spirit of frater-nal Christian charity, as we are enjoined, by our calling, to display toward our fellow-beings, be they ever so wanting in those ideals and standards which an unrealistic hankering after perfection may dictate.

My duties, I must admit, were not onerous. The village of Grisbury was an under-populated one, inhabited, for the most part, by the dwindling progenies of the original and earliest settlers in the village. The populace was subjected to a particularly sudden and large diminution in numbers following on the large-scale migration of villagers to the cities that were rapidly springing up in the environs in response to the demands of the industrial revolution underway in Britain. The out-migration was scarce-ly matched by any noticeable in-migration, for who would want to bury themselves in this already God-forsaken village, far from the amenities and comforts (and dare I say dubious enticements) of the city? And so it was that my parishioners, to whom I tended (or so I am told) with all the energy and earnestness at my command, were still so manageably few as to make their demands upon my time and effort a matter of no very great exertion for me.

I have continued, over the last thirty years from the time of my for-mal retirement, to stay on at the manse—or The Manse, as it came, quite simply, to be called: for there was no-one, really, prepared or available to take over my ministry, such as it was, and it has been left to me to provide such sustenance as I have been able to muster in the cause of the Church's upkeep and worship in it. What has helped me to discharge my functions, however informally and inadequately—especially in the last decade or so—has been the good health it has been vouchsafed me to enjoy. Still, I am ninety-three years old; and while the peculiar circumstances attending my robustness of health should stand me in good stead for at least a few years more, I am aware that the time has come for me, almost quite liter-ally so, to separate myself from the corporeal existence which we are wont to call 'life'. Whence also the urgency, with what I believe to be less than twenty-four hours of mortal subsistence left to me, to prepare my statement and leave it in my desk, for the edification of any, after my allotted time, that might come upon this document and so learn the secret of Grisbury. But here I am, despite my warnings to myself, again running ahead of my story.

It was in 1857, the year immediately preceding my official retirement, that the first of those macabre incidents occurred for which Grisbury became notorious. The reader should know that The Manse was an extension of the Church, with which, and in that part of the undercroft that had been built beneath my own bedroom, it shared a portion of the vaults to which Grisbury consigned its dead. From time to time, and as part of my functions requiring oversight of the Church and its premises, I would visit the crypt, to ensure that all was in order with the mortal remains of the souls that lay interred in their coffins. It may be imagined how, on one such nocturnal visit, the very hair upon the nape of my neck stood erect when I seemed to sense a movement and a noise behind a coffin in the far corner of the crypt that abutted on my underground cellar.

Suppressing a strong desire to drop my candle and bolt back up the wooden steps that led to my bedroom, I summoned the faith and the resolve needed to investigate the phenomenon that had so disturbed my senses. In advancing toward the far corner of the crypt, I had to pass by an ancient coffin; and as I did so, I seemed to feel a rush of air, a gust of unwholesome wind, such as of some impure and malign spirit, emanating from the coffin and momentarily taking charge of my being. I had not the time nor the occasion to respond to this experience, for I stumbled upon an obstruction extending beyond the coffin, and in so doing nearly fell down upon the cold stone floor of the crypt, with my candle in my hand. Fortunately, I managed to regain my balance, to discover that the obstruction over which I had tripped was a pair of human legs, attached to the body of a man whose face must have reflected, quite exactly, the terror I myself felt as a consequence of this bizarre confrontation.

Shortly thereafter, I could have laughed at my own fears, for I realized in a trice that the unhappy being upon whom I had blundered must be some homeless and impoverished tramp who had sought sanctuary in the Church, and found his way, in the cause of a night's sleep shielded from the icy cold without, to the relatively secure protection offered by the solid bulk of a coffin in the crypt. I was the first to recover; and I believe it came as a wondrous relief to the poor wretch in front of me to be addressed in a kind voice. Before long I learnt that the vagrant in the crypt responded to the unadorned appellation of 'Bill'; and that he was a hungry and exhausted way-farer who, finding that the latch on one of the windows on the far side of the Church was not proof against a bit of determined manipulation of the window from the outside, had climbed in through it. Letting himself down on the floor of the Church near the vestry door, he had found his way, by the light of a candle grabbed from a holder on the wall, to the staircase leading beneath to the crypt. Here he had laid himself down to sleep through the night by the side of the coffin where I found him.

Quite soon, and after making a mental note of shutting and re-latching the Church window, I returned to my room up the stairs, and ferretting about, found an old unused mattress and blanket, and the leftovers of the evening's soup, which the man Bill accepted with eager gratitude. He fell upon the soup with a savage sort of appetite; and with the keen edge of hunger blunted somewhat by the sustenance provided by the make-shift meal, he was happy to curl up on the mattress and go to sleep next to his coffin, ensconced comfortably in the blanket. I suppose he made for a pathetic sight, lying there and looking so contented in his sleep to be a recipient of the rough comforts of the crypt. But it was not only pathos which the sight of the man stirred in my bosom; it was also a sense of provocation—unnamed and unnameable—that was so far removed from and alien to my natural temperament and the persuasions of my calling that it was all I could do to suppress an involuntary cry of both fear and disgust. Stifling my disquiet as best I could, I regained my bedroom where I passed the rest of the night in alternations of sleep and wakefulness.

It was the widow Henderson who discovered the body next morning. It was the weekly day of the uninspired 'dusting' to which she subjected the book shelves in my bedroom; and finding ajar the little door opening out on to the stairs leading to the crypt, she went down to investigate. It was then that I heard her blood-curdling scream, a sound at once so inhuman and so terrifying as to cause the auditor to wish never ever to hear such a sound again in his life. My heart palpitating like the broken wings of a crippled bird inside my breast, I rushed down to the crypt, to be confronted by the sight of a housekeeper with her hands clamped on her ears and cleaving the air with one unnaturally ear-splitting scream after another, while she stared with wild, terrified, unseeing eyes at the thing that lay by the coffin in the far corner of the crypt.

The thing was what remained of Bill the tramp. Upon his face was registered the indelible stamp of a terror that defies human description. The left side of his breast was torn asunder as by the implacably honed claws of some terrible bird of prey; and through the open wound in the chest was a great big gaping hollow where the human heart should have been, but was not; while all around were huge clotted gobs of blood that had been pumping through the poor wretch's veins before he met his horrible end. I somehow managed to lead the shrieking housekeeper away from the ghastly scene; and after doing what I (and a hot cup of tea laced with brandy) could to calm the woman's hysterics, I alerted the police.

For all their 'careful' examination of the tramp's body, the police missed what I hold to this day to be a vital clue to the monstrous mystery of the tramp's death. It was I who pointed out to them the two small pricks, such as might have been made by twin injections, on the side of the man's neck. The police took no account of these marks; or if they did, they chose to ignore the fact as they could find no place for it in any 'rational' reconstruction of the crime. This was not for want of the issue having been brought to their attention, nor of an explanation offered for it—both, as it happens, by myself—which were alike politely (but not without humorous condescension) brushed aside as, presumably, the unscientific ramblings of an unreliable amateur. The coroner returned a verdict of 'death by unnatural causes'; the official view that was allowed to be bruited about was that some feral animal from the adjoining dense woods had entered by the Church's open window (which, in my preoccupation with other things, I had omitted to shut and re-latch), and visited its violent assault upon the tramp; and there the matter rested.

The theory I offered was one of vampirism. It was, by all accounts, a laughable theory, tendered, ostensibly, by a man out of touch with reality and corrupted by the idiocies of superstitious belief. *O stultitia!* Who better qualified than a priest, ministering to the dying, and living in the midst of vaults and ossuaries, to be informed by the realities of death and afterlife? Or acquainted with that constant companion and inseparable twin of virtue (which is all that a man of my vocation is credited with knowledge of)—the Force of Evil, Satan Himself? The coffin that diffused the unwholesome exhalation I have alluded to earlier was that of William, Squire of Trevelyan Hall, who had tyrannized the tenantry of Grisbury and debauched its fair maidens over his long tenure from 1650 to 1712. William Trevelyan was, in his day, regarded as the devil incarnate; and when a man such as he dies, the evil spirit harboured by his body remains undead but dormant, to awaken one day to seek and find domicile in some other living mortal's frame.

Of this mortal, the dire spirit takes the most utter and comprehensive possession, that it may thrive and grow fat upon the human blood which its host, transformed by the visitation into a vampire, will henceforth suck out of unwary innocents by bestial depredations of their bodies, culminating in the plucking out of the heart and its final ingestion. The overture to these ghoulish assaults is always the preliminary drawing of blood through a bite upon the victim's neck, an invasion that is invariably verified by those two tiny puncture marks. I had felt the corruption emanating from Trevelyan's coffin, and seen the puncture marks upon the tramp's neck. At the risk, and then the certainty, of being ridiculed by the police, I had informed them—to no avail, of course—that their best course of action would be to try and isolate unnatural vampire behaviour in the village's residents, one unmistakeable sign of which would be resistance to sunlight; another, an unusual ruddiness of countenance following on an unusual pallor; and a third, proximity to the crypt after the descension of darkness.

The dolts laughed at me, and so were unprepared for the next atrocity, which occurred just three days later. This time, the victim was a lady of the night, who had apparently had a lover's tryst in the dark of the graveyard. Perhaps she tarried awhile, after her lover's departure, to set her appearance in order. That, likely, was when she was attacked. There were indistinct swirls and scuffings of dirt and mud upon the wall beneath a second of the Church's windows, adjacent to the one that had apparently been shaken open upon the previous occasion, and which suggested that the victim had been dragged by some beastly force once more into the crypt, and subjected again to those ghastly travesties upon her person which we had witnessed in the case of Bill the tramp. The mutilated body, this time, was discovered by the lad I had hired to clean out the crypt three days after the outrage upon the tramp.

The victim's neck bore those tell-tale puncture marks, even as the victim's breast was denuded of the heart within. These facts were duly registered, and duly ignored by the official investigating agency. The coroner once more returned a verdict of 'death by unnatural causes'; all the windows of the church were re-boarded and fortified with new latches; and the police assured the citizenry that the (unidentified) beast of prey responsible for the attacks would henceforth cease and desist.

Which, to save the police their blushes, the beast did. For the last thirty-one years now, from 1857 to the present day, there have been no re-visitations of those dreadful events of April and May of that distant year. This does not redeem the police from the charge of doltishness that I have levelled against them. Despite all my warnings and explanations and advice, the puncture marks on the necks and the hearts stolen from the bodies of the victims were not the only things the dolts ignored. What they also ignored was the sudden apple-cheeked ruddiness of countenance that was acquired by the presbyter; his abrupt failure to be seen abroad in the hours of daylight; and his constant proximity, not to mention undeterred access, to the crypt. Call it hubris, call it the pride of Lucifer, but I had alerted them to the clues they would need to seize on in order to do their job. Instead, they mocked and scorned and failed miserably in their duty. If only they had paid attention!

Yes, that is right: I, Aubrey Melcroft, am the Vampire of Grisbury, and I embody the spirit of Squire William Trevelyan. I did mention, did I not, that I was in the way of the emanation of Trevelyan's spirit from the coffin in the far corner of the crypt? And I did further say, did I not, that in what must have been the moment of transition of that spirit into my body, I was seized by a frightening and disgusting sense of provocation? What possessed me, I might have added, was a sensation of voluptuous bloodlust such as I had never before had any apprehension of; and the lust would not be satisfied until I had vented it upon the tramp. Shortly thereafter, I was overcome again by the same frenzy, which was assuaged only by my assault upon the lady of the night, whom I first stunned and then carried, as with a superhuman strength, through the Church window I had left conveniently open for our ingress, to the crypt below where I concluded my gruesome task.

They say that the blood and hearts of two adult humans should keep a vampire going for eighty years without further need of transfusions. I had had my fill, and for thirty-one years, from 1857 on, I have enjoyed the best of health. I know I am good for about another five decades; but one grows weary of the accumulation of years, as of the laboured tolerance of one's fellows who do little to conceal their contemptuous pity for a man whose whole condition is seen only in the light of what one might call *Anno Domini*. I have heard young Dr Morton and young Professor Seagrove, both men of Science and Rationality, refer to me as 'that demented old duffer', little knowing that my hearing is perhaps sharper than theirs. I cannot abide the arrogant young upstarts.

And so I shall will myself to die tonight. Tomorrow the village folk will find me dead in my bed, and give me a decent burial in the crypt. My spirit, I know, will travel from my corpse to that of Squire Trevelyan in his coffin. And within a week thence, I shall again prey upon the inhabitants of Grisbury. Animated by the Squire's spirit, but in my erstwhile corporeal trappings of the Rev. Aubrey Melford, I shall wreak my vengeance on Morton and Seagrove, damn their souls.

In the vulgar language I have heard employed by some of the coarser elements among my parishioners, I cannot help but 'lick my chops' at the prospect of the repast that awaits me. My spirit, now of course indistinguishable from Squire Trevelyan's, will return to the latter's coffin. To the forty-nine years I have to my credit will have to be added the eighty years that will be furnished by Messrs Morton and Seagrove. That is a hundred-and-twenty-nine years in all from now, 1888. The world will have a sign of me again in the year 2017.

Aubrey Melford

* * * *

Postscript: Excerpts from Two Newspaper Reports.

The North Cambridgeshire Gazetteer, *May 10th, 1888. The village of Grisbury was the scene of two gruesome deaths, those of Dr Edward Morton and Professor Raymond Seagrove, whose mutilated bodies, with their hearts apparently torn out of their breasts, and their necks punctured by two small holes, were discovered dead in their respective beds, with a trail of blood spots leading to the crypt under the manse adjoining St Andrew's Church. Police are investigating, but there are apparently no promising leads to a solution. The deaths of the two young scientists are reminiscent of the identical, and hitherto unsolved deaths of a tramp and a young lady, which occurred—also in the crypt beneath The Manse—thirty-one years ago.*

The Cambridge Daily, *June 1st, 2017. The sparsely populated village of Grisbury awoke this morning to an immensely high-decibel explosion. The source of the explosion has since been traced to the crypt beneath the recently restored manse adjoining St Andrew's Church. The cover appears to have blown violently off a coffin dating back to 1712 and bearing the name of William Trevelyan. Residents have complained of what they have described as an unendurable stench of sulphur emanating from the crypt. The entire phenomenon remains a mystery. Cambridgeshire Police are investigating.*

✗

ALLEN K. '91

A WINTER REUNION
by C.M. Muller

Hunched forward, hands tense upon the wheel, Ing searched the swirling white expanse for signs of movement, a taillight, anything to indicate that he was not experiencing this godforsaken snowstorm alone. He was traveling at just under thirty miles an hour, and even this was beginning to feel uncomfortable. His back ached and the radio no longer functioned as it should, emitting various shades of static. The snow had begun falling not long after he had crossed the state line, and it had only worsened as the miles ticked by. While he had taken the trip to Hettinger on numerous occasions, never had he done so during winter.

There was little doubt in his mind that Leva and the rest of them were already worrying over his whereabouts. In a perfect world, in a world without all this misery-inducing snow, Ing would have arrived in town by now, reminiscing about old times and nursing his first aquavit. But the botched weather report couldn't be blamed on forecasters alone. No, the one who really deserved an earful was his sister, who had decided to organize this year's Enger family reunion in the middle of January. And yes, as she had explained to him over the phone, there was an important historical reason for doing so.

From an early age, Leva had been fascinated with the past. She could sit for hours in their grandfather's lap, listening to the old man spin his folkloric and familial tales. In fact, Ing knew exactly what the elder would have called the event currently transpiring beyond the Volvo's frost-covered windows: *Fimbulvetr*, that mighty winter said to arrive before the end of the world. Ing had enjoyed the tales nearly as much as his sister, even if in retrospect they seemed a bit antiquated, belonging to a time when the mysteries of the world were centuries from being solved. Nevertheless, he was grateful for the memories he shared with Leva. There was a kind of comfort there, a tranquility which in his old age he had never quite been able to replicate. At certain times he had longed to retreat to that cozy Enger living room with its fireplace and wingback chairs, merely to listen to his grandfather recite some Asbjørnsen and Moe. Had the old man been along for the ride, it would not have seemed half so bad.

Then again, if Ing truly had his choice of traveling companions, his dear departed Evelyn would have topped the list. Her death that past October had been a blow from which he knew he could never fully recover. Even if he somehow managed to cull another decade from life, the joy that had been Evelyn would continue to haunt him. Her passing had been so unexpected because even at sixty-eight she had been the picture of health. She had more energy than most people half her age, and Ing had always assumed that he would be the first to go. Ideally, they would have gone together.

With Evelyn the trip would have been an ever-joyous and agreeable undertaking. She would have already started massaging his neck, relieving the tension there, venturing every now and again to tickle an ear. Ing missed her gentle touch and her soft, intelligent voice. She could talk for hours on end if the situation called for it, and never once repeat herself. Her easy-going nature and kindheartedness would have lessened the monotony of the drive, and the snowstorm itself would have been made into a heavenly phenomenon.

Ing tried to remember when he had last seen a motorist's taillight. It felt as though hours had passed. The intensity of the storm had boxed him into his own padded cell of solitude, and while he felt sure that numerous other vehicles were not far ahead or behind, he could not help but imagine that he was traversing this stretch of nothingness alone. Snow had already drifted over much of the road, making it difficult to tell where it and the land came together. Not wishing to misjudge this boundary and end up in a culvert, Ing carefully eased the Volvo to the right as much as he dared and parked. Idling there, he peered nervously in both side and rearview mirrors, fearful of a rear-end collision.

A minute became five and then ten, but nothing emerged from *Fimbulvetr's* churning maw. Even though the Volvo's heater was going full blast, Ing was starting to lose sensation in his toes. He still had half a tank of gas, and he probably could sit at the edge of the road for a few more hours if necessary, but if the snow continued at its present rate there might come a point where rescue would be impossible. As if to will the luminous monstrosities into existence, Ing imagined a pair of snowplows racing in sync across the frozen waste, patrol cars not far behind with officers on the lookout for stranded motorists.

Had he abided Leva's recommendation about obtaining a cell phone— "Nothing fancy, just something for emergencies, something to tuck into the glove box"—Ing might very well have been able to call emergency services. A voice, even if it belonged to someone he did not know, would be of great comfort. But, as with everything involving new technology, he had stubbornly refused. As always, he was left with his own wits, which at present were rapidly failing him.

As he tried the radio again, Ing quickly grew disheartened by its ceaseless scan. Clicking it off, he focused instead on the eerily-similar static of the howling wind. It seemed to shift directions at will, determined to find a way inside the Volvo. Snow was blowing with such force that it was beginning to feel as though a part of the world had dissolved. Ing wondered if he would experience a similar fate simply by stepping outside. The car was a safe haven, but it also represented little more than limbo. And *Fimbulvetr* would soon have its way.

Ing thought of the old Enger homestead where the reunion was to take place. While it was now fully incorporated into a "living history" exhibit, the rough-hewn shack had once stood alone in the middle of an open prairie, upon land claimed by his great-grandfather in 1864. Leva's rationale for holding the reunion in such an unforgiving month was simple: she wished to recall the year which had very nearly wiped out the entire clan. It had been the first winter the family had experienced in their new home, and it had been a devastating one, particularly as it involved the loss of two children. Ing could well imagine the fear and helplessness that his forebears must have gone through. They had been as isolated as he was now, perhaps even more so. But they had had each other and persevered. He had no one, nothing but his memories.

Then again, if he somehow managed to survive, he would have quite the spectacular tale to tell. One for the generations, surely. He laughed at the absurdity, and it felt surprisingly good to do so. Closing his eyes, and taking a deep breath, he readjusted the seat into a more comfortable position. He tried to clear his mind, tried to think of a way out of this wintery mess, but memories of Evelyn kept coming to the fore. To have spent so many years with someone only to have that joy fall into a daily ritual of absence was almost too much to bear. Ing felt tears welling in his eyes and to distract himself he turned toward the passenger seat, willing Evelyn into existence. He needed her now, if only to tell him that everything was going to be okay, that the storm would soon pass and the sun would shine again. As things stood, he would be buried alive in this Scandinavian steel coffin without a marker to remember him by.

Realizing his thoughts were getting the better of him, Ing turned his attention to the side-view mirror. He needed to remain focused on the present, not memories, needed to keep an eye out for help. Someone would eventually chance upon him, but until that time he needed to remain positive, as Evelyn would have. He knew that she would want him to keep tethered to hope for as long as he was able. Never would she have allowed him to give in to despair.

It seemed to have grown slightly darker. Ing checked his watch, thrilled to discover—even if every other aspect of his life had failed—that it still worked. He held it to his ear, comforted by its steady click. Evelyn had given it to him over fifty years ago, and the act of winding it each morning had always enlivened him, brought a simple solace to his day. And while it was still hours from needing to be rewound, Ing did so anyway.

Glancing up, he noticed a figure scurrying past the Volvo.

He refocused his attention, hoping for another glimpse, but the storm had already concealed the visitor. Ing uncoupled his seatbelt and, without thinking, lumbered outside. He pushed against the piercing wind to the front of the vehicle, calling as loudly as he could. The snow stung his forehead and eyes, and he was on the verge of turning back when he glimpsed a light in the far distance. It was part of an ill-defined structure about forty yards away, but as Ing squinted, hoping to see it more clearly, the shifting wind blotted it from view.

The point of light, however, remained, a star reflected in this arctic ocean. Ing was certain now more than ever that someone needed his help. A stranded motorist had made the foolish mistake (just as he was making now) of leaving their vehicle in a desperate attempt to seek rescue. More than likely they were already suffering hypothermia. How else to explain the fact that they had walked right past the Volvo.

Cursing the maelstrom, Ing tightened his meager hood and proceeded toward the light. Glancing down, he was surprised by all the undisturbed snow. While it continued to accumulate at an unbelievable rate, there still should have been some sign of a disturbance. Moving ahead, he continued his sustained plea, encouraging the unseen motorist to approach his voice if they could hear. By the time he had ventured twenty or so paces, he half turned to ascertain the location of the Volvo, but it was already gone, absorbed into the void. Not being able to glimpse that boxy but reliable refuge unnerved Ing, but nevertheless he pushed on.

"Fimbulvetr…"

He stopped in his tracks, startled by the close-sounding voice. As he stared ahead, the structure he had previously glimpsed began to grow more defined. The front door was about ten yards away, and if no one was home or it turned out to be abandoned, Ing felt confident he could backtrack to his vehicle without much effort. The storm certainly hadn't pushed him too far off course.

"Fimbulvetr…"

This time it was Ing who uttered the extraordinary word, as though its recitation might bind him to the lost soul, might somehow bring them together. He lumbered ahead, his pace infuriatingly slow. Snow continued to scrape his exposed flesh, making it difficult to focus for more than a second or two. As he brought a hand up to shield his eyes, he noticed a more expansive light emanating from a previously obscured window. Through its lit pane, the interior of the shack looked cozy and inviting, completely at odds with what he was expecting.

Heartened by his good fortune, Ing strode to the front door. He knocked a bit too heavily, and the latch gave way, leaving a semi-open doorway quickly filling with snow. Without a thought, he stepped over the threshold and closed the door. The screaming storm was muted slightly, and this new silence was unsettling. Having been lodged in *Fimbulvetr's* throat for so long made its absent howl nearly as excruciating.

"Anyone here?" Ing called, still lingering near the door. Judging by the silence, his abrupt entrance had startled the occupant into hiding.

It wasn't any warmer inside, but without the wind it certainly felt less intense. Ing could still see his breath, and now that his eyes had adjusted he was shocked by the simplicity of the one-room shack. It wasn't half as appealing as it had appeared from the outside. There was a potbellied stove in the nearest corner, though its hearth was lifeless and no kindling was in sight. Next to this stood an immigrant chest, with a name scripted in gothic lettering across the front. It was irrevocably faded, enough so that Ing doubted he could decipher it even up close. A table and two benches were set along the nearest wall, atop which rested a leather-bound book. Ing's grandfather had had a similar *bibelen*, which he had treasured to his dying day. The only other visible pieces of furniture were a rocking chair and a spinning wheel. Ing recalled the light which had originally drawn him inside, and only now did he think to search for its source. As far as he could tell there was no lamp or candle burning anywhere, nothing that could have produced that warm painterly ambiance he had originally seen.

"Fimbulvetr..."

It was the same voice he had heard from outside, but this time it was accompanied by a tattered cough and soft moan. As he stepped toward the source, Ing noticed a dark blanket draped from the ceiling in a corner of the room, in effect creating a hidden space.

"It's okay, I'm here to help," Ing said, his voice as gentle as he could manage. He pulled the blanket slowly to the side, not desiring to scare the individual any more than he already had. There was a bed beyond the curtain and laying upon it, half curled into a fetal position, was an elderly woman. She was wearing nothing more than a dirty and ragged nightgown.

Ing knelt down to have a closer look, wondering if the elder was even aware of his presence. He cleared his throat. "I saw you wandering outside and..." Even as he said this, he knew it could not be true. There was no way this frail creature could have trudged for any length of time through *Fimbulvetr*. No, she had not left this bed, this place, in a very long time.

The old woman shifted slightly toward Ing's voice, moaning as she repositioned herself to meet his eyes. Her own were startlingly familiar, reminding him of Evelyn.

"It's going to be all right. My car's not too far away. I'll take you there now." Ing stood up and undid the blanket from the ceiling. Once he had it loose, he slipped an edge under the old woman and did his best to wrap all but her face. He lifted her into his arms, surprised not by his strength but by her lightness. She weighed hardly more than the blanket.

"I'm going to get you some help," he continued, struggling past the door and stepping forth into a miracle: the blizzard had stopped. *Fimbulvetr* had moved on.

Gazing into the distance, Ing was heartened by the clarity and closeness of the Volvo. And the snow, unbelievably, did not appear quite so deep as he remembered. The sun was visible, but even its paltry rays could not have altered the landscape so quickly. A semi suddenly blasted past his field of vision, scattering snow in its wake.

By the time he reached the Volvo, Ing was nearly overcome by the new weight of his burden. The old woman felt so much heavier, though this was probably a matter of his own fatigue. Opening the passenger door, he situated the elder carefully into the seat, loosening the blanket. She peered up at him and smiled, appearing much healthier in the new light.

"I'm appreciative of your kindness," she said, her voice much clearer, more youthful-sounding. She looked so different now that she had been removed from her decrepit abode. This was no longer the withered old woman Ing had just rescued.

"I don't think it's too far to the next town," he said. "We'll have you looked at there." He shut the door and walked around to the other side, nearly losing his balance along the way. By the time he slipped inside and latched his seatbelt, he felt exhausted and uncertain about his ability to converse, much less drive. Nevertheless, he put the car into gear and started slowly forward.

It was miles until he saw the first sign indicating a town, and miles more before he felt a hand gently massaging his neck and then moving up to tickle his ear. He turned toward the old woman, seeing in her further aspects of Evelyn. Her cheeks, her smile....

"I'd been there for so long," she said, her eyes glistening like a newborn's. "So very long, in that dark, dark place, waiting for someone to come. And you did." Her smile widened.

A final coherent thought came to Ing before he returned his attention, however wearily, to the road: he would have done well to have left the crone in her rotting bed. She hadn't been sick, not really. He knew that now. Knew it with the same clarity that he knew he was on the decline, that in a very short span *he* would be the one curled up and courting death. Darkness and further isolation were fast approaching, with the growing intensity of a winter storm.

But for now, Ing tried to enjoy the sensation at his neck, the tenderness of which reminded him so much of Evelyn and death, entwined now as they were. He had a feeling that by the time those fingers ceased their magic and withdrew from his flesh, something else inside of him would end as well.

The creature at his side began to hum, the intonation of which sounded mythic and warm, a song belonging to more ancient times, a melody evoking mysteries which perhaps only Ing's forebears could fully appreciate and comprehend.

If he listened long enough, perhaps he might understand as well.

✗

LE GARGOYLE
by Russ Parkhurst

Looming softly in the mauve Parisian dusk
ambiguous even by moonlight   splitting eyeworn skies
lovers have died under   a solitary figure broods
high atop a cathedral   roosting above the naves
and above the knaves   alone   unbroken by love
kissed only by the sleetridden Catalonian wind
blowing at Christmas   pretending to disdain
the bright mad melodies of the travelers below
but secretly craving them   so that one bitter night
his ancient bonds crumble   and he falls willingly
to the cobbled street   stone meeting stone
and the crowds returning to the streets in the morning
find pieces of him scattered everywhere,
everywhere

THE STRAVINSKY CODE
by Leonard Carpenter

It was the macabre death of the choreographer, Laurenz Velkin, that drew me into the Stravinsky Code affair. Baltimore's police, having ruled out a mere accident, were vexed. It was quite obviously murder, a deft and savage snapping of the neck from behind. But there were certain peculiarities, and so I, as a recognized symbologist on the faculty at Brown University, was consulted regarding the odd position of the body.

Right there at the crime scene, happily, I was able to allay their fear of some Neo-Nazi murder conspiracy. Really, I asked them, would a cold-blooded assassin have been patient enough—and demonstrative enough—to arrange the victim's body in the shape of a swastika?

If so, he or she would certainly have taken the trouble to get it right—that is, Right-spinning or clockwise. In Hitler's "twisted cross" the arms (and, in this instance, the legs) trail out counterclockwise so that the pinwheel design appears to turn or roll to the right. In poor Velkin's case, this was reversed. The symbol thus presented was a common Asian or Navajo/southwest US pattern, usually indicating spiritual harmony and continuance. Such a shape might suggest some devout ritual treatment for the deceased choreographer, or possibly even goodbye blessings for the world to come.

Nevertheless Velkin's demise was a brutal fact. And the arrangement of the remains had been precise, and emphatic enough to involve some snapping and dislocation of limbs other than the neck. In this *maestro's* artistic works, if one of his performers had managed to achieve so *avant-garde* a *grand jete* and somehow survived to limp off the stage, the famed choreographer would have heartily applauded. There was, presumably, some very pertinent or strongly-felt motive for posthumously arranging the late dance-master in an innocuous but fractious spiral motif.

My initial suggestion to the police to seek a murderer among the ranks of dancers was frustrated, or possibly crippled, by Velkin's cutting-edge moves. The manner of the crime did, after all, suggest exceptional physical development on the part of the killer.

I noticed the framed playbills in Velkin's studio, hung high on the mirror-walls that elsewhere reflected the dance floor. The most prominent poster was for Stravinsky's Rite of Spring at Carnegie Hall. Spring maypole dancers invariably start their circling in a clockwise direction; so, if the arms of the concentric figure were seen as *leading* rather than *trailing*, Velkin's terminal posture might represent a birds-eye view of a highly seasonable ritual dance.

As I examined some curious scratches on the hardwood dance floor, my work was interrupted by a most singular individual. A woman in a gray flight suit, complete with helmet and microphone, strode up, seized my arm, and rather forcefully urged me to accompany her.

"Professor Hankins? Bud Hankins of Brown University?"

"Who wants to know?" I asked as I was dragged along.

"Agent Starkey, NSA."

"Really?" I asked, surprised she would admit it. "I thought you NSA spooks were always supposed to be, like, No Such Agency."

"This is a security matter. Come along." Though insistent, she was pleasant-looking behind her smoky visor. Judging by the cut of her coveralls and the strength of her grip, she could have been a dancer or acrobat herself.

Around us, I saw the murder investigation being taken over by gray-suited men from Homeland Security. Since Ms. Starkey assured me that my help was so urgently needed, I consented to accompany her out into the fragrant spring night.

Her craft was a Zulu, the almost mythical pulsejet copter whose operational existence was so frequently and plausibly denied. Its black stealth shape, its ability to fit on Velkin's mid-sized lawn, and its whispering speed, all made it easy to forget or deny ever seeing. Its victims, I gathered, generally did overlook its presence until too late.

In no time Agent Starkey swept us very deniably to National Security Agency Headquarters in Fort Meade, near Washington DC. On that broad roof, she shut down the silently spinning chopper blades and ushered me out. As she placed her hand in a palmprint identifier to summon the elevator, she explained our mission.

"Velkin was in contact with certain groups in the former Soviet Union that might pose a homeland security threat."

"And they killed him for it?" I balked at the vagueness of the charge. "You're saying he was a terrorist, a Communist, or both?"

"Maybe neither." Drawing me into the elevator, she shrugged. "But he had people coming and going in the context of his creative activities, sketchy individuals who may be involved in transferring intelligence, surveillance data, etcetera, to and from extremist groups in the Middle East."

"Groups? What groups? Al Qaeda, Al Aqsa, Isis? You must understand, Ms. Starkey—"

"Call me Ella." She rather forcibly led the way out of the elevator into a dimly lit basement corridor.

"Ella, this all sounds fairly Big Brotherish." Though she rolled her eyes I tried to explain, "As a tenured professor, I have to support academic and artistic contact between all countries. Travel and the free flow of information are essential. Was Velkin dealing with any known terrorists?"

"Not exactly." Her palm-print opened an automatic double door. "More likely with religious fanatics."

"You mean radical clerics, Wahabi mullahs or extremists?"

"Actually, older than that." She led us through a broad dark room divided into stacked cages and lockers, evidently an evidence storage basement.

"Older than Islam? You mean Christians or Jews?"

"Could be quite a bit older, actually."

"The Persian sun god Ahuramazda?" I speculated. "Sounds like REALLY old-time religion to me. True fundamentalists."

Starkey unlocked a filing cabinet, rummaged inside, and unrolled a drawing from a sealed plastic evidence bag. "Does this mean anything to you?"

I took the brown cracking parchment and felt an eerie sense of recognition—shades of Abu Grahib, or something much older. It was an ink drawing of a human female, chiton-clad, in the clutches of some nameless thing. The short-haired figure was spread-eagled in the grip of a large jointed device resembling an artificial tree. The woman's wrists, ankles, elbows, knees, waist and neck were each circled by cuffs or bands at the ends of spider-like arms branching out of a thick, shoulder-high trunk. Her consequent posture in the toils of the machine was a forced, garish dance-step, with her bare left foot on the ground, right leg arched high, arms spread wide and head bent back. The expression drawn on the figure was blank and submissive. A hand-crank projecting from the side of the trunk suggested that the device dictated motion as well as restraint. A bell was ringing in the back of my mind, yet I decided to probe deeper for information. "This is, what, a weapon of mass destruction, or deception?"

Agent Starkey shrugged. "You tell me. A torture instrument, maybe, used for interrogation or mind control. Or…."

"Or possibly a murder weapon," I said, "depending on who turns the crank, in what direction. It looks quite old—the drawing, too. Not exactly high-tech."

"It comes from a document cache unearthed in a castle in northern Afghanistan," Ella said. "Estimated age one thousand, five hundred years. But this photostat was found in Velkin's briefcase." She handed me a print of the same picture.

"A fax or copy…" It was my turn to shrug. "Not a WMD, presumably?"

"Professor Hankins, please, can we stop fencing?"

"Call me Bud," I parried.

"Reginald, Bud, whoever," she jabbed back well below the belt. "I'm just asking whether, speaking as a symbologist who deals with images, you can give me any background on this ancient garrote, or whatever it is."

"More a **gavotte** than a garrote," I quipped. "Tell me, Ella, did you ever hear of the Fourth Way, of G.I. Gurdjieff?" At her questioning gaze, intimidating even without the flight helmet, I went on, "Gurdjieff was a Greek-Armenian vagabond who came west from Russia early last century, to found a spiritualist institute in Paris with his disciple, Ouspensky."

I stopped and spelled out the names for Ella, who was making notes on her PDA. "Got it," she said. "Go on."

"Most of what I know comes from Gurdjieff's book, *Meetings with Remarkable Men*, He claims to have wandered the remote valleys of central Asia in search of ancient secrets, talking to monks, mystics, and some charlatans. He tells of a hidden method of communication used by the Old Man of the Mountains. Hasan, the Chief of Assassins in the twelfth century, had possibly carried it over from far earlier times. Dancers were trained to perform specific sequences of steps that had a coded meaning, and sent forth to carry secret messages from the religious leader to his agents in remote castles. The performers themselves were ignorant of the message, but rigorously schooled in the dance steps."

"You mean, their moves were coded like semaphore signals?"

"Yes, with motions added in-between. But the dances were learned by rote, so the dancers themselves didn't know what messages they carried, and even their trainers didn't understand the code.

"Instead, the dancers were taught using a tree-like device with crane arms that moved their limbs through the exact motion sequence. The tree had a slot in the trunk, into which the dancing-master inserted a series of grooved templates. Each plate represented a different letter or element of the code. The selection and order of steps were determined by the vizier, who knew the message content.

"Then, the dance troupe went forth to broadcast the code strings to highly-placed initiates who could "read" the steps. All others looked on in ignorance and were merely entertained. The dance might be a political message, to rebel at a certain hour or strike at an enemy. Or to the faithful, it could be a religious teaching, even a mystical spell. The music of the dance, its name, and the number and pattern of dancers might or might not have any significance."

"The dancers had to precisely follow the steps to preserve the message," Ella observed.

"Yes, I suppose so. Even though they were ignorant, they had to obey strict religious discipline." Seeing the grave look on her face, I said, "I imagine all this could play into your worst Homeland Security fears."

"It certainly fits the data we have." She dug in her file drawer and produced a handbill. "Here's the troupe that Velkin was principally working with."

The glossy, colored flyer for the Celestial Flame Dance Consort showed costumed dervishes spinning and leaping in the Eastern manner. The text mentioned folk dances and classics by Prokoffiev and Aleksandr Borodin.

"Here are the titles," she said, handing me a playbill. Aside from Stravinsky's work were featured the Polovetsian Dances from Prince Igor, and Borodin's entire ballet, On the Steppes of Central Asia.

"Well, well. Did they also do, maybe, From Russia with Love?" My natural skepticism was returning. "These are dance numbers, but what could it have to do with long-dead composers? Are you saying the music itself is subversive?

"Not necessarily, but certain music has always been provocative." Starkey consulted her PDA notes. "In 1912 in Paris, when Igor Stravinsky came from Russia to work with Sergei Diaghilev's ballet company and the famed lead dancer Nijinski, the Rite of Spring's premiere caused such a public furor that the uproar drowned out the music. The dancers couldn't follow the beat."

"So, Stravinsky's work was syncopated and dissonant. A new sound, so what?" I challenged her. "You mean it was nothing but Bolshevik propaganda? Like, if you play his vinyl record backward it tells you to smash the state?"

"Let's be real here." Her rebuke sounded almost plaintive. "I'm trying to find out whether, even back then, these performances contained secret messages —if maybe they've been reactivated, as a former KGB intelligence system now in Putin's hands. In your view, is it possible that Stravinsky or Diaghilev made contact with this man Gurdjieff?"

"Hard to say. They were both in New York later." I was done playing coy. "If you want to help the Baltimore police find their killer, try checking the records of movers and truck rentals at Velkin's address. The marks on his dance floor suggest that this, this—learning tree or whatever, the original Dance Machine, was present at the crime scene."

"Oh, really." Ms. Starkey got busy on her cellphone.

In a few moments she was back to me. "You were right. The cops noticed the same thing, and our Feds checked it out. Three weeks ago, Velkin's credit card was used to rent a lift truck. But the listed address isn't the same." Having locked up her evidence drawer, she was leading me out the door.

"So the Feds, FBI or whoever, are already there?"

"Almost," she said, punching the elevator button for the roof. "But I doubt if they'll beat us by much,"

* * * *

The Zulu chopper dusted down in the parking lot of a DC warehouse. A local police cruiser and unmarked FBI vehicles were already there, but Ella had radioed ahead to keep any evidence from being removed. Apparently the low-cost industrial space had already been vacated by its tenants.

"No weapons or explosives found yet," a lieutenant reported to Starkey. "It looks as if our foreign nationals were present in the last few days, and their departure was sudden, sometime after the victim's death. Very odd what we did find," the man added, walking us in.

The old brick warehouse had watery fluorescent lighting. Mirror-roll plastic had been pasted on the walls to make it a rehearsal arena; but with the patched concrete floor, it was nothing like Velkin's studio. Its central feature now was the grotesque, angular tree contraption that stood in the center of the room.

"This is it," Ella said, "the encryption device. It looks like a newer version of our drawing. Still, it must be hundreds of years old." She examined the cast iron trunk for manufacturer's marks, evidently in vain. The crane arms were hand-turned of tapered hardwood, with brass fittings, joints, and latching cuffs.

"I see it's already been dusted for prints." I tried the steel hand crank, having put on the latex gloves she gave me. "There's a lot of power in there." As I leaned on the lever with both hands, heavy flywheels rumbled and whirred slowly up to speed inside the trunk. We both stepped back to watch all eight jointed limbs flail, leather cuffs lashing at the ends, until the wheels creaked to a halt.

"Cute," Ella said. "But hardly Swan Lake."

I went back and inspected the mechanism. "I think I see the problem," I told her at length. "The code reader is faulty."

By reaching four fingers into a wide, mouth-like slot above the crank and lifting, I was able to remove the rectangular brass plate that had been left in the machine. "This is the dance step template." I traced the grooves, thicker and stronger than any player-piano roll, that would translate into specific motions of the tree limbs. "But here, do you see this one beveled corner? It's like a computer floppy disk, meant to fit inside the slot in just one way." I flipped it over and slid it back until it snapped in place. "See there, it still locks in. The blocking tab must be broken off inside the trunk." I pulled the plate out, reversed it endwise, slid it back in and locked it again, then pulled it, flipped it over and did so again. "So there are three incorrect ways to insert the template, and only one right way. The result for the dancer could be an impossible contortion —one that snaps his neck."

"You're saying Velkin's murder was a Death by Misadventure?"

"Yes," I said. "Very likely, Velkin wanted to demonstrate the machine himself. He may have known the proper way to insert the plates. But once he was locked into the cuffs, someone else had to change the template and turn the crank, someone who probably didn't know."

"Then why did they run away, and why try to hide this infernal machine?" Starkey knelt and rummaged in a nearby packing case. "Here are more templates, dozens of them. Too bad, I wish they were marked with the letter or whatever they represent. And look at this." Having smoothed out a crumpled handbill, she handed it to me. It was a cheap print job compared with the others she had in evidence, duplicated in black ink on red paper.

"Burning Bush, a Rite in the Desert," I read aloud. "Featured groups: Valhalla, The Mug Shotz, and the Celestial Flame Dance Consort. A Redrock Village Equinoctial Production by Keith Milvius."

"No date. But the paper is fresh, not faded." Starkey was punching queries into her PDA. "This could be the very next gig, the one they were practicing for."

"Hardly a big-budget production," I said, squinting into the muddy photos "This headline group must be a punk band, maybe Aryan rock. And the promoter, Milvius, is definitely third-string, after Manitoba. I didn't know he was still in business."

"After what?" Starkey asked, distracted.

"The so-called Manitoba Woodstock," I explained. "It was a disaster Keith Milvius staged in the nineties. A backwoods rave concert, with Bad Loser and other big punk bands performing. A freak blizzard struck, causing some deaths and a lot of frostbite, a few people insane from bad drugs, some totally lost in the whiteout. Plus, there were crazy supernatural rumors of Wendigos and things. Bigfoot carrying off frozen victims, the New Age gone bad. U.S. papers didn't cover it much."

"Sounds delightful. As for this event," Ella said, "the flyer must be printed for local distribution, or else meant for multiple venues. It doesn't list a place or a date." She set down the paper. "For all we know, it could be on the Steppes of Central Asia,. Maybe a USO tour."

"Not Asia, Arizona." Picking up the page, I pointed out the logo design across the bottom, a bird figure rising out of stylized flames. "That's a phoenix symbol; insiders likely know what it means. Check for a Redrock Park near Phoenix, AZ."

"If you say so." Thumbing her PDA, she seemed way less skeptical.

"As for a date, there is one. It says here, Equinoctial Productions. The Vernal equinox, the astronomical beginning of spring, is right about now."

Starkey got busy. After flurries of keystrokes she reported, "There is a Redrock Campground, south of Phoenix on the road to Tucson. As for the equinox—" more clicks— "it's today."

"Hmm. Well, it's really no big deal." I yawned, looking up at the skylight, which was already pale with dawn. "The event is obviously a very small-time ripoff of the Burning Man festivals in Nevada. Not a lot of people are likely to go."

"It doesn't matter, as long as the right ones do." Agent Starkey appeared to be sending texts, but she kept talking. "The NSA uses all its resources to monitor every communication channel in our data-driven world. If this is a new data source, unmonitored, and known only to our enemies—" she pressed Send, folded her PDA and put it away— "the threat is substantial."

"Threat level ultra-orange?" I quipped. "So in other words, you're going to have them bust this rock concert?"

"There isn't time for a full scale operation," she said. "But I, we, can monitor and report. I'll have to deputize you. Fortunately, secure transportation is available."

"What, we? C'mon, you've got to be kidding!"

Argue as I might, I found myself back onboard Ella's chopper.

$* * * *$

Twelve hours at two hundred miles per hour, my mind kept repeating. As we raced the sun westward, the time-zone changes helped. The Zulu's pulsejet was quiet enough for sleep, if not for idle conversation. Bathroom, fuel and food stops were at unnamed military hangars equipped with vending machines. Across the Midwest, Ella had a relief pilot. Presumably she was able to get some sleep, sprawled under her blanket in the back passenger seat next to mine.

When she stirred, I tried speaking without headsets, off the record. "Is this trip really necessary?" I asked over the rotor throb. "I mean, is the threat genuine?"

She shrugged drowsily. "*Semper vigilis.* It's a war without end. You've heard the latest *fatwa* by our enemies, haven't you—that the Great Satan will be drowned in heaven's holy fire?"

"Nothing new." I sighed, inaudibly but deeply. "It's just our age, I guess. The dominant theme of this new century—power corrupts, and absolute power corrupts absolutely."

She eyed me narrowly, NSA-style. "You mean, the power of fanatical, monolithic religions?"

I shrugged. "Yes. Or the fanatical power of megalithic government."

The motor noise was too loud for any more conversation.

By Arizona, the sun lay low in the west. The desert sky was a simmering red oven-mouth, even if the full heat of summer was yet to come. Phoenix spread away under a pink smoky haze, as if the place had already burned down and awaited its rebirth, or re-hatching. City lights started to prick through the smog as we turned south.

A Homeland Security radio link with the INS began coaching Agent Starkey where to land. The Forest Service was alerted, as was the Air Force, lest our sleek craft be detected and mistaken for a UFO.

Then the Zulu's stealth capability came in handy. Using night vision to skim along a dry wash, Starkey set us down there, barely a hundred yards from the glare of the desert amphitheater. Buttoned up, with canopy hooded and rotors secured, the parked aircraft soon blended into the nightscape behind us.

Ahead over a rise, the Mug Shotz were already playing, their heavy metal sound having quite effectively masked our arrival.

"This desert is incredible," I observed as we struck the Redrock camp trail. "Smell that fragrance? The wildflowers must be in bloom." I breathed in the twilight scent once again. "It all seems so fitting."

"Why? You mean, because our troops are fighting in the Asian deserts?" Starkey checked her watch. "So, our enemies might feel right at home fighting us here?"

"No, because desert is the birthplace of religious extremism," I said, waxing professorial. "Holy hermits, dust devils, mirages and divine visions. It goes back to the Book of Revelations, and beyond.

"I'm not sure it's the desert," Starkey said as we drew near the light and noise. "We have our share of loonies and American Ayatollahs back East, inside the Beltway."

Approaching the concert from the desert side, we encountered no fence around the youthful ravers. Still dressed for a murder scene myself, with Starkey out of her flight suit, we must have resembled MIB impersonators or X-Files UFO investigators. Not a problem, since dress at the event varied wildly from togas to hippie gear, to punk regalia, to little or nothing at all. I scanned the crowd for any apparel that looked identifiably ethnic—turban, fez, chador or flak jacket—but in the motley crowd and shifting light, racial and religious and political profiling were impossible. I saw medieval garb, a Trekkie costume, and one youth in what appeared to be a hooded Cthulhu sweatshirt—the quasi-religious symbology of a new pulp graphic era.

"What are we looking for?" I asked Ella over the din. "Do you have a list of suspects or targets, whoever? Shouldn't we try to get around backstage where the dance troupe is?"

"Sounds like a plan. Look for a ringleader." She scanned the purple-lit stage with pocket binoculars. "Nope, those aren't exactly the mug-shots I'm looking for. Just keep your eyes open, and stay near me." Patting the slimline holster at her belt, she threaded our way through the throng seated mostly on blankets and folding chairs.

Before we could get close, the opening band wrapped up their set and fled the broad platform, almost as if frightened of arrest. Roadies hurried out to clear away mikes and wires and drums. For a moment the platform stood empty. Then, to a dissonant recorded fanfare, the dancers came leaping and tumbling onstage.

The change of act was a signal for some in the audience to get up and move, blocking our way. But to me it didn't matter; I was frozen by the dance's slow, ominous opening. As Stravinsky's disharmonies gradually swelled, and mythic mood took over, the dance steps blended hypnotically. Above the hills a last blaze of sunset was fading, the stars beginning to twinkle forth in multitudes. The crowd grew silent as the chords and rhythmic movement mingled with narcotics to stir deep, indefinable feelings.

After the fanfare and initial flurry of dance steps came a weary choreographed trek, not a Star Trek but a steppe trek, as if toiling through the surrounding arid Arizona waste, This wore on, to be followed by a blissful interlude of peace.

And then, a musical trill of discovery—I was certain that I knew this orchestral work, though it must have been differently adapted for dance. It certainly wasn't the Rite of Spring.

"Strange moves," Ella said as a red-plumed female pranced and postured at center-stage. "Could that be the coded phonetic language, do you think? Semaphore signals?"

"Definitely, though it looks more like ritual," I watched the dancer's smooth, beckoning motions alternated with frozen attitudes of awe and submission. "There's an element of worship in it, like the invocation of a deity."

"Something very peculiar," Ella said. "I wonder what the ancient dance figure is for Semtex explosives?" She scanned the crowd. "Do you see anybody taking notes, transcribing or dictating?"

"Hard to say." As a stealthy male dancer stalked behind the red-plumed *primadonna*, I found it hard to tear my eyes away.

"The steps are choppy, stylized," Ella said. "But the music is so familiar. It's…."

"Stravinsky's best-loved work," I suddenly realized. "It's The Firebird."

Even as I spoke, a change came over the desert night. There was a rushing sound and, simultaneously, a pink glow and warmth passed through the air overhead. Before our eyes the Burning Bush effigy—a pile of dry tumbleweeds roped around a giant cloth-and-wood likeness of a politician—ignited with an audible roar on the hill beyond the stage, giving off a wave of heat that everyone could feel.

The audience stared upward, bedazzled by the sudden pyrotechnics. The dance continued, but then again came the rushing warmth. Ahead of us in the crowd, some kind of disturbance broke out—perhaps a fire, I thought, from stray embers thrown off by the bonfire's ignition? As I looked around for fireworks, rockets, or whatever source could have touched off the display, I was struck on the shoulder by a falling object.

It was sturdy and fan-shaped like a palm frond, but elongated and smoothly tapered—brushy-stiff, longer than a tennis racket. And strangely hot to the touch—a giant feather, bright red in the floodlights' glare. Just a prop from the dance show?

Around us thing were going seriously wrong. I heard cries of panic and saw people running—the audience, not the wild leaping dancers. The air suddenly stank of burning fabric and singed hair.

And over us again, the moving warmth! It seared my face until I instinctively raised my feather-fan to shield against it—and oddly, it worked! Peeking around it, at last I glimpsed the heat source, though I could scarcely believe what I saw.

It appeared to be, not a child's bird kite but the frightful mythical Firebird itself, a silent red-tufted flaming thing that swooped down from a vast height to loom over us larger than a jumbo-jet—the primeval specter itself, somehow drawn down or conjured up by this arcane dance spectacle.

The crowd tried to scatter, with blankets and garments bursting into flame as the great wings beat down searing heat onto our heads. Starkey and I kept together as we pushed through the throng. The fireproof feather, though light and pliant, helped shield us both from the heat. Only my knuckles around the shaft were scorched, though my hair and eyebrows were singed from trying to glance upward.

As we fled, the dancers finally broke up. Some beat out fires on their costumes or stripped them off altogether, while others scurried for shelter beneath light-towers and the stage. The recorded strains of Stravinsky's Firebird Suite still blasted forth in a syncopated demon-dance as, over our heads, the demon itself swooped and circled, spreading flames and buffeting us with its hellish heat.

As lights failed and went out, the creature was intermittently visible against the stars, glimpsed as a ruffled belly lit by its own fires or the occasional lash of a flaming red wingtip. Squinting up, I could make out the crested oriental shape with radiant eyes and tapered yellow beak. Its crimson feathers, like the one I clutched, looked yellow-fringed now—or was it just the bird's furnace-heat glaring out at us from within?

"Faster, this way," Ella panted, dragging me far from the stage. "We can stop it. The Zulu will take it out!"

"What, a dogfight with a firebird?" My breath and protests were used up as we dodged between fleeing music fans and leaped over those who rolled in the sand to extinguish their garments. "What do you think the bird wants?"

"I don't know—why did they conjure it?" Ella gasped. "Maybe just some ancient religious rite gone bad. Could be due to a faulty machine code. Or else a terrorist plot to set the whole western US on fire! We've got to head this thing off."

At last we blundered through scorched, spiky bushes into the dry wash. Ella was at the chopper, ripping away the fabric cover and flinging open the door. She had the rotors sluggishly turning even as I hauled myself in.

"Belt up, we're out of here!"

The first lurch was heavily forward, while I labored with my seat buckle in triple gravity. Then I dragged my headset on, to hear and talk through. Only our upward momentum held down my lunch as we spiraled past the rave-inferno where, just ahead of us, a luminous shadow soared and flapped.

"It's leaving the concert, see there," Ella said, turning to follow the retreating bird. "Her heading is north, toward Phoenix!"

I didn't take time to address the issue of him-or-her. "No more fires down below," I said, looking out over dark hills as we left the blazing panic behind. "Nothing much out here to burn."

"No, but plenty up there!" She pointed to the faint glow of city haze over the desert, against which the flapping wings were outlined.

"Do you think it knows?" I asked.

"Homing instinct," my pilot said, accelerating. "It probably wants to torch Phoenix and lay its eggs in the glowing embers. I'll have to give them a warning if we don't take it down."

"As if anybody would believe us! How do we stop it?" I asked.

"Duh—ever heard of a heat-seeker? One should do the trick." So saying, she slammed her hand down on a red dashboard control.

A blast of flame lit up our night vision, quickly narrowing to a spiraling missile exhaust as it streaked toward the target. Not much chance of mistaking the target, I thought, with the concert fires and lights already far behind us on the ground.

The projectile straightened and dove at the target. It detonated, blossoming flame and smoke with a delayed, audible thud.

But as our blinded vision cleared, no change was evident. The faint pinkish shape still capered against the stars, blithely spreading its havoc.

"Try again," Ella said, hitting the other red button and shielding her visored eyes. This time as the missile homed in, she gunned the chopper closer for a better look.

"No good," Ella announced as the second heat-seeker's bloom faded. "The heat from that bird-thing touches off the warheads well before they hit. The explosive force dissipates, barely enough to ruffle the thing's feathers. That was our last missile, anyway." She reached under the dash and extracted a pistol grip on a thick cable. "We'll have to try small-arms fire."

The chopper vibrated as tracers sprayed out at the target. The bullets seemed to flare as they neared the bird, without striking home.

"Just as I thought," Ella announced. "The rounds are melting and detonating before they hit. One more trick left, before we call in an air strike."

Plunging ahead, racing past the giant bird, she slapped a button marked "ECM."

"Emergency counter-measures?" I asked, unsure.

"It lets off shredded foil to confuse radar," she explained. "Maybe it'll distract the critter. Tell me what's happening."

Twisting in my seat, I peered back. To my alarm, the bird was now following us. Through the trail of glitter, I glimpsed the great yellow beak craning open and beady eyes gleaming against the background of scattered fires. "It's interested, all right,"

"Good," she said, hitting the ECM control again.

I craned my neck. "She definitely likes bright shiny things," I reported.

"Terrific." Ella reached down for her radio mike. "This could buy us time to call in some interceptors. There's a lot of briefing to do, just in case we don't make it."

Our pursuer, with its keen night vision, seemed enraptured by the myriad tiny specks that reflected its own fiery light. More visible now in the high-altitude blackness, the Firebird flapped and climbed like a giant condor, cavorting through each successive shower of chaff. The campground lights had dwindled far behind, and on the distant highway I could see a flashing train of emergency vehicles headed south toward the conflagration. Better if they'd gone north.

"What about smoke?" I asked with a sudden inspiration. "Do you have any of that?"

"For marking position, sure," Ella said, pointing to a white knob. "Why?"

"Can you let it out in a pattern, like skywriting?" I asked. "Try getting a good way out in front, and trail more chaff."

As I explained my concept, she balked. "What, you mean drawing swastikas in the sky?"

"Not a swastika, the reverse of it," I said. "The pattern that killed Laurenz Velkin. The coding machine was improperly loaded, but the figure he made might still be significant, the final dance step."

"I'll try it, if you really think so." Having pulled ahead, Ella spun the copter back toward the bird. As white smoke billowed, I felt us lurch sharply down, then left, then down—and then, after rising smokeless, right, down, and right. The chopper blades drew some smoke downward and sent it whirling, so it was hard to know what, if anything, the bird could see. But as we jetted clear, I could glimpse the giant pattern in the glare of our own running lights. And beyond our last twinkling chaff, the blazing stars....

"Wait." The certainty dawned on me. "I think it's gone." Scanning around us and overhead, I saw no trace of the bird, just the last disappearing flecks of chaff.

"I'm not seeing it anymore," Ella declared. "There's nothing on the proximity sensor. Impossible." She fiddled with the controls. "Your plan worked."

"I guess it was mythical after all," I said, feeling total relief. "Gone back to the steppes, or wherever it came from."

"Great," Ella said, already thinking ahead. "Just groovy! So the fires and deaths, severe burns or whatever, will be attributed to some human cause. Terrorists—a few more innocent patsies for Gitmo! And we'll have to explain the two Sidewinder missiles expended!" She put down her mike. "We'd better get our stories straight! Good thing it's all top secret."

"The bird'll be just a bad batch of acid once they debrief the survivors," I mused. "So much for the threat to Homeland Security."

"Call it a threat to Homeland Sanity," she ruefully said. "Too much old-time religion. We'll both seem flat-out crazy, even to NSA."

"We'd better hang onto this, just in case." Smiling, I fanned my sweat-damp face with a large red feather, not even singed.

⚔

SHE TALKS TO ME
by Matthew Masucci

When I pulled into the driveway, both my parents stood side by side on the porch looking like American Gothic, except my mother sported a ridiculous pained smile.

Scrit-scrit-scrit—

N-E-R-V-O-U-S

"Don't worry, Betty. I'm sure once they meet you, they'll be fine. It'll be a little awkward at first, but…"

* * * *

So, when I phoned my mother that I was bringing someone by to meet them, I warned her that it was a bit of a nontraditional relationship.

"Does she have a kid?"

"No, ma."

"Is she black?"

"Nope."

"Asian? Mexican?"

"No and no."

"Oh, dear, you're not gay are you? Not that there's anything wrong with that."

I laughed. "No."

Mother worried that I would get a girl pregnant before finishing college. My biggest concern was just talking to women at all.

* * * *

With a half glass of beer in his hand, my father leaned back in his recliner, his elbows sinking into the threadbare armrests. Mother sat on the plaid loveseat next to me. It matched the living room décor, made up of all things country: milk bottles, antique crates, various rusted metal tools. I laid Betty on my mother's lap.

"So, how does this work?" Her unsure hands hovered over Betty.

"You can ask her a question."

Mother raised her voice, like when she talked on her cell phone. "How did you two meet?"

"You don't have to talk loudly. She's not deaf."

"I've never done this. Do I have to touch the…thing?"

"The planchette? No."

"Oh! There she goes! Look, Frank! All by herself!"

Betty spelled out

P-L-E-A-S-E-D-T-O-M-E-E-T-Y-O-U

My father stood up with his empty cup in his hand and walked toward the kitchen. "This is going to take a while."

"Oh, hush, Frank."

I followed my father into the kitchen. He popped the top on a Coors and poured it into his glass. "It must be like talking to your mother sometimes. Slow going," he said.

"We use a kind of shorthand that makes it go faster." Ice clinked in my empty glass.

My father filled another glass with a pitcher of sweet tea on the counter. He took down another glass from the cabinet, the same ones that lined the kitchen walls since I was little. He tilted the glass toward me. "Does Betty, uh—"

"She doesn't drink."

My father nodded his head, handing me the one filled glass. "Take this in to your mother."

When I came back to the kitchen, I filled the awkward silence between us by pouring more sweet tea into my glass.

"I'm not sure how to say this—" my father began.

"Then don't."

"Have you thought about the future?"

"She *is* a talking board." I chuckled, trying to make things a bit lighter.

"I'm serious."

"We've talked about it." I sipped my tea and leaned back against the counter.

"At least you didn't bring home a Magic 8 Ball." Father looked at me and chuckled, offering a rare smile.

"There was that one you bought me when I was twelve—"

Father's face became a slate of granite.

"I'm just kidding, Dad."

"Jesus Christ."

"Don't let Ma hear you say that."

He let out his breath. He must have been holding it. "You had me there for a second."

"For a moment you thought this was your fault? Like there's something wrong?"

We heard Mother laughing in the other room.

"She seems to be warming up to her," I said.

"Your mother's a good woman. She loves you, and she tries hard."
I sipped my very cold and very sweet iced tea.

* * * *

Betty waited for me in the car. Mother hugged me while Father waited inside.

"Son, I respect your choices, and I just want you to have the best," she said.

"Ma, she is the best. She talks to me. We talk. Betty's really important to me."

She smiled. "Honey, people will laugh at you."

"They've laughed at me my whole life."

* * * *

All the talk shows I watched growing up emphasized the importance of communication. All of the soap operas Mother watched while I grew up emphasized the importance of French kissing. Somewhere between those two aspects was a relationship.

At a stoplight, I looked over to Betty.

Scrit-scrit-scrit—

Y-O-U-L-E-F-T-M-E-W-I-T-H-H-E-R

Scrit-scrit-scrit—

A-L-O-N-E

Scrit-scrit-scrit—

I missed what she said next because the light turned green, and I had to keep my eyes on the road.

"No texting and driving, Betty."

REM played on the radio. "Half a World Away." I tried to warn Betty that they're stuck in their ways, but they're nice people. If my mother said anything offensive, she didn't mean it. I tried to explain these things to Betty, but I realized it wasn't fair. It turned into a lecture because I just couldn't pay attention to her the way she needed while I was driving.

And I was hungry. On the right, there was a Denny's.

Once I ordered, we picked up the conversation.

"Don't say that, you can't mean it."

Scrit-scrit-scrit—

"At least tell me why."

Scrit-scrit-scrit—

"You're not making sense. You're going too fast."

Scrit-scrit-scrit—

"Every relationship requires sacrifice. We both should have something at stake."

Betty stopped talking to me. I sipped my water and stared across to the empty booth seat. I pushed Betty to the side so that the waitress could put the food on the table.

Suddenly, a woman sat across from me, hair black as wet jetty wood and eyes so dark one could fall into them for days. I recognized her from Psychology class, but I couldn't remember her name. She pulled Betty in front of her, picking up the planchette.

"This is so cool. I used to have one of these."

"Really?"

"I remember this one time I was at a sleepover, and we all went down to Beth's basement and took her older brother's Ouija board with us. We were asking the spirits who liked who at school. This was middle school, by the way. And then it started to say some really dark things, so we all ran upstairs screaming like banshees. We all pointed fingers at each other for the rest of the night about who was moving it on purpose to say those terrible things. I think it works on static electricity."

This girl flipped over the planchette. She ran her fingers along the felt circles on the planchette's feet.

"Something about the electrical charge running between two hands—" She touched my hand and –zap!– she shocked me.

We both sat back laughing.

"Sorry," she said. And when the waitress came over to check in, the girl ordered a Coke and something to eat.

WINGS OF TWILIGHT
by L.F. Falconer

"Unless one is strongly influenced by their peers into a herd mentality, we're all guilty of selective reasoning," Martin stated, smacking at the tickle upon the back of his neck. "We hear only what we wish to hear. We choose our beliefs."

"Whatever you say, dear," his wife called out from inside the cabin.

Martin's face paled as he leaned forward and gawked at his blood-smeared palm. "Dear god, what have I done?" His voice rose in pitch. "Darlene, come take a look at this."

"I'm in the middle of something," she answered. "Can't it wait?"

Martin swallowed back his gorge as the tiny, winged creature he'd just squashed ceased to stir. Disrupting the silence, a chorus of youthful whoops and cheers rose up from across the lake and an explosion of wood ducks shot into the amber evening sky. A chilled breeze washed through the pines, wrapping Martin inside a shudder.

"No," he shouted. "No, it can't. I need you—right now." He attempted to rise from the porch swing but his strength had disappeared, his stomach coiled like a hangman's knot.

Wiping her hands with a dish towel, Darlene emerged through the cabin's screen door with a tired sigh, joining her husband upon the porch. "You're not going to start harping about those kids camped across the lake again, are you?"

Martin continued to stare at his palm. "Do you see this?"

Darlene gave it a cursory glance. "It's a dragonfly. Honestly, Martin, you really do need to get out of the office more often."

"It's not a dragonfly." Martin brought his gaze upward then, staring his wife dead in the eye while raising his hand closer to her in the fading sunlight. "Look again. What do you really see?"

A distant bullfrog emitted a deep-throated *bha-rumph*. Darlene took a step forward and leaned in to look. "I've never seen one bleed be—oh my goodness!"

Her startled step backward drove Martin to his feet, his knees crackling like old cellophane. "Go get the phone."

Darlene clutched the towel, taking another step back. "There's no service up here."

"To take pictures, damn it. It's proof!"

Darlene scurried back inside and Martin sank into the seat of the swing again, staring down at the tiny body in the palm of his hand—the broken arms and legs—the bleeding skull—the crumpled, diaphanous wings, tattered, torn—the miniature humanoid torso, flattened and oozing, staining Martin's skin with the remnants of life.

The screen door squealed and banged shut as Darlene darted back out, her cell phone in hand. She leaned in close, quickly snapping off half a dozen shots of the dead fairy in Martin's hand.

"I don't suppose we have any way to preserve it," Martin said. "I imagine someone at the university might like to see it."

The university, Darlene thought with disdain. *The same university which forced Martin to take this extended vacation as the Board of Regents ponders his future there.* Martin had yet to receive the protective net of tenure. If he lost his position they could lose the house. They could lose everything. His damned obsessions could keep him from ever securing other employment at any respectable institution. Their sunset years could become more than bleak.

"We can put it in a sandwich bag in the ice chest for now," Darlene offered. "That should keep it."

The cacophony of boisterous youths continued on the far shore as Martin followed his wife inside the vacation cabin to free his hand of the gruesome evidence and cleanse the crime from his flesh.

"Why'd you kill it?" Darlene asked, carefully placing the plastic bag atop the block of ice.

"It bit me."

"Where?"

Martin pointed to the affected spot upon his neck.

Turning on the lamp and donning her glasses for a better look, Darlene inspected the area. "I don't see anything. Are you certain it bit you?"

"I'm convinced it intended to bite me."

"So, it didn't really bite?"

"It simply didn't get the chance."

"Do they bite?"

"How should I know?"

"You're supposed to be the expert. I never even thought they were real."

"You've never believed in me," Martin snapped. "If you'd allow yourself to pass through that wall of pragmatism you hide behind, you might see there's much more to this world than most people ever perceive, but no. Just like everyone else, it's *oh, there goes Martin again—seeing things that don't exist.* People think I don't hear, but I hear. I hear every damn word."

He pulled a handkerchief from his pocket and blotted his glistening brow. "I know what you think of me—what everyone thinks of me. However, the line between truth and fiction is practically nonexistent. Miniscule. Or merely a matter of perception. Who can claim to know the absolute truth? Isn't insanity only in the eye of the beholder?" He carefully folded the handkerchief and returned it to his pocket, his eyes boring into his wife's. "As I've often said before, there are those who might believe you to be more mad than I."

His lips curled into a brief, conspiratorial smile, raising goosebumps on Darlene's arms. She glanced back at the ice chest. She had seen it, hadn't she?

Martin's smile vanished, his face washing pale as moonlight. "Oh dear," he gasped. "What if this was the only one? What if it was the last of its kind?"

His rising panic spurred Darlene to her husband's side. It was always best to keep him calm. "I'm certain there has to be more, dear. Besides, it was an accident. I know you didn't mean to kill it."

"But I did. I did mean to kill it. Not that I intended to kill a fairy, but I did intend to kill whatever was crawling on my neck. It's a natural defense mechanism, to slap, you know. I thought it was a bee, or a spider, and my absolute intention was to kill it, without any knowledge or foresight as to what—or whom—I was killing." He collapsed into the nearby sofa. "But it's terrible luck to harm one. If there are others about, I'm afraid some type of retaliation could be in store."

Inwardly, Darlene chided herself for her lack of knowledge. Other than her husband's obsessions, all she knew of myths and folklore were the bedtime tales of her childhood. She sat beside him and put her arm around Martin's slumped shoulders, giving him a reassuring squeeze. "How could you have known?"

"Because it's a forest, Darlene. Strange creatures dwell in the forest. Here I was fearing to run across Bigfoot. I never dreamed I'd kill a fairy." A defeated sigh rattled his lips. "How could I have assumed it to be merely an insect?"

Darlene kissed her husband's cheek. "As you said yourself, it was a natural reaction. It couldn't be helped. Let me make you a cup of tea to help you relax."

"I don't want tea," Martin snipped, breaking free of her hold and leaping to his feet.

Darlene rose as well. "Cocoa?"

"Would you listen to yourself, Darlene? I did a terrible thing and I'm trying to vent here and you're spoiling it with offers of cocoa and tea! Can't I simply be angry for once without you thinking I'm mad?"

"I was only—"

"I don't want anything." Martin stormed over to the screen door and peered outside. Beyond the porch, a chorus of crickets had begun to sing. "I didn't want to come here in the first place. There's no peace here. Why did you force me to come?"

"I didn't force—"

"I didn't want to vacation in the woods." He turned to face her, his cheeks ablaze. "You knew that, yet you booked us a cabin anyway."

"You needed to get out—"

"I did not need to be in a forest! We could've gone anywhere else."

Darlene could argue this point till the end of the century, but had long since run out of steam. Why had she chosen the woods? Was she simply embarrassed to take him into public anymore? Biting her tongue, she put on a kettle for tea. "May I remind you," she spoke quietly, measuredly, "our vacation options are growing limited. I would have preferred another cruise, but no—we can't do that anymore. Not after what happened last time."

Martin slithered back to the sofa, sinking into it, shaking his head. "Mermaids," he muttered. "There are far too many mermaids in the sea." He gazed back up at his wife and wrung his hands, his eyes welled with tears. "Thank god you were there." Removing his handkerchief once more, he dabbed at the moisture in his eyes. "You are right. We could never go on another cruise. And flying is much too dangerous."

Darlene settled onto the sofa beside him, patting his knee. "I know. Gremlins."

"We're lucky we survived."

Darlene stared over at the ice chest. How much longer must she suffer his whimsy? It had taken her three years of marriage before she'd come to realize her husband hadn't been joking when putting a bowl of cream onto the back step every night to appease the brownies. She'd always assumed he'd merely been spoiling the neighbor's cat.

Then came the Caribbean cruise. She'd awoken in the night to find Martin missing from their cabin. After a short search, she found him perched upon the railing, flirting with the dark, salty waters below. He claimed the sea sirens were luring him to join them in the watery depths. She'd been able to convince the alarmed ship steward that Martin was prone to occasional sleep walks, but they were put permanently ashore at the following morning's port of call. On the subsequent short flight back to Florida, Martin became thoroughly agitated, convinced he'd spied gremlins scurrying about the jet's wings before an engine fire forced the plane into an emergency landing in Miami. Air travel was now fully out of the question.

Driving after dark had become nearly impossible. Martin would randomly jump like a frightened deer, claiming to see the ghosts of those who'd lost their lives to the roads. Last week, he'd released all the lab animals at the university under the explicit orders given him by a cat named Bastet on the quad. Yesterday he was certain he'd seen Bigfoot wandering through the trees near the lakeshore. Today—he killed a fairy.

He needed proof that his mind wasn't failing him and he believed that proof now lay safely nestled against a block of ice, shrouded in plastic. He could show it to the Board of Regents and his position at the university would no longer be in jeopardy.

Darlene could swear that she'd seen the purported creature Martin had killed. For a brief moment. Perhaps. Or had she merely *wished* to believe? For years she witnessed her own father lose himself to dementia. What cruel, clenched fist of fate allowed her to end up with a man like Martin? A man so seemingly brilliant, gradually losing possession of his mind. Yet with whom did the fault truly lie? Had she merely seen what he wanted her to see because she, as well, needed to prove he wasn't delusional? Or was it only a desperation to prove her own sanity?

"They'll probably come after us," Martin said, gazing toward the window into the gloaming. "Fairies are not known for their kindness—especially to those who've done them injustice."

She had her glasses on now. Should she look at the photos? Look inside the ice chest? She feared to confront his proof again—feared she might, once more, actually see the tiny, mythical creature instead of the dragonfly she knew it had to be.

"If we lock the door and windows, we should be safe." Darlene tried to reassure him. *To reassure herself?* "This cabin seems pretty solid."

Martin glanced over at the fireplace and shook his head. "We can't keep them out. If they want in, they'll get in."

A dead blackbird upon the empty grates the day they'd arrived had nearly ended the vacation before it ever began. Martin claimed it a bad omen and nearly demanded they leave then and there. If a bird could get in, then…

A deep, rhythmic *boom—boom—boom-ba-boom* rumbled through the air across the lake. Martin's eyes widened and he sprang to his feet, racing to the window, staring out at the growing darkness.

"Do you hear them?"

Darlene crossed over to the door and swiftly closed and locked it. "It's only the music of those kids again," she said. "Please, Martin, there's nothing to be afraid of." Within her chest, her own heartbeat did its best to outdo the bass beat of the music. A shrill whistle sang out behind them and they both jumped, wheeling around. Upon the stove, a jet of steam screamed from the tea kettle.

Laughing relief, Darlene hurried over and turned off the fire beneath it. "Tea, or cocoa?" she asked once again.

"Tea," Martin acquiesced, staring back out the window. There was little to see in the blackness beyond. The *boom—boom—boom-ba-boom* slightly rattled the window glass. Martin pressed his palm upon the pane, feeling the pulsing beat. In a moment, he leapt back when a thump, tap-tap hit the glass. A fleeting glimpse of wings evanesced into the dark. He turned a cold eye to his wife.

She easily read the fear etching lines into his face.

"They're coming," he said. Martin stepped away from the window. "They are bound to punish us."

"Us? But I didn't do anything. It was you who killed it."

"Mere semantics. It won't matter who they punish, as long as their vengeance is served." Martin stripped off his shirt, turning it inside out. "Quickly, Darlene, reverse your clothing." Martin slipped back into his shirt and removed his trousers.

"Whatever for?" Darlene set the tea bags aside as her husband proceeded to turn his trousers inside out.

"It's for protection," he stated. "Just do it. For your own safety."

He was mistaken, wasn't he? Allowing his imagination to rule over logic? Here's Martin, always so certain of himself—solidly assured of his self-convictions while she could only ever doubt her own. What had she truly seen upon the palm of his hand? What had she placed into the ice chest?

"Turn your clothes inside out," Martin commanded, pulling his trousers back on.

"This is ridiculous." Darlene wrested the tee shirt up over her head. From across the room, she heard Martin scream. Pulling free of her shirt, she watched her husband duck and swat at the moth that flitted about, seeking the lamplight.

"For crying out loud, it's only a moth," she spat as she slipped her reversed tee shirt back over her head.

"With a Mason jar and a few drops of honey, we could catch it." The excitement in Martin's voice edged into giddiness. "A live specimen would truly exonerate me."

Another thump rapped against the window.

"I don't have any honey." Darlene backed up a step. "And all we have is an empty soup can."

The moth flitted above her, then zipped toward the light. A second one emerged from the empty fireplace, jouncing across the room to join the other as they danced in a light-induced frenzy.

"We have to get out of here," Martin whispered. "We can't stay."

"We have the cabin for two more days."

"We have to leave now." Martin's voice rose. "Do you understand? Now."

"It's only—" Darlene swallowed her words as she glanced toward the lamp. Those were moths, weren't they?

Another thump at the window pane.

"Grab the ice chest and the phone," Martin shouted, hefting the half-filled suitcase from the corner chair. "Leave everything else." A third set of wings fluttered in through the chimney.

"It's after dark," Darlene pointed out, tucking the cell phone into her purse.

"It's a risk we must take. But you must drive because—you know…"

"I know." *Ghosts.*

In a flurry, they gathered their necessary belongings and hurried out to Martin's restored '64 Chevy Impala, stuffing the suitcase and ice chest into the back seat. Darlene slid behind the wheel and turned over the engine as Martin scooted into the passenger seat beside her.

Darlene's hands shook and she gave her husband a sidelong glance. Here they were—two adults, running like scared children in the night because of a few lousy moths. Again, she questioned: why the woods? Had she secretly hoped he'd get eaten by a bear? *Or Bigfoot?* After all, his life insurance was up to date.

Above the purr of the engine, the *boom—boom—boom-ba-boom* came to a sudden stop. A veil of dull silence melted down from above.

"Go," Martin demanded. "What are you waiting for? Just go!"

Shifting the Impala into first gear, Darlene pulled away from the cabin on the lake, heading through the tree-lined access road for the main forest highway.

Martin leaned forward, glancing up toward the darkened sky. "Oh, my god," he gasped, frantically grasping onto the dashboard. "They're gathering."

Darlene cursed his infectious panic. "What do you mean, they're gathering?"

"Look." He pointed toward the sky. "That rainbow ring around the moon. They're gathering."

Darlene wanted to cry. His obsessions were growing completely out of hand. She was losing him, just like she'd lost her father. Just like she was losing herself. Caught in a vortex, the swirl in the eddy had been slowly, steadily increasing as Martin approached the center. Now he was inescapably caught in the sucking downward spiral. And he was taking her with him.

"It's only moisture in the air, Martin." The quiet explanation she struggled to keep controlled. She would not let him drown her in his own nightmares. "The reflecting sunlight off the moon causes a halo. That's all. That's all it is." Darlene turned onto the highway and quickly brought her speed up until the needle reached 60 MPH.

Martin glanced over at the speedometer. "Can't you go any faster?"

"Do you really think they're capable of jet speeds? Deer come out at night. I'm already going faster than I'd like."

Martin sank back into his seat, closing his eyes. "It doesn't matter. You can't outrun them. Our only alternative is to give it back."

"Give what back?" Darlene eased her speed up to 65.

"The body. The one I killed. We've got to return it to them."

"Your proof?" Proof that he was insane? Or proof that he wasn't? *That she wasn't?*

She tried to recall what she'd truly seen in the twilight on the porch, needing to satisfy her own fears. To prove to herself she wasn't sliding into a Neverland of the mind. Like her father. Like Martin.

She slipped her hand inside her purse, searching for her cell phone while Martin shimmied around and reached into the back seat, fumbling with the ice chest. Popping off the lid, he fished around for the sandwich bag.

Darlene located the phone and set it on her lap, steering with her left hand and swiping the front screen of the phone with her right index finger. A soft light illuminated the dark interior. She had to see the photos. Martin's leg nudged against her, nearly knocking the phone to the floor.

"Be careful," she scolded, maneuvering the phone back in place.

"I've got it," Martin cried. With a ragged jerk, he twisted back into his seat knocking the phone off Darlene's lap once more with his knee. She scrambled to catch it.

"Damn it, Martin, I asked you—"

"I'm saving our lives here," he shouted, rolling down his window and tossing the sandwich bag out. "You should—oh, dear god—ghost!" he screamed.

Darlene glanced up at the road. Illuminated in the headlights, the giant figure appeared just left of center on the narrow, two-lane highway. Darlene swerved hard to the right. The front end of the Impala glanced off a granite boulder on the shoulder. Darlene's head thudded against the side window glass.

The car juddered through the dirt and rammed headlong into a towering Ponderosa pine. Darlene's chest slammed into the steering wheel. Her head collided with the windshield.

Within a smothering silence, a liquid gurgle rattled from Darlene's throat. Electrified jolts of pain wracked her head—her shoulders. Unable to move, she could only endure the sparking moments, her sight slowly blinded by a steady stream of her own blood, smudging the vision of her husband as he crawled from the wreckage.

Not a ghost. The thought blinked on through the fear that soon she would haunt this very stretch of desolate road herself, all alone, consoled only by the knowledge that she was not insane.

The amorphous mass of tiny winged creatures which had gathered upon the road slowly drifted apart. Martin trundled to his feet, the unified drone of beating wings descending upon him with a deep *boom—boom— boom-ba-boom.*

Not one of your damn ghosts at all. In the twilight of consciousness, Darlene laughed in silent madness.

A PANTHEON OF TRASH
by Thomas C. Mavroudis

Lester heard it beating in the tree all night. It thrashed in his sleep, and when he returned to bed from a trip to the toilet, the noise prohibited him from relaxing, from falling asleep again. He pulled the window shut, but he could still hear it flapping. He sat on the side of his bed, his back curved like a sickle, watching it with scorn. He could barely discern its outline in the darkness, still he could see the flash of its eye and beak, or silver glint off its feathers when it shuddered.

When he let Oliver out for his morning perimeter check of the front yard, Lester saw that what he mistook for a restless night bird was but a plastic bag tangled and impaled on the high branches. He was especially agitated because he wouldn't be able to get to the tattered detritus himself. It hadn't been there the day before, and he couldn't remember there being enough wind to place it there; in fact, he recalled that the previous day was as mild as the current morning.

He was confounded, for he suddenly noticed the yard was littered with garbage. Littered by his standards, which were pristine and dauntless. He glanced at the neighbors' yards, noting their perfection. With his growing decrepitude, he wondered if the pieces of dirty paper and plastic defacing his lawn were signposts for the beginning of the end. He snickered—he was already bent halfway to the ground. He went around the yard and daintily picked up the garbage, disposing it with Oliver's waste.

Then it was time for his morning customs. He sat in the shower on the safety bench he was embarrassed but grateful to have with the arc of his back to the water. He carefully washed his feet, scrubbing away the pads of dead skin that seemed to return like toadstools. He shaved at the mirror above the sink, doing his best to get his neck smooth; it was getting more difficult every week. He looked fondly at the rack of ties in his closet. He told himself he would wear one tomorrow. Before he left the house, he reminded Oliver to be a perfect gentleman. The dog sighed and blinked, his head tilted on the floor, reminding Lester he wouldn't be anything but.

Lester could still drive, but it was uncomfortable, so he reserved that feat for distances of a mile or more. The McDonald's where he read the newspaper was four blocks away and down a hill.

For a couple fleeting but good years, he met two other widowers every morning at the restaurant. Once and a while, another elderly gentleman or couple would join them. The conversation was more entertaining than anything, for at their age, fewer and fewer of the issues mattered to them directly anymore. When he was the only one left, Lester considered going to the Starbucks instead—it was on the side of the street closer to home—but he thought that was a sign of defeat.

It was such a quiet morning, that Lester kept looking at his watch. It occurred to him, in a flare of panic, that he might have gotten his days confused, that what he thought was Wednesday was somehow Sunday. How could he have lost so many days? He had no way, presently, to confirm, so he continued his ritual path, albeit in a layer of unease.

The morning was vivid but motionless, flat as though he traveled an elaborate diorama of his world. It looked real, but absent of tangible angles and curves. The further he walked, the more the world seemed a collage of precisely torn papers, colors and shapes filling in correctly, yet manufactured and unnatural.

At the hill, the illusion was reassuringly broken by the traffic at the bottom. The walk was not steep, but long, curving around a mound of earth too small to develop, too big to keep clean. Besides chunks of broken glass, the weed speckled hill was a catch-all for every sort of floating refuse. Where did it come from, all these pieces, these remnants of something else? They were like colossal specs of dust, dead scrap sloughed from some great, unimaginable entity.

Lester shuffled over the crosswalk at a swift clip to prove he could. The entire McDonalds front counter wished him good morning. They had his pancakes, sausage and orange juice ready. "Good morning, good morning," he said coming through the door, a hand raised like a diplomat.

The dining room was empty, and he checked his watch again. "Wednesday, isn't it?" he asked, placing dollar bills into the cashier's hand.

"Yes, Mr. Backus," the manager said.

"Quiet today."

"Drive-thru's been busy."

"Good to hear." Lester took his tray to the table he used to share with his companions, retrieving the paper. The newspaper itself was merely a station in his ritual, as most of his news was acquired by national radio in the afternoon and local broadcast before bed. Someone had been through it before him; a section was missing—the innermost piece with the obituaries. He read the boldface headlines, then the story, but the words wouldn't connect. The fragmented newspaper made *him* feel incomplete, and he left the restaurant earlier than routine.

Lester would usually continue walking south to the park, stroll around its lake a few times to aid digestion, but he was uncharacteristically tired.

He braced himself against the traffic pole, waiting to cross and work his way back up the hill. He thought if he sat in his chair with his eyes closed for an hour, he would feel up for a more spirited walk later.

He crossed the boulevard slowly, stepping onto the curb just as the signal for the cars turned green. Winded, he peered up the hill with contempt. He motivated himself saying, "Come on, old boy," and began the ascent, his eyes on the worn concrete, stopping midway to catch his breath. There was movement at the corner of his eye, a flicker over the bare dirt. It was the shadow of a large butterfly. He turned, craning his neck up to see the creature. It was a moth with faded white wings like the bottom of a Styrofoam cup. It fluttered clumsily to the sidewalk, alighting on the toe of Lester's shoe. "Oh," he cried, kicking the thing away. It crumpled to the gutter, nothing but a ragged shred of cotton cloth. Across the earthen mound, the debris imitated insect life. He could almost hear the din of buzzing, the edges of paper and plastic vibrating in the wind—if only the air stirred at all. He hurried to the crest of the walk and away from the mocking filth.

But it pursued him. Scattered over his lawn were clutches of long grey feathers. He plucked a feather from the grass and saw that they were strips of newspaper, the newsprint reveling itself as the day's mislaid obituaries. Above in the tree, the plastic bag snapped and crackled of its own accord. Lester locked himself away behind the front door.

He fell into his chair and closed his eyes. He heard a familiar *click click* approach, but he was afraid to open his eyes and see an unfamiliar thing. He was relieved to feel Oliver nudge his hand, his mass settle beside his feet. And when he opened his eyes, unable to hide in total dread, Oliver was there, the canine expression of concern on his face.

"Oliver," Lester said, stroking the dog's muzzle, "this is a very ugly day."

The dog licked his hand in agreement.

* * * *

Oliver whined, waking Lester. The dog sat at the door, facing the old man. The entire day had disappeared and the murk of twilight painted the world inside and out. "What happened, Ollie?" The dog padded over, sat, pawed the man's knee. "Yes, yes," Lester said, rising from his chair in cracks and pops of sinew, "I'm sorry." He turned on the small lamp by the door and the porch light, but before he let the dog out, he remembered the waste outside.

The dog scratched the door. "Come on, Ollie, let's go in the back."

The dog turned to Lester. He whined and yipped.

"No, Ollie! This way. Come, come."

The dog hung his head, stretched prostrate on the floor.

"Damnit, Oliver."

Lester looked out of a front window. It was difficult for him to determine the state of the world outside, the glare of the porchlight too bright to see beyond into the heavy murk. The dog released a sorrowful sound, then stood, going to the door.

Lester looked at his companion. "Don't leave me."

Oliver barked, wagged his tail.

Lester opened the door and the dog trotted out, lifting his leg at his preferred spot adjacent to the step, then made his rounds.

"All right," Lester said, with a little relief. But as his eyes adjusted, he perceived that creation had only disintegrated further. The block was covered in flecks of the world like a layer of grimy snow, but the night sky above was clear and calm. And dark, absent of heavenly bodies. Other houses had their lights on, but to Lester they seemed like paper lanterns, disposable. The brick and vinyl under the gloom was worse, rotten, thinned like worn-out fabric. He looked at his own house. It was solid, complete.

Oliver plowed through the tattered ephemera, sniffing, gleaning information.

"That's good, Ollie. Come in, now." Lester's voice echoed back off the hollow dwellings lining his street.

Oliver was excited by a rustling in the hedge. He howled and shot his head into the dry foliage, drawing out a rodent in his teeth, shaking it furiously so that bits of it speckled the air. He laid it before his master—a greasy paper sack, knotted by secret forces.

"This is uncalled for," Lester shouted. Oliver put his tail between his legs, but Lester was speaking to God, or Death, or Nature. Man and dog went inside.

Lester turned on the digital radio, expecting to hear static, or nothing at all, but it was the evening music program after the nightly headlines. Viewing the radio's display, he saw it was much later than he presumed, even the local news had passed into late-night talk.

In his chair, with his back to the window, he felt safe. He didn't want to leave the room. That Oliver was unaffected should have been a comfort, but he was merely a beast. Not merely; he was a beast, unlike the human animal, and knew and did not know certain, intricate details of existence.

Lester's bladder was full, drop by drop collected over half a day. When he couldn't take the pressure any longer, he crept to the bathroom, bent more so with the abdominal strain. He relieved himself—sitting as usual because his prostate wouldn't allow for anyway else—beneath yellow incandescent light fixtures. Tiny insects clinked between the lamp and bulb, blinded by the sudden light, yet yearning for it. Lester knew they were only little pills of paper and he hoped they wouldn't ignite, incinerate the last real thing remaining.

The dog trailed him, waited at the doorframe with care. "Well, Oliver, I'm going to lay down now." He looked at himself in the mirror. There was nothing else to do: he wasn't tired, he wasn't hungry. "I hope I see you in the morning." He said the words to the dog every night, but this night, they sounded more true. Tears welled in the old man's eyes and Oliver snorted.

But Lester didn't lay down. He sat on the edge of his bed, watching the black birds in his tree. There was a flock now, a murder. Birds that were not birds, not even animals. He could see their eyes and beaks. They hopped from branch to branch, silent except for the snap of their wings. In the sky beyond the tree he could see the silhouettes of other birds, of bats and insects drift past in clumsy, roiling patterns. More trash.

The next morning, Lester woke without realizing he had fallen asleep. He was dressed, curled on top of the covers. After decades of reading the sunlight on the ceiling, he knew it was around 8am. Oliver should have woken him by then. He called for the dog and he trotted in happily. He scratched behind the dog's ears. "You let me sleep." He stretched, as best his body would allow. He asked his companion, "Did you make a mess?" But he knew better, the dog was worriless.

Outside, Oliver was unfazed by the accumulation of clutter, but Lester was awestruck. Straw wrappers, cup lids, receipts, envelopes, flyers, business cards, chip bags, voided checks, sandwich baggies, surgical masks—it was everywhere. And not just the trash. The entire world was flaking away, shard by shard. The houses on the block were peeled back in brittle strips, their windows warped and cracked. The automobiles alongside the crumbly sidewalks were tarnished and rusted. Everything smelled bitter. He was frightened to see another human, but when he examined himself, he was still fleshy and flush, if worn out in his own way.

He waited. He stepped onto the litter, stood beneath a cloudless sky. There was little sound: no traffic, no wind, only the rustle of the waste itself and Oliver's fresh study of it. Lester crossed his yard to the sidewalk and stood. He moved up the sidewalk stopping in front of his neighbor's house. "Come, Ollie," he called. Oliver looked up, ears perked. Lester patted his knees and the dog's ears went flat—he cautiously walked out of the yard, sided up to his master.

They walked to the hill, which was a rubbish heap, a landfill. The empty boulevard at the bottom was like some polluted river. No, a dry riverbed layered in whorls of debris. Further, beyond the empty, collapsing McDonalds, he could see the park and the lake, plastic and paper skimming the surface in place of ducks and geese.

Lester rubbed the loose skin on the back of Oliver's neck between with his thumb and forefinger. "What is it, Ollie? What happened?"

The dog panted, then yelped his remarks. Lester couldn't agree or disagree.

They walked the opposite direction, past their home a few blocks to another main street. It was the same; not dead, but lifeless, everything a leftover, a line of dust at the edge of a dust pan.

Lester was going to knock on his neighbor's door, but what did it matter? He went to the most immediate house instead and knocked, afraid the door would collapse under his frail fist; it shook like cardboard and felt the same. "Hello?" He rapped on a window. The glass was firm but not hard—more congealed—and made almost no sound.

They crossed the dirty street into another neighborhood, walked to the park there. The grass reminded him of carpet remnants, uneven patches of faded color assembled in odd arrangement. All of it spotted with litter. In the trees, the avian watchers: white, brown and black plastic grocery bags. Even in the daylight, if he didn't look at them directly, Lester could sense their eyes and beaks. He surmised they were birds of prey or carrion birds.

Fatigued, perhaps in shock, Lester sat on a splintered park bench. "What do we do now, my boy?" Oliver yipped, wagged his tail, snarled playfully. Lester corrected himself, "What do I do?"

The dog trotted under the bench behind his master. Lester, stiff, rotated to his right, leveraging his hands on the cracked wood. He could barely discern Oliver's head bent low. He put his hands on the back of the bench, pulled himself around so his posterior barely clung to the seat. Oliver sniffed from puddle to puddle, thirsty, except the puddles were scraps of bubble wrap.

"Ollie, no! Come, Oliver!"

The dog looked back impassively, continued on.

Beyond the dog, at the far edge of the park, a line of translucent figures drifted down the street behind a wind break of evergreens. Lester could tell they were plastic garment bags, the thin sort used by dry cleaners, yet they held vague human form and paraded as mourners.

"Oliver!" Lester called, taking to his feet. The dog ignored him completely, furthered his distance. Lester groaned, shuffling across the expanse of trash toward the animal, straining his eyes and neck to look forward. "No," he begged. The broader the gap became, the more supplicant his muttering.

In no time, Oliver joined the throng of plastic shrouds, obeying their silent commands. He heeled at their side, appearing blurred through the billowing window of their gowns. Lester's face ran with tears and snot. His mouth brimming with moisture, he cried, "Please, Ollie."

The dog stopped and looked around, tail between his legs. Lester gathered his waning essence, galloped in pained micro-steps to the row of trees and stood in the stale shade of the cardboard armatures covered in needles of dingy felt and dust.

"Oliver." Lester approached the far curb, wiping his face with the anger of shame. He commanded the animal, "Stay."

The dog whined, put his head to the ground. Likewise, the garment bags halted, suspended as if captured in a photograph.

"Now," Lester began, attempting to call the dog over. Instead, Oliver rolled on his back in submission. The old man hobbled off the curb and stooped to rub the animal's belly. Oliver's tongue lolled to the side of his mouth, one of his legs trembled in contentment.

When he was finished, Lester stood; it was the first time in over a decade his posture was aligned. "Well," he said, confidently. As though he were a puppy, Oliver sprang to his feet and bound to the spectral plastic. "Let us commence," Lester declared. And he began to drift.

JULIET'S MOON
by D.C. Lozar

"Wake up, Juliet."

The Moon's voice was feather soft inside her mind. She moaned and rolled over, hoping he would go away. She knew he wouldn't.

He never did.

"There was a young boy at the party. He liked you."

Juliet knew the boy. He was a Montague.

"He's hiding in the bushes beneath your window. Come look."

She squeezed her eyes shut. She wanted nothing to do with the boy. He had cornered her behind a pillar. He had snuck his hand up her skirt and stolen a kiss before she broke free. Even then, he would have pursued her if Tybalt hadn't interceded. "He's not there. I saw him run from my father's men."

"He is a boy in love. He will not rest until you are his."

Juliet shook her head and mumbled into her pillow. "Stop talking to me. You're not real."

"Because your nurse said so? Because she's scared people will think you're sick." There was a hint of anger in the Moon's voice. "I warned you about the arrangement your Father struck with Count Paris. How would I know you were to be engaged if I weren't real?"

"He's old," complained Juliet, "and he has a wart on his chin the size of a thumb."

"He's royalty. Don't you want to be a princess?"

"Shut up," begged Juliet. "Just let me sleep."

"If I'm wrong about Romeo, I swear to be silent until morning."

Rubbing sleep from her eyes, Juliet rolled out of bed. The floor was cold beneath her bare feet. "Will you protect me from the Count?"

"Do you love me?"

Juliet pulled a shawl over her shoulders as she moved to the balcony. The Moon never lied to her, never made her do things she didn't like, and he always listened to her complaints. They were friends, good friends, but how could she love him? He lived in the sky, while she was a prisoner inside her father's home. The Moon was powerful and free. She was a trinket, a bargaining chip to be given away or fought over. They were from different worlds. "I'm just a girl."

"You drive men insane with your beauty. Your heart is as innocent as it is strong. Tell me you love me, Juliet. Tell me, and I will free you from the chains of men. I will make you immortal."

As she stepped out through the patio doors and onto the veranda, his magical light washed over her. He knew her, loved her, and the distance that separated them meant nothing as long as they could see and talk to one another. "I do love you."

"I knew it." Searching hands closed over her shoulders from behind. The voice was coarse and young. It was Romeo. "I knew you felt the same way."

"No," Juliet's protest failed to escaped the calloused hand he lay over her mouth. She tried to scream but couldn't breathe.

Romeo's embrace crushed her chest.

She pulled and twisted. She tried to inhale, but only a thin trickle of air entered her lungs.

"I told you he wanted you," whispered the Moon from the shadows. "I told you, he was hiding."

Romeo's hot tongue caressed her neck. His lips sucked desperately at her tender flesh.

Juliet's vision blurred. Her heartbeat echoed in her ears. She stamped her bare foot down on Romeo's boot, and gulped as his grip lessoned. "Help me."

Romeo laughed and pulled her closer, his teeth nibbling her ear lobe. "I'll help myself."

"I need to know you love me. I need proof," hissed the Moon so softly that Juliet had to strain to hear. "What is your freedom worth?"

Juliet stared up at the sky, at her Moon, and croaked, "anything. I swear I love you, and I will do whatever you ask of me."

"So be it," answered the Moon.

"So be it," said Romeo.

"Juliet," came the formidable voice of her nurse from the bedroom. "Juliet. I heard voices."

Romeo's arms unraveled, and he vaulted over the parapet and disappeared into the underbrush.

Juliet fell to her knees, gasping.

"Go see Friar Laurence tomorrow," commanded the Moon. "Spy on him from behind the hay barrels in his apothecary. Remember as my lover, you are not bound by the rules of men. Marry, kill, plot, or deceive, the weird sisters are now your family."

"Why are you out of bed?" The nurse's search brought her to the balcony. "My dear, what's wrong? Are you sick?"

"I can't breathe."

"Come away from the draft. I fear the party was too exciting for one as delicate as you." The nurse helped Juliet to her feet. "Still, you do need to practice. The Count will expect you to entertain his guests once you're married."

"He has a wart," whined Juliet.

"If men were perfect, what purpose would women serve?"

* * * *

Juliet's arms and legs itched from the hay, but she refused to move. She had promised to do whatever the Moon asked.

Unaware of her, the friar crushed herbs at his desk while humming an inanely simple tune. Thinking he was alone, the burly cleric passed gas and scratched in places that made Juliet avert her eyes.

"Friar!" The voice came from the door. It was familiar and demanding. "Friar Laurence. Are you within?"

The friar took a pinch of the powder before him and inhaled it into his nose before brushing the rest into a small claw bowel with a knife. "Who is it?"

"Count Paris. Open this door."

Suddenly on his feet, the friar hurried to unlatch the wooden door. "My Count, this is an unexpected surprise. Welcome."

"I need a potion." Paris was a powerful man, broad of shoulder and stature, but his appetite for fine food had left him with a rotund belly that all but negated his heroic charm. "Immediately."

Friar Laurence's beady eyes locked on the wart, a hairy bulbous growth, upon his master's chin. "It is too large for a poultice."

"What?"

The friar wiped his knife against his dirty robes as he advanced. "There will be blood, I fear, and a sizeable scar."

The Count put up his hands. "Not that, naive. I need a love potion, something that will make me irresistible."

Disappointed, the friar nodded. This was not the first time a man had come to him with such a request. "I have just the thing."

Annoyed, the Count paced. His steps carried him dangerously close to Juliet's hiding place. "It irks me to make the request, but I know without it I am lost. I fear it is my appearance, the whole of who I am, that conspires against my heart's desire."

"To be a man, is to be a beast in human attire. Would that the world did not dress us in the finery of civilization so that we might explore the flesh that is our right."

"Well said," agreed the Count, regarding his conspirator with renewed respect. "I had taken thee for a fool but perhaps I misjudged."

"The slight is undone." Friar Laurence placed a silver flask in the Count's hands. "As no man knows the struggles of a fellow as well as one who is equally afflicted."

"You lust for another? Are you not a man of the cloth?"

"Are you not one of the state? We are wolves cloaked in the skins of sheep. Should we not help our pack brothers when we recognize their scent?"

"Truly, you know me." The Count's voice shook with appreciation as he held up the silver flask. "It is with thy help, thy magic elixir, that I will feast upon my prey. Would not that I could take a bite for thee in gratitude."

"It is my duty to serve," bowed the friar, "and hope the Count finds my skill worthy of his continued patronage."

A knock came at the door.

Both men froze.

Then, silently, the friar motioned for Paris to follow him to a hidden exit door at the back of the room.

"One moment," he called out to his waiting patron.

From her hiding place, Juliet bit her lip as she glared at the flask in her betrothed hand. Her father had given her body away, but the Count wanted her heart. If she drank the friar's potion, she would fall madly in love with Paris and forget her beautiful Moon.

She could not allow that to happen.

The knock came again, louder and more desperate.

"I'm coming," assured the friar as he moved to unlatch the door for a second time. "Time be no man's friend, and thus wise are those who give it away for free. Be patient."

"How can I be such when my heart is in my hands," complained Romeo as he burst past the friar. He wore the same clothes as the night before and his face was a mask of fatigue and desperate desire. "I need a potion."

"A love elixir," sighed the friar, his shoulder slumping. "Alas, I gave away the last but moments ago."

"The mother's milk of cowards." Romeo spat into the straw. "No. I need a sleeping draft, something to sedate the conscious gatekeeper of my woman's heart so that I might freely explore her body."

Friar Laurence nodded appreciatively. "Indeed, it is a shrewd man who tastes the apple before he buys the bushel."

"Well said," agreed Romeo as he strode anxiously about the room. "Better still, if the apple knows not that it has been bitten."

"Any man of herbs could give thee as much. No, my squire, for you I have something more." The friar opened the bottom draw in his mahogany apothecary and retrieved a pewter flask. "With this, she will appear as one of the dead while her mind remains wholly awake. The fruit of thy desire will know your fiery embrace, will remember your voice, but will be made toothless to impede your assault."

"A miracle for any man." Romeo snatched the elixir from his mentor's hands. "Truly, you are cupid incarnate. My heart withdraws into my chest knowing it will feed on the flesh of my dear Juliet."

"Juliet," said the friar, perplexed. "The woman the Capulets keep locked in the east tower? You saw her?"

"She was at the ball last night. She professed her love for me."

"You are mistaken, young Sir." Friar Laurence shook his head. "That woman is thy elder by an eon at least. Perhaps, it was another who gave you a false name?"

"To be sure, she wore a mask at the ball and my night vision is poor." Romeo hesitated. "But when I stole into her room at night, her body was tense and strong beneath me."

"She consented to thy touch?"

"That and more. She vowed to me her undying love."

"Never to a mortal man!" Juliet rose from her hiding place, her face flushed with rage. "I am promised to the Moon."

Leaping back, the men saw a wrath dressed in tattered black addressing them from the shadows. It's eyes burned with crimson hate.

"A witch," exclaimed Romeo, reaching for his blade.

"A demon," agreed Friar Laurence, his voice trembling with fear. "Stay your hand, squire. No earthly metal may pierce the flesh of one such as this. We must deal in words and promises if we hope to preserve our souls."

Juliet laughed, a cackle that echoed harshly in the small room. "What souls? You are men, are you not?"

"Juliet?" The friar's voice caught in his throat. "Be you mortal flesh or phantasm? Reveal yourself."

Stepping into the light, her face rigid with condemnation, Juliet faced them.

"Are you one of the weird sisters?" Romeo squinted at Juliet.

"Know me not?" Juliet scowled at the boy who had stolen her first kiss. "For sooth, a moment ago you professed your love."

"No!" Recognition dawned on Romeo, and he shuddered with revolution. "You are not my Juliet. You are a hag."

"I am four and ten years of age, fresh and ripe as a morning plum." She turned her body to the side so that the men could appreciate her profile. "I am the most beautiful girl in all of fair Verona."

"Forty years ago," added Friar Laurence under his breath. Leaning over, he whispered to Romeo. "A brick fell from the battlements and cracked her skull so that she has, for all this time, not aged a day in her mind while one would be hard pressed to say the same of her body."

"As you said, time is no man's friend," said Romeo looking away from Juliet's insistent posing, "while it is every woman's enemy."

"I will not drink it," said Juliet through clenched teeth. "I will not fall for your trickery."

"I give it back," said Romeo, returning the flask to the friar. "I beg we forget all that has happened."

"How could I forget last night?" Juliet strode to Romeo's side, her body tense with indignation. "You came to my chambers. You forced yourself on me."

"Young sir!" The friar took a step back, disgusted. "I will help thee to woo a woman, even take one, who is your peer, but this? This is dark work."

"It's not like that," protested Romeo. "Nothing happened. We kissed. Nothing more."

"I will tell," threatened Juliet. "I will tell everyone what you did when we were alone. Do you think it right grab a maiden from behind, to squeeze her so hard she cannot object as you take what you want?"

"But, I didn't," said Romeo as he motioned for her to keep her voice down. "I love Rosaline, the sweet and innocent flower of my heart. This is a misunderstanding, a comedy of errors. Do you know what people would say if they thought we had been together?"

"Were you?" Friar Laurence raised a bushy eyebrow.

"No. No. I say again. No." Romeo dropped to his knees before Juliet. "For your silence, your discretion, I will give any boon you ask?"

Juliet remembered her Moon's words. "Marry me."

"What?" Both men exploded.

"Friar Laurence will bind us in marriage." Juliet's mind raced forward, seeing the steps, the silver path her Moon lover had lain before for her. "Fret not. We will keep it secret from all but one. When Count Paris demands my hand, I will direct him to our loyal friar who will confess to our matrimonial bound. The Count, not wishing to appear jilted, will then withdraw his proposal and leave me unmolested."

"But I'm a Montague, and you're a Capulet," protested Romeo as he climbed to his feet.

"All the better," agreed Juliet. "None will suspect our collusion."

"You are a witch."

"Perhaps, but every woman is that and more. I promise you, your Rosaline has secrets to match this one and more. Tell her nothing of our marriage, and I swear to hold my tongue."

Romeo shook his head and backed toward the door. "If I refuse?"

"You think me a enchantress, one of the sisters?" Juliet glared at him and raised her hands as if to caste a spell. "Mayhap I am. Shall we see?"

Romeo cringed, trapped. "You swear to tell no one?"

"I swear."

"I will not do it," objected the friar. "She is no witch and what she asks has naught to do with love."

"This sleeping draft," said Juliet, tearing the pewter flask from Friar Laurence's grasp, "has naught to do with love. Yet, you would have your squire use it on me?"

"He didn't know who you were."

"But, you do." She uncorked the flask and advanced on the friar. "Refuse me, and I will have you drink your own poison."

"You tickle me with a peacock's feather and expect that I should tremble?" Smirking, the friar crossed his arms over his rotund chest. "The draft would give me a night of paralysis, nothing more. Still, I refuse."

Romeo withdrew his sword and advanced on his mentor. Laying the point against the friar's throat, he said. "Remember, my old friend, that even the softest feather has two ends. I will have her silence. Marry us or say ado."

* * * *

Newly married, Juliet spent the day exploring the market. People treated her with respect, if not a little fear, and many knew her before she said a word. It was more fun than she had had in years, and she vowed to get out more in the future.

As dusk fell, she returned to her chambers through the secret passage that led to her room to find her nurse waiting for her on the other side.

"Where have you been?"

"Out."

"I know that, for you were not in," grumbled the woman. "For had you been in, I would not have torn my hair out. Listen my peach, much and more has passed today and far more of it than passing concerns you."

Juliet was carful to keep the pewter flask she had taken from Friar Laurence well concealed behind her back. She would use it on Count Paris if the Moon's plan failed. "Pray tell."

"A murder was done," said the nurse, wringing her hands. "Our fair Tybalt is no more."

Juliet gasped. Tybalt was one of the few people who cared for her. On the night of the dance, he had recognized Romeo and would have demanded the interloper's head had it not for her father's plea for peace. "Who? By whose wretched hand was this deed done."

"A Montague killed him in a street fight. A boy named Romeo."

"No!" Juliet's hands balled into fists. "It's impossible. Tybalt is more than a match for that boy."

"It was an ambush, two against one. Tybalt was caught unprepared, his back against a wall. He fought bravely but they wore him down. In the end, he killed Mercutio but his blade stuck in the man's body a moment too long. He was defenseless when Romeo stabbed him."

Juliet's mind burst into flames. She paced around the room. "The constables know it was him? They know Romeo was the one?"

"Yes," said the nurse solemnly.

"Then, the Prince will have him put to death." Juliet bit her lower lip and tasted blood. Why had Romeo fought? This was going to ruin everything. "They caught him?"

"They did, but Count Paris begged the Prince show mercy."

Juliet stared at the nurse, not believing her ears. "The Count did that? Why?"

"He said the feud between the Capulets and Montagues must end. Instead of death, he brokered a deal in which Romeo will be banished from Verona."

Juliet's heart sank. Romeo had sabotaged her plans to use him as a shied against Paris without breaking his vows to her. If he were exiled, there was little chance they could consummate their marriage, and so their union might easily be annulled. She sat down heavily on the bed. The boy was smarter than she guessed. "My life is over?"

"No, my precious heart, be not all gloom, for there is still a golden thread to follow out of the darkness. To lighten the mood, your father has moved up your nuptials to the Prince." The nurse took Juliet's hand and squeezed. "You are to be married tomorrow tonight."

"Tomorrow? I cannot," moaned Juliet. She needed more time to outsmart Romeo. "It's too soon after Tybalt."

"I know how much he meant to you, but you mustn't morn him. Your cousin wanted you to be happy. He would want you to continue."

"Leave me." Juliet's words were harsh, but she needed to be alone to talk to the Moon. "You have no idea what he would have wanted for me."

"My dear, there are things we need to discuss before…"

"Now!" Juliet rose from her bed and pointed at the door. "I wish to grieve."

Her nurse's lower lip hardened with defiance, but she saw the conviction in Juliet's eyes and decided this was not a battle she would win. Bowing, she left the room. "I am sorry, mistress. I will wake you early tomorrow."

Locking the door, Juliet went to her balcony and looked up into the evening sky. "You knew this would happen. You knew Tybalt would die."

"To be eternal, to join me among the stars, your story must be tragic."

Juliet savored the rays of her Moon before raising the friar's flask to her lips. There was only one way to escape her fate. "They will think I committed suicide."

"Thy dear cousin was very special to you. Why should they think anything else?"

* * * *

The hard marble bench made Juliet's bones ache to move, but she found the friar's draft unerringly potent. So much was she a prisoner of its power, none suspected her deception as they came to the crypt and bid her farewell.

The townspeople, despite having never known her, wept. Her parents cried. Her nurse wailed like a skinned cat. Count Paris swore never to marry for he said no woman could compare to the memory of his poor Juliet. As to Romeo, Juliet learned much from the gossip whispered over her dead body. The boy was locked in Count Paris's private dungeon and would be exiled on the morrow.

Juliet's heart smiled grimly. At least, the murderer would suffer some inconvenience for having killed Tybalt.

In all, it was a good death and an informative funeral.

That was until Friar Laurence leaned down to whisper in Juliet's ear. "I know you live, little witch, and you can hear me. You pretended to be a demoness, a student of the arts, and I trembled, I confess, before the fraud. But you are a mere mortal woman, a desperate child of clay, and I will not abide such slights as you have dealt me. You stole my sleeping elixir while I had a blade at my throat. So, know you this: When you awake, you will find a dagger in yours."

The friar's threat weighed heavily on Juliet, and so she fought boldly against the elixir's power. Even so, the most she could move were the tips of her fingers and toes.

Helpless, she waited. She waited in darkness, surrounded by the moist odor of decay, and listened to the soft skittering sounds of crypt vermin. She felt so cold, so dead.

The great-hinged door that led into her crypt screeched as powerful hands pulled it open. Footsteps on the damp marble stairs echoed about her chamber. Torchlight flickered crimson over her closed lids as the intruder approached her bench. His breath came quick and hard.

He was scared.

"Witchcraft and more I charge thee with," said Romeo into her ear, "while I beg thee, even still, to ply thy dark arts to free me from thy curse. I confess. I did conspire to murder Tybalt and in so doing I justly earned your wrath, but I fathomed not what horror it would take. I beg of you, fair

Juliet, wake from your false slumber and show mercy to one who knew not what it was to be vulnerable."

Thoughts and questions arched like lightening across Juliet's mind. Why had Romeo come? Had Count Paris banished the boy before first light? If so, why had the fool risked the hangman's noose to see her? Was he taunting her with the murder of her cousin? No. He was begging her forgiveness. He believed she had cursed him.

Fighting hard, Juliet forced open one eye in time to watch Romeo raise a small crystal vial to the torchlight. It held the seal of death upon its thin neck.

"With this sweet nectar, I will wipe away the memories and desires that even still haunt my waking mind. Ask I only that you absolve me of any wrong I did thee and grant me an eternal rest in which thy spell lays not upon my breast."

"Romeo? Sweet Romeo?" Count Paris's voice thundered down the crypt's stairs. "Why do you flee? Is this another game? Wherefore art thou, Romeo?"

"No!" Romeo broke off the top off the vial and drank the poison in one swallow. Unsheathing his sword, he stood ready. "I am no longer your prisoner, ghoul, pursue me no more unless it be through hell's open gate."

Count Paris entered the crypt with his sword drawn. "Perhaps it is the wine, or my accursed age, but I believe it was you who pursued me but scant hours ago?"

"I was not in my right mind," said Romeo. "A curse was placed upon my soul by this very witch. What I said and did were not my custom nor want. Forget all of it, I pray of thee, as I am bound to do."

"You do not love me?" Count Paris pouted. "You swore you did."

"No," spluttered Romeo as he shook his head. "It was the witch's curse."

"The dead hag?" Paris waved his sword in Juliet's direction and laughed. "She was but a pawn, a distraction, in our thirsty game of cat and mouse. In my care, did you not feed and drink as if you were a chained King?"

Juliet bent her arm slowly, raising it onto her chest. She flexed her calf muscles. Her paralysis was wearing off.

"I take not your meaning?"

"Your mentor, Friar Laurence, and I are well acquainted." Count Paris moved toward Romeo cautiously, his sword lowered. "Surely, as his squire and confidant, you know of his skills with herbs?"

"No." Romeo's complexion paled as the vial of poison did its work. "He knew of this?"

"He is wolf," gloated Paris. "Why should he care where his brother feeds so long as I am sated? Did not LyLy say, 'all is fair in love and war.'"

Finally, Juliet understood. The love potion in the silver flask had been meant for Romeo, not her.

"Come at me then," challenged Romeo, "and we will see how well you receive my love."

The clang of swordplay rang about the torch-lit chamber as Juliet rolled off the marble bench. Her body was sore and tight, but she forced it to hold her up so that she might see the fight.

Romeo's strength and anger should have surpassed whatever skill the Count retained from his youth, but the poison in his veins made the boy slow and careless. A cut across his chest and another to his cheek foretold how the battle would end. A deep wound to Romeo's leg put him on his knees.

Juliet rose from her hiding place, her face a ghostly visage, and pointed a trembling finger at the Count. "A hag's curse upon your house."

Shocked to see the dead rise, Paris raised his weapon.

Recognizing the opening, Romeo ran his sword through the older man's heart. "There now, you have found your Romeo, and with my blade, I kiss thee goodnight."

Count Paris collapsed to the ground, dead.

Juliet walked to where Romeo knelt. "Tis not the act, but the manner whereby love is attained. My Moon and I have never touched, but our souls are as one. If demons exist, they live in the flesh and so expire as we do. Die now, fair Romeo, at the feet of the woman who you so wronged. My curse is undone."

"As am I," whispered Romeo as he fell dead over the body of Count Paris.

The sounds of men, of swords drawn, approached the crypt from outside. "Who goes there? Who disturbs the dead?"

Juliet scanned the room. There was only one exit.

Silver moonlight, warm and inviting, painted the marble floor before her.

She knelt and touched it with her bare hands. "What must I do?"

"There is still time," answered her Moon from the shadows near the stairs. "Run, you can still escape if you hurry."

Obeying, Juliet ran for the door.

Friar Laurence rushed at her from the shadows to sink his dagger in her breast.

Standing back to avoid the blood spatter, he spoke. "I promised to free you from the chains of men, my sweet, and so I will."

Clutching the hilt of the knife, her mouth agape, Juliet stared at him.

He spoke with her Moon's voice. "I will make you immortal."

"This is the Prince, and I say again, who disturbs the dead."

Her life's blood spurting out, Juliet fell to the ground.

Stepping over her, blocking the moon's rays, the man who for years used the secret passage to her room to earn her love called out. "It is I, my liege, Friar Laurence."

"Pray tell why thou are in the crypt of the Capulets," demanded the voice from above.

"Come and see," answered the Moon.

Juliet's vision blackened even as her memory cleared. She reached for the moonlight and met only the heel of her first lover. It had been he who loosened the brick in a jealous rage, he whom she had spurned in her youth, and he who took up the cloth as penance.

The Prince and his guards burst into the crypt. "What manner of horror is this? Say at once!"

"A tragedy, my Lord, one that is far worse than any imagined," said Juliet's Moon. "A pair of star-crossed lovers…"

THE GARGOYLE'S WIFE
by Jean Graham

"I could kill him for you," the gargoyle said.

Ellen pulled her hand away, but stared hard into the statue's black glass eyes. "What did you say?" she whispered.

No response.

With a nervous glance at the antique store's owner, preoccupied behind the counter, she reached to touch the stone figurine again. And for a second time, a faint vibration crawled, spider-like, up her arm and murmured in her ear.

"Take me home, Ellen," it said.

"How…?"

She reclaimed her hand again and looked to be sure that the owner hadn't heard her say that out loud. He hadn't.

Too much wine after dinner last night, she thought. How else could a foot-tall chunk of black rock be speaking to me, even know my name?

And it wanted to kill Doug for her. Now that had to be the wine talking. Not that she hadn't considered killing him a time or two. Maybe three.

You know he starred in The Gargoyle's Wife, right? She mouthed the words without voicing them. *And that Mr. King of the Midnight B Movies is a lying, cheating son of a bitch?*

It—*he*—didn't answer. No doubt that the gargoyle was a he. Couldn't mistake him for anything else. Not with those bulging biceps, the six-pack chest, and oh, yeah—the anatomically correct genitalia. All of that, though, was topped by a snarling dragon's head, and its otherwise human shoulder blades sprouted two bone-ribbed, bat-like wings.

"Impressive, isn't he?"

The proprietor's question startled her. She hadn't heard him approach.

"Um… Yes, he is," she said, and hoped he hadn't noticed that her voice was quavering. "Is he… is *it*… very old?"

"Don't think so." The owner shook his head and scratched at his graying beard. "Just a copy of one of those things they used to hang on cathedrals to keep the evil spirits away."

"Gargoyles," she said.

"Yep. Ten bucks and he's yours."

Ellen could have sworn the statue's eyes flashed at that.

"Sold," she said, and paid the man. "Wrap it for me, would you?"

* * * *

Doug wasn't home. Not that she'd expected he would be. The world's self-styled greatest actor would claim, if he showed up at all, that the film shoot had run over, they'd needed extra takes, he'd had to do more voice loops, whatever. Yeah. Right.

"Bastard," Ellen muttered as she carried her bundle through the double front doors and into the cavernous foyer. "The only extra take he's getting is screwing the latest script girl out in his damned dressing trailer."

The package under her arm sent a tingling vibration up through her arm and shoulder to her ear. "Told you I could kill him for you," it said.

"Uh-huh." She began tearing the butcher paper from the statue's head. "I'll think about it."

Once she'd ripped the rest of the paper away, Ellen carried her acquisition across the mosaic-tiled floor to the foot of the massive staircase, and sat the gargoyle down on a white marble plinth to the left of the banister.

"There. You look a damn sight better than the dead plant that used to be here. And oh, by the way…" She swept both hands upward to the corbeled and chandeliered ceiling. "Welcome to movie star Doug Marlowe's Malibu monstrosity. It's an exact replica of the plantation manor house in *Nashville Zombie Apocalypse*." She crouched to peer into the figurine's black, faceted eyes. "Not exactly an epic film. In fact, it sucks. But then, all of Doug's movies suck, including *The Gargoyle's Wife*. Something tells me you might like that one, though."

She pressed a hand to the statue's base and waited for a vibration, but apparently it had no opinion on the Doug Marlowe movie suckability factor.

"Okay." She wadded up the shopkeeper's butcher paper and tucked it back under one arm. "Time for my solo microwave dinner and a glass of sherry before bed—which is, of course, also solo."

She'd never heard him come in, but when Ellen came down the back stairs the next morning, Doug was at the kitchen table, wolfing down corn flakes and black coffee. From the state of his uncombed hair, baggy eyes and rumpled clothes, he hadn't spent much time sleeping the night before.

"Must have been one hell of a script girl," she sniped, pouring herself a cup of coffee and sitting down across the table from him.

He gave her a self-satisfied smirk and swallowed a mouthful of flakes before replying. "You know it's effing June, right?" he said. And when Ellen widened her eyes in a "huh?" expression, he added, "So what's with the stupid Halloween crap in the foyer?"

"Gargoyle," she amended, and sipped her coffee before going on. "Sort of looks like the one you played in *The Gargoyle's Wife*, don't you think?"

He made a sneering face that indicated he clearly did not.

"I wandered into an antique shop after my aerobics class today, and it just sort of said, 'Take me home, Ellen.' So I did. What's the matter? Don't you like him?"

"Nope." Another gob of corn flakes went down his famous movie star gullet, this time unchewed. Whenever he swallowed, Doug's adam's apple moved up and down like a rat under a blanket. She'd always hated that. "But hey," he went on, "whatever blows your skirt up, sweetheart. Just put it somewhere I don't have to look at it, will ya?"

The word "sweetheart" had been delivered with a rictus of contempt and no trace of anything remotely resembling affection. Ellen opened her mouth to say that she'd put the gargoyle any damned place she pleased, but Doug derailed her by noisily scraping back in his chair and getting up to clatter his bowl, cup and spoon down into the sink with enough force to chip the china. Then he stalked out, mumbling something about a seven a.m. make-up call.

"Well, screw you, too," she said after he'd banged the back door open and shut. She flipped him off in absentia, put her own cup in the sink, and headed back to the foyer to visit her purchase.

It looked… well, changed somehow, as though its dragon wings and those muscular arms had flexed and repositioned themselves during the night.

Hm.

"Stretching a bit, were we?" she wondered out loud. No answer to that, even though she pressed the palm of her hand against that magnificent chest and waited. Finally, she asked it a somewhat more pertinent question.

"Just how exactly would you kill him? I mean—no offense—you're nothing but a chunk of carved black rock. How could you possibly…?"

She trailed off, feeling suddenly stupid for having asked. But just when she'd been about to reclaim her hand and walk away, the now-familiar vibration crept into her fingers and traveled up her arm.

"There are many ways," the rasping voice replied. "Place me at the top of a stairway in the dark. Prop me over a door or high on a window sill. Many, many ways."

Ellen took a deep breath. "Okay, so I can't say I've never thought about killing him. But I always wind up deciding that a divorce would be a heck of a lot easier. 'Former model divorces B movie actor' sounds like a much better headline to me than 'Former model gets 25 years to life for murdering husband,' don't ya think?"

"But a divorce," the gargoyle rasped, "would leave you with nothing. May not have been such a wise decision, signing that pre-nup."

"How the hell did you know...?" An abrupt surge of anger made Ellen snatch her hand away, only to put it back by grasping the statue by the clawed feet at its base. "I really have to think about this more," she said. "A lot more. And you know something? I don't think I should leave you down here while I do it."

She stashed it away in an upstairs closet—the one in the bedroom she was sleeping in—and decided it could stay there, out of both sight and mind, for the time being.

She needed time to think.

It took her nearly three weeks to reach a resolution. They'd been three weeks full of aerobics, long walks and shopping sprees, but had also been weeks marred by more infidelity (three new script girls), and when Doug came home at all, nothing but silent, cold indifference.

"I'm considering filing for a divorce," she told him flat out when, for the first time in a month, they again shared a breakfast table.

"Uh-huh." Corn flakes already devoured, he was nose deep in his tablet's on-line sports page, clearly not listening to her at all.

Ellen reached across to grab the top edge of the tablet and slammed it aggressively down onto the tabletop.

"I *said*..." She over-enunciated each word distinctly. "...I want a divorce."

He glared, snatched the tablet back up again, and apparently satisfied that it was still operational, grunted a single word in reply.

"No."

"I don't need your permission, Doug. I don't even need your signature on the decree. Not in California."

He lowered the tablet on his own this time, and gave her a seething look. "No," he repeated. "The tabloids already have enough dirt on me. I won't have an ex-wife adding more fuel to the fire. So, no."

She laughed. "Nobody cares about that sort of stuff anymore."

"I do. Producers are a bunch of arch-conservative old geezers who still care, too. With a divorce on my résumé, I may never get another lead role in anything."

Ellen snorted. "Oh, dream on, Mr. B movie has-been. You're not getting any lead roles now."

"Shut up!" He sprayed the table with spit when he shouted it. "Just shut up and get the hell out of here!"

"No." She echoed the same intonation he'd used on the word a moment earlier. "I'm filing. Tomorrow. And there's not a damned thing you can do to stop me."

"No? I think there is." He punched the tablet with a knuckle, turning it off. "It's pretty hard to file anything if you're effing dead."

Ellen's "what?" got stuck in her throat, and before she could dislodge it, Doug had again exercised his favorite tactic of ending an argument by storming out of the room.

Ellen sat staring at the doorway he'd gone through for a long, long time.

"Okay," she eventually said aloud to no one in particular. "I guess I've thought about it long enough."

* * * *

The gargoyle's wings had moved.

When Ellen pulled the black statue from the closet, she was sure of it. No longer held high and folded close together above his head, the wings were now outstretched, as though he might take flight on a moment's notice.

"Not much of anywhere to fly inside a closet, is there?" she said, and put him down on the bedside lamp table. She ran her fingers across the now open wings. "How do you *do* that?"

"So…" The vibration tingled up through her fingers, but instead of answering her question, said, "You've finally made up your mind, have you?"

"All right, yes. I want the asshole gone."

"Dead and gone?"

"Yes. No… I mean…" Ellen's determination faltered. "I don't know! I've never…" She had to force the word out. "…killed… anyone before. Or even helped to do it. Either way, I don't think I can, even if the piece of crap does deserve it."

"M-hm," said the gargoyle. "Well then, if death is a little too permanent a solution for you, perhaps we can devise an alternative arrangement."

Ellen blinked at that, confused. "A what?"

"How would you like…" And here, the grimacing stone teeth stretched into a wicked grin. "…to become *my* wife?"

* * * *

They waited in Doug's bed.

"Used to be *our* bed," Ellen grumbled as she crawled in on what used to be her side and propped the gargoyle up against Doug's pillow. "Used to be our room, our house, our marriage. Now it's all about nothing but *him*, the son of a bitch."

She stabbed an angry finger at the remote on the bedside table. It turned off the only-slightly-less-gaudy-than-the-foyer chandelier and left the room pitch dark.

Suited her mood.

"He may not come home tonight at all, you know," she said, then squirmed herself into a comfortable position and decided she might as well doze for awhile. Nothing else to do.

The sound of the bedroom door opening woke her. Ellen sat up, expecting the lights to come back on. But instead, heavy footsteps tramped across the hardwood floor to the bathroom. He went in and closed the door. Doug always closed the bathroom door, even when he was (or in this case, thought he was) alone. For years, that had made Ellen wonder what the heck he spent so much time doing in there...

A thin bar of bright light appeared where the door didn't quite meet the hardwood. She listened to the sound of urine splashing into the toilet bowl, then a flush, and running water as the sink tap came on.

It occurred to Ellen then that he might just leave the room lights off and expect to get into bed in the dark.

And that wouldn't do at all.

She fumbled in the dark for the remote, found it, and pushed the button, squinting in the sudden glare when the chandelier lit up and flooded the room with light again.

Less than half a minute later, Doug opened the bathroom door.

He was, no surprise, stark naked. Doug, vainly proud of his physique, never wore pajamas. When he saw Ellen and her macabre bed-mate, his face—and much of the rest of him—turned an ugly shade of red.

"What the hell...?"

"Welcome home, *darling*," Ellen said sweetly. "We've been waiting for you."

"Very funny." He stalked over to her side of the bed and snatched back the covers. "Now get out. And take that... that *thing* with you."

When she didn't move to comply, he grabbed her roughly by one arm and hauled her to her feet, shoving her hard against the lamp table.

"Ow!" She tried to shove him back, but couldn't budge him. "Damn you!" She pounded his bare chest with her fists and screamed the words at him. "Damn you, damn you, damn you!"

He grabbed her wrists in a bruising grip, shook her and pulled her away from the table, only to slam her into the wall.

"I told you to get the hell out!" He was bellowing now. "And take this hunk of garbage with you!"

He reached across the bed for the gargoyle, snagged it by the ankles and started to shove it into her arms. But when Ellen shrieked an obscenity at him, he shifted his grip on the statue and lifted it with one hand above his head, on the brink of striking her with it when...

The statue moved.

Wings and claws splayed out and then immediately wrapped themselves around Doug's raised arm, clutching, digging into soft flesh, drawing blood.

Doug screamed.

He stumbled backward, desperately trying to shake the thing loose. Blood spattered the carpet, the pillows, the bed spread. The gargoyle did not relent. Its dragon teeth clamped down on his wrist, evoking a howl of pain and a loud *crack* as he tried to smash the statue against a bed post. At once, the teeth and claws dislodged themselves and the gargoyle flew free of him for a moment.

But only for a moment.

It flew straight back at him and this time flattened itself on his chest, making a hideous sucking noise that made Ellen's stomach churn. Doug tried feebly to pry it away again, but abruptly abandoned the effort, stopped struggling and went oddly stiff. His arms dropped. The sucking noise continued for a few more seconds, then ceased, and Ellen watched in horrified fascination as Doug's eyes morphed from blue to shining, obsidian black.

The gargoyle's wings flexed once, twice, and it drew back as though preparing to take flight. It didn't, though. Doug's right hand rose slowly to grasp the thing by its waist and he held it outstretched in front of him. It writhed, and began to reshape itself in his hand. Stone crackled as it reassumed its former pose, and as it froze once more into place, Ellen could have sworn she heard a final, anguished *skreek* of protest.

But then naked Doug, his eyes blue again with just a hint of deep-down ebony, was standing in front of her, proffering the no-longer-moving statue.

"Hello, darling," he said in a sonorously deep voice that wasn't Doug's at all. "This thing really ought to go back into the closet, don't you think?"

Ellen took the statue. It seemed lighter and wasn't, she noted, nearly as well-endowed as it had been before.

Doug, on the other hand…

The gargoyle's wife smiled.

"I do," she said.

THE MELTING MAN
by Justin Boote

Kevin Dodson cast a quick, sly look around. This was the critical moment; only thirty seconds till arrival. To his left; a family of four. This was dangerous; the kids would surely beat him to it. To his right; an elderly couple-worse yet. The place was filling up quickly, he had to make a decision. With a sniper's eagle eye, he spotted a place with no evident danger, and dashed for it, just as the train pulled in.

Now, using all his cunning, and wits, he scanned the train. It was make or break time. A mad sprint further ahead, or trust his instincts, and a certain dose of luck? The train stopped. He'd already positioned himself, so that he would be directly in front of the door when it opened. His options were good, but there was still one final decision; left, or right?

No time to think. Left it was. Not being a situation to allow for good manners, he barged past the couple stepping off, and took a direct path to the empty seat. He would have hurdled over the seats if he thought he could get away with it, but fortunately, his faithful sense of judgement rendered it unnecessary,

He'd made it. A sigh of relief, another job well done. He grinned, and silently chuckled as he watched the other passengers cast wicked glances around the wagon looking for a seat. Some blatantly barging past others, others with a look of resignation on their faces as they faced another journey standing up.

Ninety percent of the time, he would prefer to stand on the thirty- minute journey to work, or if his intuition indicated little danger, perhaps sit next to Another Human Being. Depending on the state of said Human Being of course. The consequences could be catastrophic.

He knew he was not the lone member of this particular tribe. It was a global phenomenon played out by millions every single day and night, regardless of nationality. It might even have a name; the Please Pretend I'm Not Here syndrome. The trick consisted in finding an available seat on the bus or train, and avoid one of several things; A) the person next to you/opposite wasn't drunk, mad, or stunk to high Heaven, or B) the person next to you/opposite was not going to act as though you were a life-long friend and engage you in pointless conversation, which usually revolved around *their* whole life, not yours. Elderly people were particularly vicious in this field, and generally it was easier to be fooled by their harmless aspect. A drunk or nutter was easier to spot, and thus, evasive action could be taken.

By using the tried and tested trick of ignoring everyone by burying one's head in the smart phone or book worked ninety-five percent of the time, but, there was always that one person who failed to understand the hint; Leave Me Alone. I Don't Want To Talk To You. But for now, he was safe.

The train pulled into the next station; Belton. He watched as the same scenario was played out; people positioning themselves strategically to gain tactical advantage over available seats; others ignorant, lost in their cell phones. What interested Kevin was anyone of dubious character; the person opposite him had risen which meant there was a free seat.

"Oh no. Please no," he mumbled. Despite the air conditioning, a screen of sweat appeared instantaneously on his forehead. He stared at the floor as though something extremely interesting had caught his attention, yet one eye casting quick glances to his left. A Potential Nutter was boarding the train, and Sod's Law dictated that he would inevitably sit opposite him. It was mathematical. Be where thee may be, He will find you, and totally, utterly, fuck up your day until you manage to escape.

His premonition was confirmed.

It was summer-not scorching (in Bradwell, on the east coast of England it never was), but enough to require only a t-shirt to cover one's chest. The man now ominously approaching was dressed for an Arctic winter. Thick, dark green trousers covered his legs and a black jacket that would protect anyone from the most ferocious of storms. The jacket's hood was set firmly on his head, and as if to reinforce his evident allergy to the sun, a baseball cap sat underneath it. His face was almost indistinguishable; giant, black glasses covered most of it, showing only the tell-tale signs of a hardened alcoholic; red veins criss-crossing his nose and cheeks, the skin thick and leathery. To complete the disguise (of what, Kevin could not even begin to fathom), enormous headphones covered his ears, bound together with intricate and copious layers of electrical tape, giving the impression of someone who has a desperate need for music as they roamed town, yet not the finances to buy new ones. The heavy boots he was wearing however, indicated otherwise.

Kevin pretended to look out the window, but was in fact watching the guy in the reflection as his worst fears came true. He shuffled to the free seat-as though suffering serious bowel problems-and sank onto it. Kevin's heart speeded up. Time to think quickly again (he'd woke up late, and had forgotten to grab both his cell phone, or a book to read on the journey to work. His boss at the restaurant he worked at was not sympathetic to his staff arriving late).

The other two passengers in their little cubicle rose instantly, and left. No-one occupied the free space.

Ignorance. This was his only escape route. Pretend he hadn't seen the guy.

"Morning," said Weird Guy.

Shit.

Kevin jerked his head, and looked at the guy, pretending he was seeing him for the first time. He offered a feeble smile, and turned to look out the window again.

"Nice day, isn't it?"

Shit. Shit!

This was how it always started. An irrelevant comment about the weather, then things would slowly, and terrifyingly progress to the stranger's current torment; perhaps, if things went really well, Stranger might even like to discuss his latest ailment, or maybe how sad and lonely he was because his great-great grandmother had just died (full details included), and he didn't know how he was going to manage all on his own. The victim-in this case Kevin-would then have no choice but to offer full sympathies, show pity at all the right moments, and then become even more nervous at trying to think of something to say which wouldn't sound patronizing, or even worse, something that would give cause for further discussion; maybe a brief comment about he had also lost a relative recently and understood completely. An invitation.

"Yes. Fine day indeed," he said, now using all his artillery to appear distant and uninterested, but inside, he was feeling very nervous. The guy could be a damn nutter; say the wrong thing, might fucking stab you. And besides, if it's such a nice day, why are you dressed as though the next Ice Age was upon us?

Kevin could tell from the reflection in the window that Weird Guy was staring at him. What could he be thinking? That Kevin was deliberately ignoring him, and thus, should be kicked repeatedly in the head? Or was he thinking of something to spark a conversation? It was another twenty minutes before Kevin arrived at his station, and they could be very long minutes indeed. Eternal even. The train was full of people- rush hour-and to squeeze past them all to get to another wagon was a mission almost as stressful as pretending to be invisible.

Weird Guy sighed heavily, and exaggerated.

Here it comes.

"You're sweating."

Please don't do this to me.

"I said you're sweating. You okay?"

Kevin had no choice but to answer. "Yeah, fine. Thanks. Conditioning ain't working to well, I guess," and offered another feeble smile.

The smile abruptly disappeared. It was only a second or two, just enough for him to react in time and dissimilate by looking away again, but the smile had been replaced by a momentary look of shock, like when you turn to look at someone to see something terribly wrong with their features, or when someone smiles at you, and you can't help but cast a glance at the metal brace glued to their teeth, or the birthmark on their face. It was subtle and quick, but you knew that *they* knew you'd looked.

The guy was sweating also. But this was no ordinary sweat. In that brief glimpse, Kevin thought he'd seen something resembling candle wax cast a slow and determined path down the left side of his face; a single thick droplet that left a slimy trail, then dangled precariously from his chin. It reminded him of the times he had a nasty cold, and had to serve customers with the ever-present threat of snot dripping into their food, yet this was so much thicker, more *compact*.

I didn't just see that. That was my hangover playing tricks on me.

"So, off to work, are you?" came from what seemed a very distant voice.

Kevin jolted slightly.

"Looks like you're in for a long day. Too much to drink last night, eh?" followed by a cackling that Kevin likened to a senile crow.

Kevin slowly turned to face Dripping Guy once more, almost afraid to look.

"No. just a little tir…" he trailed off. More streams of wax were dripping from his face. It reminded him terribly of the empty bottle of wine he kept in his room, now decorated with coloured wax from numerous candles he'd used to decorate it with. The guy was rapidly becoming a human wine bottle. And worse yet, was that he didn't seem to realize what was happening to him. He continued looking at Kevin, evidently more preoccupied about him than himself.

Kevin looked around the wagon. Had anyone else noticed this apparent transformation? No. All were busy studying their cell phones or engaged in deep conversation, and yet, nobody had bothered to sit beside them in the empty bay. There were two precious seats available and no-one wanted them.

The train pulled into another station. Kevin silently begged for the guy to get up and leave. He was starting to feel ill, and although his mild hangover might have contributed, he thought it wasn't the main reason. His stomach was churning, and his heart was bobbing frenetically in his throat. Then, he heard a sound; *Plop*, followed by another. It sounded… squidgy, like walking through a wet, muddy field. He didn't need to look to know what that sound was.

"Yeah. I've been there. You wait till you get older. Then you'll know what sufferin's all about! Where do you work?" Candle Man said, but it now sounded as though he was talking through a mouthful of liquid of some kind. Bubbly, as if he was underwater, and trying to speak.

Kevin looked again at the guy. Now, his features were beginning to distort, melt. One eye was slightly lower than the other and warped, so that it seemed he had a permanent squint. His cheeks were ripples, waves of jelly that wobbled profoundly whenever he moved, and his lips drooped as though imitating a child's tantrum face.

Kevin was by now sweating profusely himself. He really didn't want to sit here anymore, thought of getting up and moving, but what if the guy touched him, or grabbed him by the wrist as he squeezed past? Would his hand be all slimy and *gooey* as well?

He was still staring intensely at Kevin, oblivious it seemed of what was happening, yet worse, no-one else noticed either. Panic and sheer fright overcame him. He needed to *get away*. It was imperative, because Kevin had an idea what the outcome might be of this little get-together. And it wouldn't be pleasant.

Silently vowing never to drink alcohol again (at least on a work day), he stood up, tense, expecting the worse, and tried to rapidly calculate how to get past without touching him. It would not be an easy task; the guy was pretty damn big. His hands alone were shovels. He had to fight with himself not to take another peek as he edged by, just to confirm, and found it impossible. His heart throbbing like a mad thing, he faked another timid smile, and looked.

Candle Man's face had by now practically melted into a single, featureless blob. His nose had blended with the cheeks and lips, his eyes now round, white marbles free from eyelids. The whole thing was now dripping copious amounts of flesh and fat onto its lap, leaving the cheekbones in full view and devoid of any facial protection. Kevin thought he might have produced a little squeal of horror; he wasn't sure, it seemed to come from somewhere very far away, but he had an idea it was his own failed attempt at screaming.

"Leaving so soon?" gargled the thing. "Your stop isn't for another ten minutes. Why don't you sit back down. It's been a long while since I had a nice conversation. People get nervous when they see me, you know. All these clothes…"

I want to wake up now. I refuse to believe this is happening. I had too much to drink again last night with the guys from work, and now I'm paying for it. How could he possibly know when my stop is?

Kevin gave another yelp; the guy/thing/whatever was tugging at his trousers for him to sit down. A thick droplet of mucus ran down his leg from where he'd been touched. He looked wildly, blurrily around for help. A few disinterested glances his way at least acknowledged his presence, but immediately returned to whatever they were doing.

It has to be a dream. Why is no-one else seeing this?

"Funny you know. How first appearances can create so much preju- dice. People see me in this outfit, and think I'm some kind of nutter, freak. Not once do they think I may have some disease or illness. People are scared of anything that doesn't follow the norm. They think it's contagious even. Very funny. Do *you* think that's funny Kevin?"

Kevin wanted to cry.

Kevin wanted to wake up in his bed, give thanks that it had been a terrible nightmare, and *then*, perhaps laugh. That would be funny, not this.

He looked to the abomination sitting before him. A creature that could not possibly exist, melting, a large pool of…something, already forming on the floor, and suddenly felt sad for him. He still wasn't sure if he was dreaming, hallucinating, or if a substantial stay at Northgate Hospital for the mentally-impaired was called for, but began to recall all the times as a kid he had laughed at fat old Mrs. Wilkinson, who was enormous, until she told him one day in tears that she had a terminal illness, and her weight was a direct result of it. Jonny Rice who at sixteen announced proudly to the world that he was gay, and who, eight months later, committed suicide due to the constant threats, insults, and jokes. And the elderly lady who had wanted his seat but he had pretended not to see her. Let others get up, not me.

He told himself that one thing had nothing to do with the other, be- cause regardless of what the guy was saying-and Kevin knew he was un- fortunately right-even so, people did not suddenly start melting right be- fore your eyes. So, it had to be a dream, right?

The man's clothes were now sliding onto the seat and floor, mixing with the vast pool of sludge that had been his body, now almost completely disappeared, yet his eyes remained open and alert. Pitiful; yes, but *there*. Two round balls sitting like mysterious marbles on the heavy jacket as though it were a cushion for some ancient, demonic God.

Kevin edged past, careful not to step into the puddle, and waited for the train to stop at his station. He stepped off, and, as he walked past the window next to where he'd been sitting, looked in.

A young skinhead sat defiantly where he had been, regardless of the elderly folk that looked to him with disdain and contempt for not giving up his seat.

The thick puddle that had once been The Melting Man was now gone, making Kevin wonder again if it had after all been some kind of hangover- induced hallucination, but even so, it didn't really matter anymore. He thought he might look at things in a different light from now on.

He turned to leave the station when something caught his eye. Someone was boarding the train where he'd left. Someone wearing an oversized coat with the hood up, and heavy headphones covered in tape over his ears. He bundled past passengers as though they weren't there, and sat opposite the skinhead. Kevin smiled. He thought the skinhead might be in for an interesting journey.

✗

DEAD WAVES
by Sean McCoy

The night before Bill Parsons and my dad and I went ice fishing for the last time, I stayed up late listening to my ham radio. The static came to life in my headphones and I heard the distant voices calling across the radio waves. At first, I could only recognize the Russian speakers with their soft "zh" and "vrov" and "ski" sound. But as I twisted the timer slowly I heard others: the French swallowed "r" (as in "merci") and those lisping Spanish esses.

I had my own call-sign by then. KC5ZTM. Which meant that I had taken a class and knew all the rules and a little bit about how the radio worked. Even still, I was usually too afraid to talk—to make contact with the voices on the other end. But when I listened, every voice sounded like a permanent echo, like hearing voices from a thousand years ago. The soft, foreign chatter lulled me to sleep as I doodled a picture of a yeti in my math notebook. The strange voices filled my head as I slept until I heard my dad knock softly on my door and whisper that it was time to get up.

The car was so cold that the leather seats felt like the hard plastic chairs from school. I tucked my hands inside my jacket sleeves to keep what little warm air I could inside. I tucked my head into my collar too and closed my eyes, trying to find my way back to sleep.

"How come we haven't seen Mr. Parsons in so long," I asked my dad.

My dad was quiet for a bit before answering. "Mr. Parsons and Mrs. Parsons aren't together anymore," he said. "They had to get a divorce."

"How come?"

"Well, it's complicated," he said. "But he lost his job for a while there, and it's taken some time for him to get back on his feet."

"So how come you haven't seen him?"

"Well, he was just, he was busy dealing with all that. Anyway, we're seeing him today. Try not to ask him anything about his divorce, okay?"

"Okay."

Dad listened to talk radio and again the radio voices returned and made it easier for me to get a little sleep. The words swam through my head and I drifted and drifted until I felt the car brake and my dad shifted in his seat.

"Okay buddy," my dad said. We'd arrived at Mr. Parsons's place. "Time to get up."

I wiped the sleep from my eyes and looked out the window at the small apartment complex. It was all brick, with little black rails and as I watched a large dark shape lumbered towards us, fog streaming from its hooded face like a cartoon bull staring down a matador.

"Go ahead and let Mr. Parsons sit up front, James, would'ya?"

I nodded and opened the door, stumbling out of the car. The sharp wind blew through me like a ghost and I ran to the back of the van to get back to warmth as quickly as I could. Unfortunately, they hadn't salted the roads near Mr. Parsons's place and I slipped and ran smack dab into him, whacking my tiny head against his flannel-wrapped beer belly.

"Whoa!" he said and steadied me with huge gloved hands. "Good morning, soldier! At ease." He helped me find my way to the back seat and then stepped into the front. The whole van lurched when he stepped in, and his frame took up the entire passenger's side, such that I couldn't see out the windshield on his side.

"Slippery out there?" my dad asked, eyeing me in the rearview mirror.

"I think somebody tied on a few last night," Mr. Parsons said, and then made that drink-tipping motion with his hand and winked at me. "Is that what happened?" he asked me. "You get lucky last night, soldier?"

"Bill," my dad said.

"Gross," I said.

"Sorry," Mr. Parsons said. "He's getting to be a big man. You gonna play football this season, James?"

"He's only in seventh grade," my dad said.

"They don't have football in seventh grade?"

My dad shook his head. "That's just not what James is into."

* * * *

The drive only took an hour and a half, and the whole time Mr. Parsons and my dad mostly caught up and told dirty jokes that I only half understood. I usually gave a chuckle whenever Mr. Parsons said "balls," which was a lot considering how short the drive was. My dad usually shot glances at me in the rearview letting me know it was okay to laugh at some of this stuff, even if I didn't really get it.

"Tell Mr. Parsons about your radio," my dad said, and then to Mr. Parsons, "He's been working on this day and night since Christmas."

"What you been workin' on there, bud? You know I was in Signal Corp back in the day. I didn't know kids still did that kinda stuff."

"James does," my dad said. "Tell him."

I shrugged, not sure what there was to say. "Dad got me a ham radio kit for Christmas. It's got its own transceiver and a battery and an antenna and all the stuff you need to make it. I got it working last week for the first time, usually I use my dad's—"

"He's been listening to it every night."

"Is that right?" Mr. Parsons said. "Old ham op, huh? Man that is something else, I tell ya. I did my time in the First Signal Brigade, if you ever heard of that."

I said I hadn't.

"Mr. Parsons speaks Korean," my dad told me.

"Maegjuneun eodi iss-eoyo?" Mr. Parsons crooned out in an over the top Asian accent.

"What's that mean?" I asked.

"Means, where's the beer," Mr. Parsons said and he and my dad both laughed.

"So you like radios?" I asked after they had calmed down.

"Son," Mr. Parsons said, "I tell you language is the bedrock of human civilization, we don't have nothing without we have the ability to communicate. And radio lets a lot of people communicate over a long distance in a lot of different languages. Even writing lets us communicate with the dead, and without the written word, we don't even have history. Let me tell ask you something, James, you ever heard of a number station?"

"No, what's that?"

"Oh," my dad said. "This is neat. You'll like this."

Mr. Parsons grinned and hooked his arm around the front seat to look back at me.

"There are these short-wave, at least I believe they're short-wave, radio stations, you could probably pick them up on your ham radio there when you get it up and running all the way. But the point is, they're these little stations that will just, it's a man or a woman, I think it's a woman a lot of the time, and they just read out these numbers, one after the other. A lot of time it's just a computer voice, but every hour or half hour or so you'll hear the station identify itself-"

My dad made a radio squelch sound and cupped his hand over his mouth while he said, "Six-Niner-Zero-Oblique-Four," and then chuckled.

"That's right, exactly like that, or sometimes they play a song or maybe you'll hear some Cuban or whoever say something like "*Attencion, attencion*" in Spanish and then they'll list off a string of numbers and repeat it a few times and then it'll be silent until, you know, the next, uh, the next broadcast."

I pictured a small buoy stranded somewhere out in the vast ocean on a rainy night, buffeted by huge waves, with a tiny blinking light in the dark and I heard the numbers accompanied by dits and dahs coming through the static in my head. Dit-dit-dit, dah-dah-dah, dit-dit-dit. One. Seven. Six. Seven. Three. Four. One. Seven. I heard the numbers over and over.

"What do the numbers mean?" I asked.

"Noooobody knows," my dad said and took his hands off the wheel for a second to waggle them in the air. Mr. Parsons grinned and slapped my dad on the back.

"Well, that's a good question, but they think, whoever 'they' are, and I think they're right, for what it's worth, that they're normally used for, well you know, for espionage."

"Spies?"

"Well maybe. People think that the numbers are a code and that someone out there, whether that's a spy, or maybe just a ship's captain or someone who has, not necessarily military, but maybe secret or privileged information, has some sort of decoder on the other end that they use to, you know, decrypt the message, and then they can send messages that way."

"Like Morse code?"

"Sort of, yeah sort of like that. It's a code probably, with the different numbers meaning different things on different days."

"Here's the thing," Mr. Parsons said. "Some of these stations though, some of them may be automated, just running on an endless loop forever. Maybe during the Cold War there was some spy and he was lost and they couldn't find him and so they send out instructions on the loop for him, looking for him in case he's ever found. And then, you know, maybe that radio is just in a basement somewhere repeating the same numbers over and over again. Completely forgotten about."

I thought about that and it made me very sad. The idea that someone was lost and couldn't be found made me sad, but more than that the idea that the radio didn't know that it was over. That the person was gone and wasn't coming back. And that it was programmed to keep sending its signal out into the waves forever. That made me really sad.

* * * *

We made it to the lake while it was still dark out and my dad paid a guy who owned a snowmobile to drive us out to the darkhouse he'd rented for the day. The sky was dark as judge's robes and the wind slapped my face hard as a nun. There were a few other ice shanties on the lake, but it was close to the end of the season and not a lot of people were out. My dad tapped my shoulder and pointed out the constellation Cetus, the sea monster. I smiled and nodded, though I thought Cetus looked more like a broom with a pommel like you'd see on the end of a sword instead of a sea monster.

The inside of the darkhouse was just like it sounds, except there was a worn patch of wood floor where a portable gas stove would go and several steel hooks to hang your coat or a lamp, and a few rickety shelves for the tackle box and the cooler and all that. My dad and I stacked up the tackle boxes while Mr. Parsons used an auger to drill a big hole in the ice. I watched him crank the auger while it slowly bored into the white ice and drew the circle deeper and deeper down. The ice was a little over three inches thick and my dad went over all the rules of ice fishing again with me again for the thousandth time. The most important rule was always that when we were out on the ice, I had to do whatever my dad said, no hesitation. No matter what. People could drown or freeze or crack their skulls or any number of bad things dads always mentioned but never happened.

When they had the hole cut and the lines dropped in, my dad and Mr. Parsons cracked their first beers (I was given a Dr. Pepper) and Mr. Parsons made a toast.

"May the best of your yesterdays be the worst of your tomorrows," Mr. Parsons said and my dad said "here, here" and they clunked their cans together and then Mr. Parsons tapped my can with his and my dad smiled and did the same and we all drank.

It took a while for the fish to start biting and the whole time the cold slowly set in. At first it froze my butt where I was sitting until my legs shook. Then it crept through my chest like a skeleton rising from the dead, and grasped my arms until my fingers turned to stone and I had to breathe on them to keep them wiggling. My dad and Mr. Parsons didn't mind though and their cheeks got red and I could see their breath every time they laughed, which was a lot.

My dad caught the first fish, a bluegill, and Mr. Parsons toasted the fish and even poured some of his beer on it. My dad laughed and they put it in the ice chest to gut later. I caught the next few fish, some sunfish and a perch. Then my dad again. Then me. Halfway through the day my dad took a break and gutted and cleaned the perch and then grilled them on the portable stove for some sandwiches with cheese and tomatoes. I cut the tomatoes into thin slices near the grill to warm up while my dad worked and Mr. Parsons watched the lines. Nothing bit while we ate and Mr. Parsons got quiet and wouldn't eat at first.

"We'll catch more, Bill," my dad said. "Eat your food."

"No we won't," Mr. Parsons said.

"It's only lunchtime," I offered, not really sure of the nature of when fish congregate or what their patterns were. "We can switch to a new darkhouse too, right?"

"We sure can," my dad said.

"Won't matter," Mr. Parsons said. "It's me."

"Bill."

"I'm cursed."

"Don't start this again."

Mr. Parsons took another swig from his can and stared down into the hole in the ice. The water was dark down there and I could see his reflection coming off the water. His face and jowls looked sunken, not like the rosy cheeks he'd had in the car, or when we first got here, when he was telling stories and jokes.

We ate and then cleaned up, but Mr. Parsons sandwich just sat next to him on some crinkled up newspaper my dad had brought to wrap the fish in.

* * * *

We fished until it was dark again and then the cold really set in and I asked my dad if we could do something to warm up.

"What's wrong there buddy you uh you uh cold?" Mr. Parsons interjected before my dad could answer. He was swaying on his seat and his breath came out in big warm clouds when he spoke, which wasn't as often as when we first got here. "You want a sip of my scotch? Put hair on your chest and warm you right up."

"Maybe next time," my dad said. Then to me, "Let's get you moving a bit."

"Fair enough," Mr. Parsons said. "S'good for the blood. Moving. Man's gotta keep moving. Can't stop for nothing. They won't let you stop."

"Yeah," my dad said. "Maybe we could all use some fresh air."

"Won't it be colder out there?" I asked.

"Yeah, but you'll be warmer inside by comparison," my dad said and smiled.

We all buttoned up and went outside. It was as dark as it was in the morning and the only light came from the stars and the little lanterns that hung above all the rows of darkhouses on the ice. I thought of the number stations from before, each one of the darkhouses now looked like a tiny buoy on the frozen lake. The wind bit my nose and I pulled on the drawstrings to keep my hood tight. I even closed my eyes to keep my eyeballs warm and besides, it wasn't that much darker with my eyes closed anyway.

I paced softly across the ice away from the darkhouse while my dad told a story about jumping naked into snow after getting out of a sauna when he was an exchange student in Finland.

"Hoo-ee-Shit!" Dad said, which was one of the only times I ever heard him curse. "There'd be steam jumpin off your parts and everyone was laughing. I mean over there its guys and girls. But man, that would wake you up."

I didn't know what to say to that. But at least Mr. Parsons was chuckling again.

We got out far from the darkhouses where the halos wouldn't reach and looked up at the stars. We pointed out constellations again, my dad showing me Orion, which I already knew, and Mr. Parsons pointed out Perseus, which I had never seen before.

"He fought the Medusa," Mr. Parsons said. "She turned people to stone, y'ever heard'a that?"

I nodded my head, I didn't want to bring my muffled mouth out to speak and risk the cold. I felt like it would take over my lungs and steal my breath and turn me into ice from the inside out. I pictured Superman's Fortress of Solitude and all its crystals and ice and I was afraid that I'd be trapped like that inside my own body.

"But he showed her her own face with a reflective shield, like a mirror y'see and she saw what she was and that just about shut her down. Turned her right to stone."

Mr. Parsons was quiet then for a while and the only sound came from my dad turning in place on the ice, scraping his boots trying to get a better look at all the stars, and from the wind that blew with a dull whispering chorus.

"We're way out here," Mr. Parsons said to me and took a knee. He put a hand on my shoulder and then stretched the other one out over the ice wobbling it slowly like a see-saw. "So you be careful, okay? That dark ice'll getcha. It's slippery. Okay? You're walkin and you think it's safe and then the ice just falls out from under you. Stay inside the lines there."

He pointed out the orange lines stuck to poles in the ice where the game commission had come out and pointed out the weak ice now that the season was ending.

"Don't scare him," my dad said. "He'll be fine."

"People die every year, you know that, don't you?" My dad didn't hear Mr. Parsons whisper to me and I wouldn't have heard him either if I didn't see his cloud of breath rise up from his facemask.

"I know," I said, but it just came out as, "Mo," from inside my hood. Mr. Parsons nodded and stood up again to stretch his back. We were quiet for a while and I thought we'd all just freeze to the ice there and somebody would find us in the morning like sculptures. Like Medusa.

"Somebody's already way too far out there," Mr. Parsons said.

"What's that?" My dad asked.

Mr. Parsons stuck a finger out towards the horizon.

"Out there," he said.

I looked where Mr. Parsons was pointing and squinted. I couldn't see anything at first, all I could hear was the whipping wind and then slowly in the distance I saw a dark form come into focus out on the ice.

"I don't see anything, Bill," My dad said, then he walked over to Mr. Parsons and put a hand up over his eyes like he was staring into the sun.

"Who is it?" I asked.

"Drunk fisherman?" my dad asked Mr. Parsons. "I can't see it."

"Is he okay?" I asked.

My dad didn't answer. He and Mr. Parsons just looked out over the ice at the dark form that stood there.

"Dad."

"What's that?"

"Are they okay?"

My dad looked down at me.

"There's no one there," he said. "Just some shadow. Let's go inside."

My dad turned and started the long walk back to the darkhouse and I followed behind. Mr. Parsons stayed out a bit staring at the horizon. When he made it back to the darkhouse he was muttering to himself about the Medusa and the dadgum fool out there on the ice.

"See isn't that nice and warm by comparison," my dad said when we got inside.

"Yeah," I said. And it really was. I had a few crackers and a part of an apple and my dad said later we could make s'mores and burn up what was left of the propane on the stove.

"It'll be lighter to carry back to the car," my dad said.

"It's just gas though, why does it weigh so much?"

"It's compressed inside. It actually has a mass to it and they stuff a lot in it. The gas actually wants to expand, that's what makes it so explosive."

I said I thought I understood and Mr. Parsons came in and baited the hooks and we set our lines again and waited for a couple of hours. You couldn't hear anything inside the darkhouse except for our breathing (my dad was getting sleepy and sometimes he snored) and the wind, which had started to howl. Mr. Parsons just stared at the lines and I thought he stared so hard he might actually move them.

A little after midnight a fish bit on my line. I struggled to pull it out and Mr. Parsons came over to my side and tried to take the line from me.

"Here let me get at it," he said.

"I got it."

"You've been gettin fish all day. Let me try this one. Help me break my streak."

"Dad."

My dad lifted his eyes and tried to sum up the situation quickly but looked lost and confused.

"He's got a big one here," Mr. Parsons said. "I'm gonna help him get it out."

"That's not fair," I said. "It was my fish."

"Let him have a turn," my dad told me. "You won't always be so lucky.

It's good to share."

I said fine and huffed and went to Mr. Parsons seat, which was some-how colder than my own. Mr. Parsons had a greedy looked on his face and smiled as he brought the fish in. The shadow looked big under the water and a cold light reflected against Mr. Parsons's grin.

The thing he pulled out of the water was black and big and slimy and it had a gash running down its side. It flopped once when he pulled it out and I couldn't tell what kind of fish it was but it was dead when it hit the ice and lay very still.

Mr. Parsons just lost it and kicked his chair and yelled at the fish and stepped on it.

"Cocksucking son of a bitch! I can't get even ONE fish! One fish you won't even let me have!"

"BILL," my dad stood up and he used a voice I had only heard him use once before and it had involved me and the dog and a lot of mud in the house. I felt frozen to the chair and steam rose from Mr. Parsons body as he yelled and threw his hulking body around the small darkhouse.

Mr. Parsons sat on the ground next to the black thing and put his head in his hands and started to cry.

"Why don't you go outside," my dad said to me. I looked at him and he nodded and went to Mr. Parsons and sat down on the ice floor with him and patted him on the back. I hugged the wall and went around them both and didn't even have time to wrap myself up again before I opened the door.

The door flung open from the wind and my dad yelled and me to move and shut the door and I did.

Outside was very dark and even the stars seemed lost behind the fog and the clouds. All the lights were out from the other darkhouses except for ours. Everyone else had just gone home.

I walked out to the edge of the halo from our darkhouse and looked up at the stars and tried to find Perseus again. I thought about what Mr. Parsons said about the Medusa and I pictured a naked lady with snakes crawl-ing all over her body and with bite marks all up and down her neck and I thought of her laying on a bed of stone statues that stretched out farther than I could see and I felt very cold and afraid.

I heard the wind pick up and I looked out again to the horizon and there I saw it. I saw the figure, what Mr. Parsons must have seen, but closer now. A light grey thing wrapped in some kind of grey sheet with a dim white face. I couldn't tell if it was a man or a woman and all the time it seemed to be walking closer and closer to me but it didn't ever seem to get any closer. I got real scared that someone was out there and that I was all alone and so I went back to the darkhouse, at first walking slowly like I was supposed to do on the ice but then I could feel the prickling at my back like the thing was right there behind me, that it had flown across the ice on the wind and I started to run.

I slipped and fell on the ice and I heard my knee make a sound against the hard ground and I yelled. It was stupid to yell, the thing might hear me, I thought. I felt so afraid, I started to crawl and tried to stand at the same time, just trying to get to the door of the darkhouse, get back to dad, but then a shaft of light fell across me and I saw that my dad had opened the door and Mr. Parsons was still sitting on the ground behind him.

"Are you okay?" My dad yelled. Snow had begun to fall it snowflakes peppered the side of my dad's head.

"It's still out there!"

"What?"

"That person on the ice they're still there!"

My dad walked to me and picked me up and dusted the snow and ice chips off my back.

"No one's out there," my dad said. "Just come inside."

But when we got to the door Mr. Parsons was standing there, his face had lost all redness and had turned a cool purple color. No more steam came off him and none rolled out of his mouth when he spoke.

"It's her isn't it," Mr. Parsons said.

"Bill, go back inside. We're done here."

"She can't just let me have one fish can she. She has to have it all."

"Bill, you're scaring James. There's nothing out there, it's just a trick of the ice. Let's go." He looked at me and grabbed my collar. "Come on," he said and we pushed past Mr. Parsons to go inside.

Once we got inside my dad started to pack everything up. He cut the lines and rolled them and put them back in the tackle box and he covered all the food in the ice chests with the fish we had caught and all the trash he tossed into a bag.

"Mr. Parsons is having a hard time," he told me. "And he and I probably drank too much. It has nothing to do with you, okay? This has nothing to do with you."

"Who's that person out there?" I asked.

"There's no one out there," my dad yelled. "I don't know what you thought you saw, but there's nothing there. Mr. Parsons has put stories into your head. It's time to go. Let's get Mr. Parsons, we're going."

We went back outside but Mr. Parsons wasn't out there. The wind was blowing fast and I could hear the other darkhouses shaking, their empty lightbulbs clacking against the aluminum roofs.

"Stay here," my dad said. "In fact, go back inside."

"I don't want to be alone."

"Just, just listen to me okay? It's not safe out here."

"Dad, look!"

I pointed. Mr. Parsons was out on there on the ice, walking towards the place where the thing was, only nothing was there now. He walked stiffly, both hands out to his side like he might fall at any moment. He was shouting at something, but we couldn't make out his words.

"Bill!" My dad yelled and went after him. Only then the wind picked up and we had to hold our eyes to shield ourselves from the snow. My dad yelled and went after him anyway and I stayed by the darkhouse holding onto the cold walls.

When we got home that night my father was so tired from answering all the questions about Mr. Parsons and talking to the police that my mom took my dad to their room and told me to get to bed. I just wanted to go to sleep and get the image of the thing out there on the ice and of Mr. Parsons's grim face and the way he walked, I wanted all of that out of my head.

I turned on my radio on and faced the window, aiming my antenna out and trying to get a good signal. Only static came through for a while. Static like sheets of snow. The static kept doubling and repeating back on itself until I couldn't hear anything else except the static and the wind. And then I heard it. A voice from nowhere, quietly, softly. A woman's voice. British. Repeating over and over and over.

Numbers.

✗

THE PROPOSAL
by J.D. Brink

James stepped off the curb on Bleaker Street and stuck his hand in the air to hail a cab. A checkered yellow Studebaker drove past him, paying him no mind. In the back seat was an exotic looking woman in a broad-brimmed hat and pearls.

She looks nice, James thought to himself. *Guess I wouldn't have stopped either.*

Then again, I have Pauline. So I wouldn't have picked up that high-priced dame in the first place.

Pauline wasn't like most women James knew. Oh, she had all the feminine qualities that others had. She had beauty: curly raven locks, crystal blue eyes, and the curves of a rather short hourglass. She had brains: the mind of a university professor, the knowledge of a librarian, and the adventurous heart of an archeologist. And she fragility. She was a soft flower, drawn into a tight bulb most of her life, just now beginning to open up and blossom into womanhood.

James wasn't the only one to notice Pauline's own personal spring, either, but he was right there. At her side. Working together, exploring together. He was her sun, she his rose. And though he was six years her senior, they were meant to be together. He was sure of it, and certainly she was, too.

Even though there had never been any actual, blatant expression of romantic feelings between them… Well, he knew it was true. *Certainly* she shared that unspoken bond.

Another cab passed him by, this one with no passenger in the back seat. It simply didn't stop for him.

James shifted the bundle of white daisies (he couldn't afford a dozen roses, not on a research assistant's stipend) from his left hand to his right, as well as the tiny wooden box he held.

Wait. Fragility? Pauline?

James chuckled. Would a fragile flower of a girl have survived that whole big scaffolding collapsing out from under her? The sarcophagus and weight of ages falling on top of her?

He saw the whole terrible scene again in his mind. Pauline, stout and curvy, in her working apron and flat-bottomed shoes, ten feet aloft on that bamboo scaffold. The stone chamber was lit by torches, flickering shadows everywhere. The huge stone mural of hieroglyphics loomed three-stories tall. Pauline was armed only with a coarse, horse-hair brush against the fearsome fate that was about to befall her. She swept away the dust and stones, clearing the negative space that spelled out something important in standing figures and balancing cranes and swimming crocodiles. A warning, she had said. Pauline was reading it, translating it, as she went, and she had called his attention because she thought she had finally figured out what had been worth so much time and effort on the part of Egyptians two-thousand years dead.

And then it happened. The wall cracked, spontaneously broke open, and the sarcophagus spilled forth from its hiding place into the dim torch light. It practically landed on top of her, though in his mind's eye he still swore that the scaffolding had buckled first; Pauline was already in the act of falling when the vessel that would carry its cargo into the afterlife appeared from the crumbling wall.

Although that didn't make much sense. If not the weight of the coffin and rubble, what would have caused such a thing to happen?

The scaffold, the opening sarcophagus, and Pauline, all piled up on the tomb floor. A wave of dust roiled outward. James had been so frightened that his eyes had played tricks on him. He swore that he saw faces in that thundercloud of dust and debris. A beautiful woman one instant, a withered, cackling skull in the next, there and gone in the space of a blink as the particles hit him in the face. He had already hurtled himself into the chaos, was tasting and choking on the airborne remains of a deceased priestess and ages of lost history.

That had been the end of the expedition. Pauline—poor lovely, delicate Pauline—had suffered bodily injury and was unconscious as he carried her from the cavernous tomb. The guides and their camels, supposedly waiting for them outside, were in the act of fleeing when he emerged carrying his burden of love. Had he been a moment later in making it to sands and sky, he and Pauline would have been trapped there, alone. He'd have held her in his arms and watched her slowly die there in the deserts east of Cairo.

James's heart reacted again—speeding up, pounding against his ribs, the green taste of dread surging up his throat, thinking the girl he loved but had never told so had just been killed before his very eyes. His hands tightened involuntarily, crunching the green flower stalks and testing the sturdiness of the small wooden cube.

After a brief hospital stay in Cairo, they were flown back home to the States. James went to his lonely apartment, and back to the university to deliver their treasures and report his findings to the board of regents. Pauline went to Gothic General. There she slept in the care of physicians and nurses who couldn't say what was wrong with her. She appeared to suffer no serious injuries, and yet was oblivious to the world. Comatose.

Until today. When James had phoned the hospital today, they'd told him that Pauline had woken up and discharged herself from their care. The doctors could see no reason to hold her, as she'd spontaneously awoken from the only ailment with which they could charge her.

But why did James have to find out this way? Why hadn't Pauline telephoned him to assist her home? Or invited him to see her once she was safely back to her apartment?

Had her deep, death-like sleep robbed her of the feelings she once held for him? (For, surely, she loved James as much as he did her. Surely, her endless fever dreams were fantasies about their finally professing their undying love for one another, and about their wedding day, and their future children.)

Finally, a yellow cab declaring itself of the Acme Taxi Service eased to a stop next to where James stood in the street. The driver's face must have been a reflection of James's own flustered, hopeful, and heartbroken expression, for he gave him quite an inquisitive and puzzled look.

James gave the cabbie the address, following with, "My girl's just been released from the hospital. We are reuniting today after nearly two weeks apart."

"Congratulations, mac," the driver said. "But, in that case, don't you think you could have sprung for roses?"

Eighteen minutes later, the cab deposited James outside her building.

But he wasn't the only one there waiting.

A swarm of cats, dogs, pigeons, and even rats were amassed at the stairwell door.

The cabbie sped away with curses of confusion and disgust. James stood at the edge of the street, gripping his gifts, half afraid to step up on the curb. Several of the beasts turned around to stare him down. A mangy hound and a fierce Dachshund growled at him. More than a few cats hissed in his direction—not at the rats or canines, their natural enemies, but seemingly at James.

Finally a jet-feathered rook squawked at him, perched on a lamppost above his initial field of vision. It cawed again and the savage peanut gallery cowered. The black bird flicked its head from side to side, sizing James up with one eye and then the other. He had the strange feeling that he was being assessed for worthiness. James fidgeted with his bowtie.

Suddenly a Roadster blew past him, blaring its horn. James jumped onto the sidewalk.

The menagerie of creatures gathered there, however, did not budge. They flipped around en mass to face him, to keep him from reaching the door. Only when the rook fluttered down among them, hopped around and swept its wings in shooing arcs did they take the hint and move aside. A few seconds later, the way was cleared. The animals had all retreated to the open alleyway, crouching around the corner, or peeked on from behind a blue postal box. Then the winged usher flew back to its perch and squawked a final time, as if to order James inside.

"Damnedest thing I've ever seen in my short lifetime..." James muttered, hurrying through the door and mounting the first few steps in a single bound.

Pauline's apartment was number 2B. He had never been there, but he knew it from the university records. And she must have told him herself once, as well. He was certain she would have.

James cleared his throat, smoothed his hair, and checked his bowtie one more time. He inspected his daisies and found one stalk fractured and drooping where he'd clutched it too tightly. That one he tossed, primped the rest, and poised his fist to knock.

But the door eased open of its own accord, just enough to allow her bid to enter to reach the hallway.

"Um, hello?" he called, gently pushing open the door. "Pauline? It's James. Come, uh, come a-calling. Of a sort."

Her apartment was small but nice. The foyer merged with the parlor on the left and kitchenette on the right. There was a sea-green sofa and chair in the parlor. A Zenith radio sat on a small, circular table beneath the window.

Something black uncoiled itself on one seafoam-colored pillow. A black Persian cat lifted its head, probing him with yellow eyes and pointed ears. The thick furball climbed up into a sitting position and glared on, watching him defensively.

"Oh, you have a cat," James said nervously. "You never mentioned that before."

"I always keep one vassal close," came Pauline's voice, rougher and more determined than he was used to hearing, "and several more in waiting."

She strutted into the parlor and went immediately to the Persian, stroking its head between the ears. She looked... good, he supposed. Pauline stood slightly taller than he remembered, wearing a strapless blue dress, black sandals, and what must have been every piece of jewelry she owned. He recognized some, simple necklaces and a few inexpensive rings that she'd inherited from her grandmother, she'd said. But Pauline usually went modest on her adornments. Today, seven fingers wore rings of various styles and the pale, bare skin of her chest held almost as many chains, lockets, and brooches. A thin tiara was poked into her curly raven hair with interlaced triangular silverwork centered at her forehead.

Her face... Her face was pale, too, cheekbones more pronounced, and her eyes appeared sunken, made worse by the darkening application of cosmetic eyeshadow and thick, ruby lip gloss. Pauline almost never wore make-up, and he'd certainly never seen her put it on so heavily.

Two weeks asleep, he reasoned. *Not eating, not taking care of herself, just... Just the illness. And two weeks of famine. That must be it.*

Pauline glared at him. "Well?" she demanded.

"Well, uh," James stammered. "I wish you'd have telephoned me, Pauline, I could have helped you home."

"Are those for me?" she asked expectedly.

"Oh, yes!" He clumsily stumbled forward, flowers out-stretched. When she didn't take the bouquet, he simply lowered his arm. The tiny wooden cube he gripped even tighter now, consuming it in his hand. He almost hoped she didn't see it, that he hadn't brought it.

"So, uh, how are you feeling?"

"Better," she said. "Better than I have in years. Thousands and thousands of years."

James chuckled. "It's only been two weeks. Two long weeks, granted. They seemed a lifetime to me, too." He felt his cheeks blush and hated himself for it.

"Oh, the treasures!" He looked around for somewhere to place the flowers, found nothing, and continued. "The tomb, the artifacts, everything we brought back from Cairo."

"Oh, Cairo," she breathed. "Poor ignorant, vengeful Cairo..."

"Uh, yes. Well... Not sure what you mean there, dear." He'd slipped in a *dear*! Had she even noticed? Did she mind? "Professor Clark has analyzed what we found and determined that the tomb belonged to an excommunicated priestess—"

"Hecateptra," Pauline said, stepping nearer. "The Stillness of the Water. The Emptiness of the Night. The Cold in Men's Hearts."

She was close now—*very* close, inches from him. A dark passion flared in the deepness of her blue eyes. Her ruby lips pursed provocatively as she formed each syllable. She stood so near to him now that the heat of her body... Well, actually, he felt a rather chill vacuum coming from her direction, but James certainly felt warmer.

He flushed and licked his lips with a suddenly dry and anxious tongue. "That's right," he whispered.

Her fathomless blue gaze locked on to his. He felt as if he were swimming in those dark pools.

Swimming.

Sinking.

Drowning.

Her powerful, entrancing glare broke away and glanced downward. "What do you have there? What are you keeping secret from me?"

Slowly, he raised his hand and unfurled his fingers. A tiny wooden box, two cubic inches, rested on his palm. He dropped the daisies to the floor and used his other hand to slide open the lid. Inside, nestled among a packing of shredded paper, was a ring. A scarab of tarnished turquoise, hastily polished as best he could, clasped to a circlet of pure gold.

"Ah," she said. "My ring. After all these long years of slumber, you've found it for me."

James nodded wordlessly. It seemed to him that he'd wanted to say quite a bit more about the ring when he'd come in, but those thoughts were all lost now. His tongue lay idle and nothing came to mind. He was lost within himself. And soon, he somehow knew, everything else would be lost, too.

"I'll be happy to reclaim it. But, my dear…" Her cold, clammy hand with its bright red fingernails caressed his cheek. "Why don't you kneel for me?"

The chill of her touch shuddered through his entire body, settling like frost in his joints and in his heart. James lowered himself silently, planting his left knee on the floor—right on top of the bouquet of daisies—and held the ancient scarab in its box aloft.

"Thank you, my love," she purred, staring down on him. "With this ring, I claim you, and this world, as my own."

DARK ENERGY
by Kevin Hayman

'I see it,' Jameson said. 'Over there!'

He pointed at the circular object in the distance.

Dawson focussed his eyes. 'That's it.' He twisted the control lever, heart thumping as the ship gathered speed. He pulled back the throttle. Somewhere on that fast approaching planet was the fugitive they had spent months trying to find. Adrenalin surged.

'Looks like a pretty desolate place.' Jameson gazed through the telescope. 'If he's here, I hope he's brought enough lunch.'

'He's here all right.' Dawson was usually right about these things. His intuition was a sound tool, one that had helped him track down many criminals over the years and bring them to justice.

* * * *

A speaker started beeping.

Jameson flicked a switch. 'Yes,' he said, reading from the monitor. 'The systems located movement.'

'Focus in on it. I want coordinates.'

Jameson tapped something into the keyboard. 'We're too far off for it to make an accurate reading.'

'It's him,' Dawson said calmly as he brought the ship in closer. 'I know it's him.'

They were orbiting the planet when the beeping stopped.

'We've lost it?' Jameson shook his head. 'Must be a course atmosphere? Want me to ring it in and get permission to land?'

Dawson nodded. 'He's down there, Jameson. Only right to bring him in.'

'All right.' Jameson picked up the radio.

Abruptly, the ship nosedived. The fuselage shuddered, rivets screeched. They juddered in their seats.

'What the hell was that?'

'Turbulence,' Dawson said. 'Fasten your belt.'

The ship lurched again. Jameson hastily fastened up. The control lever began shaking uncontrollably, their seats vibrating. Locker doors sprang open spilling out their contents. Grey streams blurred past the windows as the ship was tossed, erratically. Dawson clenched his body rigid in fear—he was no longer in control of the ship. He scrunched his eyes closed and thought of Rebecca. God, he hoped to see her again.

'Brace—'

There wasn't time to say more. The ship arched in violent convulsions, plummeting wildly. Their heads jarred back. An almighty crashing sound burst through the ship with impact. It scraped along the surface like a skimming stone, sand whipping up against the windows. Then they were thrown forward as the ship halted. Smoke rose quickly from the engines. Escape pods slid open.

Dawson looked over to Jameson. He looked pale and shaken, but was lucky to be alive. Miraculously, both had survived unharmed.

Jameson grinned. 'Guess permission's granted.' A poor joke in delivery and timing, but the mind dealt with shock the best it could.

Fire spread across the ship. Dawson tried to think. 'Spacesuits,' he said. 'We need to gather everything we can.'

There wasn't time.

In a mad panic, the two spacemen suited up and hurried out of the burning ship grabbing what they could. Then, almost as soon as they were out, it exploded into a ball of orange flames. Hot shrapnel tore through the sky.

Dawson watched with horror; mind consumed hopeless doom. Everything they needed to survive was being slowly devoured before them. And somehow, like Jameson, the hopelessness of the situation seemed almost comical. A smile touched his lips before it was blasted away with yet another explosion, snapping like a firecracker.

His stomach twisted. He looked up, shaking his head at the cloud of black smoke that hovered over charcoaled metals. That was all that was left of their ship now on an otherwise unblemished planet.

'There's nothing but sand here,' Jameson said. He seemed almost glad about it. 'It's like the bottom of the ocean. Only, without the ocean.'

Dawson admired his optimism. Would surely have told him so had his mind not been cluttered with worry. Instead, he gazed silently out to the flat sandy horizon shimmering in to the distance.

'It's like a sand pit in outer space. Say Dawson, you think there's an ice cream stall out here somewhere?'

Dawson didn't answer. He crouched and took a handful of the warm white sand. 'I hit the panic switch before we crashed,' he said, allowing the grains to sift through his fingertips. 'The nearest ship was days off. We've only got eight hours' water. Maybe nine?'

'And I'll bet you didn't pack a single ice cream?'

He hadn't, of course. But in the mayhem he had managed to grab a bag.

He slung it to the floor to see what might be inside. He hoped he would find radio and rations, but knew there would be little more than a first aid kit.

He opened it. 'This is a survival situation we find ourselves in. We'll have to make everything count. Keep your phone on. If it picks up signal, it might attract a passing ship.'

'Yes boss.' Jameson checked and saw that his phone had not been damaged.

There was more in the bag than Dawson thought. 'Canteen, tent, flares—'

'Ice cream?'

'First aid kit, suntan lotion, protein pills, iron pills.' He pulled the drawstring closed.

'Not one ice cream? Dammit, *Dawson*!'

Next Dawson checked his phone. It had no signal and the compass app seemed off. 'Our best chance of satellite signal is to head out that way,' he pointed in no certain direction.

Jameson shrugged. 'You're the Major,' he said.

There was something about the way he said it that made Dawson realise that, apart from all the kidding around, he was actually scared—little more than a terrified boy up to his neck in a situation he couldn't handle.

'We'll be all right,' Dawson said. 'There's more in the bag than I thought. Who knows, if we head west we may even find you an ice cream stall?'

Jameson smiled. It was a nice touch.

Before Dawson stowed the phone away he switched to another app—his photograph album. The picture of Rebecca posing at the beach. He kissed the screen affectionately before sticking it in his pocket. Looking up, he saw that Jameson was doing the same thing. He threw the bag over his shoulder. 'Come on, lover boy,' he said. 'She'll still be there when you get home. Time to move.'

Jameson grinned, pocketing the phone. 'Do you think they'll have rum and raisin?'

* * * *

Their ship was nothing more than a dot in the distance. They must have walked the Sahara Desert and back. Felt like that anyway. The suns baked down on them like a magnifying glass over ants. Perspiration broke out over their brows and dribbled uninvited salt goblets to their mouths. Their armpits and groins were chafed raw, their feet blistered, their faces burnt, and still they walked on until Jameson could take no more.

'I've got to stop,' he yelled. 'I need water.'

Dawson handed him the canteen. 'Just a drop though,' he said. 'We're on a schedule.'

Jameson pressed the canteen to his lips and let the warm water fill his mouth.

'That's enough!'

Jameson gulped at the water, savouring it. He gurgled it around his mouth as he handed it back. 'How long before the next drop?'

'Long enough,' Dawson said and took a sip.

'Hallelujah!'

They walked on in single file, Dawson leading the way, Jameson trailing a few yards behind, their phones still unable to locate signal.

'Dawson, do you get the feeling we're being watched?'

Dawson looked around at the open landscape. Sun, sky and sand is what he saw and nothing else. No cities. No skyscrapers. No civilisations of any kind. No people, and yet he did feel like he was being watched. He felt like he was being *studied*. 'Out here?' he asked, arms raised, 'must be kidding.'

* * * *

Their ship was no longer visible.

Jameson had started to sing, almost dementedly. Something about being rescued and given complimentary ice cream, to a tune he'd invented as he went along.

Dawson was wondering about home. What was happening there now? What was Rebecca doing? Waiting patiently for his return, he hoped.

He took out his phone again and opened the album. There she was, bronzing in the Hawaiian sun, smiling for the picture. But his stare looked passed her beautiful green eyes and focussed on the turquoise sea in the background. God, it looked so cool and inviting. Good enough to drink. His dry tongue licked across his cracked lips. But you couldn't drink the sea, he knew. It was good for swimming and sailing and surfing and snorkelling and splashing about. But you couldn't drink it. Marooned sailors lapped it up during World War Two, he remembered reading, and those that weren't violently sick inevitably died of dehydration.

He put the phone away.

Maybe Rebecca was walking the sandy shores back home somewhere? He watched his feet moving along the sand. She wouldn't be, of course. Not without him. She would be at home, far away from all those staring eyes. Maybe she would be sunning in their garden, but not at the beach. Their garden was nicely secluded. There she could get her sun fix and not be bothered. Higgins the gardener was the only man who'd be around and he was in his sixties, far too old and busy to notice her basking in the sun. He thought of her wonderfully pert breasts and slender legs freely exploring the luscious green lawns. Higgins wouldn't look, he told himself. He just wouldn't.

He shook his head. 'Must be time for another drink.' He was telling Jameson, but it was a little for his own benefit too. Jameson was no longer singing. 'Jameson. *JAMESON?*'

He was staring off vacantly in to space, his eyes wide and dull.

Dawson held up the canteen. *'Drink?'*

'Yes,' he said eventually, his voice a mere whisper. He took the canteen and sipped at it. Then he wiped an arm across his mouth. 'Dawson, do you think our partners are behaving at home?'

'What?' It was startling how closely Jameson's concern mirrored his own. 'Why do you ask?'

'I don't know. I was just thinking that's all. We've been away long, I just worry. What if we don't find water or a signal, we'll—'

'Jameson,' Dawson's tone was clear and confident. 'I have absolutely no doubt Joanne will be waiting for you *when* you get home. We know there was movement on this planet, right? So we'll arrest our fugitive and fly his ship back.'

It was not a good plan. They were weak and tired, had little strategy and no weapons. Even though Jameson was a new officer, he wasn't stupid. He made a grunting sound at the comment and Dawson felt compelled to reason with him. 'Listen, it's a plan, okay? But I'm sure backup is already on its way.'

* * * *

Dawson's feet were becoming unbearable. His heels were like walking on hot coals. His weakening muscles cramping. The suns were still high in the sky and showing no signs of relenting. Sweat ran down his face. There would be no night here, it occurred to him. No coolness to look forward to. Jameson was so far in the distance now that he felt sure he would give up. If he could just get a bar of signal from one of the roaming space satellites they'd be saved. Or at least, have hope.

His phone had no signal and he found himself looking once more at the picture. Something about the sea made it look as if it were moving, rippling, flowing in the breeze. Waves building and crashing into white beads on the shoreline. Back and forth they came, rising and falling. Rising and falling. It was hypnotic the way they came and went.

In the foreground, Rebecca's beautifully full red lips parted slightly to reveal pearly white teeth. She was incredible. Her eyes, so clearly resembled the ocean. Her crimson cheeks were high and rounded like the suns. Her skin was as soft and smooth as the fine delicate sand. She lay like a marble statue in front of the tumbling waves. Waves that built up and shattered in to white surf.

Kids were moving now. Rushing up to touch the sea and splash their friends. Young couples passed by, their feet treading carefully along the shallow shoreline. Swimmers swam, snorkeler's snorkelled, surfer's rode on distant waves. An old man in khaki shorts limped along in the background. He was pale and gaunt and wrinkled. Out of place in the picture. He stopped, suddenly interested in the woman sunning on the beach. He stared at her. It was Higgins!

Dawson felt his grip tightened on the phone. 'No,' he growled. 'Move on. *MOVE ON!*'

But he didn't. Instead, he stood there watching her. Grinning. His thin quivering lips creased with lurid pleasure. His haggard sunken eyes gleamed at the sight of young tender flesh. He was ogling her.

'You bastard!'

Higgins stepped a gangly leg forward, a purple tattoo of varicose veins. Rebecca turned. She smiled.

Dawson tensed. He tried to yell something but it was muted in the dry cavity of his throat.

They started to chat, happily. He thought he could hear their laughter echoing in the chamber of his mind, like a tennis ball bouncing between walls. He watched as she brushed a palm playfully over his bony yellow arm and sniggered. They were flirting.

It triggered his mouth to open in a ridiculous snarl. '*NOOOOooooo!*'

'What? Jameson asked. 'What is it?'

He couldn't talk. His mind had been rattled. He stood there, gazing blankly, drawing in deep breaths, unable to think properly. He ran his hands over his face, forcing himself to ignore the hallucinations. Demanding it, almost. Very slowly and carefully, he managed, 'Let's put up camp.'

He was overtired. Over worked. Dehydrated. Suffering from the repercussions of shock. He wasn't mad. It was very important he reminded himself that. His survival, and Jameson's come to that, required clear thinking and good decision-making. Those were not key characteristics of the insane.

He took back control, overseeing the construction of the tent and insuring they took their protein and iron pills. He wanted to give them the best chance at surviving. Then he laid back his sunburnt head and rested.

Jameson lay next to him, looking up. 'Tomorrow's do or die, isn't it?'

There was no easy way to answer that. 'Get some sleep,' was all he said.

* * * *

Jameson jerked upright, panting. His eyes alight with panic.

'It's all right,' Dawson whispered. 'You were dreaming.'

'A-A nightmare,' he said between breaths.

'I know.'

He grinned, bitterly. 'Can't say I'm pleased to wake up here.'

'No.'

'What's doing this to us?' He turned to Dawson. 'The dehydration?'

Dawson stood and pulled back the tent flap. He looked out at the desert. That's what was doing it he now knew, the dammed planet. It had a life all of its own. It was watching them and worse, it was tormenting them. 'Don't know,' he said.

Something in the distance *moved*. He shielded his eyes from the bright suns. It was almost impossible to make out...

It *was*!

'My God!' The words fell out of him. 'Jameson, get up.'

Jameson sidled outside. 'What? What is it?'

'Look!' He pointed at the thing moving. 'It's a space buggy.'

Jameson squinted 'Yeah. Yeah, I think it is.'

They stood for a moment, the two of them, staring out into the vast dessert without moving. Paused in disbelief—rigor mortis of the mind.

Then they were moving for it with renewed strength in their legs.

'Stop the vehicle!' they shouted. 'Stop!'

They had no weapons to force the issue and the driver did not comply. Instead, he circled them, straightened out, and then drove directly at them.

'Get back!' Dawson yelled at Jameson, instinctively grabbing his canteen.

In one quick motion he threw it hard at the approaching buggy. At school he'd been a pretty average pitcher, nothing out of the ordinary. He expected to miss his target by some distance. Then it cracked the driver slap-bang in the centre of his face, forcing him to jerk suddenly at the wheel. The buggy swerved on to two wheels, and then snagged to its side. What a shot!

He couldn't quite believe it. He looked to Jameson who seemed equally perplexed. Then he turned back to the buggy and approached cautiously. If this was their fugitive, he was known to be dangerous. It was, but there was no worry of that. He'd clearly been dead for some time. His decomposing body must have applied pressure to the accelerator. The buggy, charged by solar panel, seemingly moved at random unless...

'Jesus,' Jameson said as he approached. 'What the hell happened to Brian May, here?' He did look a little like Brian May. Though the suns had dried his skin to a leathery brown and rotted away his nose. His sunglasses barely clung to his face.

Dawson switched off the engine. 'Suicide, I guess.' He made the assumption based on the condition of the man's slit wrists and the knife that lay a few yards from the overturned buggy.

'It's our man, isn't it?'

'Maybe.' He was looking for some form of evidence before he confirmed it. On the small black dashboard above the steering wheel, he found two words that had been repeatedly carved. They read: DARK ENERGY. DARK ENERGY. DARK ENERGY.

Dawson pursed his lips. 'Come on,' he said, finally. 'Let's get this thing back on its wheels.'

Two large blue containers had been strapped to the back of the buggy. During the crash, one had rolled free.

Jameson inspected it. 'Hey Major, what do you think's in here?'

Dawson wrestled the container upright, unscrewed the lid and gawped in.

'Well?'

He couldn't contain his smile. 'Christmas,' he said, plunging in his hands. They came out cupped and dripping wet.

'Water!'

* * * *

They got the buggy back on its wheels and ditched the driver. He was rigid and still in his sitting position when they laid him out on the sand. Then they opened the second container. This one was loaded with supplies like tinned food and packet snacks. There was even some freeze-dried ice cream, albeit not rum and raisin. Still, it was another welcome treat. Dawson tossed it over to Jameson and told him to 'Go crazy!'

But that would come later.

* * * *

Before they sped off in search of the fugitive's ship, they returned to camp to collect their equipment. They loaded it onto the buggy and were then off at high speed, bouncing along the rough surface. It was a joy to feel the air breeze past their burnt skin like soft silk.

'So what was your nightmare about?'

'It's stupid, really.'

'Go on,' said Dawson. 'Can't be any more ridiculous than mine.'

'All right,' he said, 'try this. I dreamed that Joanne was cheating on me with the maintenance man.'

'Maintenance man?' Dawson choked out a laugh. 'Isn't he nearly seventy?'

'He's nearly eighty, actually. But it just felt so real. And then—' the jovial smile left his face, 'then she merged into the elements.'

'What?'

'Yeah, she became the beach and wanted to… to kill me, I think, by luring me in and swallowing me up?'

Dawson felt himself go cold. He'd had the same dream, only with Rebecca and Higgins. That too had seemed real.

'So what was *your* dream about?'

Dawson shook his head, dismissively. 'Nothing as freaky as that.' He hoped he'd sounded convincing.

* * * *

They found the remains of Brian May's burnt-out ship a few hours later. It appeared he'd crashed upon landing and escaped in the buggy before it caught fire. With the food and water containers hardly touched, it couldn't have been long before he gave up and slashed his wrists. Dawson thought about the strange message on the dashboard as he opened a can of beans, watching the suns shine over the wreckage. Any hope of leaving the planet now depended on their rescue. But they had food and water supplies, and shelter. They had a vehicle. If they could only find a signal they could make contact with Earth.

Dawson checked his phone—nothing. A little further west, he tried to convince himself. Then he quickly stowed his it away, forcing himself not to look at the photo album. Even though he was now fed and watered, he knew not to look. He washed down the beans with more water. It was the first time he'd taken more than he felt he needed, but he wanted to drown out those terrible thoughts of Rebecca and Higgins.

* * * *

They drove along in silence for a while. Dawson's hands, tight fists that gripped the steering wheel. His hold was so tight that his knuckles turned white. He glanced at the rear-view mirror and froze. Rebecca stared at him from the backseats. Instinctively, he cocked his head to the rear. He saw only the containers, bobbing about in the back. He swallowed. Don't lose it, he told himself. But his mind had started wavering again.

'*Joanne?*' The voice came from beside him.

Jameson was staring out into the distance as if his young wife was lingering out there somewhere. There was no one, of course.

'It isn't,' he shouted. 'Keep looking ahead. *Keep looking ahead.*'

He couldn't. The intrigue of his wife was just too great. Dawson had experienced the same thing and had struggled to fight it.

He grabbed Jameson's jaw and straightened his gaze ahead. Jameson kept it there only momentarily, then his eyes crept to the side and his head soon followed.

'*Darling,*' a voice whispered sweetly. It was the unmistakable voice of Rebecca.

Darling!

It wasn't, he knew. He was on a planet a million miles away. Blot it out, he told himself. Blot it out. Drown it out. Get rid of it!

He started to sing—anything to focus his mind. It occurred to him he was singing the same song that Jameson had conjured up yesterday, the one about being rescued with copious amounts of ice cream.

'Sing with me, Jameson,' he rattled him. 'Sing!'

In the distance was a ship—a large circular ship, not a bit like the one they had crashed in. Dawson forced his foot down on the accelerator.

Jameson's hands were clasped to his ears, as though trying to keep out the voice of his wife. 'Could you fly that thing?'

'I could fly anything.'

Darling! Her voice was soft and inviting. *Come to me, darling. Come to the beach!*

He focussed his eyes on the ship ahead. Focus!

It was a mother ship, capable of manning a crew of a hundred or more and staying in space for long duration missions. There would be help inside.

He pumped the brakes as they neared the ship. The buggy skidded sideways on the sand and halted. The men ran for the ship with their hands pressed to their ears. They were singing.

The ship's sensors picked up their movement and opened its doors. They hurried up the stairs and into the fuselage.

The doors closed behind them.

Despair!

'No!' screamed Jameson. Dawson could not scream. He was muted with terror.

The ship had been sabotaged. The engines had been ripped out. The crew lay dead on the floor, their bodies stripped with cuts. Blood, flesh and mechanical pieces lay strewn in a disastrous jumble. The fridges were open and their contents rotting. And the walls were a mosaic of frantic scribbling—a scribbling of two unforgettable words: DARK ENERGY.

They knew what it meant now. This crew had known what it meant. Brian May had known what it meant. You couldn't fight what you couldn't see—a dark energy. This place, this entire planet was surrounded in it. It was a sea, they realised. A sea of dark energy and it washed out everything around it.

Dawson's phone started to vibrate. Soon after, Jameson's followed.

'A signal,' Dawson said. 'It's a message from Earth. Help is six hours away.'

Jameson snatched the phone, frenzied. 'You fool,' he snarled. 'It's the dark energy. Can't you see? It's in our minds. It's in our minds!'

They stood staring at each other, trembling.

Just like the insane.

* * * *

After encountering strong turbulence, the ship from Earth was able to land safely. The crew separated in to two parties to search for the spacemen. The first party returned after a few hours. They had found the remains of two burnt out ships and a poorly decomposed body, thought to be that of a well-known fugitive. The second party returned having found a ship that had been internally destroyed by its crew, who had then committed mass suicide. They also reported finding a space buggy a few miles from the ship. Though the bodies of Major Dawson and Officer Jameson could not be located, they did, however, find footprints in the sand near to where words had been scribbled.

Two words.

DARK ENERGY.

CHRISTMAS AT CASTLE DRACULA

By S. L. Edwards

You think I am evil.

I can tell by your eyes. So pointed, so full of hatred, bile and revulsion. You look at me and you see innumerable sins, unforgivable crimes against both your species and your God.

This is fine, and I do not blame you. You'll have time to come to understand me, my friend. And I *do* consider you my friend, despite what you might think. We've already been through so much in your days here, and you are not going anywhere any time soon.

You'll thank me after, when all of this is over.

But before that I want to tell you that you misunderstand me. You hold up your cross and you believe that I cower away in fear, in vulnerability. But I will tell you, it is not with fear that I look upon the sword of God…it is with *reverence*. I look upon this instrument of torture, the symbol of the cruelty mankind inflicts on anything it sees as greater and more divine than itself, and I feel *kindred*.

I was just a child when my *devout* Christian father gave my brother and I to *devout* Muslims in slavery. It is no wonder that when I finally returned home I acted so cruelly. In their dungeons I learned hatred, the sort of hatred of an animal adopts in its cage. It does not know why, it does not know how, but the caged animal knows that *something is not right*. It knows it *does not* belong in a cage. So it paces, back and forth, biting at every hand whether they feed it or beat it.

To be certain, our cages were gilded, our jailers thought themselves merciful men. Eventually we were removed from the dungeons and placed amongst a sort of limited society. They taught us things which they should have not. Arts of horsemanship, literature, their very language.

But above all else, their cruelty.

The cruelty which despite any other virtue, I will always remember them by.

They would open our doors at night and whisper into our ears as we cried that it was our *privilege* to be their prisoners.

They taught me more there, more than my brother, who came to love his captors more than he ever loved our family. I do not blame him, given the loyalty of our father. But I never could understand, and I could never sympathize with his choice. I loved my brother and deeply wish that I had been a better keeper.

If there is one regret which immortality has given me; it is that I bear upon myself the mark of Cain.

I prayed often there. To my God, to my father. Little did I know, my father was no godly man. And my God was always with me.

Our captors released me onto the world and I brought with me the hatred which had grown for so long. You look at me now and I know you see a monster. But you are born off of the sins of monsters such as myself. What is the difference between the impalement of a hundred men, the slaughter of widows and children, compared to the suffering of one child? You look upon me and see some Eastern barbarian, some vaguely Asiatic warlord. You put distance between yourself and I, but you do not take into account the sins of your own fathers. Surely, you must look upon what your country has done in India, and certainly you must know what happened to the people who stood to protect their homes when your ships arrived. And in these actions, my dear friend, you may believe that you see my influence on history. But this is not the case.

I was a man before I was ever any sort of 'monster.'

How shocking is a banquet amongst corpses when every meal, every success and excess you consume is built upon the lives and sufferings of millions?

I have given you much to think about. I pray you consider it while you hang there. I encourage you to sleep. It will make the time go so much faster.

I will return when I can. Goodnight.

* * * *

Greetings, my friend. You look much better. The change will progress, will heal you.

I, however, must apologize.

I never wished to make another man my prisoner.

You might perceive hypocrisy, and you would not be entirely wrong. I was still a man when I was voivode. Murder, slaughter, genocide. These were small concerns in one of the bloodiest tracts of land in my time. The dirt at the crossroads of civilizations is always hungry, and must be watered accordingly. I was made to believe that I was part of a great clash of two civilizations, and that I was the tortured child of both.

And despite all of the garments and vestments, I had given up on God. I was a faithless man in the armor of the faith, a wolf in sheep's clothing.

My animal hatred burned against every Turk who represented my childhood jailers, against every European who represented the godless father who so willingly surrendered my innocence.

But then, this changed on the road from Bucharest to Giurgiu.

There, I beheld the same blinding light that Paul had beheld before he became Saul. I was thrown from my horse, crushed underneath and killed in the light of something far greater than any man could ever be.

Surely, my friend, you have read the word. But to read of the resurrection is one thing, to experience it is another entirely. I have looked upon the word with eyes which have truly been reborn and I have seen the secret meanings passed down to those given the true gift of eternity on earth. There are scripts there, invisible to those who are confined to a mortal life. Between the lines, in the sacred and hidden meter of the truly divine.

Now…looking back on my past as Saul, I see that mankind will always attempt to consume itself. Every man alive is a Cain, and any Abel is slaughtered long before he has a time to become old.

The differences you make between yourselves are truly superficial, purely cosmetic. The blood of an Englishman tastes the same as any other. Inside you are each a series of innards, defined not by any nationhood but by *pipework*.

And yet you cannot overcome your differences because you are born into them, inheriting the prejudices of generations before. And so, burdened with ancestral hatreds you and your leaders will always seek to begin wars over small infractions, matters of ego and fabricated prides.

When I awoke, after decades of cold, long darkness, I climbed my way from my tomb and held myself up in the mountains, in the ruins of my old life. And there I studied, grew and waited with my new form. The word was a frequent subject of study, and I grew more sympathetic to a God willing to suffer for his world rather than condemn it. And I studied languages, philosophy, for a hundred years I lived alone with my library.

It is true, though, that eternity requires a sacrifice, requires a devotion and commitment which would make the lesser folk tremble. I sought to pass eternity on to those worthy. Those who were not worthy…they were only men, only women. I climbed down from my tower walls, slithered into their villages and killed them as they slept. And as I did so, I whispered prayers and thanks into their ears, sending them on their way to their maker with mercy and blessings.

You call vampirism a sickness and you are as blinded by prejudice as your species ever was. It is pure, unabashed egotism to think yourselves the superior creatures on this planet. How can an entire species, an entire race, be a *disease*? We will burn in the sunlight, surely, but we will not die by gunshot, nor by any of the other ailments which make humanity so frail. We need the blood of others, but no water, no food. You think of our existence as impossible, as a wretched contamination. However, we are in fact the *advancement* of the human race.

We are more *holy*.

Think on my words. I will see you tomorrow night.

* * * *

You might think it strange, my friend, but I do not hold any ill will towards those who have killed me.

Each time I learn something new, a vulnerability which I was unaware of or a method that somehow escaped mention in any of my books. Then, when this information is passed down to the inevitable children of those who will oppose me, I will be more prepared. In this way, I owe you and the others many thanks.

And then, each time I die, I come closer to my Lord.

Death is only a temporary pain, after all. It is one which, as you see, can be recovered from.

But those who fight me look upon me and they saw what you see. They compare me to Genghis, to Napoleon. But I tell you now that in all of the history of this world you will have never seen a ruler such as a Dracula. Never before has one been so clearly been sent by their maker to dominate and lead mankind.

I will take control of this world; the matter merely lies in the waiting.

And that is precisely the problem with humans, with leaders of men. They are made of breakable bones, malleable minds, and conquerable spirits. They only live so long before they make their irreparable mistakes, and not knowing the extent of history which years of studies brings, they commit the same errors as their fathers. The spend the blood of sons, the lives of men and women on things which they do not need. Their sight only extends years, decades if a man is truly wise. But a decade is no time at all to someone who does not die, or to someone who will not *stay* dead. And the preservation of your children will be a very different cause than the preservation of your great-great grandchildren, ancestors who you will never know.

But I will know them.

We will not make humanity cattle. The notion is ridiculous. Our culture would thrive by night and be dead during the day, our planet would be losing half of its time. It is true though, that we will need to feed. And we will not apologize for this. There are more than enough people on this planet to feed every vampire for over a century. And at the rate populations grow, the more we seem a natural check. They will die, and it will be necessary. Progress has always come at the price of blood, and the end of history is no different than what preceded it.

But we will not turn them into us. Should we do that, there would be too many of us.

And then we would become them, we would become mankind. With all of its fictitious schisms and all of its careless violence.

No…no I am content to rule from a distance, content to sit on an invisible throne with my shadow-laden crown. I need nothing more from my subjects than that blood which I must take to survive. I am willing to outweigh the lifespan of nations, of empires, of any of those who have any hope of killing me. And when they are gone, I will give their children…my children, a new earth.

Here, drink. This is the blood of my covenant, which is poured out for you.

Eat. My flesh, given for you.

Sleep well friend, for when you wake it will be with new eyes.

Welcome to my home. To *your* home.

And, of course, merry Christmas.

THERE WAS FIRE
by M. Ravenberg

Harlon was young and full of dreams and vigour, and this night, he told himself as he paced down the street, would be the night he had sex with a woman. He did not particularly care which woman it was with, only that she be youthful and pretty and able to match his superficial desires.

It was dark. The air smelled swampy and toxic, and he was afraid that the odour would bleed into his expensive clothes. The moon was hiding behind a clump of silver clouds. No doubt, Harlon thought, that the roof of the art institute would be crawling with frivolous students and their easels.

He wanted sex partly for enjoyment, partly for inspiration. After studying Van Gogh and his unfortunate hearing loss, he had the idea to visit a brothel his colleagues had spoken of. Without a second thought he made plans to visit the harlot's house.

His destination was in a less trafficked part of the city, in which the loud jingle of coins in his pocket made Harlon uncomfortable, and where few respectable people were to be found at day, though seemed to congregate there by night. He saw a familiar face or two on his way, all of whom turned away from him in a gesture as if to say "We will not see you, if you will not see us." He expressly took them up on the unspoken, mutual agreement, forgetting faces as he passed on his way. Besides, he had more pressing thoughts on mind.

He imagined the woman he would find himself with: and in the cold of that night it would be difficult not to think about her warmth. Not that he was pushing her from his mind. This woman he dreamed was a darkly brunette, firm breasted and full of flare. Red lips—naturally crimson without gloss. Eyes that shined like lanterns down mineshafts or the great beacons of lighthouses, guiding lost sailors. Her voice, a shiver of wind. The simple thought of being inside of her flushed his body with an uneasy, giddy feeling. He wondered if the excitement showed in his eyes.

He turned down a byway that shielded him from the sharp tongue of the wind. Actually, he perceived a warmth about the alley. The door to the brothel was at the other end. He knocked. A girl answered.

"I am here for women," he said quietly, not knowing what else to say. "I have money," he added.

The woman seemed to understand, sending him a curt, almost plaintive, nod, opening the door wide, and he found himself in a warm, plain room. There were no hangings or garnishes. It was a cheap brothel.

"Your money," the plaintive girl said; "let me see it. As proof."

He swung a fold of his coat over, revealing a hidden inner pocket from which he extracted a purse containing a hefty sum. She fingered through the purse, counting mumly under her breath. When she counted to a number high enough to please her, she smiled, first to herself, then to Harlon, saying:

"Yes—this is enough. See that door? Through there. Take your pick."

"How much—how much do they each cost?"

"No matter: you will have enough for whoever you choose, maybe two."

"If I choose you?"

"I am not a choice. Now go, have fun. Your money will be safe—and clothes if you wish to leave them here. Some do."

He did not wish to.

Through the door, the quality of décor noticeably and sharply improved. There were long lavender sheets in the corners, dimmers fixed to the lights, creating a gloomy mood of lurking shadow, and long, sheeted sofas. At least ten half-naked women reposed around the room. They eyed him sensuously. Some kissed at him. A tall redheaded girl—no more than twenty-three—approached him.

"Who do you desire?" she asked with a pleasing, opulent tone of voice.

"I've never done this before. I don't know." He could not rip his eyes off her bare chest.

"Do you want somebody who is gentle, or more…rough?"

"It is my *first* time," he reiterated.

"So you don't know your way around a woman? I can show you, if you can afford—"

"The girl outside said I had enough for any of you…"

"Yes, but do you have *enough*?" she threw back her head in a short giggle, making him uncomfortable.

Bashfully, he hurried her on: "I am young, twenty, I have enough."

"Well, then, who do you want?" she giggled out.

"I don't know, I said. Let me consider."

"Choose one now, you can always come back."

He impatiently scanned the prostitutes, eager to get the decision over with. None of them were particularly fabulous. Some pushed out their chests to make their breasts look grotesquely large and misshapen. Some wore soiled corsets and some nothing at all. All of them seemed to blend together in one streak of bland, uninteresting colour, save for the redhead girl. The choice was obvious.

At last he shyly said "I'd like you" to the redhead.

"I'll be gentle for your first time. I'll make it worth it." She allowed a slim smile cross her pink lips.

The other women looked at him with a mixture of disappointment and jealousy as the redhead led him up a flight of stairs by his shivering hand.

She said, "I'm Abby, and you?"

"Harlon," he said with anticipation. The excitement was mounting.

"I've had a man with that name before. Nothing like you. Old, decrepit. I thought he would die before we finished. He was a scholar. Not a successful one, mind you. He tried to write books about rocks."

The light of the stairway was tenfold brighter than the room before. He could see Abby now in her fullness. She was gorgeous. Her body was pale, red hair like fire cascading down her sensuous back, trailing over her ass, which was covered only by a thin, dazzling skirt. Around her neck hung a beaded necklace. Face and chest were splotched with rusty freckles that made a spade down her nose. Almost timidly he reached out and massaged her left breast. It was firm, covered in tiny, soft hairs. He wanted desperately to kiss it. Admirable how she could walk around bare breasted and exposed. He could never feel comfortable naked in the presence of a stranger—but then again, he was about to be, wasn't he? Did she even care to see him naked? It was her job, most people do not like their job, it goes without saying.

They reached a closed door. Instinctively he reached over and held it open for her. With an air of faux gentility she ushered in. When he turned in, she was spread over the bed. Her skirt was folded upward to her waist; he could almost glimpse…

His eyes were adverted as she spoke: "Come. Sit. I'll help you undress."

He was drawn like a moth to flame by her and her hair. It was such a lively hue of orange, almost a red. On the bed he kissed her nape, running his teeth over her quivering white flesh. Did she enjoy this, he thought, and stopped to look at her in the face.

She had worked his coat off, when he said: "Who *are* you?"

It surprised him as much as it surprised her.

"I told you my name…" she responded dismissively.

"What is your life?"

Suddenly he was possessed by something other than libido. By curiosity.

She paused to contemplate the strange direction things were going.

"I am a poor girl, as you may have guessed. I live and work here, because there is nowhere else for people like me. What about you? What is *your* life?"

"Mine?"—he was now resting on the bed, hands supporting head—"I am an artist, or hope to be. I am a student at the institute not far from here."

"My father, he fancied himself an artist."

"Might I know him?" he sniggered.

"No, he died in a fire with the rest of my family, when I was thirteen. All his work was lost. None of it, really, was good, anyway.

He stopped smirking, "That's tragic. I'm sorry."

"I alone survived. The firemen say they found me passed out among the ashes. They mistook my hair for embers. They say a fallen beam shielded me from the flame. But I know better. I know the truth."

Now she was back in action, driven to lighten the mood after a spirit of solemnity had overtaken the room. She flung off his shoes, socks, and, as his fingers were too shaky, helped to undo Harlon's belt buckle. She complained: "Silly. Why do people wear such fancy clothes when they know they'll be taking them off? I don't see the point."

In nothing but underwear and a shirt, he watched her dance on top of him. Her skirt was beginning to fall down, he helped it off. He ran his fingers through her hair, appraising its smoothness. It was a physical manifestation of the inner flame she encased.

"So red," he said succinctly.

"It used to be brown."

"I'm glad it isn't. It makes you look so unique....unlike the other whores here."

She kissed his face, bit his nether lip. He wormed out of his shirt and underwear. Inside of her, they became one. One movement. One person. They were in unity. A single will with a single goal. He felt her warmth enclose him; he filled her with passion and pain. They bucked in throes of sexual pleasure. He held her buttocks, her blazing hair streaming over his hands. She was a fire, consuming him, burning him through. Her expression seemed to widen as her eyes and mouth opened as far as possible in a deep groan. They surged with spasms of love and lust. He kissed her nipples again and again, sucking, almost as if begging or pleading....

This was sex. This was pleasurable, enlightening. This was so much more than he had envisioned. This was his element. Where he could unfurl his emotions at their rawest and perform at his best.

When he finished, she rolled off him, leaving him suspended in place, heaving for air....

"Do you mind if I smoke?" he asked her when he had recovered.

"Go ahead," she said nonchalantly, as if nothing had just happened. "Unlike most girls here, I like the smell of tobacco."

He lit a cigarette from out of his coat pocket.

"Did you like your first time?" she inquired.

Before responding he huffed musingly on the cigarette, making a face in mock-imitation of a bust of a Greek scholar, "Like it? Abby, I loved it. You were like a fire."

"I'm glad you enjoyed yourself. I had a Russian who kept repeating: 'You are fire, you are fire' over and over. He was dreadfully drunk."

"Did you enjoy it?"

"Why do you ask? You know I'll say I did whether I did or not. May I have a drag?"

He passed the cigarette to her.

"This is good. I'm not just saying that. Must be expensive."

"Very," he said. "I don't normally share them—I give other people the cheap kind. But you—you're special."

"In that I'm your first?"

"Not just that. There is something more to you than what I can see. I feel it. I could really feel it before, when I was inside of you. I could feel it flowing through you, into me. It was spreading. It was growing, expanding. Blossoming. We were connecting on a more than physical level. I felt this subdued energy opening up to me. You know what I felt?"

He was now holding her gently around the shoulders.

"What did you feel?" she asked, curling a coppery brow.

"I felt love," he said adoringly.

"Love?" Her lips wrinkled in an ugly, sarcastic smirk.

"Yes. I'm in love with you. And you with me!"

She laughed. "You are mistaken. You have sex for the first time and you think it is love? It is not. I don't doubt you felt something, dear, but it was not love. My past clients have talked to me about this. They have though it was love when it was not. One man said, I made him burn. I made him so hot he began to burn. I guess you felt that same fire."

Her eyes were large, wet globes. He began kissing her again, all over her body. She laughed as if deriving some sort of pleasure from this. So he continued, attempting to please her so she would love him. He knew she could. He knew she would. His head lowered to between her hips, where he began to lick gently. She smiled mischievously at him, exposing a row of gleaming, moon-silver teeth.

"You're a fascinating lover," she groaned.

"Ah, we're lovers," he confirmed.

"We are lovers. We make love, though we may not have it."

This seemed to anger Harlon, as he immediately ceased his activity, broke away from her, reposing in a chair away from the bed. She could see that he was still visibly aroused, moved over to him, sitting on his lap.

Looking him in the eyes, Abby said, "You're brooding. Try to enjoy this. Sex is not for the heavy hearted."

"But love is."

"No, love is for no one." She placed a single, slender finger over his mouth.

He began to buck, and they moved in a steady rhythm. His mind began to ease. Abby rustled his dark hair. He had that feeling. Almost embarrassed, he came to the conclusion that it was not love he had felt. All he had ever heard and read about love was that it was emotional. What was now happening was not emotional; it was primal, physical, titillating, unrelenting, deep and sunken, exuding a strange, languorous spell over his mind. His head was giddy with thrill. He was enraptured and, on a deeper level, terrified. The idea of mundane domestic life where he was not always feeling this way—it depressed him. He felt he was as high as he could be, now the only place to go was down.

Her tantalising appeal forced him closer to her. He was obsessed by the primal physical-emotion she radiated. She embodied everything suppressed in him: immaturity, sex, arousal, perversion. He drank in her aura and felt he could conquer the world.

Abby was no longer a cheap whore with a blessed body. She was a god of fire. Omnipotent and everlasting. She could burn humanity to ash, resurrect it in her image. There was fire in her very being. She was linked to it. She was touching fire, and by touching her so intimately he was in contact with the eternal, sublime flame that exists behind the veil of everyday life. Centuries of damnation and sin fed its ever-mounting inferno. The erotic, the perverse, the destructive—it all fit in with the fire.

"I do feel hot," he managed to gasp as this epiphany hit. "Hot on the inside."

"It's alright…. Take it slow."

"It feels amazing. I want to paint…to paint this…you."

"You want to paint me?" she said as he came.

"Yes, I do. I want to somehow capture this heat on the canvas. This is revolutionary!"

"Revolutionary?" she grunted.

"Yes. It could change the world, if only I can contain, somehow quantify, it as a painting. This energy and all it entails—can change how we think!—how we act!"

"You're making so much of so little," she said in a tone entirely unconvinced. "Are you seeing reality? Do you realise what is actually here?"

"Oh, yes I do. You are a whore, this a house of whores. You provide sex to lazy, desperate men. Is that not true? I want to show that. I want to show how debased life is. I want to paint a fire that strips away the glitter we see covering everyday life."

"It sounds so complicated. Why not paint flowers?—or fruit? That would make me happy."

"I am happy—now." Then he proposed: "Will you be my model?"

"Your model... I don't think I will be. You are an agreeable man, but that's out of my area of expertise. I'm no model. My place is here. I've carved out a living here that I enjoy. I have my regulars who keep me fed and clothed. I fear I'd be misplaced if I went with you. I could never fit in."

"Please," he begged. "I can help you settle in, make you comfortable."

"No," she said firmly. "It simply wouldn't work. Where I am is where I want to be. I would die if you tore me out of here. I need sex to survive. I may enjoy your company but you could never satisfy me. Sex fuels me, keeps me going. I live on sex and all the sex I need is here. One man would never be enough. You're at the peak of your vitality and you alone are not enough. Stop trying to convince me. It will end badly, for both of us."

"Please, I could make it work..."

"No, you can't," she stated definitively.

That broke him. Anger flared and dominated his other emotions. He hit her. He left a red sore across her soft cheek. Instantly he regretted it. Her lips parted momentarily then quickly closed. Looking to the ground confusedly she moved over to the opposite corner of the room, sitting on the floor, arms limp on her lap. She did not even shed a single tear.

He lapped up the water out of a glass on the nightstand, moving silently round the room like a vulture high above in the air, avoiding her. The wildness in him was slain. He went about pulling his clothes on without motivation. Abby caught him sneaking short, remorseful glances at her. She thought he was crying a little and trying to hide it.

Her hair draped over her face, and her eyes were gleaming from between curly locks. They were black. Every second seemed hours long. He felt inadequate and small, as if every piece of himself had been closely evaluated and nothing of value was found in him. He didn't want her to see him. He was ashamed of himself, his actions, his body. Ashamed to be present at a whorehouse. Ashamed that he was never good enough at what he did. His insecurities flooded him. He felt crippled.

He wanted to apologise but didn't know how. He wanted to rescue her from this pit. Hoping to draw her out into conversation he put his hand on the brass doorknob.

"Wait..." she gasped, doing exactly what he had hoped.

He turned on his heel to face her. She was standing. Their eyes locked. He waited for her to say something.

"Don't go," she steadily began. "You paid for a night. It is only one o'clock..."

"After I—after I hit you, you'd still take me?"

"Others have done worse."

"Then why don't you leave? You could make a decent living."

"Hush. I can deal with *them*. That *you* hit me is what frightened me. When I saw you, you seemed naïve and innocent. I would have never guessed you'd be violent to me. I felt a connection."

"I felt a connection with you, too. A physical connection. Something real. I understood the fire that burns beneath your skin. You can leave with me tonight."

"I can't."

Her face was drenched in sweat and masked in desperate aggravation.

"Why not?"

"I feel sick…"

She fell against the wall with a thud. Harlon, frightened, helped her over to the bed.

"It came on so quickly. My stomach. And chest."

"You look terrible."

"I hear strange things at night"—her voice a whisper, eyes unfocused— "not coming from out of the dark. From within my own skull. Crackling. Please don't leave me."

"I won't."

"This happens sometimes. When I get stressed. Normally I keep it under 'til my clients leave."

She was gasping—gasping for air.

He dipped a handkerchief into a pitcher of cold water, began rubbing her forehead.

"No, stop," she screamed weakly. "It hurts more."

"You've a fever. It'll help," he insisted, pushing down the cloth.

"No, you don't understand!"

Then she did something he hadn't expected.

* * * *

When the firemen had finally arrived on scene, Harlon was long gone. Over the next few days he would read about it mentioned in the gazette. The mysterious fire that ravaged a brothel. People theorised about what had really happened. Regulars would lament the deaths of their favourite prostitutes. But that did not matter to Harlon. When he entered his room that night, it did not matter. It was almost morning, he couldn't sleep, didn't try to. Tea tasted stale in his mouth. Any eating was in vain.

His mind was too occupied to pay attention to anything that was happening around him. That night he was haunted by a myriad thoughts and ideas. They were overwhelming and fought for attention. The longer they were kept supressed, the more they increased in ferocity. Nothing solid passed through his mind—nothing of Abby or the earlier night—but shapes and impressions, vague in outline, but intense. Out of all the confusion and mental mayhem one insatiable image reared its presence. One focused image that clawed to be freed.

Dizzily he prepared his tools and strung on his apron. With mechanical precision he mixed paints and selected a few clean, dry brushes. He positioned a comfortable chair at the window, through which the first luminosities of dawn were peeking. This image, fresh on his mind, was more glowing and brilliant than any sun. Then with everything in place he sat down at his easel and began to paint. There was fire in his eyes.

THEM

by Sharon Cullars

The whiskey was biting tonight. Not smooth as before. The liquid grasped the walls of Kayla's throat, crawled down her gullet as though it anticipated the acid juices of her stomach.

Lately, her food refused to settle right causing her extreme gastrointestinal distress. Eventually the warmth of the liquor reached its destination and the acids devoured it.

The phone sitting on the table next to the futon rang. She refused to get rid of the landline despite the fact that her whole life was on her iPhone. She picked up.

"Kayla?" Her mother's voice was a strident whine, her usual tone but tonight there was an underlying urgency to it.

"Yeah, Mom, what's going on?"

"Did you see the news tonight? About Tom Thackery?"

Kayla's stomach tightened. She hadn't seen Tom in a couple of weeks since they had gotten back to Frisco from the Tusayan Ruins in Arizona.

"No, I don't have the TV on. What's happened to Tom?"

The liquor was making a racket in her stomach. Or maybe it was the desiccated steak she'd choked down for dinner.

"He's disappeared and his family…oh my God, those poor babies."

'Those babies' would be Tom's two girls, Leah and Reagan, two and four, respectively.

"Mom, tell me what's happened and don't get weepy on me!" Kayla said with her no-nonsense voice, the tone she'd used since she was ten and her mother was finally diagnosed as bi-polar and their roles reversed during those times her mother refused to take her meds.

"The news report was just on. Tom's kids and Charlotte…they're dead, Kayla!"

The sudden wave of nausea almost overtook her but she forced it back, her stomach rioting even as her brain tried to process what her mother had just told her.

"Dead…but…they can't be. How…how? Where's Tom?"

"Tom isn't there. The police are still at the house. They think the bodies might have been there all night. Kayla, they think Tom is responsible somehow."

"But that's ridiculous! Tom literally couldn't hurt a fly." Which was so true. It was something she'd teased him about at the last dig where they'd been brought on to extricate a dinosaur cranium that a tourist had discovered by accident and to search for any relative fossils. During the two weeks there, flies had swarmed them horribly. She'd set her sights on the vermin, swashing them with relish while Tom gently swatted his attackers away.

"That's why I can't believe what the newscast is implying. I've known Tom almost as long as you have, Kayla, and this...well, this has to be some horrible mistake."

"Mom, I'll call you back. Let me turn on the news, see what's going on."

Kayla abruptly placed the phone on its cradle, retrieved the remote lying on the futon, hit the on button. Her screen flashed to a wrestling bout between two beefy opponents, one man already on the mat as the other man screamed and hovered. Letting out a sound of impatience, she surfed past the bout until she hit the nightly news channel.

The picture of Tom's quaint blue and white Queen Anne was in the background, cordoned off by yellow police tape. Several uniformed officers stood sentry as a well-coiffed newswoman identified as Beverly Mains spoke to the TV audience.

"...as you can see, the police are out in force at the site of a tragic triple murder. The cause of death is not yet known, but at least one witness has told Channel 3 that there are three bodies, one an adult woman, the other two young children, girls. They have been identified as Charlotte Thackery, age 34, and her two young children, Reagan and Leah. Family members who have come to the scene say the girls were four and two. All of the bodies are said to be so badly mangled that police may have to wait weeks to determine what caused their deaths. At this point, police are searching for the husband, Thomas Thackery, an archaeologist on the staff of San Francisco State."

The camera panned the front of the house again as the newswoman signed off and the story went back to the anchor desk. Two anchors, an attractive black woman and white man, looked sympathetically at the camera and gave follow up murmurs of condolences in tones that said this was just business as usual before they moved on to the latest carjacking.

Thoughts raced through her mind. There was no way in the world Tom had killed his family. He and Charlotte had been sickeningly in love even after nine years, and no one doted on those girls more than Tom did. She could hear their voices in her head, a chorus of "Aunt Kayla" spoken with adorable lisps. Just a week ago, Tom had phoned her to invite her over to the house to talk about the dig and their subsequent findings, something they had done dozens of times after each of their projects. She'd been looking forward to getting together with Tom and Charlotte, who had a knack for brewing her own beer. She couldn't believe the next time she would see Charlotte or the girls would be in their caskets (if the state of their bodies allowed for an open casket). Her stomach roiled, the nausea pushing its way up. She pushed down the bile rising up her throat.

She picked up her iPhone, hit the button to call Tom. It rang three times then went to his voice mail greeting.

"Hey, not able to talk at the moment. I'm probably digging up something dead and decomposing. Just leave a message and I'll get back with you."

She started to disconnect, but she was desperate.

"Tom, it's Kayla. Please, please call me. I need to hear from you right now."

Even as she pleaded, she knew it was useless. Wherever Tom was, he wouldn't be picking up. Maybe he was on the run because he had actually killed his family. As soon as the thought formed, she violently pushed it away.

Or maybe he was dead, too.

This thought was worse than the thought of him being a murderer. Or was it? Tom as murderer would be another type of death entirely.

No! He was alive somewhere, he had to be. He was probably in hiding out somewhere in a state of shock. He'd probably discovered his Charlotte and the kids lying dead in the house, panicked and ran.

Except that wasn't the man she had known and worked with for nearly fifteen years. Even before Charlotte and the kids, they had been fast friends. They'd met as undergrads at Stanford studying paleontology together, both eager to travel the world, to discover ancient worlds, to uncover the past, find answers to universal questions. And they had traveled to many places including the Sudan, Egypt, Southeast Asia as well as most of the U.S.

Their travels hadn't been without risk. A couple of years ago when they had been excavating in a cavern in Vietnam, one of the local men had come at them with a machete in an attempt to rob them. Among their crew of five, Tom had been the one to disarm the man, not by might but by prudence, talking the man down until the would-be attacker had dropped his weapon.

Tom wasn't one to run. He stood his ground no matter what. And he wouldn't have run from his own dead family, not without a good reason.

The last time she'd seen him face to face was at the Flagstaff airport where they had parted ways because they hadn't been able to get on the same flight..

Nothing had seem out of place, no indication that anything was wrong although both of them had been a little subdued.

She thought back to their conversation.

"I'm not sure about the report. It doesn't seem kosher, you know."

"I told you it was a hallucination. There's no need to include it in the write-up..." she'd said.

"A hallucination? What type of hallucination is it when more than one person experiences it?"

"Like that french term, what's it called? Folie a deux?"

"Yeah, but this delusion involved more than just two people," Tom had insisted. "Jim and Cheryl...all of us experienced the same damn thing. It isn't right leaving out something this vital in the report."

"Look, we were sent to work with the University of Arizona to extract the Dilophosaurus fossil and that's just what we did. That's all that was required and we fulfilled our contractual obligation. Whatever happened out there...well, it was probably due to the extreme heat, and maybe more than a little dehydration. Adding anything like this to the report is simply going to result in more red tape."

He'd look uncertain, but after a few moments, he finally nodded.

"Maybe you're right. The sun played some trick with our brains."

"Exactly."

That had been the end of the discussion and soon after Tom boarded his plane. A week later he'd called to invite her to dinner and neither one of them had brought up the subject again. The subject had been moot anyway. The University had already taken possession of the fossil by then, and the report had been submitted with the standard language. As far as anyone was concerned the excavation had been incident free.

Except that wasn't true. And despite what she'd told Tom, she hadn't been able to convince herself.

Kayla couldn't remember when she'd first noticed that something was different. Out of place. The site had been cordoned off to keep out tourists and curious onlookers. Jim had set up the coordinate grid and soon after began digging around what appeared to be a full vertebrate. The sun was the enemy that day, waves of heat distorting the horizon. The type of heat that cut breath short, seared the lungs.

Chipping away at the granite embedding the dinosaur cranium had been more difficult than she'd anticipated, the exertion causing her to sweat profusely.

Which is why she'd thought she was hallucinating through the sweat dripping from her lashes.

And then Tom and Cheryl paused from digging, stood erect.

"What the hell?" Tom said under his breath.

"What is that?" Cheryl asked as she pushed a dark strand of hair from her wet brow. Jim didn't say a word. He too was standing erect.

Something shimmered in the heat-warped horizon miles away. An outline of a body that had yet to be filled in, like an unyet colored-in figure in a child's coloring book.

The indefinable shape stood nearly eight feet.

"Are all of you seeing what I'm seeing?" Cheryl asked.

"I don't know what the hell I'm looking at," Jim answered.

Kayla had remained the only one without anything to say, her tongue stilled by a fear edged by curiosity. She couldn't be sure that a leviathan hadn't reanimated from the earth, it's bones merged together again, it's outline wavering between the corporeal and the ethereal.

It took a step toward them, the step covering a mile. For now, it was so much closer. And Kayla saw that there were more than two legs, more than four. Not a leviathan then. The ghost of a shape was starting to fill, a figure that seemed to have wavered under some cloak of invisibility and then decided to emerge as total flesh, a flesh that was not true flesh. It shimmered in the sunlight.

Why wasn't she afraid, she'd wondered to herself after the shape emerged fully, more arachnid in form.

Her companions stood obedient as well. They all should have been running, but something stilled that impulse.

The whisper in her head was a strange voice, it's cadence neither female or male, its timbre neither human or animal. Not any animal the earth has known in its millions of years of existence. Carbon had not formed the monstrosity approaching them.

There should have been fear, though her pulse raced and the air became more suffocating than it had been.

And the whisper grew louder, more insistent, its decibel striking through her brain, interrupting synapses, throwing off neurons.

The message was transmitted, a language beyond time or the existence of the universe. Strangely, she understood.

"Really," Cheryl had muttered in response to nothing, a statement underwhelming given the circumstances. But she too was mesmerized by the thing walking closer to them.

A star exploded in Kayla's vision, a planet crumbled sending debris through the unnamed galaxy. Interstellar garbage traveled light years, shooting through the Milky Way.

Those not ripped apart existed beyond the black holes, watching this newly formed universe with hungry eyes.

Eventually, the survivors chose a new home.

Millenniums passed, epochs came and went. The leviathans and mammoths ruled for a time then died, falling victim to the detritus that was the remnant of an exploding planet far away. Bones melded into rock, carbon merged into the earth, eventually to be discovered and extricated.

The hungry ones waited, and most eventually died out. All but a few. Yes, there at the horizon stood another shape, then another.

One who had hidden and waited, marking the passage of time. Until the moment arrived when it revealed itself, revealed the future of the Earth.

A smell arose, something like meat rotting in the sun.

Then the sound of flesh being eviscerated, of blood spilling as skin was ripped apart.

Kayla, standing in her living room, remembered the heat, the smell of blood. A singular light burned through the dimness of the living room, so much cooler than the atmosphere of that Arizona day. She mentally leafed through memories that had been torn from the original Kayla.

Then rebirth. Death followed life which followed death.

Kayla remembered the message inside her. That had traveled with her through the passages between universes. A message of survival, promising a new home.

They had almost died out. But through the few left would come many in this new world.

She walked to the landline and dialed her mother.

"Kayla, did you find out anything about where Tom is?" the woman asked.

"Don't worry Mom. Everything is going to be alright?"

"Alright? How can you say that when Charlotte and the kids are dead? Murdered, maybe by Tom?"

"I'm going to come over, have something to eat."

"Eat?! Kayla you're not making sense. It's way past dinner time and besides I hardly have anything in the refrigerator."

"Then we'll talk, mother."

"You sound…strange. What's wrong?"

"Nothing. As a matter of fact, everything is right."

"Kayla, I don't understand you."

"I'll see you in a half hour."

She didn't give her mother a chance to protest as she disconnected.

So much was coming back to her as her lives merged together.

Kayla Simmons stood in this room.

The Kayla Simmons who lived two weeks ago…well, her bones would settle into the landscape of Tusayan, her carbon would feed the earth as had those of the mammoths and leviathans. Until she was discovered, bones amid bones.

But her thoughts and memories would live on in the incarnation that had risen.

The memories had confused her these weeks, had made her forget who she was.

But she remembered now. Because the message was inside her.

Of course, Tom had killed his family. Because the message was inside him, also.

There would be more deaths because death fed life. Cheryl and Jim would leave their own pounds of flesh, torn asunder.

And from the carnage would rise new ones, with memories of another earth, with memories of this Earth.

Charlotte, Reagan and Leah, eagerly devoured, were reborn and were with Tom somewhere. And surely death would follow them wherever they traveled. And that death would birth life. Until all of this Earth was born anew, a host to the ancients.

They, who had lived for millions of eons, had come home.

Her stomach was much better now. No more indigestion. With her memories restored, her system had settled.

But she was hungry again.

Time to drive to mother's.

Death. Then life. The message of survival.

✗

ALLEN K. '13

FOR LOVE OF LYTHEA
by C. I. Kemp

"Bring me Lythea."

"Sire…"

"BRING! ME! LYTHEA!"

The bellowed command reverberated off stark grey walls.

At the foot of the throne, the mastiff, startled by the booming decree, growled. Faron stepped back, aware that the king's next words might well be directed at the massive hound to rend the Court Magician.

Instead, King Mallios spoke in a near whisper, no less menacing for its softness.

"You have three days, milksop, or else…" Mallios gestured towards the one spot on the walls which was not unadorned and bare. Here, hung broadswords, axes, spike mauls, flails, and maces. All were coated with a rust-colored residue, not from Mallios' enemies, but from those guilty of petty or imagined slights against the monarch.

Faron bowed and took his leave.

The mastiff resumed gnawing a bone, the source of which, Faron dared not guess.

* * * *

It was Faron's custom to walk in his garden when troubled. In his years of service to King Mallios, he often took such walks. As Court Magician, he was bound to his king by an unbreakable Blood Oath, one that had never been violated over the centuries that magicians served kings.

As Court Magician, he must only use his magic as commanded by his liege lord, no matter how objectionable those commands might be.

As Court Magician, he had the power to make clouds spew snow on a midsummer's eve, but could not raise so much as raise a boil on the king's arse.

Faron walked amidst the labyrinthine rows, bounded by towering vegetation. Normally, the fragrances of rose, lavender, sage, and bay soothed him, after an audience with Mallios. Now, however, their sweetness had no such effect.

"Bring me Lythea."

Surely, Mallios understood the enormity of this command. Surely, he relished the anguish it would cause Faron.

For Lythea was not only the loveliest maiden in the kingdom, she was Faron's godchild. Seventeen summers ago, Faron spoke a different Oath, one no less binding than the Blood Oath he'd sworn to his king: to keep his godchild safe from all harm for all of his days.

Safe! What safety would there be in the chambers of a king whose greatest pleasure lay in the seizing of beautiful women? No young mother, wife, or daughter was spared Mallios' predations. When Mallios tired of them, he disposed of them in ways best left unsaid.

How Faron wished he could turn Mallios into a foul liquescence to be absorbed into the earth. He could not, of course. The Blood Oath constrained him as fetters constrained ordinary men.

Sickened by the king's directive, he felt the bile swell within him. He was making for the plot which held wormwood, mint, and balm - herbs that would ease his rising gorge.

From the corner of his eye, something caught his attention.

A mouse had emerged from the shrubbery, its tiny limbs trembling, its body convulsing. Most likely, the poor creature had nibbled one of the poisonous toadstools Faron used in his potions.

As Faron watched, one of the palace cats pounced upon the dying mouse and devoured it. Within seconds, the cat began to shake and gasp before stumbling at the Magician's feet, a lifeless mass.

Faron contemplated this end-of-life drama. In its death throes, the mouse had doomed an enemy which had only acted according to its nature. Was it not possible that Faron could use Mallios' own nature to ensure Lythea's safety without disobeying his king?

An idea began to take shape, one that would never have occurred to him had not Lythea been in such imminent danger.

* * * *

Faron adjourned to his quarters where he doused all torches and drew on the floor a mystic symbol, one meter by one meter. He sat, cross-legged in its center, closed his eyes and whispered an ancient spell. The symbol glowed a soft yellow in the darkness. Beneath closed eyelids, Faron summoned an image of Lythea; gold-haired, azure-eyed, Lythea of the flawless complexion. When he opened his eyes, she stood before him, yet not before him—a mere image to whom he projected his sorcerous warning:

Flee the kingdom. Go along the mountain roads by night when there are no patrols. Seek refuge in the Southern Realms of good King Licaan.

Still standing before him, yet not before him, her image faced him, fear and bewilderment in her eyes.

Make haste, child!

For an instant, she stood unmoving, then nodded, her lips forming words of obedience and love.

The image faded. The symbol ceased to glow.

Faron stood, gestured, and the torches sprang again to life, their flames casting flickering shadows throughout the room. Removing one of the torches from its sconce, Faron made for an antechamber. Its shelves were stocked with vials of powdered bones, desiccated animal remains, dried human entrails, and other arcana. For this venture, he required very specific components, applied in very exact measures at very precise intervals.

Next, he placed a cast iron tub, one by three meters atop the symbol he had drawn earlier. Within the tub, he began pouring the ingredients he had gathered. He spoke words in a forgotten tongue and once again, the symbol began to glow, not with a gentle yellow, but with a glaring orange.

Before many hours had passed, the tub itself began to radiate an angry red heat. As its contents oozed and bubbled, Faron gestured above the rising miasma.

For nearly three days amidst the infernal heat, Faron stood over the tub, neither eating, drinking, nor sleeping. He spoke the necessary incantations, performed the necessary hand motions, and added the necessary ingredients at the right moments. At the tenth hour of the third day, the contents began to cool and congeal. A grey residue, with pulsing, glowing embers lined the bottom of the tub.

At this crucial point, Faron leaned over the tub and whispered:

"Gilded rivers, sprung from thy crown—take form!"

Yellow hair appeared from the uppermost part of the residue and streamed downward.

"Cornflower orbs 'neath crown of gold—take form!"

Eyes that glowed like sapphire appeared.

After many such invocations, a fully realized naked likeness of Lythea rose from the tub. Though lifeless, she possessed (and would exhibit) the characteristics, both physical and temperamental of the true Lythea.

Faron clad her in garments he had set aside for this moment. "Come. It is time to meet your king."

* * * *

"You have deceived me!"

"Sire?" Faron drew back, in fear. Was it possible that this lout had seen through his subterfuge? That the Lythea he had been bedding these many moons was, in fact, *not* Lythea but an ensorcelled duplicate?

"Deceived me!"

Faron knelt, fully expecting a command to the king's guard, followed by a stay in the dungeon, and finally, his own death.

"Aye," Mallios continued, slouching on his throne. "I expected a shy, timid, maiden, and what do I find? A lass as versed in the arts of love as the most accomplished courtesan! You have deceived me, Magician!" With that, Mallios emitted a laugh which carried fumes of the mead wine the king had been drinking in great volume.

Faron raised his head. "I do not understand, Sire. Are you angry?"

Another bellow of laughter. "Angry? By no means, Faron. You goddaughter is a temple of amatory delights. You have done well!"

Faron lowered his head again, a gesture he knew the king would interpret as one of discomfiture, upon hearing his godchild so described. In truth, Faron was gratified. In addition to her true characteristics, Faron provided Lythea's image with great skill in the erotic arts.

There was something else Faron had bestowed upon "Lythea," that the king had yet to experience.

Mallios lifted the flagon of wine and glugged it down. Wine dripped down his chin and stained the cushion of his throne. Once the flagon was emptied, his jovial manner changed to one of rage. He hurled the flagon against the wall where it clattered to the ground. Rising from his throne, stumbling, Mallios roared, "Begone, milksop!"

Faron departed, watching as the ruler staggered his way up the stairs. Only when Mallios was out of sight, did Faron allow himself a brief chuckle.

And so goes the cat to the mouse.

* * * *

Mallios dismissed his guards and unlocked the bedchamber where his plaything awaited.

Upon his entry, Lythea rose from the couch went to greet him. She wore nothing but a gossamer shawl which did little to hide her ample endowments.

"I am pleased to see my lord…"

"Silence!" Mallios backhanded the girl across the face. The strength of his blow propelled her against the wall, where she crumbled to the floor, whimpering, a flow of blood trickling from her lip.

Between sobs, she managed to say, "Have I displeased my lord?"

Mallios covered the width of the room in two strides, and lifted the cowering girl by the hair. "Did I not say SILENCE?" He hurled her against the wall and began pummeling and kicking her. Lythea tried to protest but each effort aroused the besotted king to a greater fury and arousal. His hands closed about her throat, shutting off her protestations.

He began to squeeze.

A mighty blow from unseen hands backhanded Mallios across the room, his head hitting the wall with such force that his vision blurred.

"You damned little...."

Before he could rise, something grasped his beard and wrenched him upward. He opened his eyes to see grey shapes surrounding him, one of which held his beard in a formidable grasp. The others converged and Mallios realized that they were not solid forms, but semitransparent wraithlike things. Through these, he could see the tapestries adorning his chamber, the lattice on his windows, and the wall against which he'd hurled Lythea. Lythea was nowhere to be seen.

A fusillade of blows cut short his cries of fear and bewilderment. What felt like fists of chain mail pummeled him. What felt like legs in iron greaves propelled vicious kicks at his trunk and groin. What felt like fingers encased in iron gauntlets squeezed his throat shut. His cries became whimpers through swollen lips, pleas for mercy even as he choked on dislodged teeth.

As Mallios flailed, his limbs encountered naught but empty air. He thrashed, he floundered, he felt the foul wine trying to disgorge itself without success. His lungs screamed for that which would not come. His vision was failing. Everything in the room was fading, fading...

* * * *

"A most violent fit."

Such was the cause of death pronounced by the Court Physician the following day over Mallios' shattered body.

Mallios' lands were absorbed into the Southern Realms. And Faron swore the Blood Oath to King Licaan whom he served with honor and gladness for the rest of his days.

Printed by Amazon Italia Logistica S.r.l.
Torrazza Piemonte (TO), Italy